The Clima

A N

Susan Whiting Kemp

Matt and Laurel,
I hope you book lovers
enjoy this! All the best,
Susan Kemp

Enormous gratitude to Nancy Bonnington and Evelyn Arvey for tirelessly reading and critiquing the different versions of *The Climate Machine*. This novel wouldn't have been possible without your wisdom and creativity.

Thank you Dr. Alan Whiting, for scientific input about the world we live in, and for helping me be as accurate as possible in a story that can't actually happen (that we know of). Your knowledge of the ocean, physics, astronomy, and other sciences were invaluable.

To early readers Frank Monahan, Mary Beth Hughes, Jim Bonnington, and Elaine Roe–thank you for your suggestions for improvement and for your caring encouragement.

Thank you Tiffany Yates Martin at FoxPrint Editorial. Your astute edits and comments helped me shape and refine *The Climate Machine* into a more approachable story. It would have been a very different book without your guidance.

Special thanks to my husband for support all along the way. Your love and humor sustain me.

Chapter One

W*as that a raindrop?* Marella Wells felt her arm, disappointed to find her skin dry. But of course it wasn't raining. The sky above the bakery was a cloudless powder blue, interrupted only by the flying saucer-like top of the Space Needle. The windows of the city's towering icon gleamed silver in the morning light.

A dozen shiny gold objects clung to the saucer's edge. From several blocks away they looked like beetles, though they had to be much larger. One detached from the Space Needle and began to fall, edges rippling in the wind.

Its arms flailed.

Marella gasped...it was a person!

A human being, plunging toward certain death, seeming to fall for an eternity—the Space Needle was six hundred feet tall, after all.

Marella's shoulders tensed for the landing and remained tight. The person disappeared out of sight behind dead trees—trees that, like so many around the Pacific Northwest, had withered during the drought.

Now another person fell.

"Tell me this isn't real." A woman behind Marella had seen it too.

A man joined them. "Are those window washers?"

"Not dressed in gold robes," said the woman.

Marella struggled with her cell, hands shaking as she dialed 911. "People are falling off the Space Needle!"

"We've had multiple calls," said the dispatcher. As if to confirm, a siren sounded, then another, wails weaving and blending as they neared the Seattle Center.

The man scrolled his phone with quick flicks. "They're jumping on purpose. This is unbelievable. It's an apocalyptic death cult. Zokara's Chosen. Fifty members."

Marella leaned against a sidewalk planter, her leg muscles weak. Dead foliage scratched her arm; she rubbed the pain prickles absent-mindedly.

The next figure launched itself. Again, a fluttering of shiny gold. Marella's hand shot up to her face to hide the sight. "Why would they do this?"

The man read from his phone. "They believe the drought is signaling the end of the world. It's a show of faith to their leader and a guarantee of their own salvation."

Dozens of sirens yowled from all directions. They would soon converge on the scene, and Marella could only imagine what they would find. Cracked skulls. Broken bodies. Gold robes soaked in pools of scarlet blood.

Another cult follower flung himself from the Needle. This one pedaled in the air, as if trying to bicycle back to the top. Had the poor soul changed his mind? It was too late now.

Another figure jumped. Then another. Still shaking, Marella couldn't look away.

Finally, when there were no more, the three watchers shifted and fidgeted. It was time to disperse, but a spell tethered them to one another.

"I counted fifteen jumpers," said Marella.

"Something's very wrong," said the man. "Maybe this drought isn't going to end."

That's ridiculous, thought Marella, though for a tense moment the idea lodged in her head. It was July so of course it was hot, but her lips had been cracked for months. It took a glass of water less time to evaporate. Deep-rooted evergreen trees were turning brown and dying in record numbers. But the five-month drought was an anomaly. The rain would return.

The emergency vehicle sirens stopped shrieking. The world was quiet.

Several pigeons burst up from the sidewalk, breaking the spell. Her appetite gone, Marella skipped the bakery and returned to her truck. She rolled her shoulders back, started the engine, and grasped the steering wheel tightly to stop her trembling.

It was unbelievable what brainwashing could do. *Flapping robes. Flailing limbs. Falling bodies.*

She would have to deal with the horror of it some other time. She was late for work.

Chapter Two

Employees stiff-walked across HemisNorth's main lobby. Marella caught herself doing the same, taking deep breaths to decompress from what she'd just experienced. She was already edgy about the explosion that had happened the week before, although management was taking measures to keep employees safe. There would be no more research done at company headquarters, which meant no more fuel tanks. They even planned to move the company vehicle gas tank offsite.

She also needed to stop worrying about getting laid off. The trade wars would end soon. As soon as tariffs lifted on HemisNorth products, things would be better. They could even hire back those who had been laid off.

After climbing three flights of stairs, she paused before the door to the environmental compliance offices. She gathered herself into her work persona, the confident office assistant who got things done. It wasn't easy to be that person. Six months in, she still felt like a newbie. She thought she was doing well, but wasn't sure others saw it. She was particularly proud of having found a major error in a contract, a decimal in the wrong place making six thousand dollars read as six million. She had hoped for praise, but had gotten only a nod. Still, she was grateful to have a job when unemployment was rising.

She checked her clothing. No spots on her lavender blouse or grey slacks. Pulling open the heavy door, she whooshed into a world of turquoise walls and artfully curved white desks. The clock said nine o'clock. Thirty minutes late. She set her backpack on her desk next to the now dried-out fern she'd bought on a whim back when she was excited to get her first office job. She'd stopped watering it because the dry spring and early summer brought less mountain snowpack, so the city was asking people not to use water unnecessarily. Next time she would get a cactus.

The desk across from her was empty, its occupant laid off the week before. The entire company had five thousand people. This local office had two hundred, until ten percent of them were laid off for belt-tightening. Her mother identified it as proof that corporations were evil. Treating people as numbers. Sloughing them off like dry skin.

Luckily Diana, Marella's neighbor, a chemical engineer who had helped her get the job, hadn't been part of the layoff. Later at lunchtime Marella would tell Diana about the suicide jumpers. Her friend would probably respond with something warmly brash. "Yes, that happened, now put on your big girl panties, we've got other fish to fry." The thought fortified her.

Through an interior window Marella saw her boss, Elizabeth Fehr, framed by an abstract painting resembling a desert, its dunes edged in the same shiny gold as the fluttering robes. It jolted Marella, as if Elizabeth were somehow connected to this morning's tragedy.

She blinked hard. She needed to get past it—needed her brain power to focus on her job. Proofreading reports, cross-checking documents, and putting the sections together correctly took concentration. Typos and missed deadlines could have serious consequences when a report was sent to the Environmental Protection Agency, the Washington State Department of Ecology, King County, or the City of Seattle. She was just shy of her job's probationary period so HemisNorth would have an easier time letting her go if her work wasn't up to par.

Seeing Marella, Elizabeth beckoned with the brusque hand gesture of a fifty-something-year-old established in her career. As Marella approached, Elizabeth's expression was as unreadable as an iguana's, but then it usually was. She rarely smiled at Marella directly.

Of course after the death of her coworkers in the explosion, not to mention the layoffs, she had less to smile about these days.

Marella cleared her dry throat. Talking about the suicide jumpers would make her break down in tears. She couldn't do that. She couldn't look weak, undependable. "I'm sorry," she began as she trotted in. "Traffic..."

"Never apologize," interrupted Elizabeth.

This flustered her. She had forgotten one of Elizabeth's most-repeated maxims, that apologizing gave subsequent words less value. She was supposed to thank Elizabeth instead. For her patience? For her time? She wasn't sure, and the words that came to mind seemed awkward. *Thank you for your patience with my being late because of traffic.* Or, more truthfully, *Thank you for your patience with my lateness due to people splattering onto the concrete after jumping from our fair city's 1962 World's Fair leftover.*

To make matters worse, Marella's eyes landed on the artsy glass replica of the Space Needle that sat on Elizabeth's desk. She nearly expected to see miniature glass cult members tumbling off.

"Are you all right?" asked Elizabeth.

Marella snapped to attention. "Great," she said brightly.

Elizabeth tilted her head as if she didn't agree. "Glad to hear it. I have some data tables for you to cross-check, and more copying and pasting into the database. Plus the human resources department is short-staffed so they asked if you could input this list of people who took the health and safety training. It all has to be done by the end of today. It's a lot, but you're a fast worker. I have every faith in you."

Elizabeth's tone was encouraging. As usual, Marella wanted to prove herself worthy of that faith, but it would be a challenge. Taking the documents from the desk, she felt their weight. This was a lot of work. And the copying and pasting out of the electronic documents would be tediously slow because it was important not to make a single mistake.

What if she didn't accomplish it? Would it be a mark against her, a reason to let her go in the next round of layoffs? Or would her boss understand that it took time to do things right, and be fine with finishing the rest on another day? She swallowed. "No problem."

"And I need you to download a form for me. I tried to register on a website and it closed before I could create a password. So now it won't set up the account because it says my email is already assigned. It's going to be a real pain asking you to access the website every time I need something but I can't see a workaround. I'll send you the link."

Surely there was a better way. Marella's mind felt like a roulette wheel, its ball bouncing as it spun, not landing...not landing. Finally an idea struck. "What if you go into your browser history and get back into the website that way?"

As she clicked at her keyboard, Elizabeth said distractedly, "That won't work because it'll ask for a password." She pulled her head back in surprise. "Oh! I'm in. Nicely done!" She looked up, almost smiling. "I need to talk with Belinda. Is her car here yet?"

Marella marched to the floor-to-ceiling window. HemisNorth headquarters had six main buildings on a campus-like setting, nestled in a profusion of rhododendron bushes—their leaves dead. Rhodies normally made it through Pacific Northwest summers just fine, but apparently five months without rain had been too much for them. The wind blew the parched fir tops, which seemed to fight back, slicing uselessly at the gusts.

There were parking spots in front of each building for VIPs and visitors. From where she stood on the third story, Marella could see Elliott Bay, which was part of Puget Sound. Its gray water was threaded with silver ribbons. Rip rap lined the shore, made of refrigerator-size black rocks.

As a child Marella thought Puget Sound was a noise, until her mother explained that a sound was a large ocean inlet, like a fjord. She showed Marella a map. Puget Sound slashed more than a thousand miles through Washington State starting from the West Coast, then veered south. It made the northwest corner of the state look like a giant jaw opening upward. Puget Sound wasn't open ocean, but was so large it felt like it.

She turned her attention to the building-front parking below, where Belinda Waverly, HemisNorth's CEO, was emerging from her Tesla. Marella thought of her as a tornado. Her hair for sure, but also the way she swept through the office, and the way people watched warily for her.

"She just arrived," said Marella.

Elizabeth joined her at the window. Belinda strode across the pavement to a building used for research and development. Building C, wrapped with yellow danger tape. The building where the explosion happened. The building where Eshana Collins and Len Janderson died.

One week earlier Marella had been at her desk trying to make sense of a sentence in a report. Just when she realized it was missing a noun—probably "analysis"—she heard a boom. Not merely a noise, but something she felt in her insides, making her organs seem to settle into a new configuration.

She leaped to her feet along with everybody else, rushing to the window, where she had a full view of Building C. When the security guard opened the door from the outside, smoke poured from the building. He backed up, holding his arms against the rush of smoke.

The fire alarm sounded, its harsh blare making everybody cover their ears. She joined hundreds of evacuated staff members flowing down the stairs. They gathered by the water, which sparkled quietly in contrast to the scene it bordered, snuggling against the embankment rocks as if nothing was wrong. There were people rushing about. A profusion of black smoke. Police cars. Ambulances.

Later they learned two people were dead because of a faulty fuel tank.

Now Elizabeth's fingers grazed the window frame. "Eshana and Len were the most brilliant minds in the universe and then some."

Marella didn't know Eshana, a physicist, or Len, a computer scientist. They had been working on a confidential job called Project Athena. Perhaps a new product of some kind. She imagined a miracle cleaning liquid or something that could be used in advanced technology. HemisNorth was a chemical company, but there were rumors that it was reinventing itself, morphing as times changed, like Nokia, which started as a paper mill and now made cell phones, or Nintendo, which went from playing cards to computer games. When she tried to make the mental leap, Marella wasn't sure what that meant. A playing card to a computer game was like a cleaning fluid to a—what?

She wasn't sure of Elizabeth's role in Project Athena. As the Director of Environmental Compliance, her boss made sure the company adhered to the laws. She oversaw staff who took water samples near HemisNorth plants, and tested fish to make sure stormwater discharge wasn't making them all grow two heads or something.

She suspected Elizabeth was involved with Project Athena, since she often saw her with Eshana and Len. When the three emerged from a discussion, they always seemed animated, as if they had been playing ping pong across the conference table.

With Eshana and Len dead, what would happen to Project Athena? Had it died along with them? And what did that mean for the company and its employees? More layoffs?

Now the security guard in front of Building C, framed by smoke damage around the door, nodded at Belinda as she entered. Marella had once gone to that building looking for Elizabeth. That same guard had drawled in the nicest way, "Nope, can't go in there. Not gonna happen." What was in that building before the explosion, and what was left to guard?

Marella was unsure how to respond to Elizabeth's comment about Len and Eshana's brilliant minds. She wasn't competent at corporate small-talk and banter, especially when death was concerned. Movie-like phrases came to mind. *The world will be a poorer place without them. HemisNorth has lost two of its finest.* She finally landed on "I bet you'll miss them."

"I will," said Elizabeth. "They were good friends."

While Elizabeth's interior was usually hidden, the words opened a crack through which Marella could peek, showing that Elizabeth was human, struggling to make sense of a tragedy.

* * * *

IMMERSING HERSELF IN work distracted Marella from her worries. She had to get familiar with the human resources part of the database so she could check the right boxes for those who took the training. Then she had to make sure she did the copying and pasting correctly. Copy a title here. Paste it into the database there. Copy a dollar figure here. Paste it into the database there.

She was sure that tonight she would dream about copying and pasting. But tomorrow would be better because it was Saturday and she was going to visit her family. At least she had something to look forward to.

At lunchtime, she went to Diana's office on the fourth floor as she often did. They would usually head to the exercise room where they could walk the treadmills side by side, jawing about this and that.

But Diana wasn't there, and neither was the toylike yellow, red, and blue carbon atom model that usually graced her desk. Her flip calendar was also missing. So was everything else except for a paper clip and a tape dispenser labeled *Do not remove from copy room.*

She stood at the door, not wanting to believe what she already suspected.

"She got laid off today," said a voice behind her, jolting her like a missing stairstep. She turned to see Emmett, a chemist who resembled a friendly milkman in a classic sitcom.

"I heard they might get rid of more people but I didn't expect..." Marella trailed off.

Emmett's voice lowered while his eyebrows raised, giving him an air of dramatic intensity. "If they could lay Diana off, nobody's safe. Mind your P's and Q's and get your backup plan ready. The economy might tank. Did you hear about the drought spreading and the lake levels dropping? It's getting serious."

She texted Diana. *U okay?*

Diana replied, *I guess.*

Need company?

Busy today. Come over tomorrow at 4.

• • • •

AN HOUR LATER MARELLA was passing the Lake Sammamish conference room, named for one of many local bodies of water. Through its window she saw Elizabeth and Belinda poring over a dozen folders fanned out on the table. The same viper green folders that the Human Resources department used. Marella squeezed the report she carried so tightly that its comb binding dug into her palm. They had to be discussing more layoffs. Perhaps the next ten percent to go. Would she be one of them? Her folder could be the one that Elizabeth was pointing to even now. She turned her head away as she walked past so they wouldn't see the alarm on her face.

At her desk, she sipped a glass of water, which she drank instead of juice to save cash. She couldn't get laid off. She lived month-to-month. She had to do something to convince Elizabeth to keep her. But what? Offer to work harder? Later? Smarter?

It occurred to her that she could get ahead of this. Find out their criteria for layoffs. Why might they choose one person over another?

Was it something she could control, like efficiency, punctuality, or productivity? Or something she could do nothing about, such as seniority? Irrationally, she thought that just asking for their criteria would give them the idea to get rid of her.

If she could only hear what Elizabeth and Belinda were saying. She watched them surreptitiously from her desk. Their gestures were dramatic, their faces concerned. She imagined their comments. *Marella doesn't have much experience. There's a lot she doesn't know. She's just an assistant—the technical staff could take on her duties. Why keep her instead of one of them?*

When she and her sister Brielle were young, they would play spy, putting a glass to the wall to hear their mother's conversations. A supply room adjoined the conference room. Would it be possible to eavesdrop from there?

Normally she would never consider such a thing. As Mom would say, "That would be all kinds of wrong."

But as Elizabeth said, "Information is everything."

She weighed the chance of being caught. Not too high, as long as she was careful.

Downing the last of the water from her glass, she retrieved the key to the supply room and unlocked it. The automatic light burst on, illuminating shelves of paper and pens on one side and goodies for meetings on the other. Bottled water, pop, juice, cookie packages, potato chip bags.

She shut the door behind her. She couldn't hear Elizabeth or Belinda. She would have to put the glass against the wall to listen in, which would make her transgression obvious. She glanced back through the narrow window in the supply room door. Nobody there.

Shelves ran the length of the room. After moving a shrink-wrapped stack of facial tissue boxes, she placed the glass against the wall, flinching when it made a dull clunk. She leaned awkwardly between the shelves to put her ear against the bottom of the glass. Her heart began pounding. What would she say if she were caught? *This shelf sure needs dusting!*

She concentrated, feeling like a quack doctor listening for the building's heartbeat. She could hear them, though the voices were tinny. She kept watch through the door's window as best she could while she strained to make out the words.

"Normally I would trust your judgement," said Belinda, "But this is not a typical situation."

"It's not like you to make a decision without more information," said Elizabeth.

What information? Overtime hours worked? Tasks accomplished?

"Without information," continued Elizabeth, "we can't be sure it's safe."

Safe. They weren't talking about layoffs.

"It was most likely a faulty fuel tank," said Belinda, "just like we announced. We only need final confirmation."

"I'm not convinced the tank caused it. Its destruction could have been a secondary effect. I only agreed to say it was to keep speculation to a minimum."

Marella could hardly breathe. They were talking about the recent explosion. They had lied about it. Outright lied.

"I know you suspect the machine," said Belinda. "But how could it have caused an explosion? The fuel tank is much more likely."

Machine? What machine?

"I wouldn't know because I don't understand Project Athena's complexities," said Elizabeth. "Nobody truly did except Len and Eshana, and they're gone. We don't know what they were doing when it happened."

Marella shifted her feet anxiously. She should stop listening. This was overstepping. Yet she was already here. And the explosion had affected her. Plus they had lied and she deserved to know why.

"It wasn't anything they did," said Belinda. "They had just walked in. They were only there for a few minutes."

"There are too many unknowns," said Elizabeth. "If the prototype caused the explosion, the full-size machine is so much more dangerous. Think of the enormous size of such an explosion. Nobody would make it out alive."

Marella nearly gasped out loud. She felt herself slipping and grasped the shelf to steady herself. Belinda was worried about a gigantic explosion. Because of an experimental machine that produced—what? Could Seattle become another Bhopal, India, where many thousands of people had died from a chemical plant explosion? Had she already been contaminated from the first explosion?

And if Building C had only held a prototype, then where was the full-size machine? HemisNorth had manufacturing plants nearby. Was it one of them? How big was the machine? Would its explosion wipe out all of Seattle? And if so, how far would its contamination spread?

"Again, we don't know what Eshana and Len were actually doing in there," said Elizabeth. "What if they made an adjustment that caused the explosion?"

"That's a big leap. They wouldn't want us to give up on all their hard work. Don't let their deaths be in vain. They were trying to save humanity."

Had she heard correctly? Not save the company, but save humanity? From what?

"We'll wait for the rest of the results," said Belinda. "Two more days."

It was quiet. She imagined Elizabeth pinching the top of her nose between her fingers as she sometimes did. "All right."

"I'm flying to Houston tonight. We have complex issues to work out with production there. But I'll call you when the results come out. In the meantime, hold down the fort here. I'm relying on you."

Marella straightened quickly, shoving the glass behind a box of Post-It notes. She picked up a notepad, pasted a pleasant smile on her face, and scurried to her desk, where she furtively watched Belinda tornado across the floor and into the elevator.

She stared at the title on a spreadsheet without comprehending its meaning. It was starting to really sink in. Elizabeth thought some machine linked to Project Athena could have caused the explosion. She thought they could all be in danger.

She imagined Eshana Collins and Len Janderson as mad scientists in Building C simultaneously pouring beakers of neon yellow liquid into a rivet-lined steel tank. The tank exploding, the blast spreading, gaining strength as it traveled across the city.

Was HemisNorth more concerned about money than people? They were leaving people in danger while they waited for test results. What did that say about them?

Nothing, she told herself. She was overreacting. If Elizabeth really thought there was danger, she wouldn't have agreed to wait for two days.

Elizabeth emerged from the conference room. One of the field staff, a biologist wearing a yellow safety vest, headed her off. "We couldn't get any water samples."

Elizabeth frowned at him. "Why not?"

"There wasn't any water."

Marella's ears pricked up. More drought problems?

"Is this the Bremerton facility?" asked Elizabeth. "Of course there wasn't any water in the pipes. You're only supposed to sample after a stormwater event."

"But..."

"Come into my office."

The biologist had screwed up. She felt sorry for him, but at least it had nothing to do with the drought.

She tried to concentrate on her work but couldn't push away worries about the explosion. When an employee dropped a cup Marella leaped out of her seat at the noise. Still, she managed to finish most of the cross-checking Elizabeth had given her, and every single bit of the copying and pasting. She hoped that would be good enough.

Chapter Three

During the two-hour drive south to Centralia the next morning, the suicide cult deaths dominated Marella's thoughts, triggering memories of her father, who had died falling off a cliff during a camping trip in the Olympic Rain Forest. Mom didn't like camping, so she had stayed home with Brielle. Five-year-old Marella was the only one nearby when he died.

At the time, a babysitter had taught her that everybody who didn't believe in God was a sinner, and Hell awaited sinners. When her father died, she had thought Hell was going to open up. Demons would come carry him off, and her too. So she ran. She was lost in the rain forest for three days scrambling through thick fern patches, thinking every noise was a demon coming after her. Finally she made it to a road and a car picked her up. She'd hated being alone ever since.

The images spooled, alternating. The people in gold robes, falling. Dad's body sprawled on the ground, his back bent all wrong. Demons with dagger teeth and bright red skin. Too clear in her mind's eye. A feeling of hopelessness grew until it was suffocating; she had to tell herself to breathe.

Finally she passed a junior high school and then rolled onto the driveway of the house her mother was renting. It was such a relief to arrive. Mom and Brielle would distract her from all that death, at least for a little while.

This was her first time seeing the new place. The house seemed to have more moss than roof, but at least there was no junk car body and no toothpaste-colored paint splotch barely masking fresh graffiti. Blackberry vines overran the brown lawn, but that wasn't so bad, really. In fifty-two moves, her family had inhabited worse.

Her twenty-year-old Ford F150 had come with a dashboard GPS. She slid it into the glove compartment to keep it out of sight of thieves, then jumped out into the summer heat. Trotting to the door, she passed a hut-size greenhouse, its windows dusty and cracked.

"Mar-Mar!" Fourteen-year-old Brielle opened the door, nearly knocking Marella over with a big hug. She wore tie-dye workout clothes and smelled lemony. The wind blew her light brown hair in her eyes. She swiped it away. She was so animated, so like a gymnast at the "ta da" moment, Marella felt slightly better. It seemed like they hadn't seen each other in years, though it had only been a month. It was supposed to be easier to be apart from family at the age of nineteen, but not for Marella.

Their mother appeared, dressed in jeans and a light blue button down shirt, her nose a touch red—she could never be bothered to reapply sunscreen. If Brielle was the "ta da" moment, Mom was the steady effort to get to it. Always there with good advice or a helping hand.

"I've missed you so much," said Mom. Wrapping her arm around her daughter, Mom walked her though the door and into the kitchen. The familiar crock pot sat on an unfamiliar cream-colored counter. The familiar straight-back chairs sat on an unfamiliar red and black checkered floor. The familiar cups sat on an unfamiliar green shelf. A few moving boxes still sat in a corner.

"It's not the same without you," said Brielle. "I wish you still lived with us."

"Me too." Marella had lived on her own for six months and it still felt wrong. But even if she could endure four hours of commute every day, her wallet couldn't. Plus that would make her more likely to arrive late to work. And then in a few months Mom would get antsy and feel the need to move again.

In the living room, Brielle threw herself onto the paisley couch, knocking away the book that was serving as its missing leg. The couch corner dipped, making her snort with surprise.

Mom seized the book—a mystery novel with a magnifying glass on the cover. "What was that doing there?"

"I couldn't find the couch brick," said Brielle.

They all searched. Marella spied the chipped red brick in a still-unpacked box, next to the baseball bats. "It's right here." She shoved it under the couch corner.

Brielle scooped up a hair brush and a cornflower blue canister. "Look! I've got hair powder so we don't have to use as much water washing our hair. We can do our part to conserve water."

"Great idea," said Marella. "Mom, you can go first."

"Are you kidding?" joked Mom. "I don't want to look like some eighteenth century wig guy."

"It really works," said Brielle, flipping her hair in a shampoo commercial parody. "The trick is you brush it a lot."

Marella sat on the newly leveled couch. Brielle sprinkled the citrus-scented powder on Marella's hair and set to work with long, slow strokes. It felt like floating on a cloud.

But there were no clouds. Only blue sky, the Space Needle, and people falling to their deaths. Marella put her face in her hands. Even among her family, she couldn't seem to forget.

Mom sat next to Marella. "What's wrong?"

Marella moved her hands to her lap but kept her face down. "Did you hear about the suicide jumpers on the news?"

"The Space Needle ones?" asked Mom. "What about them?"

"I saw it happening," said Marella. "I was a few blocks away."

Brielle's voice was breathy. "Wow, you watched fifteen people die? That must have been hard to see."

"Oh honey," said Mom. "Why didn't you call me?"

"I had to go to work," said Marella, "and ever since I've been trying not to think about it. But I can't stop."

"Maybe telling us about it will help you let go of it," said Mom.

"Yeah, tell us." Brielle patted Marella's back encouragingly.

Lifting her head, Marella described how she'd stopped the car to get breakfast, and happened to see the falling people. "They went one by one, and each time I thought there wouldn't be another, there was. And they had gold robes that fluttered, and it was weirdly beautiful and surreal except that you knew they were going to die. And I couldn't see them hit the ground because the trees were in the way, but I still can't stop imagining what it must have been like."

"I'm so sorry you had to go through that," said Mom.

"Yeah, that's rough," said Brielle.

"Don't let it get to you," said Mom. "You didn't know any of them. Just put it out of your mind."

"But the thing is..." Marella's throat tightened.

"Yes?" asked Mom.

"I can't stop thinking about Dad either. When he died."

Mom looked away, then back at Marella. "I thought you stopped dwelling on that years ago."

"I did stop. But then that cult leader conned people into killing themselves and it's all coming back. It's stupid. It's not the same thing. I don't understand why I'm being so pathetic."

"But it is the same thing," said Mom. "They're both random and tragic. If your father hadn't tripped, he'd be alive today. And if those people had never met that psychopath they would still be alive too. It was all just chance."

"It's not really the same," said Marella. "If their families had gotten them away from that guy in time then things would be different. Their families should have...oh shit."

The real connection between the two events was suddenly clear to Marella, so that she couldn't speak.

"What is it, Mar-Mar?" asked Brielle.

"Take your time," said Mom.

She didn't want to say it out loud. She never had before. But she'd gotten this far, she might as well. "I should have stopped Dad from dying."

Mom put her hand on Marella's arm. "Honey, you couldn't have. You were a little girl, and you weren't near him when it happened. You said he told you to stay at the campsite."

"Yes, but if I'd helped him get firewood he wouldn't have gone off so far."

Brielle's eyes widened. "No way. Then you would have both fallen off the cliff and I wouldn't have a sister."

"I could have told him I didn't want a campfire." Marella's voice grew hoarse as she tried to keep from breaking down. "Or I could have refused to go camping in the first place. He wouldn't be dead if it wasn't for me."

Mom blinked fast. "Oh my girl, is that what you've been thinking all these years?"

Marella nodded, tears finally spilling.

"Why didn't you say something?" asked Mom.

Marella just shook her head.

Mom launched herself at Marella and hugged her tightly. "It's not your fault. It's just not." Her voice warbled with emotion.

"I wanted to go camping. I asked him if we could go. He wasn't that interested but I keep begging him."

Mom let go and leaned back. "He was just teasing you, pretending he wasn't into it. He was the one who brought it up in the first place. I remember him saying, 'Sleeping in a tent, that's no fun. Roasting marshmallows, that's no fun.' He loved camping. I just wish he hadn't taken you to the middle of nowhere. Then you wouldn't have gone off and gotten lost."

Marella wiped her eyes. "Still. I went along with it."

"You can go through the 'what-ifs' endlessly, but you can't see the future, and so there was nothing you could have done."

Marella let that sink in a little. She'd spent so much time telling herself what she should have done differently to have a father in her life, that she never looked at it as something she couldn't have controlled.

"Don't blame yourself," said Mom. "You're not responsible. Do you hear me?"

Marella nodded, partly because that's what you did when your Mom said such a thing and partly because she was beginning to think it was true.

"All right," said Mom. "Now we've got that established. You grieved for him and now you've grieved for these people. Give yourself permission to move on."

"It's not that easy," said Marella. "I can't just forget about it."

"Sure you can," said Mom. "You need to distract yourself."

"I know," said Brielle. "Let's do batting practice. We're right next to a school and the ballfield is practically in our backyard."

"Good idea, Brielle," said Mom. "That'll put her in the moment. She won't have time to think of anything but what she's doing."

Marella waved the idea away. "I'm too tired after that long drive."

"You were sitting the whole way." Brielle strode over and picked up a baseball glove and ball. She tossed the ball into the mitt several times, making thunk sounds. "Come on, it's like Mom says, you can't think about other stuff when a ball is coming at you."

Mom picked up a bat. "Let's go. Activity always makes you feel better."

"I don't know if anything will help," said Marella.

"You won't know if you don't try," said Mom.

"That's such a Mom thing to say," said Marella.

"Because it's such a true thing to say."

Brielle retrieved more mitts and a batting helmet. She handed Marella a bucket of baseballs, chanting, "Too slow, let's go," as she headed out the back door. Marella and Mom followed her through a gate and across a field to a baseball diamond.

Marella gave a few practice swings, feeling the solid weight of the bat, then positioned herself at home plate, presenting a bravado she didn't feel. "Gimmee all you've got."

"And more," said Brielle, in a comically gruff tone. She pitched a ball right to the sweet spot. Marella swung. There was a satisfying thwack of bat against ball, then a straight drive down the middle of the field.

Mom cupped her hands around her mouth. "Run!"

"It's just batting practice," said Marella.

"Run!" insisted Mom, coming at her with a ball her hand. So Marella did, rounding the bases, with Mom—a former track runner—right behind, tagging her just before she reached home.

"Safe," said Brielle.

"I got her," said Mom.

"Five-second rule," said Brielle.

Mom sputtered in mock indignation. "That's for food on the floor, not baseball!"

Brielle held Marella's hand up as if she'd won a boxing match. "Ladeeeeez and gentlemeeeeeen, the winner, Marella 'the Slugger' Wells!"

Marella went along with it, somewhat limply, but with a smile.

After all the balls had been hit—or not hit—they stood at the pitching mound back to back for the retrieval contest. On the count of three, they scurried to get as many balls as they could. Brielle—the first winner—stomped out a happy dance full of overdone swagger. Marella and Mom draped themselves over each other laughing at her awkward movements.

Later they took a break, sitting in the shade on the stubbly brown grass. Marella's woes had been put on pause for a time, and while they now flowed back, they weren't quite as overwhelming as before. Also, she was able to let Mom's statement sink in even further. She couldn't see the future, so she wasn't truly to blame. Perhaps it was true that there wasn't really anything she could have done to save her father. She felt buoyed up with gratitude. What would she do without Mom and Brielle?

"The wind made it tricky today," said Brielle.

"Wind is good," said Mom. "It'd be too hot otherwise."

"But it's weird how it's windy all the time," said Brielle. "And it's weird how dry it is. You can sit on the grass without getting your butt wet, even first thing in the morning."

"We've had extra-dry summers before," said Marella.

"I know," said Brielle, "but it was like this before summer got here, and it feels so different. You hang up a washcloth and it dries so fast. It's rained in California but not here. That's wack."

"It's climate change," said Mom. "When I was a kid it hardly ever got above eighty degrees here, and now it gets above ninety for days in a row. Eventually it'll dry up and we'll have scorpions instead of slugs. We'll have to move to Alaska."

"That won't be better," said Brielle. "The Arctic is heating up twice as fast as the rest of the planet. And five million people die every year because we have more hurricanes and forest fires and floods and..."

"New subject," said Mom. "What should we have for dinner?"

"Something you don't need the oven for," said Brielle.

Marella reached up to wipe sweat from her forehead but it had already dried.

Chapter Four

During the drive back to her apartment building on First Hill, Marella thought less about the suicide jumpers, but now dwelled on work worries. The explosion, the mystery machine, the layoffs. She wondered if Diana could help her make sense of it all.

When she was almost home, she stopped for gas. The pump ran slowly, as if powered by a lazy hamster on an exercise wheel. Still, she filled the tank so she would be able to visit her family again soon. She wished she didn't have a four-door gas guzzling truck, but it was the best deal she'd found for the money she had.

At four o'clock she went to the fifth floor and knocked on Diana's door. Her friend opened it looking like a big-cheeked Amelia Earhart, her hair brushed back as if propeller-blown, giving her an on-the-verge-of-adventure look. She wore a banana-yellow t-shirt and pajama bottoms dotted with happy llamas.

"Hello, former workmatey," Diana's voice slurred with drunkenness, even though it was only four o'clock in the afternoon. She waved an arm to indicate Marella should enter.

Marella followed Diana past her papasan chair to the kitchen, where her friend splashed rum into a three-tone glass and basketball-tossed in a sprig of mint. "I'm thinking of going into bartending." She forced a lemon slice onto the rim; it slipped to the floor.

Marella gave a grunt of a laugh. "I think you should stick to chemical engineering."

"Fair enough." Diana kicked the lemon slice away and slapped another one in its place, where it hung precariously. "That's for you."

Marella took the glass, straightening the lemon slice. She didn't feel much like drinking, but a little wouldn't hurt. It would still her racing mind. "You got anything to mix this with?"

"No. Drink it straight up."

They sat on the couch. Diana's expression turned morose, her shoulders slumped. Marella always thought that if her friend were a superhero, her power would be to repel adversity rather than bullets. Bad luck, insults, and lies would bounce off, straight back at the fiends who launched them. But the mere appearance of strength didn't give a person the ability to avoid all woes. It was hard to see such a strong person beaten down.

"Listen, I know this was hard on you," said Marella, "But you're so smart. Somebody's going to snap you up. Later you'll be telling me it was the best thing that happened to you."

"I don't think so. This was such a kick in the gut. I worked so hard. HemisNorth was my life. I was loyal. I passed up other opportunities. And now..." She touched a finger in the air as if pressing a button. "I've been deleted."

"Wow. You make it sound like they offed you."

"Yeah, well, feels like it. Someday when you're a manager, don't let it change you," said Diana. "Stay compassionate."

Marella wasn't sure she deserved such a compliment when she was disappointed to be propping Diana up instead of working out the explosion mystery. "Who says I'm compassionate?"

Diana nearly did a spit take. "Trust me. You're compassionate. I saw you bring Laurie a cup of coffee when she had a hangover."

"It was no big deal. Coffee's free at work."

"You miss my point. You exhibited an indicator trait." She spoke the words slowly so that she wouldn't garble them while drunk. "Bringing people stuff instead of laughing at their pain and foibles. We should have had more like you in management."

"I'm not the management type. I'm terrible at getting people to do things."

"That's not how I'd sum up managing. And anyway, you'd be surprised at what you can do when you look at things in the right way. But here I am, giving you advice when I let this happen." She gestured as if waving away a mosquito.

"It's not your fault. Emmett said if you got laid off the rest of us wouldn't be far behind."

"They won't get rid of you. Elizabeth would fight for you. She says she only has to explain something to you once. And you always find a workaround. She talks about you like you're the future. And you are. Cheers to the future." She was starting to brighten up.

Marella raised her glass high. "To the future. It's going to be a better one." She took a tiny sip.

Diana wiggled her fingers at Marella. "Drink up! We have sorrows to drown. How are we going to have the hair of the dog that bit us tomorrow if the dog doesn't bite us today?" She was even more joyful now. She'd turned a corner. Maybe Marella could ask her some questions after all.

"I should get a dog," said Diana. "Maybe a Dalmatian. I think they have rescue Dalmatians."

Marella took another small sip. "I have to ask you about something. You worked a lot with Len and Eshana. Do you know much about Project Athena?"

Diana tilted her head, gazing directly at Marella. "If I did I couldn't talk about it."

Marella felt a flash of shame to be asking a friend to reveal company secrets. Still, if she had been contaminated, she needed to know sooner rather than later. Maybe there was something should take, like iodine for radiation. "So you do know."

"Why?"

"I just want to know how dangerous it is."

Diana took a deep breath and let it out through duck lips. "Dangerous. Well, yes, in the sense that everything is dangerous." She thrust her hand forward. "Hurtling down the street in a two-ton car is dangerous. Yet we do it every day. Eating food is dangerous. You

can't see botulism, salmonella, e-coli. It could be lurking in any food."
She examined her lemon garnish as if it were evil. "Yet we eat all day
long. What are we thinking?"

"So Project Athena is no more dangerous than eating?"

"What triggered this?"

Marella stared at her drink to avoid Diana's gaze. "I just...was
wondering if Project Athena might have had something to do with
the explosion."

"No. It was a faulty fuel tank."

"But what if that's not true?"

Diana touched her chin the way she did when she was
calculating numbers in her head. What did that mean? Was she
deciding whether or not to tell the real story? But she merely
responded, "It is true."

"I heard it might not be."

"Well then that was just a rumor. Like the one that Elizabeth
bites the heads off of birds."

Marella kept a straight face. "What makes you think that's a
rumor?"

Diana laughed like a lawn mower that wouldn't start, which
made Marella laugh too.

Marella continued. "Anyway, the danger thing was more than
just a rumor. Somebody high up said it might not be the fuel tank.
That it could be the Project Athena machine."

"Seriously?" asked Diana, leaning forward a little too far and
then catching herself with a start. Her drink sloshed. "Who said
that?"

Marella hesitated.

"For god's sake you can't say something like that and not tell me.
Who was it?"

"Elizabeth."

Diana leaned back slowly so as not to slosh her drink again. "Elizabeth actually told you that she thought Project Athena caused the explosion?"

"Well...yes." Marella felt her face redden. She had just told Diana a sideways lie to get her to tell her more. It felt horrible. She shouldn't treat a friend that way.

Diana raised her eyebrows, then looked up at the ceiling, seeming to process the information. She didn't immediately deny Project Athena could be the cause. Did that mean it could be?

"Shit," said Diana. "If they don't go forward with Project Athena." She looked distraught.

Diana seemed to be on the verge of opening up. Marella felt a flutter in her stomach. She might not like what she heard, but she needed to keep Diana talking. "What if they don't?"

"How much do you know about the project?"

Marella shrugged. "Not enough." Now she was telling the truth.

"Well for one thing, Project Athena is the answer to all our prayers. It will save humanity."

There was that term again. *Saving humanity*. If Diana was using it, then the words were more than just corporate pretention. Project Athena was supposed to save them all. From what?

Her friend continued. "And killing Project Athena would ruin my life. I spent the last five years on that project. If it goes forward and I can put it on my resume, I can work anywhere I want. I'll be in high demand. But if it doesn't, I'll be in limbo. They might hold me to confidentiality. I'll have a big gap where my resume will read, 'Can't tell ya.' And then everybody will say, 'Can't hire ya.'"

Marella cleared her throat. "That was just a prototype in Building C. If the real thing exploded, how bad would it be? As bad as Bhopal?"

"Bhopal! Wow." Diana wiped the air with her hand, dismissing the idea. "You don't have to worry about that."

"People didn't worry about Bhopal and then it blew up."

"Project Athena can't blow up Seattle or any other city. It's off in the middle of nowhere." She waved a floppy arm.

Marella closed her eyes, took a deep breath, and let it out. She felt grateful to Diana for easing her worry somewhat. But what about the employees who worked onsite? And what about any contamination from the explosion in the research building? "Project Athena is in middle of nowhere? So, Tacoma?"

Diana laughed the lawn mower laugh. She was from Tacoma. "Very funny."

"But seriously. It must be in eastern Washington then. In the desert, away from people."

Diana shook her head to the beat of her words. "No no no no no. It's off the coast."

"You mean in the Pacific Ocean? On a ship? What if docks at a port? Then it could be dangerous."

"No. Not on a ship."

"So on an island?"

"I'm not playing twenty questions until you get the right answer. Anyway, you'll find out soon enough. They initiated the project five months ago. Every month they started up a module. Today they planned to start up the final module. If they did, then soon there'll be a huge public relations thing. And then you'll know everything."

They were silent for a while. Questions stacked up in Marella's head. She wanted to know now. But she would have to have patience.

"What a kick in the gut," said Diana, her good mood fading.

"I don't understand why they laid you off. Wouldn't they need your expertise if they needed to troubleshoot something?"

"That's what I thought, but I guess I was wrong. If Eshana and Len were still alive, maybe they would have fought for me. That's what I get for being so heads down. I should have spent more time with the bigwigs. Gone to lunch with them, gone to ball games. My social game sucks. I realize that now."

Marella's shoulders slumped with guilt. She'd been holding Diana back from spending time with more important people by taking up her lunch hours. "I'm sorry. You should have been networking instead of exercising with me."

"That's the one thing I don't regret. I could have done both. It's too late for me at HemisNorth, though I'm trying to learn from failure. It's a good lesson for you too." She wagged a finger too close to Marella's face. Marella pulled back. "It can't hurt to have friends in high places." Diana leaned forward and pinched her friend's cheek like a grandmother. "Make friends. You're good at it. People like you."

Marella pulled away from the pinch, smiling at the compliment. She tried to imagine herself lunching with Belinda the tornado and Elizabeth the iguana. Or any of the managers. She saw herself dabbing the corner of her mouth with a cloth napkin saying, "We need to do something about our numbers," then spilling coffee on her blouse.

"Anyway," continued Diana, slashing her arm like a window wiper. "I'm done with the whole thing. I wouldn't go back even if they begged me on bended knee. I'm going to move to Micronesia and lie on the beach all day. I never want to hear the word HemisNorth again."

"Micronesia? That's random."

Diana downed the rest of her drink and smacked her lips. She smiled conspiratorially. "Not as random as you think." She lay back on the couch, closing her eyes. Her breathing became even. She was asleep.

Marella tapped on her glass. It was confusing. Project Athena was supposed to save humanity but could explode instead. Which would it do? Well, she wasn't going to find out tonight.

She took her glass to the sink and dumped the half she hadn't drunk so she could rinse the glass, but none came from the faucet. Typical. Things were always going wrong in this building. Broken heaters, stuck windows. She hoped her apartment wasn't affected too. She let herself out.

Chapter Five

After the visit with Diana, Marella went to her own apartment a few floors down. It seemed particularly bare. She needed Brielle to be perched on a stool near the old-fashioned sash window, cracking silly jokes about the people outside, while Mom invented whimsical stories about where those people were going and why.

Moving to this apartment had given her a taste of stability, though it made her understand how lost she was without her family. Lost without the very mother who had made her life so abnormal by moving them from place to place, fifty-two moves and counting.

The apartment also felt empty because she had so little furniture—no couch, no tables, only her bed and a dresser. The down payment on her used truck had been her priority, so she could visit her family wherever they happened to move to. She was lucky the building's age and lack of amenities kept the rent low in an otherwise expensive location or she couldn't have afforded it on her own.

She touched the clean edging of the leaded glass window in the cupboard. Ran a hand over the decades-old avocado laminate counter. Except for living alone there, she liked the apartment. It was small, but it had character. Plus, at six months, she'd lived there longer than any place she could remember. It almost felt like she had begun to grow roots.

She wandered to the map of the North American west coast she kept on her wall. It had a red dot on every town she'd ever lived in, most in Washington, a few in Oregon. The fifty-three dots gave the map a case of the measles. When she first marked up the map four years earlier, at fifteen years old, it had been to confront her mother. To make her face daily that she uprooted her family needlessly. Instead, it had become a source of reassurance, showing that she had been *somewhere* all that time, even if it wasn't *here*.

She ran a finger along the coast. Project Athena—the apparent savior of humanity—was there, somewhere in the ocean. Why? Had they discovered something out there? Perhaps a deposit of something under the sea floor, like oil but different. Whatever it was might require an oil-rig type structure to pump it out. Maybe several of them, and that might be why they talked about starting up different modules. What could they have found there that would save humanity?

A fountain of youth! Marella chuckled at the fantasy, imagining Elizabeth drinking such a liquid, morphing younger and younger, until she was seven years old yet still just as formidable. Handing out work assignments wearing pigtails and that iguana stare.

Perhaps it wasn't a product at all, but the location of a great experiment. A biosphere where people could live under the sea to practice for living on Mars, which humans might have to do if the Earth became too fouled. That could require modules and machines.

Or what if they were saving humanity by redesigning it? They could manipulate genes now in ways had been impossible not long ago. That would explain why they were offshore, to bypass any individual country's laws. She shivered. It was the stuff of horror films, especially since it involved a machine.

She broke off her musings. She could concoct one fantastic scenario after another, but the truth was Project Athena was likely something much more pedestrian. She remembered when the HemisNorth staff had made a big production about a new product to be unveiled. Then, as now, she had imagined great things, but it had only been a new type of food packaging.

She went to the sink to get a drink of water, but nothing came from the faucet. She stared at it meanly, as if it were a bad dog. No water at Diana's; no water here. The water in the entire building had been shut off. She leaned on the counter and sighed. She was thirsty and needed a shower. She texted the building manager. *When will the water be back on?*

The reply was immediate. *Water shut off in Seattle.* She pulled her head back in dismay. What?

She sat on her bed, clicked a local TV news channel app on her phone, and called up a piece about the drought. "Breaking News" ticker-taped across the bottom of the screen in thick red letters. An announcer with a jutting chin was speaking in the urgent, professional tone used for serious news. "The water level of lakes and rivers across the Pacific Northwest dropped drastically today, in some places by half."

Half? She couldn't have heard correctly. That would be impossible here in the Pacific Northwest, a place so well known for its rain that a local company made rain globes instead of snow globes.

The screen showed a dock with a swimmer cannonballing into a lake, and a sunbather jerking away from his splash. The announcer continued. "That was Lake Sammamish this morning. Here it is now." The camera showed the same dock now high and dry. A seagull landed then took off again, as if disappointed by the scene. "At eight miles long, Lake Sammamish is the sixth largest lake in Washington."

Her throat tightened. She covered her mouth with her hand. She sat riveted, waiting for a logical explanation. Half of an eight-mile lake gone. That was a phenomenal amount of water to disappear in a short amount of time. Where could it have gone? She imagined a chain lifting a giant plug from the bottom of the lake, the water whirlpooling into the Earth's bowels.

A camera panned across a river. Boulders protruded like iceberg tips from its rushing water. Cedar trees stood sentry right up to its banks. The announcer continued. "This was a Cedar River tributary this morning. Its watershed supplies Seattle with the majority of its water." Newer footage showed the boulders dressed in algae where the water had abandoned them. The river was now half its previous size, meandering through ash-gray rocks dozens of feet from the cedars. "Here is that same tributary, live. Experts are trying to determine why water has disappeared throughout the Pacific Northwest and beyond." A map appeared. A grid covered most of Washington and Oregon, plus sections of British Columbia and northern California.

A montage played: half-drained lake beds the color of aged concrete. Shrunken rivers. Boats sitting crookedly like abandoned toys. Her horror mounted with each new image.

"Why did the water disappear?" asked the announcer. "Will it continue to vanish, and for how long? Utilities throughout the Pacific Northwest turned off the water without warning today. Some have labeled this the Aguageddon, but officials assure us that stockpiles will get us through until the solution is found."

She hunched, pressing her hands to her temples to try to make sense of it. Aguageddon. Yes, the name fit. Already it hadn't rained in five months, which had never happened before. And now this. Half the area's fresh water gone. Just like that. Would the other half disappear tomorrow? And what then? How would they survive?

She straightened. Emmett had mentioned the lakes but she had been distracted by Diana's layoff. And the biologist had told Elizabeth there wasn't any water to sample. Why hadn't she paid attention? She could have prepared. Filled some containers, and her bathtub. But now she had nothing to drink at all. She had no pop or juice, and was out of milk.

Was there any water left in the reservoirs? What was the city's plan? She rubbed her temples. She and her family would have to move away. The Midwest, or the east coast. The thought of having to pick up and go again was devastating.

She dialed her mother. "Mom. Did you hear about the water?"

"What about it?" Mom sounded calm.

"They turned it off in Seattle. Is yours off too?"

"I don't know. Let me check. What's going on? Has it got E. coli or something?"

"No, it's disappearing. The lakes have shrunk by half. Rivers drying up. It's crazy. Things like this don't happen."

"By half? Are you sure? That doesn't sound right. I didn't think the drought was that bad. They were only saying not to water the lawn." She made a noise of dismay. "Oh no, it's shut off here too. What's going on? Why is this happening?"

"No idea. It doesn't make sense." Marella couldn't bring herself to suggest moving out of the area. She needed to know more first.

There was silence. She could imagine her mother twisting her shirt hem while she thought. When Mom finally spoke, her tone was pinched. "I can't clean houses without water, that means no work. You know what else, most of our power is hydro. The electricity will go off. Charge your phone."

This new thought only added to Marella's alarm. No water meant so much more than just no water. Problems would radiate like spokes of a wheel. "Have you got stuff to drink?"

"Let me think. A quart of milk. A couple of cans of pop. I'll have to go to the store."

"Me too."

"Better hurry. It'll be a madhouse."

• • • •

SHOPPERS SPRINTED PAST Marella as she rushed a cart with a stubborn wheel down the grocery store aisles. "Time after Time" played on the sound system, the same as the last time she'd been here. Back then the shelves were overflowing with cases of beverages. Now those aisles were bare.

She hurried down other aisles, her mouth as dry as chalk. Surely there was something to drink somewhere in the store. Some liquid item others had missed. She screwed up her face at the sight of potato chips, crackers, and salted nuts. No, no, and no.

She had been through most of the store when she remembered that the imported goods section had canned guava, pineapple, and papaya juice. Her heart thumped harder than it should. Grocery shopping wasn't supposed to be spinetingling. Still, she felt like a bloodhound on the scent trail.

She arrived at the spot only to see bare shelves where the drinks should have been. She slumped over the shopping cart, her forehead on her arm. "Come on. Come on." She straightened. Took a rallying breath. *Don't give in that easily.* Dropping to her knees, she pushed aside jars of cocoa powder.

There, hidden back behind, was a can of papaya juice, looking yellow and orange and beautiful. Stifling a shout of relief, she peeked up and down the aisle to make sure nobody was watching, then grasped it, feeling the coolness of it in her hand. She could almost taste it. Tangy. Sweet. A bit thick for as thirsty as she was, but a godsend.

She continued moving cans aside. That was it. No other drinks. This would have to do. This would be the stopgap she needed to get through the evening.

Abandoning the cart, she headed for the checkout area, but felt vulnerable. She grasped the can in both hands, hiding its label to avoid attracting the attention of other shoppers. Even so, a businessman in a pinstripe dress shirt appeared suddenly beside her, making her start. He had the gaze of a religious fanatic, which contrasted oddly with his professional style of dress. Her stomach flipped the way it did at the sight of roadkill.

"Where did you get that?" asked the man.

"Aisle ten." She named the first number that came to mind. When he moved on, she blew an extended breath through her lips, feeling as if she'd dodged a confrontation. This was much too stressful. She couldn't wait to buy the juice and get out.

At the checkout counter she set the can down. Out of nowhere a hand grabbed it. She wheeled; the businessman in the pinstripe shirt had stolen her salvation. "Hey, that's mine!" Marella lunged for it, grabbing onto his arm. As he yanked himself away she tripped, twisting awkwardly and falling to her hands and knees. Pain shot through her left ankle.

She was about to jump up anyway, but a knife appeared in the man's hand.

"What the fuck?" She scooted back against the checkout counter, flipping up a hand-held shopping basket, brandishing it like a shield. This was too surreal. A businessman couldn't really be threatening her over a can of juice with what appeared to be a steak knife, and she couldn't really be about to fight him for it. But her throat was as sticky as flypaper. She had to get the drink back.

She needed a weapon, fast. She scanned the area for something, anything, seeing candy bars, pine tree shaped car air fresheners, breath mints. The shelf labeled "batteries" was empty. She could at least have thrown those at him, or used them as a kind of brass knuckles. There was nothing. But she had the basket. That would have to do.

She scrambled to her feet. Her ankle ached but she lunged forward anyway, heaving the basket at his knife hand, trying to knock the blade away. He leapt back as nimbly as a ballroom dancer. She had missed completely.

He ran, circling around another checkout stand, nearly colliding with the automatic door as it opened, then rushed off into the parking lot.

"Bastard!" she yelled. The other shoppers eased away. She must have looked as wild and angry as she felt. She took a few steps back, favoring her ankle. Everybody was staring at her. She felt hot. Setting the basket down, she limped for the door.

What had she been thinking, attacking an armed man? She could have gotten stabbed. As she hobbled, the last half-minute spooled in her mind. Would he really have knifed her over a single can of juice? Were things really that bad, or had they both overreacted? Her mind wheeled with confusion. All she knew was that she was damn thirsty and there seemed to be nothing she could do about it.

• • • •

AFTER GETTING HOME from the grocery store, Marella sat on her bed, a frozen gel pack on her ankle. She wished it had actual water instead of whatever goo it contained. She was still riled up from the encounter with the businessman.

The news app on her phone showed live footage of the Red Cross distributing water to a group of thankful citizens. The screen now split in two. On the left, the announcer with the jutting chin was still at a news desk, gazing into the camera with professional intensity. On the right was the subject of an interview, a man in tortoiseshell glasses with an air of profound knowledge. Maybe she would learn why this was all happening.

The announcer raised a palm quizzically. "This is the Pacific Northwest. We set world records for rain. Why has there been a drought, and why is it suddenly worse?"

The expert shook his head as if to say he'd known it all along. "The fact is, climate change has finally caught up with us."

"How can it be climate change when the problem is localized to the Pacific Northwest?" asked the announcer.

"This area has always been an outlier," said the expert. "It's a geographic exception on so many levels. Its position on the Pacific Ocean brings warmer water up from the south, which keeps this area temperate when it's actually farther north than Maine and Montreal. That's why we rarely get frigid temperatures, and have minimal snowfall at sea level."

Marella shook her head. This was nothing new. It didn't seem like a strong enough explanation.

The expert continued. "Climate change predictions showed that while other areas would get drier, here it would be even wetter in the winter, and drier in the summer. This follows the prediction exactly. It's summer. It's drier."

Marella looked out the window at the clear sky. This didn't explain why things ramped up so quickly, and it didn't tell how to solve it. Climate change was massive, without a clear, obvious solution. It wasn't like a hole in the roof that could be patched. It was like having no roof at all, and nothing to build one with.

"And when the rain does return in the fall," continued the expert, "there will be too much of it. If we're smart, we'll be prepared for that. We need to act rather than react."

She was so thirsty. She just needed something to tide her over until she could get the Red Cross water. An idea struck her. She took the ice pack off her ankle and stood. It felt better. She crossed to the toilet and lifted off the tank lid, revealing gray rings and a brown-caked float. The smell of mildew wafted upward. She had often had to fiddle with the workings in old toilets to get them to stop continuously flushing and they never smelled this bad. She screwed up her face and replaced the lid. She wasn't that desperate. And this building didn't have water heaters in the individual apartments, so that wasn't an option either.

Her phone showed the closest distribution location as Occidental Square, in the historic district of Seattle. The water would arrive at eight o'clock PM.

It was now seven-thirty. She would have to get moving.

Chapter Six

Marella drove through downtown streets for twenty minutes before finding a place to park, in a lot ten blocks from Occidental Square. It was five minutes to eight. Ankle aching, she hurried down the narrow sidewalk. She'd hoped to get enough water to last at least a week, and also to bring to Diana and to her family if they needed it. A ten-block trip to her car would make that impossible.

She rushed past a window placard that ordered: Get your game on! The demand for fun seemed idiotic under the circumstances. She just wanted to be done with this task. She didn't want to be here at all, getting her game on or getting her water on.

Others were also heading to Occidental Square. The sidewalks grew more and more crowded. Except for the strained look on people's faces, it could have been a summer festival. There were just too many people. Why hadn't they named more locations? They should have had one up on First Hill where she lived.

Marella heard the murmur of many voices ahead. Turning onto South Main, she stopped cold, her heart sinking. Hundreds, maybe thousands of people filled Occidental Square, yet more continued to arrive. Even the carved faces on two towering totem poles seemed startled by the throng. How much water would she be able to take away with so many people in need?

Where should she go? Where was the water? It didn't appear to be there yet, but where would it be handed out? As new arrivals pushed past her she scanned the square for some kind of staging area. Would there be a tent, or tables? Was there a sign explaining how the handout would work?

There was nothing. It was ridiculous to expect it. This was a disaster, not an open-air concert with velvet ropes to point the orderly way forward. Still, they would need to keep control somehow. She scanned for people who looked official. She saw only teaming masses.

On one side of the square, thick ivy trunks clung to an old brick building. Across from it stood a newly built glass-walled office building. The water would probably arrive in trucks, which would have to park on either of the streets on the opposite sides of the square. She decided to wait in the middle, so she could head one way or another depending on where it showed up.

She made her way to one of the few spots not already occupied: a tiny patch of brick near the bronze fallen firefighter memorial statues. The four life-sized firefighters struggled to fight an unseen fire. She touched a statue, then jerked her hand away from its blistering heat.

She considered sitting, but the people around her were standing. She needed to be able to see the water trucks and move quickly once she spotted them.

Breathing shallowly, she tried not to inhale the stink of so many bodies. Mom would find this difficult; she avoided crowds. To be honest, that had been fine with Marella. She had always viewed it as her mother's anxiety, but she felt it sometimes, especially now. There were just too many people stuffed into one place. Hopefully things were different for Mom and Brielle in Centralia.

The sun beat down on her, but soon there would be shade. The wind, although annoying in its persistence, made the heat tolerable.

She brushed dust from her forehead, her shirt, her pant leg. Adjusted her backpack on her shoulders. Still more people arrived. Her anxiety built. It was claustrophobic. So much need. Even if they brought semitrucks of water how would there be enough for everybody? How would they control such a big crowd? What would she do if she had to leave empty-handed?

"Patience," Mom would say when Marella was tense. Brielle would add, "Try to be in the moment." Marella tried, but couldn't help agonizing about how her family was doing.

She tried to have faith that things could run smoothly. But people seemed jittery, just like the businessman who had attacked her. A woman with stained teeth looked Marella up and down, as if evaluating her fighting ability. A craggy-faced man cracked his knuckles. Her stomach felt heavy, a mass of misshapen clay.

When a semitruck rumbled up and stopped on the street, a woman pushed past, knocking her against a brass firefighter and bruising her shoulder blade. "Hey," shouted Marella, but the woman didn't look back, and nobody paid any attention. Their focus was on the truck. People surged past, but she didn't join them, leery of the way they were packing together. It looked dangerous. People might get crushed. The water handout wasn't worth all that.

Or was she underestimating her quandary? Where was she going to get water, if not here? Lakes and rivers had lost half their volume in one day. What if she didn't get water here tonight? Elliott Bay, only a few blocks away, would have been a fallback, except it was salt water and not particularly clean at that. Should she drive to Lake Washington instead? What was the closest spot, and how much water was there now?

She called up the news app again, and saw the headline, "Lakes and Rivers Vanished." She froze, staring at the words. Thinking they couldn't be real. But they were. She moaned out loud as she scrolled through the details. No water in the Pacific Northwest. Lakes bone-dry. Rivers empty.

There was hope. The Pacific Northwest was still the only place with disappearing lakes. Going east would solve her problem. Maybe she could work for HemisNorth in a different city. All was not lost.

But she needed water now, and her phone now showed all other water distribution locations as closed. This was her only option.

The semitruck moved on. The minutes went by. Eight fifteen. Eight thirty. The sun was lower, its golden light giving the buildings a lovely tint that didn't fit the situation. A disaster shouldn't be so lovely. So picturesque.

Shade slunk across the square as more time crept by. The air felt stiflingly heavy. The general murmur of the crowd intensified, becoming louder and angrier. Nobody seemed tired anymore. People bobbed and hovered like cobras about to strike.

Should she go home and drink the toilet tank water after all? She imagined dipping a cup in. Sipping the mildewy liquid. Would it be any better if she boiled it? Her stomach lurched at the thought.

A voice boomed out, loud and commanding. "There's no real water shortage."

Marella whirled to see the speaker. A woman in a red shirt had commandeered a bench near the totem poles, her arms raised high. Elizabeth had once said people tended to listen to those who wore red. Marella would have listened to this woman regardless of what she wore. Her bearing was that authoritative, her expression that fierce. "The government has stolen our water. They've stocked it all away, and now they're going to dole it out little by little to make us dependent."

Marella felt a shiver skittering down her spine. Had she been duped so easily? She wanted to believe the woman, welcoming such a straightforward explanation. If "they" were taking it away, "they" needed to give it back. It would feel so good to fight for what was hers. It was her right to drink water. Like it was her right to breathe air.

But this woman was wrong, so wrong. The government couldn't have taken the water. That would be a scientific marvel. How could they siphon away such a massive amount of water and where could they have put it? It wasn't physically possible. This was a natural disaster, not an intentional one.

The crowd was silent now, hanging on the woman's every word. Even the totem pole creatures seemed to listen, eyes narrowed with ire. "They took our water to make us docile. To turn us into robots who will follow them blindly."

"That's right," replied a man in the crowd. Many others shouted agreement. Marella could feel the horde massing into a single entity, as if a colossal net was gathering them, packing them in with the woman and her false accusations.

How could they believe her? She gave no proof. But they didn't need it, she realized, to believe what they wanted to hear.

"We're not going to stand for it," bellowed the woman in red, her voice filling the space. She continued in a preacher-like singsong voice, chin lifted to the sky, hands clenched into fists. "They *created* a problem to make us fall in line. They *created* a problem to distract us from voting them out. They *created* a problem to make us love them. Oh, thank you governor for bringing us water. Oh, thank you mayor for bringing us water. Thank you, thank you, thank you."

People were responding with shouts of anger. A man wearing a "mean people suck" t-shirt began pumping his arms as if lifting weights, crying, "Fucking assholes." Alarmed, Marella shrank away to avoid being accidentally punched.

Others were just as frenzied. A man with a bulbous head was shouting himself red in the face. A woman with turquoise hair let out a torrent of obscenities as if they'd built up inside all her life and were only now being released.

It was all happening so fast. And still the red-shirted woman's voice boomed over the growing mayhem, urging fury.

Marella looked for police. She thought she saw a couple of them across the square, but couldn't see what they were doing. There were not enough of them to keep order if things went south. But if more came, that could be bad too. She didn't want to be corralled or tear-gassed.

Her mind whirled, trying to predict the next few minutes. Every scenario seemed to involve an eruption if this woman kept vomiting hate out into the square. There would be a riot. She wouldn't get water. Nobody would.

She felt as if a massive pool of magma raged under the square, determined to burst though. Something had to be done quickly. One of Elizabeth's phrases came to mind. *"No action" is an action.* Not doing something about a problem had just as much consequence as causing the problem in the first place. And anyway, no random rabble-rouser was going to keep her from getting what was rightfully hers. She'd have to stop the woman herself.

She balled her fists, stomping forward. People were so riveted by the woman they barely noticed Marella pushing her way between them.

At the bench the woman loomed above her. Up close her eyes radiated danger. Marella's gut tightened. It felt like she was about to provoke a lightning storm, but she had to act anyway. She gathered her courage, pulled herself up to her full height, and bellowed over the din, "Stop riling people up. If there's a riot they won't bring the water. People will get hurt."

The woman turned her attention to Marella, hate in her eyes. She spit her words. "I'm talking about injustice. Evil. If you're not one of us, you're one of them." She flicked her fingers, dismissing Marella, and returned her attention to the crowd.

Marella growled in fury. She wasn't a bug to be waved away. She gripped the woman's ankle to get her attention once more and spoke each word distinctly. "It's not possible. The government couldn't take the water."

The woman kicked out of Marella's grasp, nearly hitting Marella's face. "Back off, bitch." She then planted herself more firmly on the bench, legs at shoulder width. Addressing the crowd, she pounded her fists in the air. "We do not thank you. We do not thank you for letting our children go without water. We do not thank you for letting our families suffer thirst." The crowd whooped back.

Marella breathed quickly. Anger catapulted her onto the bench, where she shouted, "Everybody stay calm. We're not going to get water by starting a riot."

Her words boomed louder than she thought they would. The cacophony lowered.

Abruptly it sank in. All those faces were looking at her. Such a variety of expressions. Surprise, expectation, anger, despair. All directed at her. Marella's legs shook. She went from being enraged to being struck with stage fright in a matter of seconds. What should she say to them now? She wasn't good at persuasion. She spoke the first words that came to mind. "If we all stay calm the water will get here." Stupid, she thought. As if the water was late to a party. But they were listening to her. Paying attention. This was her opportunity to set things right.

She took a deep breath, shouting from her gut. "The government didn't take the water. What makes you think they're that smart? If they couldn't solve the homeless problem in years how could they hide billions of gallons of water in one day?"

The people seemed rapt. Listening to her. Encouraged, she continued. "We all need to help each other. Get through this together." They watched her. Marella faltered. What else could she say? This was like the actor's nightmare of being onstage without knowing the lines. Without even having read the script. What was the name of the damn play? She didn't know what else to tell them.

The red-shirted woman chanted, "Wa-ter, wa-ter, wa-ter." Others added their voices until the sound was deafening. Just like that, Marella's influence dissolved. She felt invisible.

Still, she waved her arms, yelling for calm, but the mob drowned her out. She regarded their faces, now all bearing the same expression of menace, lips curled, eyes glaring. Not only had the crowd become one, but it had transformed into something nonhuman. There would be no convincing it. No logic could affect it now.

Get out. She had to leave before the riot began. She tracked the path she needed to take. Past the firefighter statue to the edge of the square and from there to the street.

A fire truck came into view. She inhaled abruptly. There would be water in the fire truck. And when everybody else figured that out there would be chaos.

She leaped off the bench, scowling at the pain in her ankle. She squeezed between two men who smelled of machine oil and past several teenagers who smelled of pot, but was held up by a solid row of people who pummeled the sky with their fists. She pivoted right, then left. Too many tall people. She couldn't see. Which was the best route out?

Then suddenly a voice boomed over the chanting. "There's water in the fire truck!"

The crowd roared, then snapped shut around Marella like a bear trap. Claustrophobia seized her with invisible claws, making it hard to think. She pushed with all her strength, trying to move forward, sideways, backward, but was stuck in place.

An elbow jabbed her in the gut, making her "oof" with pain. A hand pushed at her face, snapping her head to the side and wrenching her neck. She screamed, her voice drowned out by shouting. The multitude pushed her this way, then that.

She became wedged against a man's back, her face smothered in his armpit. She managed only short gasping breaths that were filled with his stink. She could feel his back muscles working to free himself, his buttocks squeezing and moving. She felt squirming behind her. An elbow jabbed her ribs once, twice, then again and again. Tears came to her eyes from the pain of it. She grunted, "Stop, I can't move," but the elbow kept jabbing. Somebody kicked her shin. Somebody stepped on her foot.

Then the mob was moving. She could only lurch along with it, with no perception of direction. An overwhelming sense of failure made her eyes tear up. What had made her think she had any power of persuasion? She should have left earlier, but now she would be hurt or maimed, or even die.

Space opened up to her right. She was terrified that she would lose her balance and fall into it, get trampled. She lurched sideways into the break, managing to stay upright. The crowd pressed against her once more, penning her more solidly this time, jamming her arms to her sides and lifting her. She wiggled her feet uselessly. The pressure tightened steadily like a trash compactor. Somebody's nose was above hers so that the little breath she could get was his expelled air, its oxygen depleted before it got to her. Now the crowd squeezed her so snugly that her chest compressed.

Dizziness. Helplessness. She could die. Crushed by fellow human beings. Her terror mixed with anger with the idea of such an unnecessary demise. A buzz whirlpooled in her ears. She made a herculean effort, trying to pound her arms, twist her torso, kick her legs, writhe, but she was locked in position as if buried alive. She could do nothing except plead silently. *Help me. Help me. I can't die this way.*

The crowd shifted. Her feet touched the ground. She took a deep, aching breath, extending her elbows to protect her chest. Taking more wheezing breaths, she pushed forward through a slight gap. If she could just keep going, she might get free of the crowd.

But now she saw a woman on the ground, curled up around an object. People were stepping on her. She was wailing, crying, shouting, trying to protect whatever she was holding.

A tiny fist appeared. That was a baby! In a pale green front pack, in danger of being crushed and trampled. Marella made a noise of anguish. She already knew this riot was madness, but now it seemed to be a special kind of insanity. The kind that would cause an innocent baby to perish in its anarchy.

One thing was for sure, if the woman remained on the bricks, she and her child would die. But she was too busy protecting her baby to rise to her feet.

"There's a baby! Look out for the baby!" Marella's words were lost in the racket. She squeezed through to the prone figure, then knelt, grasping the woman's shoulders, tugging upward. The mother resisted, screaming, eyes closed tight.

A knee struck Marella in the side, making her grunt with pain. The crowd was tightening up around them. She didn't have time for this. She would also be trampled if she didn't pull the woman to her feet.

She shouted in the woman's ear. "I'm trying to help! Get up!"

The woman peeked upward, her face contorted with fear. Marella tugged on her again. "Up! Up!" This time the woman allowed the help, shifting her body. Marella managed to pull the woman onto her knees.

A man was falling toward the baby. Marella threw herself in the way. The man's knee slammed against her ear. The pain was excruciating. Her head rang. She panted. Such a blow might have killed the baby. She herself couldn't take another hit like that.

Enough dilly-dallying around. Marella clamped onto the woman's shoulders and gave a giant heave, pulling her to her feet.

The crowd closed in further. The baby was still in danger. Marella braced her arms on the woman's shoulders. In turn, the woman braced her arms against Marella's. Together they formed a fortress to protect the baby, but the woman's arms were weak. Marella provided most of the strength.

She could see the top of the baby's head, smaller than a grapefruit. It smelled of baby shampoo. Was it a week old? More? Marella couldn't tell, but it couldn't have been long since the woman gave birth; no wonder her arms felt so weak. The woman's expression seemed hopeless. It threatened to pull Marella under. How were they going to save such a tiny creature among all this lunacy? "We can do this," shouted Marella. "Don't give up. Hold on." The woman gave a quick, short nod.

Marella resumed yelling, "Don't hurt the baby!" but she was just one of many shouting, swearing, wailing, and crying. There was a jab in her side; a sharp blow that made her arch with pain. It happened again. She held her position. The baby oblivious. Not knowing the danger. Not understanding that this riot would have been unthinkable only the day before.

Her arms shook with effort. She couldn't do this indefinitely. She wasn't stronger than the combined force of thousands. If they stayed where they were her arms would crumple and she would be pressed against the baby. It would be crushed between her and the mother. She would feel its death against her chest. The mere thought sent a wave of grief through her being. She couldn't allow such a thing.

The baby moved its tiny head. She could see its face. The itty-bitty nose, a wisp of hair. Though it wasn't possible, she thought she heard a tiny sigh woven into the noise of the crowd. Marella thought her heart would break. The baby didn't deserve this. It was innocent.

She spotted a wall to her right, with ivy trunks as thick as her arm. Could they climb to safety? It would be a desperate move, but it was all she had. "This way!" she shouted, steering the woman. They made small gains toward the wall. Slowly they scooted until they reached it. She felt a frisson of victory, but they weren't free yet. The mother needed to find the strength to pull herself up. The woman grabbed hold of an ivy trunk. Marella positioned herself behind, blocking the crowd as well as she could and pushing her upward.

The woman and baby rose to safety. A feeling of triumph welled up. She had saved a life. Because of her, the baby would grow to be an actual person, with dreams and feelings and experiences.

But there was no time to bask. The crowd knocked Marella to the side. She recovered, latching onto the ivy trunk. Arms trembling, she rose one handhold high, then another, then another. Two feet high. Three feet high. Her heart soared. She felt the roughness of the ivy trunk against her hands, the scratching of dead leaves against her face. She was free.

Somebody bashed into her legs, knocking them off their purchase. She grunted in surprise but held fast, legs dangling. The ivy in her right hand ripped away from the wall. She fell backward, hitting a man's shoulder then landing hard on the bricks. She arched with the pain in her back.

A kick caught her right in the midsection. She gasped for breath, closing into a fetal position and covering her face with her hands. Somebody fell over her.

She had the sudden, terrible notion that she had somehow been chosen to die in the baby's place. But she hadn't agreed to that. It wasn't right. This wasn't how she should be repaid for saving a baby's life. Instead, it was like the devil was conspiring against her, literally kicking her when she was down. Dragging her to her death. Huddled on the bricks she felt inches from the devil's knobby scarlet fingers. She could feel his hot breath on her neck. Smell his sulfurous stench.

Terror drove her. With a heroic effort she wrenched herself to her knees and maneuvered to face the wall. Clutching the ivy once more, she pulled herself to standing, then continued upward. This time she clambered above the crowd, where she clung, shaking with effort. The woman with the baby still hung onto the ivy trunks, a strained expression of relief on her face—for her baby, yes, but also for Marella. The Devil had been trying to take her, but the woman had been hoping she would make it. Marella hadn't been alone.

Marella gave a grunt of a laugh that felt slightly insane. She looked down to see the people in the crowd still pushing at one another. For a time, she had thought of the crowd as a single entity, something to be overcome. But she had just been a part of it, pushing, thrusting, probably hurting, on her way to save herself. She was guilty. She was part of the monster.

A rooster tail of water arched over the crowd. Somebody had taken control of the fire hose, turning it on. Voices called for the water to be sent in their direction. People raised cupped hands, trying vainly to catch the liquid, which drenched them, then splashed to the ground. It was such a waste. All that suffering for the water to spill and be gone.

The spray neared Marella, sparkling in the sun. When it struck her, the stream was so strong she had to squeeze her eyes shut and turn her head. She opened her mouth to taste the rivulets of lukewarm water running down her face, desperate to get it into her parched throat.

It was salty. She gagged, spitting it out. The fire engine's tank had been filled with seawater, not fresh water. She would not get the slightest bit of relief.

There was a clattering of breaking glass, somebody smashing the glass doors of the building she clung to. People poured inside like stormwater into a drainpipe. *Good. That will make more room for everybody.*

Gunshots rang out. She jerked with surprise, then flattened herself against the wall, looking wildly in all directions, trying to pinpoint the source. The crowd was a shifting kaleidoscope, impossible to read. The shots could have come from anywhere; up here she was a prime target.

With people scattering the crowd thinned somewhat, but a fight had broken out. A man with a black eye was brandishing a broken bottle at a man waving a two-by-four. They circled in an odd dance right below Marella. She felt like a migrating wildebeest trying to judge when to jump into a crocodile-infested river.

The woman with the baby began to climb down. "No!" said Marella, but the woman dropped to the ground, which distracted the man with the bottle just long enough for the other man to swing the two-by-four like a baseball bat. He smashed the man's head. It sounded like a tree trunk snapping. Marella cringed, tightening against the wall.

Blood cascaded down the man's face as he dropped limply to the ground. His eyes were open. She tried to control her breathing but was now gulping air. The crowd widened around the dead man like a camera iris opening. She scrambled down, then stood frozen, unable to take her eyes off the body.

It took so little to turn a human being into a packet of flesh. And so little to make her imagine demons reaching upward to take their due. Red beings whose fists would punch through the brick and spear the man with their claws, then reach for her too, eyes glaring, mouths slavering.

Somebody bumped her hard, eliciting a grunt and nearly pushing her over. The spell broke. Marella ran, shoes slapping on the bricks and then on the concrete of the road. The crowd opened up even more. She shot ever forward, her body racing, her mind churning. She ran for a block, then another, finally stopping to rest her sore ankle and take in great, gulping breaths.

What now?

Go home. Drink water from the toilet tank. Pack essentials. Drive to her family and get the hell out of the drought zone.

• • • •

WHEN MARELLA ARRIVED home and turned her key in the lock there was no resistance. She remembered locking her door when she'd left earlier that day. Turning the key clockwise. Stashing it in the small pocket of her backpack.

Heart thudding in her chest, she pushed the door open using her fingertips. She hoped against hope that her landlord had entered for some unusual reason, accidentally leaving it unlocked. Because if he hadn't, she had been robbed.

Chapter Seven

Marella listened for movement inside her apartment. It was quiet. She peeked in. There didn't appear to be anybody inside. She stepped gingerly forward.

She had been robbed, but in a way she didn't expect. The toilet tank lid was now on the floor. She trotted over. The thief had taken the water from the toilet back, leaving nothing but a series of dingy gray watermark rings. The toilet bowl was also empty.

Nausea welled up. She understood how people felt violated after being robbed, and this went even deeper. This was stealing the stuff of life. This was somebody stating cruelly that they didn't care whether she lived or died.

She pounded the wall. "You bastard. How could you do this to me?"

She rushed to the bedroom. Her laptop was on the bed where she'd left it. Her jewelry was untouched—just cheap stuff, but they would have had to open her jewelry box to find that out, and they hadn't. Her dresser drawers were closed. Supposedly thieves made a big mess looking for pricey items, but these thieves didn't care about anything but water.

In the kitchen the cupboard doors were ajar. The cans of string beans and fruit cocktail her mother had left when she moved out were gone. For the water inside the cans, she realized. She felt stupid for not having understood her canned food had value. It was like not realizing she owned gold ingots, which made the loss all the more infuriating. At the grocery store all the canned vegetables had been bought out and now she understood why. She felt stupid. One step behind.

Diana. Had they broken into her place too? Had they hurt her? She called on her phone. No answer. She rushed up the stairwell and to Diana's door and pounded on it. No response. She tried the door and it was locked. Hopefully that meant she was safe.

Marella was so dehydrated. Surely a neighbor would help, if they hadn't all been robbed as well. Marella went back downstairs and knocked on several doors, calling, "It's Marella, your neighbor." There was no answer. She heard arguing in the stairwell, threatening voices. Heart thumping, she rushed back to her own apartment.

She dropped onto her mattress, holding her head. *Get it together. Think. Do something.*

The light went out. She slumped. Her mother had warned her that the electricity would go out.

She called her mother's number. The connection wasn't good—Mom's voice sounded small and distant—but she could still hear relief that Marella had called.

"Did you get water?" asked Marella.

"Yes, but only a gallon and then the store sold out. Did you?"

Should she tell her mother what she'd been through? Or would it upset her too much? "I went to a distribution location but the water didn't show up." Marella rubbed her sore ankle. At least it was her left one. That meant a long drive wouldn't be painful. "Listen, Mom, I'm coming there. We're going to get out of the Northwest. We can't stay here any longer."

"No you can't come here." Her mother's strident tone made Marella grip the blanket. "It's too dangerous."

"Why, what happened? Are you all right?"

"We're fine, but we heard there are gangs of robbers on I-5 near Tumwater."

Marella felt something jolt her psyche. First a single thief in a grocery store, then a couple of burglars in an apartment, and now gangs out in the open. Any sense of safety she retained was only an illusion. She remembered reading history books where people had suffered famine, wondering why they didn't just leave. Go where there was food, or in her case, water. It was easy to suggest it. Much harder to do.

Mom continued, "Tomorrow things will be different. The National Guard is going to be called out. And also they're going to airlift in big shipments of water from other parts of the country."

She felt hot as resentment boiled up. The National Guard should be here now. The airlifts should be here already. There was no reason for everything to take so long. Didn't they learn anything from Hurricane Katrina? They were supposed to be ready.

"Okay," said Marella. "Be careful. Don't let anybody in the house."

She should be with her family. She should have moved to Centralia with them. She'd be there now. They would be stronger together.

"Brielle wants to talk to you. I'm putting us on speaker."

"Okay."

"I don't get it." Brielle's voice sounded affronted, as if she'd just been insulted. "How could the water just disappear?"

"They said climate change." It felt lame to repeat something she didn't understand.

"But when it's too hot and the snow melts in the mountains, then there's more water, not less," said Brielle. "The water should be up to our ears. Okay, not really, but you know what I'm saying."

Marella scrunched her forehead. Her sister was right. It just didn't make sense.

Mom spoke up, her voice breathless. "It must have evaporated or something."

"Water doesn't evaporate that fast. I think aliens are taking it." Brielle spoke seriously.

"Aliens!" said Mom. "Are you crazy?"

"Have you got a better idea?" asked Brielle. "Maybe they have cloaking devices. *Somebody* took it. It's gone. Where did it go?"

Marella twisted the blanket uneasily. How could the water just disappear? What was different about the Pacific Northwest that would make lakes disappear so quickly, while the rest of the world's water bodies remained normal?

"Maybe it drained into underground cracks," said Mom.

"Not all that water," said Brielle. "The earth is too dense. There are whole layers of rock and dirt."

"But there's room in some places," said Mom, sounding defensive. "It's all that fracking. Businesses just come in and do whatever they want to the land, and ruin it for everybody. And we just let them. You see what happens. They aren't accountable. Anyway, our power's out. We have to save the batteries on our phones. I'll talk to you tomorrow."

Marella tossed her phone onto the mattress, consumed with helplessness. She could do nothing for them right now. She felt stuck. She wanted to be out of there, out of the danger area, out of the Northwest. Put the riots and the Aguageddon behind. She'd never wanted to move so badly before. And now she couldn't.

It was just as well, she supposed. She was exhausted and in pain. She collapsed backward on the bed. Tomorrow would bring an answer. Tomorrow she could act.

• • • •

MARELLA AWOKE WITH a gasp. She'd dreamed of demons rioting, the devil clutching her as mayhem raged all around.

Only three thirty in the morning. She got up to shake off the dream shards. She wished that babysitter had never told her about demons. So what if they weren't real? They still frightened her after all this time.

The power was still out. Her mouth still dry. She grabbed her flashlight and checked the faucet, turning the handle on and off like a pump. Even a drop of water would help. There was nothing.

She looked at her phone. No text from Diana. Hopefully she was all right and in the morning she would hear from her.

In the living room she shone the flashlight on the map with pins in all the towns where she had lived. The northwest corner of Washington State still looked like a mouth, with the Olympic Peninsula as its massive lower jaw. Above it Vancouver Island served as its giant, detached tongue. She ran her finger along the area where the water had disappeared, top to bottom. Southern British Columbia. Washington State. Oregon. Northern California.

She wondered about water sinking into the ground. It seemed an unlikely theory. The Cascade Mountains ran north and south smack in the middle of the drought area. They would be a geologic barrier.

She opened her laptop, calling up a government map that showed the extent of the drought. The polygons marking the affected counties gave it a chunkiness that made it seem angular, but the area generally appeared to be a half circle. If she imagined the rest of the circle, the center of it would be off the Washington Coast, in the Pacific Ocean.

Project Athena was also off the Washington Coast, in the Pacific Ocean.

A shiver ran down her entire body. What if the epicenter of the drought were the location of Project Athena?

No. It couldn't be that simple. But then the drought had gotten drastically worse yesterday, the day Diana said the final Project Athena module was starting up. Project Athena had been running for five months. The exact length of the drought.

This was ridiculous. It was just a coincidence. A perfectly aligned coincidence, but still false. If Project Athena had caused the drought, smarter minds than hers would have seen it first. Brilliant minds. She was wrong.

Project Athena causing the Aguageddon was like a conspiracy theory. A desperate attempt to make sense out of something nonsensical. And what was more, it wasn't her job to solve the Aguageddon. That was way above her pay grade. For smarter people than her.

Still, she couldn't get the idea out of her head. She walked to the window, her ankle twinging. Still dark outside.

It would be easy enough to prove her theory wrong. It occurred to her that a drought meant less humidity. Could she see its progression by looking at humidity data? By doing that she could prove that the two timelines didn't actually match, and then get the idea out of her head.

On her laptop she searched online, looking for numbers, finding them on the United States' National Weather Center and the Government of Canada websites.

She began with Seattle. On February thirteenth Seattle's humidity dropped to zero. Portland, Oregon's humidity went to zero one month later. Forks, a town near the Pacific Ocean that should have had high humidity, zeroed out three months before Seattle.

Before Seattle. The drought started west of Seattle. And came to Seattle later. The Aguageddon could truly have started off the coast and expanded from there.

She took her map from the wall and spread it on the floor. Using colored pencils, she marked main cities and towns with the first date they each dropped to zero humidity.

With a drawing compass, she sketched a circle, which connected Forks, Washington to Zeballos and Port Alberni in British Columbia. These cities had all dropped to zero humidity on May tenth. She marked the center of that circle, which was off the coast of Washington, out in the Pacific Ocean.

Hoquiam, Port Angles, Nanaimo, and Campbell River were next. They had all dropped to zero humidity exactly one month later. That circle was wider than the first. Its center was in the same spot as the first circle, off the coast of Washington, out in the Pacific Ocean.

It felt as if electricity charged the air. She had connected the dots, literally, and found two concentric circles around a mystery spot in the Pacific Ocean. She continued, drawing a third circle to connect Astoria, Olympia, and Port Townsend, which all zeroed out in humidity on the same day one month after the cities in the second circle. The circle's center was the same as the others.

Her heart racing, she now drew a forth circle to connect Crescent City, California with La Grande, Oregon; Spokane, Washington; Prince George, British Colombia; and Terrace, British Columbia.

There was no denying it. The four concentric circles created a bullseye, matching the progression of the Aguageddon exactly. Every month the drought expanded, pulling more towns and cities into its ever-widening orbit around the exact center of what could be Project Athena's location.

She backed away from the map as if it were radioactive, breathing quickly. She clasped her hands to her collarbone. How would HemisNorth have done that? And why? She rose and paced, huffing, ignoring the pain in her ankle.

It had always troubled her when her mother paced, and now she was doing just that, telling herself to stop the way she sometimes told her mom. She regretted those times now. Trying not to move was like trying not to vomit. Easier said than done.

What did Diana know, and could it have something to do with why she was laid off?

She dialed her friend's number. It rang and rang. "Come on. Answer." Marella texted, "Call me, it's important."

She took a photo of the map with her phone. Should she text it to Diana? Or maybe even Elizabeth?

A thought struck her. Eshana and Len, Project Athena's creators, had been smart. More than smart. Genius. Such brilliant people wouldn't have started the Aguageddon by accident. Did they create a drought deliberately? Was there actually some corporate scheme? Were they sequestering water on purpose? Was she a naïve pawn in a nefarious scheme, coming to work each day to support something she would never have purposely signed on for?

But no. Elizabeth and Belinda weren't evil. She had overheard them plotting to save humanity. Not conniving to dominate it.

And furthermore, this whole train of thought was stupid. Her imagination had led her astray. She wasn't qualified to solve the Aguageddon. And even if HemisNorth had done it, they would know it, and they would fix it. They didn't need her, and anyway her responsibility was to her family.

She slapped her palm on her forehead. There was water at work. And pop, and juice. The supply room was full of it, and she still had one of the only keys, forgotten in her pants pocket. Why hadn't she thought of that before? She dressed quickly and rushed out the door.

Chapter Eight

It was still dark outside at four in the morning. At HemisNorth a lantern hung on the closed entrance gate. There were lights on in the main building, but they were dim. Perhaps they were powered by an emergency generator.

A man in a security uniform held up a palm to stop her, as if the fence wasn't there. Having a guard should have made her feel safer, but it only pointed out the precariousness of the situation. The way he held his arm up, almost a Nazi salute, added to her disorientation.

"ID," he said briskly when she rolled down her window.

She fished her wallet from her backpack, pinched it out of the too-tight slot, and held it out, her hand trembling. She leaned her arm on the truck to keep steadier. The guard's eyes bounced back and forth from her face to her photo, which she now realized might not look much like her now. In it she wore short hair, makeup, and a huge grin. She curled the corners of her mouth in a strained smile in an effort to match it.

The guard didn't smile back, but thankfully opened the gate. She drove through and into the parking garage under the main building. She was here. In minutes she could drink something. It wouldn't be long now.

Inside her office building, the lobby was cave-like in the low light. She took the stairs two at a time.

There was no need to compose herself as she usually did before opening the door. She dashed in. The usual smell of coffee was absent. Surprisingly, Elizabeth was in her office concentrating hard on her computer screen, as if trying mind control to make it levitate.

Marella rushed between clusters of workstations, which seemed messier than usual, drawers left open, cupboards ajar. She unlocked the storage room door and yanked it open. A dim green emergency light came on.

The cartons and shrink-wrapped packages were gone. Only dust remained, in perfectly shaped rectangles as if to show her exactly what she had missed out on.

"No, no, no." She trotted into the room, scanning the shelves for any stray bottle that might have been left behind. She scoured the corners, the bare floor, the area between the boxes of pens and staples and notepads and binder clips, until she was sure there was nothing left to drink. The only bottles were tiny ones full of white-out that nobody used anymore, though she would have gladly drunk even that much water.

"Damn it!" She kicked a shelf; pens popcorned up and onto the floor. The bottles that were supposed to be here for the employees were all gone. Taken by somebody with no concerns about Marella's welfare. No concerns for anybody else, no matter how desperate they might be. Only thinking about themselves, like the men at the gas station who had almost gotten to her. She was breathing too fast now. She was in danger of hyperventilating.

"I gave it to employees to take to their families," said a weary voice behind her. Marella wheeled. It was Elizabeth. Wearing jeans and a t-shirt instead of the suit she had on earlier.

"I need water," blurted Marella. "I haven't had anything to drink since yesterday."

Elizabeth shook her head. "There's none in the building. The emergency stores are gone too."

"But then...what about you? What are you drinking?"

"I had enough to get me through the night. I worked into the wee hours trying to keep things together here. What I had is gone now."

Marella ran to a nearby desk and pawed frantically through its drawers.

"You won't find anything," said Elizabeth. "We searched it all yesterday."

Marella felt like a runner waiting for a nonexistent starting gun. She turned one way then another, finally leaning back against a desk and putting her face in her hands. She felt her jaw quivering. She had never imagined she would be in such dire need. Every idea failing. Every direction blocked.

She felt a hand on her shoulder. "There's a solution. I was waiting for it to get light so I could get water from the bay to distill. I'm glad you're here. You can help me."

Marella took her hands from her face. A bit of hope broke grudgingly through her despair. Water distilling? She thought of TV clips showing distilleries with big vats of alcohol. Specialized stainless steel equipment. "How?"

"We'll get a pot and foil from the kitchen. We can use the gas barbeque in the courtyard."

A memory flooded in. The environmental compliance group had gathered for an employee appreciation picnic only a month ago. She remembered the ice-filled cooler stuffed with bottles of mineral water. The feel of sweating glass in her hand. The smell of lime flavoring, the bubbly crispness of it going down her throat. The carbonation rising into a burp.

She had been disappointed they didn't have cherry cola. Now she would happily drink radiator fluid if it would quench her thirst.

"A pot and foil?" asked Marella. "We don't need special equipment?"

"Of course not." Elizabeth turned, marching across the room.

Marella trotted behind, excited, feeling a touch like a mad scientist. Yes, they could make water. Her voice came out breathy. "How long does it take?"

"The sooner we get started, the sooner we'll be done. The sky looks lighter now. Let's get some containers to carry the water in from the bay. Why are you limping?"

"A guy took a can of juice from me in the store. I tripped trying to get it back."

Elizabeth seemed alarmed. Marella said quickly, "I'll be all right." They passed a crop of curved desks and a sitting area with eggshell chairs positioned around a yolk-colored coffee table. Marella glanced out the window toward Elliott Bay, then stopped. Something didn't look right. "Elizabeth?"

"What?"

Marella pointed. "Look. The water always comes up to the embankment. But I see sand. Lots of it."

Elizabeth came back to where Marella stood rooted. She gasped. "The water must have receded at least a hundred feet."

"Puget Sound is disappearing. That means the ocean is disappearing."

"That's not possible," said Elizabeth. "That's a phenomenal amount of water. Maybe there's been an earthquake somewhere and the water is receding before a tsunami."

Marella fumbled with her phone. As she scanned the headlines she felt a pricking on the back of her neck. "The ocean is lowering like this all over the world."

Elizabeth's eyes grew wide in fear or disbelief. Perhaps both. "The ocean itself is disappearing?"

Marella nodded, unable to speak. She held the phone up to show Venice's empty canals.

Elizabeth took the phone carefully as if handling a bomb trigger. "No," she whispered.

The world seemed to tilt. Marella understood, truly understood, that she and her family might die. Everybody might die.

Elizabeth handed back the phone then turned abruptly, rushing toward her office.

Marella's phone rang. It was her mother, her voice frantic. "The oceans are disappearing!"

It was heart wrenching to hear Mom's voice right after realizing they could all die. "I just found out," said Marella.

"They're setting up a refugee camp on Mount Rainier where there's snow. Lots of water up there still."

Marella's spirits raised slightly. There was a stopgap. A possibility of survival. "I'll come get you. Are the gangs still on I-5? Should I go a different way?"

"No, don't come here. Things are dicey here."

"Dicey? What do you mean?"

"We've heard gunshots. We need to go."

Marella's voice caught in her throat. "I'll meet you at Mount Rainier. A neighbor is driving us. Be careful. I love you."

"I love you too."

Marella hung up, feeling like she would never see them again in this life. She should have been there. They were stronger together. She imagined seeing them again in Heaven, wearing ill-fitting chalk-white robes and crooked costume halos. Brielle asking her why she didn't tell anybody that she figured out what caused the Aguageddon.

She pulled out her phone and looked at the photo she had taken of the map with the concentric circles. She wasn't capable of solving a world crisis. This couldn't be the answer.

Or could it? The feeling she'd had when she first connected the dots began to return. The feeling of things falling into place so elegantly, so reasonably, with no loose ends. She could be right after all. Appallingly right. And there was a very simple way to know whether it was true or not. Elizabeth could tell her if Project Athena was in the center of that circle.

She burst into Elizabeth's office. Her boss standing next to her desk, land line to her ear, saying, "Come on. Answer."

Marella blurted, "I think Project Athena caused the drought."

Elizabeth eyed Marella as if she'd said the moon was made of cow dung. She made a huffing noise. "Don't pay attention to rumors. People make up lots of things about HemisNorth. It comes with the territory. You'd better go home."

"The timeline for Project Athena implementation matches the events of the drought."

Elizabeth cocked her head, hanging up the phone. "What are you talking about? What timeline?"

"Every month a new Project Athena module started up. And then yesterday the rest of it started up. It matches the drought." She watched for Elizabeth's reaction. Would she see the connection?

Elizabeth put her hands on her hips. Her eyes bored into Marella. "Who gave you the startup schedule?" Her expression seemed to say that if Marella didn't give a satisfactory answer, Elizabeth would reach into her brain and dig out a better one.

Marella stood straight. She couldn't let Elizabeth intimidate her. "I figured it out."

"You figured it out." Elizabeth raised her palms, sounding exasperated. "Based on what?"

Marella felt a little nauseous. Was that thirst or embarrassment? Was she wrong?

She fumbled with her phone, bringing up the photo of the map, then handed it to Elizabeth. "That's humidity data from the US and Canada. You can see the progression. The circles show that every month the drought suddenly spread. I thought maybe Project Athena could be there in the center if it matched the data."

Elizabeth's nails were an abalone-shell color that alternated pink and silver as she widened the photo on the phone. A look of alarm spread over her face. *She sees it,* thought Marella.

"Marella, you shouldn't have been able to obtain specific information about Project Athena. This is a highly confidential project."

Marella breathed shallowly. "So it's true? Is that where Project Athena is?"

Instead of answering directly, Elizabeth replied with exasperation. "Do I really have to explain misattributed cause and effect to you? Just because two events align in time doesn't prove one has anything to do with the other. And furthermore, our schedule was superseded. The actual module start dates were different than we originally planned."

Marella's face felt hot. If the dates didn't align after all, then she was completely mistaken about everything. Elizabeth was an actual scientist. Marella was not. What had made her think she had the answer?

Elizabeth sat at her desk, the chair cushion whooshing loudly. "This lack of water is causing severe problems with our manufacturing plants. I've been up all night trying to help mitigate the damage so that people don't get injured. And now I can't seem to get in contact with anybody. I seriously don't have time for this. You should go."

That was it then. This was all a waste of time. There was nothing to drink, and she'd humiliated herself for no reason. She turned and walked away. When she reached the door, Elizabeth spoke. "Wait. Show me that again."

Marella swallowed thickly. What was the point if the timelines didn't match? Or perhaps they didn't have to match exactly. Could she still be right? With mounting excitement and dread, Marella showed her the photo of her map once more.

"What am I looking at? Explain."

Marella pointed to the center of the circles. "Five months ago, humidity was suddenly zero right here, in the ocean where there should be moisture in the air. Then a month later there was suddenly no humidity here." Marella indicated the first ring. "Then a month later none here, then none here."

"What are all these dots?"

"Um, something else. Places where I've been."

"Where did you get the data that you used for this?"

"From the United States' National Weather Center and the Government of Canada."

Elizabeth's eyebrows knitted. That meant something to her. Were those the right sources? Or not?

Elizabeth rubbed her forehead, sighing loudly, then said, "Sit."

Marella dropped into the chair opposite the desk. She waited as her boss opened a file drawer and thumbed through some files. Marella leaned back, then sat straight. Crossed her leg, then uncrossed it.

Elizabeth set a few pages on the desk. "Sign this."

Marella's first thought was that that HemisNorth kept a confession template the same way it kept other document templates, and Elizabeth would require her to state how she'd learned secret information. But that was absurd. And now she saw the heading on the paper. *Nondisclosure Agreement.* Elizabeth was going to tell her about Project Athena.

Elizabeth slid a pen across the desk like a bartender serving beer in a saloon. Marella began to read. Her emotions wouldn't let her do more than identify random words on the page. *Information. Penalty. Substantial.*

Elizabeth seized the papers and flipped to the last page. Her expression was one of resignation. "It says you won't disclose to anybody what I'm going to tell you." She slapped the paper. "Sign."

Marella scribbled her name on the line.

Elizabeth slid the papers into a desk drawer. "We're going to make a call."

Chapter Nine

Elizabeth twirled a finger to indicate that Marella should face the large TV screen on the wall. Marella swiveled. A screen saver image showed the Grand Canyon and its parched orange, red, and tan layers, which made Marella even thirstier than she already was. So there was enough power in the building for this. For some reason, that gave her hope.

It felt odd sitting there with Elizabeth behind her as if preparing to watch a movie while the world was falling apart. Like she could settle an oversized drink into a cup holder and reach for a handful of buttery popcorn while the epic disaster they were experiencing played on the screen.

That screen now showed an image of Elizabeth and Marella, who saw herself clutching the pen in both hands like a microphone. She looked as terrified as an amateur singer about to go on stage for the first time. Were her emotions really that easy to read? After wiping the expression from her face she tossed the pen onto the desk.

"We're going to talk with Victor," said Elizabeth. "He's on Wisdom Island with Project Athena." Marella nodded too rapidly. Project Athena was on an island. So that meant the circles on her map could be pinpointing it.

She had met Victor before. He had worked in the Seattle office but was relocated, apparently to Wisdom Island. But why? What was there?

Elizabeth continued. "Victor will confirm that we changed the schedule, and then you'll know that I was telling you the truth. I'm only including you to keep you from spreading false rumors. It's important for scientists to determine the real cause of the drought, not be misled by false leads. Do you understand that?"

Marella nodded, shifting uneasily in her chair. She suspected Elizabeth wouldn't be taking the time for this if she didn't think it was possible for Marella to be right.

A face appeared, bumping Marella and Elizabeth's to the side. She barely recognized Victor. She'd overheard other employees referring to him as Doctor Babyface, an unkind reference to his PhD and big cheeks. He'd been welcoming when she first started the job at HemisNorth. Then he was the picture of health. Now his eyes were sunken. All she could see besides Victor's head were gray utility cabinets and a white board with equations.

"Elizabeth." Victor's voice was hoarse. "Thank god. I've been trying to call you. Get me out of here. Who's that with you? Is that Athena?"

Elizabeth's brow furrowed. "It's Marella Wells."

"You've got to help me. Save me from Athena. She's furious with me." Victor looked crazed. Was he on drugs? He touched his fingertips to his brow. "Send a helicopter for me. Our boat is grounded."

Elizabeth nodded. "I'll get you some help. Just one thing first. Marella heard some rumors about Project Athena and I wanted to make sure she was wrong. I need to know about the implementation schedule."

Victor coughed. "Athena won't listen to me. She was born from Zeus's head. That's why. No, born from Len and Eshana's heads."

"You're babbling," said Elizabeth. "Are you on medication?"

"I'm sorry. I keep hallucinating. I'm sick." Victor lowered his head on the desk as if it were heavy as a barbell, then lifted it. "Please get me out of here."

"Confirm that the implementation schedule was changed."

"It was changed," said Victor.

Elizabeth nodded. Marella felt heavy. She had been wrong. All wrong.

Victor coughed again. "Then Belinda changed it back."

Marella stood abruptly as Elizabeth put her hand on her heart. Her eyes widened in alarm. "Back? To the original schedule?"

Victor nodded. "Said we couldn't afford to wait. HemisNorth stock was dropping."

"Okay then," said Elizabeth, looking away, then looking back at Victor. "What could have caused the humidity to drop to zero at Wisdom Island?"

Victor straightened, suddenly more coherent. "So you found out." He rubbed his forehead. "I thought you would. Just come get me. I don't care what the punishment is, I just have to get out of here." His voice warbled with fear.

You found out. Marella's blood chilled, as if a ghost had just passed through her body. Victor had done something. And he thought Elizabeth knew what it was. Marella could see that she didn't because she paused, mouth open, before reverting to her iguana self. Calm, unreadable. She said, "I need an explanation. Tell me why."

Elizabeth was leading Victor along. Making him think she knew what he had done wrong. Marella held perfectly still so as not to miss a word.

Victor rubbed his eyes. "Len and Eshana were close to giving up on Project Athena. We couldn't let that happen."

Elizabeth glanced at Marella, then back at Victor. "Why not?"

Victor tried to talk but no words came out. He drank from his water bottle, his Adam's apple bobbing. "Because the sampling instruments showed carbon dioxide coming out of the atmosphere, just like it was supposed to. Project Athena was working. But they said it wasn't doing enough so we would have to shut everything down." Victor stumbled over his words, voice strained with anguish. "You have to understand. We changed the sampling instrument settings for the greater good. We had to make it look like it was taking more carbon dioxide so Len and Eshana wouldn't give up. We knew they could improve Project Athena to do better. We were going to adjust the settings back after they changed their minds. Athena was going to save humanity."

"So you recalibrated the sampling instruments for the prototype here as well as the full scale version on the island to make them both read inaccurately," said Elizabeth, unable to keep amazement out of her tone. "You, Arnie, and Delphine? Everybody was in on it?"

"We were trying to save the world from the disasters that will be brought on by global warming. To save my family. To save you. To save the millions—no billions of people who would die when the waters swallowed coastal areas around the world."

Elizabeth's voice started to waver. "Before you changed them, did the sampling instruments show water disappearing?"

"Yes," said Victor. "But so little. How could we know it would empty the ocean?"

Elizabeth had the panicky look of somebody realizing the tiger's cage was open with the tiger nowhere to be seen. "And so. You made it look like Project Athena was working correctly, when instead it was depleting water from our world."

Marella could feel her pulse beating in her neck. HemisNorth had led the world to the cliff's edge. It was turning the world into a desert planet. Her bones felt like rubber.

"Turn Project Athena off," shouted Elizabeth "Shut all the modules down! Now!"

"I tried," said Victor. "I couldn't. Athena won't let me. She won't listen to reason. Gods and goddesses never do."

"Where are Arnie and Delphine?" asked Elizabeth. "Tell them to come talk to me."

"Athena killed them."

"You're hallucinating again."

"It's true. They're dead. I'm next. Athena deceived us. We shouldn't have done her bidding."

Elizabeth's mouth opened then shut, as if she didn't know what to say.

Victor looked winded. He struggled for breath. "Tell my wife I love her."

Marella froze. Those were the words of a man who knew death was imminent.

"It's the shutdown program called EndAthena.exe," said Elizabeth. "You know the passwords, right?"

"I don't have the program." Victor's voice was so weak. "And the facial biometrics require two different employees."

Marella spun toward Elizabeth. "Can you turn the machine off from here?"

"No," replied Elizabeth. "The machine modules are a closed system. There's no connection off the island. It's because of the Spokane and Raleigh incidents."

The previous year hackers had remotely shut down the system that ran one of the HemisNorth plants in Spokane. It had cost HemisNorth millions of dollars. There had been much talk of closed systems after that. Then a week later a rogue employee in the Raleigh plant—possibly paid by a competitor—had caused another shutdown. Project Athena's two-person biometric requirements must have been a reaction to those attacks.

"At least send him the shutdown program," said Marella. "That's a start."

"Hold on." Elizabeth ran to her computer and hunched over her keyboard, tapping the keys. She shook her head. "It's too big."

"Use a file sharing platform."

Elizabeth tapped the keys some more. She shifted in her chair, waiting, then sat straight, frustration creasing her brow. "File refused."

"Refused?" asked Marella. "How is that possible?"

Elizabeth pressed her lips together in apparent consternation, then replied, "Some of our programs are untransferable to keep them out of the hands of our competition."

Victor stretched his arm across the table and laid his head on it. His eyes looked blurry.

"Victor!" shouted Elizabeth. "Stay awake."

His mouth hung open, his breathing raspy. The sound delay didn't quite match his motion, as if they watched a poorly dubbed movie.

"Damn it, Victor," said Marella. "You did this to us. You have to fix it."

Victor didn't respond.

"He's dying." Marella could feel her panic rising. "He needs help. What do we do?"

Elizabeth dialed her phone. "I can't get the police."

Marella turned one way then another. There had to be something they could do. "Helicopter company?"

"You try while I call the Coast Guard."

Marella searched for a helicopter company and dialed. A man's voice answered. Marella spoke fast and furiously. "This is Marella Wells, I'm from HemisNorth. I need a helicopter right now..."

"They're all being used," said the man.

"This is an emergency. If you could divert one..." The line went dead. Marella huffed with anger. She kept searching. Trying another company, then another. "Nobody else is answering."

Elizabeth threw an arm up in frustration. "I've tried the Coast Guard, the Army, and the Navy. I can't get a person."

Victor's breathing slowed. "Victor," said Marella, "How are you doing?"

He stirred, whispering words she couldn't hear. He reached toward them, the camera angle making his arm long in the shot. His eyes bulged. Marella had the odd notion that Athena was strangling him.

"Hospitals," said Marella. "Do they have their own helicopters?"

"No idea but it's worth a try. I've got Children's. You try Harborview."

They each searched and dialed. "No answer," said Elizabeth finally.

"I can't get through," said Marella. Then, "Listen."

The sound of Victor's breathing had stopped. He was still, eyes open.

"I think he's dead." Elizabeth's voice was uncharacteristically dumbfounded. She grasped the desk, her eyes wide, her anguish so defined, so melodramatic that under other circumstances it would have been comical.

Dead. He was dead. Although miles away, Victor was somehow right there with them. Marella was shaking and couldn't seem to stop. She felt herself spiraling into despair.

Elizabeth wrung her fingers together. "Victor, you fool. You damn fool." Seeing the look on Marella's face, she said, "Well. Let's keep it together. We can fall apart later when it's more convenient."

Marella nodded, trying to get her thoughts in order. "You're right. You're right. We can't help Victor. And he can't help us. So you have to find another way to turn off Project Athena. You can't get a helicopter. So you need a boat, while there's still ocean left to float on."

"If you want something done right..." Elizabeth usually finished with *delegate it anyway*. This time she said, "...do it yourself. I'm going to take the shutdown program to the island."

Hope seeped through Marella's despair. Of course. It was so simple. HemisNorth owned research boats that the staff used to get water and fish samples. "Take the *Northern Hemisphere*."

"It'll be stranded at the dock."

"It's not at the dock. It's on a trailer at Warehouse 27. I just updated the schedule. You can pull the trailer out to the water."

"Yes," said Elizabeth. "That will work. Warehouse 27. That's north of here." She yanked her purse and a bag from the desk drawer. "Get me a flash drive. A waterproof one."

Marella rushed to her desk and retrieved one. It was silver, with the blue and purple HemisNorth logo. It was mind-boggling to think that this two-inch, trinket-like object would help avert a disaster. She brought it to Elizabeth, who loaded the shutdown program and then placed the thumb drive gently into a pocket of her bag, which she zipped shut.

"If the island computer isn't connected to the mainland how does it know to accept your biometric?" asked Marella.

"They bring updates physically. Like I'm about to do. I've got the warehouse key. I think that's everything. Except—I need a second employee to come with me."

Marella felt heavy with disappointment. There were no other employees here, and time was of the essence. She needed to be with her family, yet she was the only choice. "I'll come with you to the island."

"Excellent," said Elizabeth in a tone she'd never used before. Thankful with a touch of despair.

There were loud voices outside the building. Marella and Elizabeth rushed to the window. The gate was open, the security guard gone. A Land Rover zoomed away.

"They stole my car!" shouted Elizabeth. She slapped the wall angrily. "Why, why, why?"

They weren't safe. Nothing was safe. Nobody was safe.

Elizabeth turned to Marella. "Did you drive your truck?"

Chapter Ten

Fifteenth Avenue was bustling in all the wrong ways. Its businesses were closed, but pedestrians scurried along, glancing suspiciously about. A clump of people heaved bricks at a storefront window, which shattered like a waterfall just as Marella was driving past. Marella flinched. Elizabeth held up an arm as if the glass would hit her.

What was it like for Mom and Brielle? Were they seeing scenes like this? Or worse, were gangs of thieves stealing whatever water they had? Society had crumbled in a day. How was that possible?

"What did the machine do to the water?" asked Marella. "How did it make it disappear?"

"It's complicated."

Marella rolled her eyes. The world was in a shambles and that was Elizabeth's response? "I'm-too-stupid-to-understand complicated? Or you just don't-want-to-tell-me complicated?"

Elizabeth sighed. "You're right, you didn't deserve that. Project Athena is based on quantum physics. Let me think about how to explain it."

Marella's knee-jerk resentment morphed into unease. Quantum physics. Any time she'd read about it she understood at first, but then that understanding would dissolve and she could no longer make sense of it. She was smart, but quantum physics was weird stuff.

They passed a boarded-up restaurant with striped awnings, then slowed at an intersection. Traffic lights were out, and cars weren't waiting for each other. She waited for the right moment, then lurched forward and through the intersection.

"What do you know about the theory of multiple universes?" asked Elizabeth.

Multiple universes? "I never really took it seriously. It's science fiction."

"Multiverses aren't just invented concepts. When physicists do the math that is involved with quantum physics, it leads them to different possible versions of multiverses. Some physicists believe that universes are adjacent, like squares of a quilt. Some believe that universes take different forms, with universes tucked into others. They call them Calibi-Yau manifolds. Calibi-Yau shapes. A universe could be curled up like a snail shell, right in front of you, too tiny to see. Many of them, in fact. Endless numbers of them, right here." Elizabeth held up a fingertip.

"How can it be a universe if it's that tiny?" asked Marella.

"You perceive it as tiny. From your perspective, it is."

A woman whose cheeks were scuffed like a shoe stepped out in the road and eyed Marella as if she were an evil spirit that needed to be exorcised. Marella felt like making the sign of the cross, though she never had in her life. The woman continued across the road and Marella drove on.

"Okay, so what does that have to do with the water?" asked Marella.

"Project Athena uses the concept that a particle doesn't have defined properties until you measure them. A simplified way of looking at it is that at any moment in time, the components that make up a given carbon dioxide molecule could be in our universe or in other universes. Project Athena was built to make sure that the locations of specific particles remain undefined. A molecule is not in our universe but also not in a parallel universe. It has the potential to be in either one, but is not."

"Not here, not there. So nowhere."

"Essentially. And the machine was working. The initial studies showed a small amount of reduced carbon dioxide in the atmosphere, so they continued to try to improve Project Athena to do better. But when Victor and the others recalibrated the sampling instruments to show different results, it must have kept us from finding out water was being affected along with the carbon dioxide. Water molecules also became not here and not there."

The words seemed too strange to believe. Like a fairy tale explanation. Next Elizabeth would be explaining how humans can grow wings. "How would you make molecules be not here and not there? Isn't it a scientific law that you can't make matter disappear?"

"You might be thinking of the Law of Conservation of Energy, where energy can't be created or destroyed in an isolated system. It's not the same. And anyway, the molecules haven't been destroyed, and they haven't vanished either. They still have the potential to be somewhere."

"So you're telling me our water is in a sort of suspended animation."

"Not quite. But if it helps you can think of it that way."

"Basically, you tried to make a machine that would save humanity by taking carbon dioxide away. A climate machine."

"You could call it that. Look out!" Elizabeth pointed to a man sprinting into the road lugging a duffle bag.

"Oh no!" Marella swerved to avoid him, then swerved again to avoid a man who was chasing him. Both men disappeared between two buildings.

It happened so suddenly Marella was filled with adrenaline. She was quiet for another block as she tried to calm herself. They passed five people who were on the sidewalk. It felt like the moment in a zombie movie when the zombies notice the living. Their hungry, devouring gazes. Marella shivered.

"We can get the water back, right?" asked Marella.

"I don't know that we can."

"What? Are you serious?"

Elizabeth spoke in a level voice as if to keep from faltering. "The machine was supposed to put the carbon dioxide away indefinitely. Otherwise, what would have been the point? Our mission now is to stop more water from disappearing. I'm not sure about getting back what's already gone."

Marella felt cold inside. "So if only half the world's water is left by the time we get to the island, that's that. The shorelines will be in different places. The continents will be huge. It'll be a different world."

"Possibly. I don't know the extent to which the meddling affected the data. Since we had false data, I can't be certain of anything."

"We need to get the water back. It's not good enough to just stop it from going away."

"But that's where have to start. After we get the flash drive to the machine and use the shutdown program, then we'll determine any further action." Elizabeth cleared her throat. "There's something else I should make you aware of."

The hesitation in her voice made Marella anxious. She was about to drop a bomb. Tell her that things were even worse. "Something else? Exactly what would that be?"

"We just discovered that there's a tipping point. We can only remove a certain amount of carbon dioxide at a time before the machine will start a runaway reaction. We learned Athena has to be regularly shut down or there will be a point of no return where it will continue to take carbon dioxide out of the atmosphere. I expect the same holds true with water."

"A runaway reaction? What do you mean? Like a chain reaction? How is that possible?"

"You could think of it like a thermal runaway reaction where there's too much heat and not enough to cool it. The pressure increases. The heat increases the reaction rate to the point where it's impossible to stop. This isn't a thermal reaction and so the process is different, but the result is that molecules would continue to be removed from the world."

"Endlessly?"

"Yes. Endlessly."

She couldn't be hearing Elizabeth right. Was Elizabeth telling her matter-of-factly that a yet another sword was dangling over their heads? "Let me see if I've got this straight. You just found out that Project Athena could screw up and take all of the Earth's carbon dioxide away. All of it. Down to the very last molecule. Even if you didn't know yet that it also took water, why didn't you shut it off immediately? We would all die without carbon dioxide."

"Of course, but you have to understand..."

"And now it's even worse. If we don't stop the machine in time, a runaway reaction will make all the water in the world go away."

"In theory, but I won't let that happen."

"So when is the point of no return?"

"Eight days from now."

Marella slapped the steering wheel. "Eight days? Are you kidding me? Only eight days?"

"That's not unreasonable at all. Or it wouldn't have been without the water disappearing."

An Irish setter staggered into the other side of the street and collapsed. A car veered away from the dog, nearly smashing Marella's truck. She swerved just in time to avoid an accident. Her heart was pounding. She tried not to look at the dog in the side mirror.

She slowed down at an intersection. Cars crossed randomly. Stopping, starting, honking, veering around each other, zooming onward. A pedestrian thumped both hands onto her window, making her jump. "Jesus!" she cried.

"Please," shouted the man, his voice full of anguish, "I need water for my children."

"I don't have any," she shouted.

The man backed up holding his head. Another car bumped him. Elizabeth choked back a shout. The man staggered away.

"Look what you've done," said Marella. "This is truly evil. Why would you build such a machine? You should have called it Project Death instead of Project Athena."

Elizabeth leaned close to Marella, speaking firmly: "Every technology is a balance of risk and reward. People live with the potential of runaway reactions every day. Nuclear plants. Electrical systems. Chemical engineering. They have all caused spectacular explosions due to runaway reactions but those are the exceptions."

Marella made through the intersection. Elizabeth continued, "Athena could have saved humanity. Its potential was enormous. With climate change people are blindly moving forward on a path of doom. It's like watching them willingly march to the edge of a cliff. You have people saying they're happy if things get a little warmer. They don't mind getting drier or wetter. Pure ignorance. In the last decade one hundred and twenty-three million people died from natural disasters, and as time passes it will get exponentially worse."

Climate change. She suddenly realized why Diana had mentioned Micronesia. The islands had been drowning because of global warming and sea level rise. Diana had thought Project Athena would save them from that. But now it was the opposite. They would be high and dry. "But you were gambling with our lives."

"You're not looking at it correctly. It's like surgery. It's dangerous to cut into a human body and take out a tumor. The body bleeds, tissue gets damaged, there's a risk of complications and even death. But leaving the tumor in place may be even riskier. You balance the risk and reward. When we started Project Athena, climate change was the bigger risk. Victor recalibrating the sampling instruments and changing our data was a variable we could never have factored in."

"And now the tipping point is only eight days away," said Marella. "We should go to Joint Base Lewis McChord and see if they have any spare bombs. Just blast it out of existence."

"Absolutely not. That could cause the runaway reaction that we're trying to avoid."

Marella was speechless. The way everybody at HemisNorth talked about safety in staff meetings, she had thought it took precedence over everything else. She had fallen for the corporate line. She felt stupidly naïve.

The truck rolled to a halt behind a long line of cars. Elizabeth craned her neck to see around them, tapping on the armrest in a Morse code of impatience. She scrolled through the GPS map on the dashboard. "There's something wrong with your GPS. Every single road can't be blocked."

"Maybe they are. Everybody trying to leave town."

"But only north?"

"Look." Marella pointed at the sky. In the distance a gray feather of smoke fluttered upward.

"Fire! How are they going to put it out? There's no water."

"They're not. There's another plume. And another." Marella's stomach felt heavy.

"I see five plumes now," said Elizabeth, her voice anguished. "So all the streets really are blocked to the north."

"How are we going to get to the warehouse?"

The smoke roiled sickeningly as if Hell was venting. Marella told herself not to think like that. Things were bad enough already.

Elizabeth put her hand on the dash and craned her neck. "Something's happening up ahead."

Marella turned her attention back to the road. Two purple-masked women rushed to a truck three vehicles ahead of them. Pointing a gun at the driver's side window, one shouted, "Water! Give me water, now!"

"Oh shit!" barked Marella, twisting frantically, looking for a path out. Cars ahead. Cars behind. Traffic island on the left. An obstacle-lined sidewalk on the right.

"There's nowhere to go," said Elizabeth. "Do you have a weapon? Anything?"

"Pepper spray." Marella gestured at the glove compartment.

"Not good enough." Still, Elizabeth whisked it open, spilling contents as she grabbed the black tube, then twisting to look at the back seat.

"Just laundry back there," said Marella. "Oh shit, what do we do?"

The driver ahead apparently had nothing for the robbers. One of the masked women shot into the car. The bang made Marella and Elizabeth jerk back.

"Move, move!" Elizabeth flailed her arms. Marella spun the steering wheel and reversed, bumping into the car behind. Horns were honking.

The robbers sprinted to the next car, two vehicles ahead of Marella and Elizabeth, again shouting, "Water!" Somebody in the car held out a bottle out of the window.

"Get ready to run for it," said Elizabeth. "Scoot over to my side."

Before Marella could comply, the driver flew out of the car just ahead and ran several steps. One of the robbers aimed a gun at him. "No!" Marella hunched. Elizabeth cowered.

The robber shot. Marella and Elizabeth both jumped at the noise.

The man jerked, then fell to the ground.

The retort rung in Marella's ears. She clutched the steering wheel hard. "She shot him. She really shot him." She felt weak, as if her blood had drained away in an instant. This didn't happen in real life.

"Do something," said Elizabeth. "Anything."

Marella glanced at the sidewalk. Bike rack. Newsstand. Trees. "Hold on." Marella spun the wheel to the right.

Elizabeth grasped the dashboard. "Hurry."

Marella lurched the truck over the curb onto the sidewalk, pushing the newsstand aside. She barely managed to squeeze the truck between a tree trunk and the bicycle rack. Shots sounded. She jerked with each one. She heard two hit the truck with sickening clunks. Hyper-aware of her body, she expected to feel a bullet strike her at any moment.

The truck sped along the sidewalk and around the corner, where it bounced off into the street, jolting them in their seats. Marella breathed hard, trying to keep herself and the truck under control. They careened eastward.

Two blocks away from the shooting, Marella asked, "Are we okay?"

Elizabeth twisted, looking this way and that. "I think so. I hope so."

"All right. We made it. We're okay."

"We can't get caught like that again." Elizabeth leaned back against the headrest.

"That was too close."

"You don't look well," said Elizabeth. "Can you manage?"

"I'll be fine. Which way? Navigate."

"Keep straight. I-5 North might be clear."

"Wouldn't they blockade it because of the fire?" asked Marella. Even as she said it, she wondered who she meant by "they." Where were the firefighters, police, and national guard? Why were they so alone in this struggle?

"I guess we'll find out." Elizabeth sounded longsuffering. "Keep an eye out for trouble."

Trouble wasn't hard to come by. A block later they could see concrete barriers, twisted rebar, and all manner of debris stretched across the road. "Oh, shit, a blockade." She slowed.

"There's a man with a gun. Two men. Three."

"It's like we're in a war zone," said Marella.

"They're aiming at us." Elizabeth gestured wildly. "Go right."

She obeyed, rocketing up a ramp, which curved around and onto a freeway. There were few other cars going in their direction, but the freeway on the other side was packed.

"Oh no," said Marella. "We're on I-5 South. The exact opposite direction we want to go."

"Damn it. Look how jammed it is the other direction. We can't go north. Maybe we need a new plan. One that doesn't involve getting to Warehouse 27. What's your workaround?"

No pressure, thought Marella. But an idea popped into her head. "We can still get to the warehouse. We go downtown, and from there onto the beach where Puget Sound has dried up. We drive on the seabed to the warehouse."

Elizabeth tilted her head, considering the idea. "That's creative, but there's a steep seawall at Elliott Bay. And even if we found a way onto the seabed, just past the piers there's a sudden drop-off. We need a revised workaround. Another route down to the seabed. Think!" She seemed to be telling herself as much as Marella.

"What about the Duwamish River? It's half dry. It leads right out into to Puget Sound from West Seattle." One of the many places she'd lived. Her overly mobile lifestyle had finally come in handy.

Elizabeth bobbed her head twice. "That could work. It's south of here. Yes. Let's keep going."

• • • •

CROSSING THE BRIDGE to West Seattle Marella could see the Duwamish River's empty bed. The last time she had been there, boats made comet tails through the waterway. Now there was no flow at all, not even a trickle. Beached vessels were scattered like forgotten toys on the sand below and in Elliott Bay beyond.

The sight of the dry ground made her even more thirsty. A wave of nausea threatened. "How long can you live without water?"

"You might take a week to actually die but by three or four days you'd reach the point of no return."

Marella shook her head. Another point of no return. And after nearly twenty-four hours without liquid—except for alcohol, which was dehydrating—she was a third of the way there. A third of the way toward death. Unless somebody killed her sooner. How could the disaster have changed everything so fast?

Once over the bridge, she drove south on a street that ran alongside the riverbed and the railroad tracks. They passed several blocks of fenced businesses with giant industrial buildings. A grocery distributer, a tool fabricator, and other manufacturing facilities, yards full of heavy machinery.

"I don't see anybody," said Marella.

"Most people are with their families."

Like she should be. "Where's your family?" asked Marella. "Are they okay?"

"None of them live around here except my ex. We don't talk much."

Marella took that in. She hadn't known her boss had been married. "It's spooky around here."

"Agreed. Try that narrow road."

After turning onto it, Marella stopped the truck at the top of a slope. Brown-leaved laurel bushes and dead shrubs zigzagged in front of them, making it hard to see a way through. They got out of the truck. The wind whipped her hair into her eyes. She brushed it back anxiously, then pointed to where the foliage was thinner. "Maybe I can get the truck through."

They trudged down the slope. Elizabeth stopped abruptly. "There's a ten-foot-high retaining wall holding back the bank. We can't drive to the riverbed from here."

Marella scanned the dry bed, which was now stretched out in front of them. "Even if we could, look at all that stuff in the way. I see an anchor that's bigger than my truck." Huge barges were beached both upstream and downstream. There were patches of rocks and boulders, entire tree root tangles, and a multitude of objects that she couldn't identify from a distance. If they found a way onto the riverbed, would they find a path down to the bay?

Marella's head hurt. She didn't know whether it was from thirst or the enormity of the task. But there was no giving up. Doing nothing—standing right where she was until she turned into dust and blew away—was no option.

"I've always loved a good challenge," said Elizabeth drily.

Returning to the truck, they continued driving. Several times they turned down roads toward the river. Each route was blocked.

They passed more enormous industrial buildings, all fenced off, with many trees blocking the view. Marella remembered a news report about clearing the overly thirsty non-native plants from the riversides to get five percent more water. They were far beyond such piddling efforts now. Five percent of nothing was nothing.

They reached a park entrance. Beyond a paved area loomed a dense barrier of brown bushes and trees, interrupted only by a single narrow footpath. "I've been here before," said Marella. "It's all lawn alongside the Duwamish. If we can get past the trees we can reach the riverbed."

"Your truck won't fit on that trail," sighed Elizabeth. "Keep driving."

"We're getting too far from Elliot Bay." Marella felt her bitterness rising. There was a time she could merely stroll into a convenience store for a bottle of juice. Unscrew the lid. Tip the bottle to her mouth and taste the sweetness. That seemed so long ago. Now getting liquid was a monumental task. Soon it would be an impossible one.

But that was why she couldn't give up. She had to get Warehouse 27, or the Aguageddon would never end. Everyone would die. Marella. Mom. Brielle. Everybody she'd ever known.

She drove straight for the footpath.

"Don't," boomed Elizabeth. "The truck will get stuck."

"No it won't." Marella tried to sound confident, but her voice cracked. The truck lurched onto the uneven surface and into the woods, slapped by dead brown foliage, as if an automatic car wash was going haywire all around. They lurched up and down over potholes. Marella kept going.

Finally the foliage opened up onto the brown lawn they had seen from downriver. "We made it!" said Marella.

"Don't do a victory dance yet." As they drove across the lawn, they could see logs askew on the gently sloping beach ahead, amid patches of scull-size rocks.

Marella stopped the truck and scrambled onto the truck's bed. She swiveled her head looking for a path forward. The logs seemed to form an unsolvable maze. Over the riverbed the hot air shimmered. A pool of water seemed to lie on the sand. Only a mirage.

A crow squawked, making her start and hold her hands out for balance.

"I don't like this." Elizabeth was half in and half out of the truck.

"Yeah, it's creepy out here." Marella glanced back at the tall bushes that rimmed the lawn. The air smelled of dust with a hint of sage. Wind whipped the dry leaves, making them clatter. The sun streamed through them, creating dozens of tiger eyes that disappeared and reformed over and over.

"Quick reconnaissance." Elizabeth trotted to the right side of the lawn. Marella bounded down from the truck and ran to the left. The logs were old and rotted, rising from the dirt like narrow coffins after a graveyard flood.

"My truck might get stuck here," called Marella. "What's it look like over there?"

"Not good. I'm wondering if it's possible to get to the riverbed at all. Others would have the same idea as you did. We would see cars there but none have driven by."

A snap like a breaking bone made Marella jump. She scanned the bushes. So many shadows.

To her great surprise, a little boy, maybe five years old, emerged from the bushes. He held onto a baseball cap to keep the wind from blowing it off his head. "I can't find my mommy and daddy. Would you come with me?" When Marella and Elizabeth only stared in surprise, he repeated the words.

Elizabeth took a step toward him.

"Wait," said Marella. There was something off in the singsong way this kid had spoken. Like a child actor reciting adult lines.

Something was wrong. Terribly wrong. "It's a trap," said Marella.

Chapter Eleven

Marella swiveled toward the truck. As if she'd stepped on a detonator, a man exploded from the bushes brandishing a knife. Wearing a button-down shirt and Dockers, he looked more like an insurance salesman than a robber. A woman with a crowbar came right behind. Dressed in a pastel blouse and paisley leggings, she could have been a soccer mom.

Adrenaline shot through Marella's body. Her heart pounded. Her mind whirled. She was terrified of an insurance salesman and a soccer mom. The world had gone mad.

"Son of a bitch." Elizabeth jumped into the passenger seat.

Marella dove into the driver's seat. The man reached her before she could shut the door, taking hold of her upper arm with a vise-hard grip. She managed to turn the ignition key anyway.

Her world narrowed to a single moment where she saw only the man's face with its tiny eyes and cracked lips, smelled only his stink of sweat, felt only his hand locked onto her. As he thrust his knife at her, she stepped on the gas.

The truck shot forward; the man lost hold of Marella but his knife slid across her arm, searing it with pain. The truck bounced across the dead lawn and over a dip in the ground, leaving the man behind, but also knocking her sideways and lifting her foot from the gas. The truck came to a halt, engine still running, door wide open.

She struggled to right herself. The woman reached the truck, crowbar raised to smash Marella's head.

The world narrowed again. The woman's mouth stretched into a grimace of determination. All trace of soccer mom vanished. Everything modern, caring, thoughtful was long gone. In its place was an ancient resolve, a Viking determination. Marella raised an arm to block the blow.

Elizabeth leaned across Marella, letting out a high-pitched war cry. She shot the pepper spray, which hit the woman but also blew into Marella's face. Her eyes and throat were on fire. She was blind. Her eyes burned no matter how hard she squeezed them shut. Still she had the presence of mind to jam her foot back onto the accelerator. She felt the truck zoom forward. "I can't see."

"Not that way." Elizabeth's words shot out. "Veer left."

"How much?"

"Here, I'll help." Marella felt the wheel turning. "More gas."

Marella obeyed. The truck jolted over something. She bounced in the seat, thanking her lucky stars that the air bags were somehow not deploying. Her open door hit something, making an earsplitting grinding noise. She shrieked.

"Keep going," said Elizabeth. "There are logs but they're half-buried."

Driving blind felt so wrong. Like the earth had opened up and she was about to shoot into a chasm. The pain in her eyes, nose, and knife-nicked arm made her puff and pant. She wanted to curl up into a ball and moan. Still, she lumbered over the logs. Each time she tried to open her eyes the pain screwed them down tightly.

"Rock patch, slow down." She felt Elizabeth turning the wheel; they zigged, then zagged. Marella's door slammed closed, making her jump.

The truck skidded to a stop. "Go, go!" said Elizabeth.

Marella jammed her foot on the gas pedal, but the wheels only spun in place.

"They're still coming," shouted Elizabeth. "I'm putting it in reverse! Okay go." Marella stepped on the pedal. The truck shot backward. "Turn the wheel," ordered Elizabeth.

"Which way?"

"Any way."

She turned right, then felt the truck tipping. The sensation of being about to go over a cliff intensified. "What's happening?"

"We're on a slope."

"What do I do?"

"Nothing."

"That's too hard!"

The truck bounced crazily; she shouted as it tilted one way then the next as if the world was folding in on her. Finally the slope leveled.

"We're on the riverbed," said Elizabeth.

"Really?" Marella tried opening her eyes. "I can see a little." After putting the truck in gear she veered around a picnic cooler, a tire, a washing machine, and Styrofoam floats that were linked like sausage casings. Her tears made the scene hazy like a cheap effect in a low budget movie.

Elizabeth twisted, looking back. "They're giving up!" Her voice was jubilant.

A manic laugh burst out of Marella's mouth. They'd done it. They'd escaped the evil soccer mom and diabolical insurance salesman. "Last week if anybody would have told me I'd be driving in a damn riverbed, I would have said they were crazy."

"They used a child as bait," said Elizabeth, her voice both angry and incredulous.

The words sobered Marella's jubilation. In only a day, humans were reduced to attacking each other for their basic needs. What did that mean for her and her family? What did their future look like? She couldn't imagine, and didn't have time for it; driving took serious concentration, like a video game with objects popping up out of nowhere. Battered oil drums. A rusted storm grate. An alligator-shaped log. Car-sized orange floats. She maneuvered between them, doing her best to pick out a clear path with Elizabeth's help.

Marella blinked fast to see through watering eyes. The view from the bottom of this dried-out industrialized urban river was strange and jarring. On either side of them, pier pilings towered. Fortress-like buildings huddled beyond massive rock jetties. She felt puny and out of place. More than anything, she wanted to be back with her family, telling them about the ten-story silos, endless conveyor belts, and mountains of gravel.

Where were Mom and Brielle now? Had they made it to the camp at Mount Rainier? There were plenty of cliffs there. They could be dead and she wouldn't even know it. She imagined them falling to their deaths, like the cult members at the Space Needle, which now seemed so long ago. Or like her father. Lifeless on the ground.

She tried to shake free of her dread by losing herself in the task, concentrating on finding a path for her truck between mounds of barnacle-spattered rocks and man-made detritus. Watching for thieves who might be hiding in wait.

The bridge they had crossed earlier now arched high above them, solid and gray. They lumbered under it, reaching Harbor Island, a mass of concrete that split the riverbed into east and west channels.

They were approaching the river's mouth. Gigantic blue and orange shipping cranes lined the island's concrete edges. She'd heard they were three hundred feet high, taller than Godzilla. Some of the skeletal structures stood straight; others leaned, as if poised for attack.

Below the cranes a ship lay askew. Dozens of blue oil drums had fallen from it. She smelled something acidic. Some kind of chemical had spilled from them. Nothing too toxic, she hoped. She would have to drive right by them.

"Someone's there." Elizabeth pointed upward.

Marella looked, still squinting. At the base of a crane stood a figure like an angel, holding a torch aloft, the wind rippling its flame. The sight sent a shiver along her spine. "It's one of those cult people."

"Oh my god," said Elizabeth. "Zokara's Chosen?"

"Yeah." It couldn't be real. She had already experienced this moment, cult members on high. How could it be happening again?

"I thought they all jumped off the Space Needle."

"Fifteen jumped from the Space Needle. There were fifty in the cult."

"I heard they believe in fire cleansing. They walk on hot coals and have fire rituals as part of their religion."

The figure threw the torch down dramatically, as if smiting the evil below. Marella's stomach fluttered. Elizabeth jerked in surprise.

The torch dropped onto the spilled oil drums. Flames sprung up. In no time the ship was engulfed. As they approached its nearest end, the ship groaned like a waking monster, angry at being disturbed.

"I don't like this." Marella pushed herself back against the seat.

Elizabeth slapped the dash. "Hurry up. Get past it."

"I'm going as fast as I can."

Marella had to skirt a beached gravel barge, forcing her closer to the ship. The air felt wrong. As if the atmosphere were turned inside out. "It's going to blow up."

"I'm too old for this nonsense," said Elizabeth.

Marella's voice warbled as the flames rose higher. "You're not old, you're seasoned,"

"I hate that term. I'm not a pile of paprika."

Marella reached the ship's midsection, which rattled as if lightning ricocheted inside. They might make it past without harm. If only nothing happened in the next few moments. But the ship was as long as a soccer field. "Come on truck. Come on. You can do it."

"Good truck," added Elizabeth gingerly, as if addressing a fierce guard dog. "Be a good truck."

They passed the downstream end of the ship. Marella didn't feel relief. They were still too close. She kept glancing in the rearview mirror.

The ship exploded into chrysanthemums of fire. The sound seemed to rip the very air into fragments. Marella bellowed in fear but couldn't hear her own voice. Elizabeth cowered.

Red smoke surged outward in a great cloud, only a hundred feet behind them. It seemed alive. Coming after them in attack. Marella's palms were so sweaty they slid on the steering wheel even in the Aguageddon dryness.

"Just get away, just get away," cried Elizabeth. It was more prayer than directive.

Marella zoomed onward, the cloud of smoke chasing them down the riverbed.

"Go, go." Elizabeth pounded on the dashboard as if to push them along, then punched off the truck's air recirculation.

A bumper scraped a boulder; the sound of metal on rock made Marella shudder. She nearly hit an outboard motor, then a pile of Styrofoam.

Elizabeth inhaled sharply with each swerve. "I swear if I get my hands on those cult arsonists, I'm going to shred them with my bare hands."

"I'll help you," said Marella.

The smoke overtook the truck; one moment they could see ahead, the next they couldn't. It was hot, as if they'd driven into an oven. She barreled forward into the blood-red murk. It was more terrifying than driving blind with the pepper spray in her eyes; this time Elizabeth couldn't help navigate. Marella flicked the highlights on. Tendrils of red smoke seeped into the truck through the damaged door, highlighted eerily by the light.

"Hold your breath," said Elizabeth. Marella heard her inhale deeply; Marella did the same. The air in the truck began turning red. How long could she continue like this? Ten seconds passed as she floored the pedal. Twenty seconds. The smoke in the truck thickened. They struck something, rumbled over it. Thirty seconds.

They were going even faster now, but seemed motionless without perspective. Marella stopped counting.

She could no longer fight her need to breathe; she sucked the air into her lungs. It tasted of burnt rubber and plastic and felt like filthy cotton batting stuffed down her throat. Her mouth tasted like burnt coffee dregs. She tried to breathe shallowly, but her lungs wouldn't allow it. The air stung. She coughed and the pain intensified. Beside her, Elizabeth coughed too, raspy as a crow.

Marella was so terrified that she yearned to stop the truck to jump out. Her body automatically wanted fight or flight, though she knew she couldn't outrun this smoke, and she certainly couldn't battle it.

The truck burst out of the smoke and into a swirl of clear air.

Marella rolled down the windows. The wind swept through, taking much of the smoke with it. Marella and Elizabeth gulped deep breaths.

Suddenly the truck lurched to a halt. The wheels spun in place with a loud whine. "No, no!" Marella put the truck in reverse and gunned the engine; the wheels only dug in deeper.

"We have to get it free quickly," said Elizabeth, "the smoke is still spreading." They piled out of the truck. Tornados of red smoke twirled around them, soiling the air into sheets of haze. Fresh air gusted intermittently. Again Marella fought the urge to run. Her eyes teared even more, making it harder to see, though she could make out the wheels half-buried in the sand. Using both hands, she began to dig out the back wheel, the loose sand slipping through her fingers. She grew dizzy but forced herself to dig faster, which made her even dizzier.

"We need traction," said Elizabeth.

It was getting hard to think; still, an idea sprang into Marella's mind. "Floor mats." She staggered to the front, hauling one from the driver's side. Elizabeth pulled one from the passenger side. They wedged them under the wheels.

A burning ember fell from the sky. Then another, and another. It was terrifyingly beautiful. The glowing bits, along with her light-headedness, gave the world the air of a dream. Maybe she *was* dreaming. The real world wasn't like this. Disaster and thirst. But of course she was wrong: the real world was full of such things, and always had been, just not where she lived.

Her thoughts blurred further. Where was she? Watching fireflies acting oddly, flying straight downward as if on an elevator. But there were no fireflies in Washington state. So those had to be stars. Falling stars, which she'd seen before, but they too were misbehaving. Falling stars shouldn't drop on her, searing her arm. She yipped in pain, as did Elizabeth.

Just then, out of a vortex of smoke, an apparition appeared. She could only see its outline, but could tell it was tall, with flames sprouting from its body. Marella backed away, horrorstruck. The red smoke, the otherworldliness of her surroundings. Was she dead? Was there really a Hell, and was she there?

The figure advanced on her, crying, "Help." A man, she realized, not a demon. His arms dark brown, not red. And his shirt was on fire.

She lunged for her truck. Yanking out the top item on her laundry basket, a t-shirt, she rushed to the man, throwing it over him. He flailed about, knocking it away, still pleading for help.

"Hold still!" She retrieved the shirt and renewed her attack, but it was like trying to bag a feral cat. Elizabeth joined her and together they pulled him to his knees and tamped the shirt down onto him until the flames were gone.

"Get him in the truck," said Elizabeth. "Hurry, the smoke is getting thicker." They guided him to the back seat. Elizabeth followed him in, not taking the time to jump in the front. Marella dove in and pushed on the gas pedal. The car struggled, not moving. The phrase "toxic asphyxiation" repeated in her head.

She thought of her mother and Brielle hearing about her death by chemical smoke. She could picture their faces, see their pain. And what about them? What kinds of trials were they enduring? Tears spilled down her cheeks, spurred by smoke and anxiety.

The tire treads grasped the mats. The truck eased forward.

Emerging from the haze felt like an evil spell lifting. Yet it felt as if a blanket swaddled her brain, tucking its wool around each lobe, wrapping each thought to keep it from stirring. She fought it as best she could. "We did it," Marella croaked. "We're moving."

"Thank god," said Elizabeth.

The man in the back groaned. "Thank you. Thank you so much. Thank you." Marella looked in the rearview mirror. He was probably about her age, his long face accented by a curly top fade, high cheekbones, and a square chin. His gray polo shirt hung in pieces. He had an expression of anguish.

Elizabeth examined his back. "Could have been worse. Second degree burn or less."

"It hurts like hell," said the man.

"What were you doing out there alone?" asked Elizabeth. "It's dangerous." She peered back into the smoke. She sounded worried. "Was there anybody with you?"

"Just me. I was trying to get to Elliott Bay to get water. I thought if I went by myself I'd be able to go faster." He paused for breath. "I'm quick. But I kept almost getting ambushed. People wanted my bottles. I made it to the mouth of the Duwamish. There was an explosion and the smoke was everywhere. I dropped the bottles."

"A whole ship exploded," said Elizabeth.

"Thank you for saving me. I could have died." His throat tightened on his words. "I owe you big time."

"You're welcome. I'm Elizabeth Fehr. That's Marella Wells."

"Noah Mburu."

"Noah what?" asked Elizabeth.

"Mburu. My parents are from Kenya."

Still dizzy and disoriented, Marella drove onward. The world around her seemed to be locked in a dream state. Hundreds of flames sprouted from the bay floor as if Earth had sprung leaks. Without river water to douse them, they burned freely.

Noah groaned as if trying to shove the pain away. "Were you getting water too? Do you have an extra container? I'd hate to have gone through all this for nothing."

"We don't have any containers at all," said Marella.

"Can you take me home so I can get some? You can have some of ours."

Marella took a deep breath and coughed. "We can't go back. We have to go north. We're going to a warehouse so we can..."

"We're on a confidential mission," interrupted Elizabeth.

Marella glanced at Elizabeth, who stared at her pointedly. That was annoying. She was only going to say they were getting a boat. Surely Elizabeth didn't think she would tell a stranger her boss was taking a HemisNorth flash drive to shut down a secret project named after a Greek goddess? But then their passenger was a stranger. It was probably best not to give him too much information after all.

She slowed at a dip in the ground. They lurched down, then up. She went around an odd looking dirty white mound—plastic bags, she realized, caught up in an eddy perhaps then clumped together in an accidental sculpture.

They left the riverbed, rumbling down the dry slope where the Duwamish River used to pour into Puget Sound. No more embers fell. Here the bay floor was surprisingly flat. Dozens of other vehicles were also driving along the dry bed, having come from other directions, but not as many as there could have been. Elizabeth must have been right, the drop-off would have been too steep to come from the downtown area.

Marella eyed the vehicles warily. Who was dangerous and who wasn't? It was impossible to tell. She veered around a bus fender, a dog crate, and a marble slab jutting up like a monolith.

The northern part of the Seattle skyline suddenly came into view: Magnolia bluff and north Seattle. A wall of fire burned along its length, with a massive cloud of black smoke roiling above. They all gasped.

"Oh my god," said Marella. She felt helpless and unreal. As if her brain had separated from her body and somebody else was driving the truck, ferrying her forward into a fake landscape.

"I can't believe what I'm seeing." Elizabeth's voice was strained.

"They can't put that out that much fire." Noah clutched the seat in front of him.

Now the Space Needle came into view. It made Marella shiver. Golden robed people jumping to their deaths. She would always associate the one with the other.

The downtown skyscrapers, ferry terminal, and the Great Wheel—a twenty-story Ferris wheel—came into view. She had seen this scene before from the Bainbridge Island ferry as it returned to Seattle, except that the waterfront's giant piers now jutted out over sand rather than water.

Elizabeth blurted, "Look at the Smith Tower."

Orange flames sprouted from the building's side, midway up. A fat caterpillar of black smoke rose. As they watched it climbed higher and higher.

Marella slowed the truck, staring. Every Seattleite knew the nozzle-top shape of the Smith Tower. In the early 1900s it dominated the skyline as the tallest office building west of the Mississippi. Now it was tucked in among much larger metal and glass high-rises.

To Marella, the Smith Tower represented the stability she longed for. It had always been comforting to know that while many things changed—old buildings demolished, new ones taking their places—the Smith Tower remained. But soon it would be gone. It disoriented her further, as if she'd just spun in circles.

The wind tugged the smoke column, weaving its gray ribbon among the other buildings. She shivered in spite of the heat.

"I see fire on First Hill," said Elizabeth. "By the hospitals. Patients will have to be evacuated."

"I live up there," said Marella. "So does Diana." It felt like a hand was clasping her heart, which frightened her even more. Surely she wasn't having a heart attack so young?

Marella turned the truck radio on, but picked up only prickly static. She tapped to cycle through stations, but nothing would come up. Things were that bad. "Nothing's working."

She looked back at Noah, who was tapping on his phone. "No network service. Messaging doesn't work either. I can't warn my roommates. They're in danger. We have to get to them before the fire does."

"We can't go back," said Marella.

"They're my friends," said Noah. "I've known them all my life."

"What we're doing is too important," said Elizabeth.

"It won't take long," pleaded Noah. "You can go to your warehouse afterward."

Elizabeth emphasized each syllable. "We can't go back."

"They could die," said Noah, his voice breaking. "Don't you get it? They could die."

"We're trying to save lives too," said Marella.

"At a warehouse? Are you kidding me?" He clutched Marella's headrest, leaning forward. "I'm talking about human beings."

Elizabeth put a hand on Noah's arm but he held his position, much too close to Marella, who shrank away. Had they made a big mistake by saving him? What would he do now out of desperation for his friends? He could take the car from them. Where had Elizabeth put the pepper spray? She couldn't see it. What if he had a weapon?

Should they have let him burn?

How could she think such a thing? Her frustration built. It was his fault she had such evil thoughts. He wasn't listening, so she would have to make him listen. Marella stopped the truck suddenly making them all lurch in their seats. She turned, yelling, "I'm leaving my family behind." She jabbed her hand south. "I don't know where they are or if they're even still alive. Because what we're doing is that important and will save a whole shitload of people. You can come with us or you can get out right now."

His teeth clenched, Noah shoved the truck door open and jumped out. Still clutching the open door he twisted around, scanning the area. Fire. Smoke. Devastation. He seemed to deflate.

Elizabeth leaned toward Noah, her voice matter-of-fact. "Your friends aren't helpless, right? They can save themselves. Look at the way those fires are moving. We wouldn't make it there in time to help them."

Noah let out a big breath of air. He climbed back in, yanked the door shut, and leaned back, jerking forward in pain when his burned skin touched the seat. "You're right. I'm sorry. I shouldn't act like this. You saved my life."

The wretched look on Noah's face sapped Marella's anger. He had no way of knowing she was trying to help Elizabeth save the entire world—including his friends—from catastrophe. Even if she had told him, he might not have believed it. She herself found it completely preposterous.

They progressed north, with the Seattle shoreline on the right and the edge of the now shrunken Puget Sound on the left. The wind whipped the water's surface into sloppy pyramids and slapped down knee-high waves. She could smell the decaying fish scattered at the water's edge.

A group of five men and women were hip-deep in the bay, filling ten-gallon water cooler jugs and lugging them into the back of a delivery truck. The wind blew one woman's hair nearly straight out. They stopped their activities, watching the truck intently. A man held a gun in view. A warning not to come near. Marella held her breath until they got past.

Noah exhaled as if he'd been holding his as well. "I always wanted a life of adventure but not this kind."

Elizabeth wiped her face nervously. "I've been wanting less stress. You see how that turned out."

"Why did everything catch fire all at once?" asked Noah. "It's been dry for five months. Now all of a sudden everything is burning."

"What if that cult set all those fires?" asked Elizabeth. "Zokara's Chosen."

"I thought they all committed suicide at the Space Needle," said Noah.

"So did I," said Elizabeth. "Until we saw one of them with a torch."

"He was wearing a gold robe," added Marella. "He caused the explosion back at the Duwamish."

Noah closed his eyes and shook his head. "God my back hurts. Where'd the water go?"

Marella and Elizabeth didn't answer. What could they say?

"I never would have thought this would happen," said Noah. "My parents almost bought a house in Fife. Then they learned that if Mount Rainier blew that whole area would be covered in lahar. They moved to Spokane instead and constantly worried about fires. They stocked up on food and water in case of disaster. A gallon of water a day for each person for a month. I thought they were paranoid, but now, not so much."

"So you're from Spokane," said Elizabeth. "Just visiting?"

"I'm a student at the University of Washington. What about you? Any chance you're a doctor?"

"I'm a biologist," said Elizabeth.

"I'm an office assistant," said Marella. *I copy and paste text for the company that's turning the world into a desert planet.*

Downtown, orange flames now engulfed the 1201 Third Avenue Building. It stood out next to its blocky neighbors; its blue windows, snowflake ornamentation, and curved features belonged in a graphic novel. Something at the base of the building exploded, blossoming into a black rose. The boom came a moment later, a menacing rumble that Marella felt in her bones. Smoke enveloped the tower.

"This can't be happening," said Marella, her voice hoarse. "Please tell me this isn't happening. I hope nobody was in the building."

Flames now spiked up along the entire length of the former shoreline. Behind them on the other side of the bay West Seattle was engulfed in smoke, as was Bainbridge Island. "It's all on fire. Everything's on fire." It felt as if all the world was burning down around them. Soon there would be nothing left but crisp black spires. The hand clasping her heart squeezed painfully. They had to get to Warehouse 27 before it burned down.

As they hastened along the dry shore of Puget Sound, with north Seattle on their right, fire still raged, propelling coils of flame and smoke upward. Hundreds of cars had made their way onto the bay's floor, all pointing different directions like bumper cars. Marella maneuvered among them. Her skin felt like used paper, dry and crumpled.

"The warehouse is just around this promontory," said Elizabeth. "Hurry. We might get there in time."

But when they rounded the bend, they saw only fire. Flames devoured tall pines, low bushes, and buildings. Marella couldn't peel her eyes away from the devastation, from this lost hope. A burning piece of awning separated from a roof, floating upward like a flying carpet, then gliding away, its lightness and poetic beauty a direct contrast to the heaviness of her body.

"The warehouse is on fire," said Elizabeth. "The *Northern Hemisphere* is gone." Her shoulders slumped.

Now they had no way to get to Wisdom Island.

Chapter Twelve

Marella had come because it was the right thing to do, but what had it gotten her? Thirst, sandpapered lungs, and a brain that seemed filled with smoke. What if her mother and Brielle died because she hadn't been there to help them? She would never forgive herself.

They descended from the truck. Flames reflected orange on their faces. The sight was too much to bear. She turned away.

There were cars scattered around. A few boats, grounded. Even if they could commandeer one they had no trailer to take it out to the water. There was no workaround for this.

Which meant they had failed. They weren't going to stop the climate machine. Marella felt dizzy, as if the world had stopped spinning but she had not.

"What were you saying about the northern Hemisphere?" Noah rolled his shoulders, then grimaced in pain.

"The *Northern Hemisphere* is a boat," said Marella. "*Was* a boat."

"What do you need a boat for?" Noah answered his own question. "You're going to ride the ocean while it recedes. But what if it keeps receding? Are you going to follow the water all the way into the Mariana Trench?"

Marella didn't answer. What could she tell him? That she had been trying to save the world? It seemed so grandiose. It shouldn't surprise her that she wasn't able to do that. She wasn't capable. Her little workarounds weren't up to that caliber of task.

"Where's our other boat?" asked Elizabeth. "Did you see the *Southern Hemisphere* on the schedule?"

"It's in Sekiu," said Marella.

"Where's that?" asked Noah.

"The northwest corner of Washington," said Marella. "Almost to Neah Bay. I was there for a summer once when I was little. It's tiny. A fishing town. I don't remember much else." Marella had vague memories. A steep hillside in front of a harbor with many long, skinny docks, Her father laughing at the statue next to the town's welcome sign: a fish wearing a pink bra, tennis skirt, and athletic shoes. If only she could go back to that time.

Noah shook his head. "It'll take hours to get there from here."

"We need a closer answer," said Elizabeth. "I need to think about what resources the company might have." She took a few steps away and stared to the east.

Marella saw a tiny ray of hope. She didn't have the answer, but Elizabeth was a leader. She might come through, though she wasn't sure how.

Noah leaned against the car. "I wish I had some ice for my back."

Retrieving her first aid kit from the truck, Marella silently thanked her mother, who had given it to her. Marella had said it was just like a mother to give such a practical gift. Now she regretted she'd been rude. She thought sadly of her mother's look of disappointment. Where was she now? Would she ever be able to tell her she had made good use of it?

Noah lowered himself onto the sand, as carefully as an old man. "What's the burn look like?"

"Australia and a bunch of islands."

"That big?"

"A palm-size Australia. The way you were blazing I thought it would be worse. But I'm never gotten a burn that big. It must hurt like crazy."

"You know it."

She applied an antibiotic, which made him hiss, then taped on some gauze.

"How did that happen?" asked Noah, pointing to the wound on her arm.

She looked down. It wasn't as deep as she feared and the blood had dried. "Some parents sent their kid out as bait, then attacked us. We barely got away." She shivered at the memory of their evil, determined faces.

"Let me take care of that," said Noah. It was Marella's turn to jerk as he cleaned her arm. "I never thought Seattle would be a war zone."

And yet it was. Marella was keeping an eye on the other cars, making sure they didn't come toward them. Ready to leap back into the car at any sign of danger. As he worked on her arm, she felt a touch of camaraderie.

Elizabeth turned back to them and saw Noah finishing up with a bandage. "Safety tip: when possible, let somebody take care of their own wound."

Noah pulled his hands away from her arm. Reaching up to pat the bandage edge down, Marella felt embarrassed, as if they had been caught kissing.

"I think Sekiu is our best option," said Elizabeth. "We go north toward Edmonds. It's shallower there, so we'll be able to stay on the seabed. We'll veer northwest before Whidbey Island and go between Point No Point and Useless Bay. Then drive west through the Strait of Juan de Fuca. The *Southern Hemisphere* is our goal, but if we manage to get hold of a boat along the way, even better. Watch for opportunities."

Edmonds. Memories surfaced. Cruising around Puget Sound with Jalen, an old friend, in his parents' boat. Marella spoke quickly. "I have a friend in Edmonds. His parents have a boat. They'll help us!"

Elizabeth's looked thrilled. "Ten miles versus a hundred and something. Well done!" To Marella's surprise, she embraced her. Elizabeth's body felt thin but strong. Her reaction gave Marella even more hope.

Noah seemed happy too. His smile naturally pulled to one side like the car she'd learned to drive in. It gave him a conspiratorial look, as if they shared a private joke. They piled back in the truck. It was understood that he would come along. To leave him here would be to abandon him to the fire.

"Driving on a seabed feels so wrong," said Marella. "I'm used to hills and trees and buildings. It's so weird and flat here."

"Sediment deposition," explained Elizabeth, sounding rejuvenated.

They resumed driving. The fires on their right made the environment bizarre. Flames wrapped the trees like exotic chrysalises from which blazing butterflies might emerge. Waterfront homes were engulfed by fire. Where were their inhabitants? In the other cars scattered along Puget Sound's seabed?

"I never thought I'd see something like this," said Elizabeth.

"It's like another planet," said Marella.

"Everything is so red," said Noah.

The late morning sun was relegated to a crimson disk, as if it were sunset, which only added to the eeriness of the surroundings. "Don't stare at the sun," said Elizabeth.

"It's hard not to," said Marella. "It's like an eye watching us."

"An evil eye," said Noah.

Marella wished he hadn't said it. She pushed away thoughts of demons. Not letting the images emerge in her mind. Instead she thought of Mom taking a bite of a doughnut, eyes closed with pleasure. Brielle telling Mom she looked like she was on a TV commercial. Mom pretending she was, taking a huge bite, garbling the words with her mouth so full, "Mmmm, delicious!"

But Mom could get so fearful about her and Brielle. Always warning them. She understood now. Marella kept pushing her worries away, but seeing the fire so far north, it was easy to obsess. She imagined her family overtaken by smoke. Her chest ached with the need to burst out—in sobs or in rage, she wasn't sure—but she tamped it all down. She couldn't do anything about Mom and Brielle right now. The island was the mission.

Wisdom Island. What a name. If they had only been wiser about all this. Foreseen what could go wrong with their technology because of the human factor.

The smoke unrolled in a thick carpet, so that sometimes they could see the water to the left and sometimes they couldn't. Marella's lungs felt as if they'd been scrubbed by steel-wool pads. She scratched frenetically at itchy red bumps that erupted on her skin.

"I'm so thirsty," said Noah. "I haven't had any water since this morning."

"I haven't since yesterday," said Marella. "I'm nauseous."

"Let me see something." Elizabeth reached over and gently pinched the skin on Marella's arm upward. "It's tenting. Not going back flat. We really need to get help from your friend. Hopefully he'll have something for us to drink. Hang in there." She tested her own skin and Noah's as well, but they weren't as bad off as Marella.

• • • •

AN HOUR LATER THEY found the Edmonds ferry terminal ablaze, with orange flames curtaining the hillside beyond.

"It's like the devil came through with a blowtorch," said Noah. "And it smells like a burned coffeepot full of dead rats."

Marella's nausea deepened. The ground seemed to tilt. "The fire is everywhere. There's no way to get to Edmonds, and so we can't go to Jalen's place. We can't get their boat."

"All right then," said Elizabeth, "We have to go to Sekiu after all, and get the *Southern Hemisphere*," said Elizabeth. "I don't see any other option. Do you have enough gas?"

"Yes but that'll take hours. I'm not sure I can last that long without water." Marella leaned her head on the steering wheel. Her head was pounding. Misery filled her, as if every cell had been injected with it. She couldn't fix the world. Why had she bothered to try? She couldn't save anybody. She couldn't even save herself.

Noah put a comforting hand on her shoulder. "There's water right there in the bay. We just need to find a way to distill it. Have you got a metal container or something? We could build a fire with driftwood."

Marella shook her head.

Elizabeth craned her neck, looking around. "There's so much garbage in the sand though, there must be something we can use." As if to prove her point, a plastic bag danced up, blown by the wind.

"You're right," said Noah. "We passed drums and other containers back at the river. There will be more."

Something glinted in the sand. "Look," said Marella, pushing the truck door open with both hands, her muscles stiff. Could it be that when they needed a metal container the most, it was there? That was how life was supposed to work: good things happened along with the bad. But when Marella and Noah rushed to the shiny object, they found only a grate.

Marella crouched, face in hands. "My head hurts. I'm dizzy. I can't think."

"We'll get through this," Noah's voice was full of compassion. "Things will get better, I promise."

Elizabeth pulled gently on Marella's arm. "We'll head west to Sekiu and keep an eye out for metal containers and fuel. I'll drive."

Marella allowed Elizbeth to guide her back to the truck. Sitting in the passenger seat, she leaned her face on her arm. She watched the ground as it rolled by, strewn with Styrofoam floats, a sunken rowboat, a plastic doll. She appreciated Noah's caring words, but she was scared. She was on the edge of a precipice. Leaning toward the point of no return. The point where all the water in the world wouldn't save her.

Her eyes closed. She opened them, lifting her head. She needed to stay awake and alert. She needed to watch for containers.

•   •   •   •

A CAR WAS STOPPED AHEAD. Elizabeth peered at it. "I see one woman. She's drinking from a can. Maybe she'll give you a little when she learns how bad off you are."

"Don't get too close," said Noah. "We don't want to scare her off."

"Good thinking, Noah," said Elizabeth. "Hide yourself."

Because he was male, and because he was black. Noah seemed about to protest but then complied, slipping down in the seat. Marella couldn't help thinking he was demeaning himself for her sake.

Elizabeth stopped the truck twenty feet away. The woman retreated into her car. Elizabeth walked toward it, hands in the air.

A car door opened. A German shepherd leaped out. It charged Elizabeth, baring its teeth and barking.

Marella gripped the dash. "Run!" Her voice came out as a whisper.

Elizabeth wheeled around, flying back to the truck, eyes bright with terror. The dog bounded across the sand like a skipping stone. There was no way she would make it back to the car in time. The dog would tear her to bits.

The horror of this moment hung over Marella like a sword. She could do nothing for Elizabeth. Why was she so weak right now when strength mattered most?

Noah jumped out of the car, waving his arms and shouting, "This way you stinking mutt, this way!"

The dog wobbled mid-jump, landed awkwardly, and changed direction. Now it was heading for Noah, and would reach him in two leaps. Marella was overwhelmed with both gratitude and dismay.

He was sacrificing himself for Elizabeth, but that wasn't a good workaround. Now he would be maimed or killed.

Elizabeth reached the truck, and threw herself inside, pulling the door shut with both hands. Noah scrambled back in and shut his door as well.

Marella leaned her head back in relief. They was safe. But the respite was brief. The German shepherd attacked the car as if it could bite through steel. Its snarling fury was terrifying even while they were protected by the truck, making them all lean away from the doors.

Elizabeth peeled away.

Noah lay down on the back seat. "I can't even deal," he said. Marella was sorry she had any doubts about him. He had proved more than trustworthy. He had been willing to brave a vicious dog for Elizabeth's sake.

The sound of barking and the owner calling the dog back dwindled. Then there was only engine noise and Elizabeth catching her breath.

"It's a no," Elizabeth finally warbled.

Marella couldn't help it. She laughed feebly, though the sound barely came out. Then Noah began laughing, and finally Elizabeth.

When they had recovered, Elizabeth set them off again with, "How did she know I wasn't a dog person?"

Marella laughed in near-hysterical catch-breaths, then settled into quiet contemplation of her desperate state.

• • • •

EVERYTHING SEEMED UNREAL, as if Marella were watching a movie of herself. She felt sicker with each passing minute. They had approached dozens of other people and were threatened or turned away each time. Was this happening to her family as well? Were they just as dehydrated as she was? How would they all survive?

The further west they went, the fewer vehicles they encountered, and now they hadn't seen any for a half hour. The seabed terrain transitioned to a combination of dunes and ridges. They hugged the water's edge, staying far away from upland flames. Even so, smoke veiled the sky. Rolling dunes only worsened Marella's nausea and sense of isolation.

Marella's thigh hurt abruptly as if stabbed. She howled, grabbing her leg.

"Muscle cramp from dehydration," said Elizabeth.

"Stretch it," said Noah.

Marella contorted herself, trying to comply. She breathed shallowly. When it finally eased her head hurt worse. As if her brain had been torn into pieces then reassembled incorrectly.

Rock ridges rose up ahead, stark, imposing, and impassable. Fire burned to the left, and the water blocked them to the right. In front of the ridges stood four vehicles: a camping van, a truck with a canopy, and two SUVs. Their last chance to get help.

"We can't go further west until the water recedes some more," said Elizabeth.

"Where are we?" asked Marella.

"Near Port Townsend," said Elizabeth. "About a hundred miles to go." She reached over and checked Marella's pulse. "Your heart is beating rapidly."

They pulled closer to the vehicles, but nobody emerged. Elizabeth stepped out of the truck. "We need water," she called. "My friend is very dehydrated. She might die."

Hearing "die," Marella weighed it, trying it on for size. Yes, it was true. She might die. What was it Elizabeth had said before? The body's point of no return was three or four days without water, give or take. It had only been one and a half. But that didn't take the Aguageddon into account. How drying it was. Marella felt feverish. She was breathing too fast.

Yes, she might die. She might leave Elizabeth to fix HemisNorth's mess. Leave this world to its troubles. But that wouldn't keep her from suffering. She felt herself sliding downward to Hell and its demons. She wanted to dig her hands and feet into the imagined slope to slow her descent.

"Go away," said a voice so deep it sounded bottomless. "We don't want any trouble."

"Please," said Elizabeth. "Save her life."

"We don't have anything. Go away. This is your last warning."

Warning. The word should have inspired fear, but instead made anger surge. Was it only yesterday she had saved a child's life? Now she was the needful one. Nobody should be warning her. They should be helping her. She pushed on the truck door handle.

"Don't Marella, they'll hurt you," said Noah.

She pressed the door open. It wasn't easy. She had to lean her shoulder against it, and then let gravity pull her out. She fell to her hands and knees, nearly hitting the ground face first. Once down, she began crawling. She was that cartoon character, the one in the desert whose clothes were shredded. There should be a wryly humorous caption below her saying...saying what? She couldn't think. Just move forward.

Chapter Thirteen

A man appeared, bent down on one knee, a look of calm compassion in his eyes. He helped Marella to sit up.

He held out a cup. It had liquid. Actual liquid.

Her hands shook too hard to hold the cup. He eased it to her lips. She drank. It tasted fresh, with a hint of coconut. It ran through her throat like water through a ditch, leaving it just as dry as before. The man poured her more. "This has electrolytes you'll need." His voice was deep, comforting.

"Small sips," ordered Elizabeth. Marella pushed her hand up to help tilt the cup and drank it all down anyway. She couldn't help it.

The world slowly came into focus, its edges solidifying. The ridge of barnacle-dotted rock sloping upward beyond the vehicles. Orange and purple starfish with lines of tiny silver dots, clinging underneath an overhang. The water to her right rippled in dull bluish-grays, with a red tinge where the smoke-veiled sun reflected. Far off to her left, the wind rippled the flames that devoured the trees.

The man, who introduced himself as Preston, looked forty, with a noble-looking face. A younger and handsomer George Washington in painter's pants and a green t-shirt. Elizabeth and Noah, cups in hand, thanked him profusely.

Marella's relief was boundless. Finally she had help and kindness from a stranger. She wasn't going to die, not in this moment, anyway. This was a safe haven in the madness of the Aguageddon.

A woman appeared. The wind wrapped her orange and pink flowered skirt around her legs and blew her long gray hair behind her.

"I'm Gabriela," she said with a slight Hispanic accent, taking Marella's hand in both of hers. They were warm and soft. She smelled of sweat and patchouli. More kindness. Marella felt soothed.

Gabriela turned to Noah. "Your back! What happened?" Her voice was full of alarm.

"My shirt caught on fire," said Noah, seeming embarrassed.

"That must hurt."

"Like crazy," said Noah. "Everything is on fire from Seattle all the way to here. Have you heard any news? How far has it spread?"

"We haven't been able to get ahold of anybody," said Preston. It didn't sound like a crisis when he spoke. It sounded like there were merely setbacks to be solved. Marella felt reassured. With a little rest and recovery, she could continue solving setbacks herself, and get to Sekiu.

Another woman appeared—Marella guessed she was about thirty years old—wearing a peony-patterned sundress and holding a baby whose eyes were closed, face scrunched in an infant's dream. The woman looked like a Madonna from an old master's painting, her head tilted just so, the cloth spilling from her arms perfectly rumpled as if arranged for an oil painting.

At the sight of Marella, her serene expression vanished. She looked alarmed.

"This is Edie and Baby Faith," said Gabriela. Edie nodded acknowledgment quickly. Her forehead creased. She didn't come any closer. Perhaps she was concerned about strangers. Marella didn't blame her, with a baby to protect.

"This is Marella," said Elizabeth. "I'm Elizabeth and this is Noah."

"Noah?" said Preston, tilting his head. "Like in the Bible?"

"Sure," said Noah.

Preston's mouth opened slightly as if he had just learned something surprising. "Noah did God's bidding during the Great Flood. The opposite of the Aguageddon. Interesting." He sat. Noah and Elizabeth joined him on the hard sand.

"It was strange to see Seattle's burning down," said Noah. "I thought it would always be there."

Gabriela made a comforting noise. "Seattle burned down before. A century ago, or more, I think. They rebuilt and made it even better. Maybe they'll do that again."

"They had lumber for that." Noah looked east. The others followed his gaze. Burnt tree spikes on a tall cliff faded in and out of view behind a curtain of smoke.

"Don't they call Seattle the Emerald City?" Gabriela winked. "Well then, they'll rebuild with emeralds, of course."

Marella marveled at Gabriela's positive outlook in the face of such disaster. How did she manage it? She smiled in spite of herself. Gabriela's comment shifted something in her thoughts so that now she could imagine herself gazing at a new Seattle, with a skyline of crystalline green buildings.

"My mom says change is good," said Marella. "It keeps you on your toes."

"Is this your mom?" asked Gabriela.

Elizabeth sat hunched. Marella got the feeling she had been Atlas, carrying the world for them, but was now collapsing under its weight.

"No," Elizabeth answered. "But I wouldn't mind having a daughter like Marella."

Marella felt a surge of gratitude. That Elizabeth would say such a thing caught her off guard. She used to think of her as one of "them." A boss, somebody separate from real life. But they were connected now, through survival, of course, but also through a common goal.

Marella had gotten sidetracked. Material losses were beside the point. There was nothing more important than getting the flash drive to the island and shutting off the machine. That was the only way her family would survive.

Wisdom Island was somewhere to the west, beyond the Strait of Juan de Fuca, past the Olympic Peninsula. It didn't matter how the world had gotten to this point. What mattered was that she was going to go to the island and help Elizabeth fix it. When they reached Sekiu they would get the *Southern Hemisphere* and tow it to the water. Go to Wisdom Island. Shut Athena down.

And then Marella would return to her family. With them she would have the courage to face the changes in their world. She brushed sand from her legs and sat up a little straighter.

Edie came closer to the group, though hesitatingly, as if they might be diseased. Baby Faith made a little noise, scrunching her face as if unsure whether to cry or not. Preston's face lit up. He took her from Edie, nestling her in his arms, cooing to her. "It's all right, it's all good."

"Where are you from?" Marella asked Edie.

"Port Townsend."

"We're all neighbors," added Preston.

Baby Faith's sock fell to the ground, revealing her tiny, perfect toes. Noah retrieved it and put it back on. Baby Faith's eyes blinked in surprise at his touch. She gurgled and cooed with great effort, as if trying to explain how her sock fell off.

Marella wanted to ask where the baby's father was and if he was okay, but Edie's apprehensive expression kept her silent.

"What do you think caused the Aguageddon?" Noah asked Preston.

Edie answered instead. "God."

Marella looked away. Perhaps God did cause it, indirectly through HemisNorth.

Another person arrived carrying a bucket and water jugs. She stopped short at the sight of strangers. She wore fashionably shredded jeans, and had large eyes, as if magnified by glasses, though she didn't wear any. Her age—she looked about fourteen—and her buoyant demeanor reminded her of Brielle. Marella liked her immediately.

"This is Olivia," said Gabriela.

Olivia held up the bucket she carried. "I caught a fish! It flopped onto the sand and I got it before a wave reached it."

Elizabeth leaned over the bucket. "A yellowstripe goatfish. What's that doing here? They normally inhabit Hawaiian reefs." She flicked her hand at it. "Get rid of it. Eating it will make you sick and give you hallucinations."

Olivia spoke in dismay. "Oh!"

Marella leaned forward and peered into the bucket. A yellow stripe ran the length of the white fish. A single black blotch broke the line, like a fingerprint of smudged ink.

Preston looked at Elizabeth gratefully. "It's a good thing you came to us." The wording was unusual. Not *showed up*, but *came to us*. The quirk was endearing. Of course it was. Preston had saved her life. Everything about him was endearing.

Olivia took the bucket away to dump it.

"A yellowstripe goatfish in Puget Sound waters," said Elizabeth. "Things are really wrong."

• • • •

NIGHT CAME. THEY LAY in Marella's truck, Noah in the front seat, Marella and Elizabeth in the back seat. Elizabeth shivered hard despite wearing extra clothes from Marella's laundry basket, so Marella snuggled up to her, rubbing her arms briskly.

"Thank you," said Elizabeth.

"There must be a reason this is all happening," said Noah.

"What do you mean?" Marella stiffened, suddenly sure that Noah suspected their connection to the drought.

"Maybe it's part of God's plan," continued Noah, "But I just don't know why he would put us through this. Is he trying to show us something?"

Marella relaxed. Of course Noah didn't know. How would he?

Elizabeth sighed. "If God's trying to show us something then I wish he would just do a PowerPoint presentation and be done with it."

Marella chuckled. So did Noah, after a pause.

"Where are you going to take the boat?" asked Noah.

"Go to sleep," said Elizabeth.

Noah made a noise of annoyance, but dropped the subject.

Marella dreamed her truck was submerged, transformed into a reverse aquarium where she could admire the ratfish, the ugliest fish in one of the biology books at work. In her dream they were purple with gold eyes. University of Washington colors. *Maybe I'll get a degree from there someday*, she thought in the dream. *I'll learn all the things I need to keep other disasters from happening.*

But the ratfish, who could hear her thoughts, laughed at her. "The UW is gone," they gurgled as they gathered in front of the windshield. "Burnt to the ground."

"They can rebuild it with emeralds," she protested, only then realizing they were really laughing at her because she was trapped underwater in her truck. Terrified, she tapped at her phone to call for help, but could only bring up cartoon bubble images.

The realness of the dream remained after sunrise woke her. Unwrapping herself from her dusty towel, she looked out of the truck to reassure herself that the water hadn't surrounded them while she slept.

In the front seat, Noah now stirred. He started to speak, but it came out froggy. He coughed. "How do you feel?"

"Like I've been spun through the dryer. But a little less brain fog. You?"

"So caffeine-deprived I'd get a contact high just by walking into a Starbucks." Noah's smile was still a bit lopsided. Charming, she thought, chuckling.

Elizabeth, who was now stirring, asked, "How's it look out there?"

To the south, the trees and land were black, flames and smoke still rising in places. Smoke covered the sun. "It looks charred," said Marella.

"They brought extra gas," said Noah. "Talk about being prepared."

Following his gaze, Marella saw orange gas cans strapped to Olivia's car. She looked beyond to the west. Puget Sound was an ugly yellowish gray. "The water has receded some more, but not enough."

"So we're stuck here for now," said Noah.

Marella tapped on her leg impatiently. Stuck here. When she should be rushing to the island. She wished she had some way to get there instantly. She imagined rocketing over the waves on a Jet Ski, leaping into Wisdom Island's shallows, and sprinting over the sand wielding the flash drive like a sword.

The three of them emerged to find Edie next to her car, pumping a lever on a contraption resembling a video camera.

"What's that?" asked Marella.

"A watermaker." Elizabeth pointed to tubes that snaked from buckets to the watermaker. "The salt water comes up here, gets filtered by the watermaker, and fresh water comes out here."

"That's amazing," said Marella. "So you can have as much fresh water as you need."

"Yeah," said Edie tiredly. "But it takes a while. You can get maybe six gallons a day but who can pump all day long?"

"I'll help," said Noah, taking over the pumping, wincing as his movement pulled at the burned skin on his back. Edie seemed relieved. Marella wished she'd offered. She wanted to show her gratitude.

Preston came striding across the sand, carrying a can. "I bet you could use a little something to eat." He gave them each a spoonful of green beans. It was astonishing how good it tasted, the waxy flavor so welcome after she hadn't eaten for so long. She thought about the green beans that had been stolen from her apartment, which now would be burned to the ground. Had Diana escaped the fire? Suddenly it was harder to swallow.

"Gas, food, watermakers...you're preppers!" blurted Noah.

Preston looked at the ground, seemingly embarrassed.

Elizabeth gave Noah a look that said *be nice*. He gave her one back that said *but it's true*.

Preston chuckled. "Well, you could say that. We don't like to tell people. They make fun of us. But you're right, we predicted a disaster was coming and we prepared for it. It wasn't difficult to imagine things would go wrong, with the world the way it is."

"It was smart to be ready," said Elizabeth. "I wish I had been."

"I think we can help each other," said Preston. "Your knowledge about the bad fish saved us from a lot of trouble. Plus we're all safer together. We're going to the Pacific. We think that the water is going to continue to disappear, and our plan is to stay with it as the shoreline recedes. We would like it if you would come with us."

While the invitation seemed heartfelt, the idea behind it was dreadful. Following the water as it dwindled away, until the last drop disappeared.

"We're only going to Sekiu," said Elizabeth. "But we'll continue west through the strait with you for a ways."

Now Gabriela emerged from her truck. "I saw you limping, Marella. What's wrong with your foot?"

"It's my ankle," said Marella. "I twisted it."

"Let me take a look." Marella sat, wincing when Gabriela took off her shoe. Holding Marella's foot in her soft hands, Gabriela regarded it carefully. "I'm not an expert, but I've learned a few things along the way. Push this way. Now that way." Finally, the examination done, she said, "It's not broken." She retrieved an ace bandage and wrapped it around Marella's ankle.

Marella stood, testing it. "It's so much better. Thank you!" Grateful, she wanted to do something in return. "I'm going to look for food."

"Are you sure you're able?" asked Gabriela. "You were so sick yesterday."

"I'll be fine."

"Well then I'll join you." Gabriela scooped up a bucket and a ragged piece of abandoned netting, and they started off.

The ridge beyond their vehicles sloped upward at about forty-five degrees; Marella tested its rocky surface with her foot. The barnacles would give her traction, but if she slipped they could cut her.

Gabriela said, "Be careful now. You don't want to twist your ankle again."

"The bandage makes all the difference."

Yellowed kelp crackled underfoot as they climbed. A seagull lay almost completely rotted, with multi-colored bits of plastic where its stomach used to be. Marella tried not to think of the sight as a bad omen. It made her own stomach feel heavy in spite of its emptiness.

At the top, the ridge was layered like a sideways birthday cake, upended by some ancient geologic cataclysm. She could see the tops of other ridges and rises, going on for miles. Directly below, at the base of the ridge on which she stood, was a tongue of sand. She spotted the bright orange of a Dungeness crab.

She scrambled down to catch it before it could get away, but slipped, scraping her calf on the barnacles. She ignored the sharp pain, rushing the rest of the way, only to find an empty carapace. She picked it up. Memories flooded in.

Gabriela caught up. "You look so sad."

"It's just that I was thinking about my little sister when she was four, putting a crab shell on her head, saying, 'Like my hat?'"

"You're worried about her."

Gabriela's empathy opened up a gate, making Marella's sadness flow. "I don't know if they made it to the refugee camp at Mount Rainier, or what it's like for them there."

"I think not as bad as here. Don't worry about them. Drowning in worry won't do you any good."

"You're right. I shouldn't." Just saying it didn't make it so; still, Marella smiled in gratitude.

Green kelp had dried onto an egg-shaped rock as if it were shrink-wrapped for an Easter basket. Marella turned it over. Whenever she had gone beachcombing before, she would find small pools under rocks, from which knuckle-size shore crabs scuttled out of sight, but there were none here. The beach dried too fast in the Aguageddon.

They kept going, climbing over one ridge after the next. Marella grew fatigued. She hadn't rebounded as well as she thought, but pressed on anyway. Hunger drove her, along with the desire to pay Preston and the group back in at least a small way for saving her life.

Then, looking down from the top of the next ridge, she saw a shimmer. A wedge of gray water lay below. "Huh." She was confused. Cut off from the rest of the sound, the tide pool should have been placid; instead it churned as if turbines spun underwater.

While she watched, a gray wedge broke its surface. And another wedge. Then a silver dart leapt out of the water. "Fish," said Marella, laughing aloud.

After climbing down to the water's edge, they each clutched an end of the net they'd brought. In one pass they picked up three fish, which they dropped into the bucket. Shockingly ugly, their gray skin seemed stitched together and their pug noses turned up oddly below glassy eyes.

"Ratfish." Marella remembered her dream of ratfish from the night before. It was unsettling to see one now. It felt like another omen, one that would render the rest of the nightmare real. "Seventy percent of the fish in Puget Sound are ratfish, I read in a book."

Gabriela regarded their snouts and strange green eyes with suspicion. "Frankenstein fish."

"The book said people call them that too."

They seined the water again, bringing up one more ratfish. But the rest of their tries brought them only hallucination-causing yellowstripe goatfish.

"This won't fill our bellies," said Gabriela. "We brought some food, but we can't use it up when we don't know what's ahead."

Marella longed to tell her not to worry, that she was on her way to stop the drought.

There was a flash of movement behind Gabriela. A rock crab, bright red, chunky, and wide as a plate. "Over there!" shouted Marella.

Gabriela clambered over the rocks, with Marella right behind. The crab escaped into the water. They waded into the knee-deep pool and reached the spot where the crab had disappeared.

There, shockingly, a stone-colored face stared up from the water. Bizarre, human-looking but with an eel body. It seemed dead except for the eyes, which were too alive. Its puckered mouth opened as if to speak, then closed. Marella couldn't help feeling it wished them evil. She took several quick steps backward.

Gabriela screamed. In her hurry to get away, she slipped and fell, her hand falling right onto the creature. There was a flurry of splashing. She called out, "It bit me!"

Marella sloshed forward and seized Gabriela, hoisting her up, then helping her scramble up the slope. Rivulets of blood spilled down Gabriela's arm.

Marella looked back at the pool. The face was gone, but Marella shuddered anyway.

Gabriela clutched her arm to her chest. A drop of her blood hit the rock surface. Her skirt clung to her legs, though it was already starting to dry. She smiled through her pain. "I'll be okay."

"Yes. You'll be just fine." Marella wasn't sure whether to believe her own words or not.

Chapter Fourteen

B ack at the vehicles, Marella cleaned and bandaged the bite punctures in Gabriela's hand and arm. It was her turn to take care of Gabriela. Hopefully they wouldn't have to keep alternating that kind of duty.

"Your description sounds like a wolf eel." said Elizabeth, "They're not generally a problem. Divers tame wolf eels. They can pet them."

"Well, I did fall on it," said Gabriela. "It must have thought I was attacking it. I should have been more careful, but I was so excited about the crab."

"Keep the wound clean," said Elizabeth.

After Edie cooked the ratfish on a driftwood fire, she handed some to Marella without saying a word. She still seemed wary. Marella took a bite. It was mushy with an unpleasant aftertaste.

Now Edie tried it, but seemed unsure. "I think we should call it something besides ratfish."

"Right," said Gabriela. "Like changing the name of prunes to dried plums. Because who wants to eat something called ratfish?"

"How about Yumfish?" said Marella.

"Yumfish it is." Gabriela took a bite. "Mmmm. You're right. It tastes better with a different name." She grimaced. Everybody laughed.

Having no toothbrush, Marella cleaned her teeth using a twiggy bit of driftwood, but the ratfish aftertaste clung to the inside of her mouth.

She watched Noah gaze at the fire. She imagined running into him down the road, not having seen each other in years. They would decide to have dinner together; there would be clinking dishes, a waiter murmuring the special of the day, and freshly baked bread, hot and steaming. "Oh look," she would say pointing at the menu. "They have fish."

He would wink. "It won't be as good as our yumfish."

"Of course not," she would answer. And they would describe their lives since the long-gone Aguageddon. The thought brought tears to her eyes, along with a sense of hope. It felt good to imagine a future beyond this nightmare, a time when fear and suffering would be nothing but a memory.

Olivia began rocking, arms wrapped around her legs, head slightly tilted, staring at the ground. She kept it up for long enough that Marella could tell she was traumatized in spite of her cheery demeanor. Where were her parents? Her family? Poor thing, thought Marella, it's all been too much for her. She imagined Brielle rocking in the same way. The thought made her anxious. She wouldn't be there to comfort Brielle.

She walked away from the group, trying to calm herself. Corkscrews of orange fire still twisted on distant hills.

"Tell me about yourself," said a deep voice behind her. Preston. Marella felt a flutter. The man who had saved her life.

She turned. "I have a mom and one sister. I worked in an office. What about you?"

"I'm taking a little break from teaching. Fourth grade."

"That's a hard job," said Marella with admiration.

"Sometimes. It can be difficult to teach when a student is closed off to new ideas. But when they allow for it, then there is a wonderful moment when things shuffle in their heads, and it all fits together, and they learn. But they have to at least let the new idea in for testing. Let it sit while they examine it. Otherwise they're finished, and it's so important to remain unfinished."

Marella pondered this. It wasn't what she had expected to hear. She had thought he might say something about kids not having basic needs met, which made them less focused on learning. But Preston's thoughts were especially true now, she supposed, during a disaster. It was time for new ideas so such a thing wouldn't happen again.

"Thank you for helping us," said Marella. "Lots of people turned us away. You saved my life."

"It's been a difficult few days," said Preston. "It's one thing to prepare for a disaster, but it's a whole other thing when it happens. I wasn't ready to see people turning on each other so quickly."

"You're right. It's been crazy. It changed overnight. Somebody broke into my apartment to steal the water from my toilet. And I got caught in a riot." Thinking of Occidental Square made Marella choke up.

"I saw a man stabbed over a quart of milk." He passed a hand over his eyes. "I tried to help him, but..."

Marella looked down. "It's got to be hellish everywhere. The water is disappearing all over the world." And what about Mount Rainier? How long before its perpetually white dome turned brown?

Preston seemed to shake off his somberness. "Enough about that. I want to get to know you. Tell me something you wouldn't tell anybody else."

Such a demand would normally have made Marella feel cornered, but Preston seemed so sincere. She longed to tell him her real secret, that they had to get to Wisdom Island to turn off that damned machine so it would stop taking all the water. It seemed a betrayal not to reveal the goal after what he'd done for her. Instead she described her mother, her sister, and their too mobile life together. As she spoke, it was like seeing herself in a different way, from Preston's viewpoint. He seemed fascinated with her. Without judgment.

She was regaining strength after the worst day of her life, but it felt as if his calm was strengthening her too.

"You might think this is crazy," said Preston, "but it feels like I've always known you..." he broke off, flustered. "That sounds like a come-on, but it's not."

"No, I feel it too."

"You do?"

His smile was so appealing. The half-circles at the corners of his mouth. She wanted to know everything about him. "Do you have family?"

Preston looked away. "I haven't seen my parents in a while. They had such ambitions for me. They thought if I was going to be a teacher instead of a lawyer then I should at least teach college. And my woodworking, well, they don't understand that. It's great you get along with your family so well."

"Woodworking? What kind of things do you make?"

He lifted a cross necklace from under his shirt. Two inches long, its thick blond wood was inlaid with dark vines. "I made this."

She gasped. "You made that? It's beautiful! You're so talented."

He bowed his head to remove the necklace and held it out. "Here. For you."

She hesitated. She didn't feel deserving of such an intimate gift.

"Oh, I'm sorry," said Preston. "I shouldn't have assumed. You're not Christian?"

"I guess I am." Marella sent the occasional prayer skyward, where it vanished into the ether. "Different churches contradict each other. It makes me think maybe nobody has it right."

"That's very insightful," said Preston. He put the necklace on her. It made her feel warm. Special.

Her eye was drawn to motion behind Preston. Olivia, watching them, her lips pressed tightly together. For a moment Marella thought she might be jealous. But then Olivia smiled and said something to Noah. Marella was completely wrong.

"You need a new bandage," said Preston. "Come with me."

She looked down and at the blood stain on the gauze on her arm. She followed him to his camper. It felt so natural to climb in. Not like entering a stranger's place. On one side was a bed, on the other a padded bench. A mishmash of cabinets, shelves, and boxes took up all other nooks and crannies. Preston retrieved a first aid kit.

He reached for her bandage, but Marella stopped him. "Elizabeth says it's safer to take care of our own wounds when we can." Preston nodded, handed her a new bandage, and held out a garbage bag so she could discard the old one. She applied the new one.

"Marella. That's a pretty name. What does it mean?"

"Of the bright sea."

He raised his eyebrows. "Both your first and last name have to do with water. The sea. Wells." He put his hand on hers, scooting closer, putting his arm around her shoulder. At first Marella felt the electric warmth of his body. His strength. But then she became uncomfortable. He could be twice her age. Or maybe he just seemed like an old soul. So was this fatherly? Or something else? She turned her head, looking in his eyes, startled that they were so close. His irises brown with sparkles of green.

She was filthy, her body rank with dirt and dried sweat. Her blouse and slacks dirt-smeared. Self-consciousness crept in. Being this close in such a state was embarrassing. To be honest, he smelled bad too. Like sweat and burned rubber.

What should she say? Ridiculous phrases came to mind. *It's not you, it's me. You're winter, I'm spring. Our love was never meant to be.* She settled on, "I have to go."

Preston took it well, removing his arm. "Of course. You've been through a lot. Get some more rest."

• • • •

AN HOUR LATER MARELLA trudged to the end of the ridge. The shoreline had retreated far enough to reveal five feet of sand at the rock base. She returned to the vehicles. "Hey everybody, we'll be able to move on soon. Get ready."

There was a general flurry, everybody making sure their possessions made it back to into the vehicles. The water receded another five feet soon after, allowing them to drive further west.

Marella's truck led the way. Olivia drove one of the cars—did that mean she was older than she appeared? Sixteen? Even Eighteen? The terrain flattened. She felt exhilarated. They were moving. They were on their way to Sekiu.

Only an hour into the drive, Elizabeth said, "There's something up there." A swath of silver stretched out in front of them.

"I think it's dead fish." Noah sounded both astonished and disgusted. "It stinks like a slaughterhouse. I've never smelled anything worse in my life."

"They're not all dead," said Marella. "Some are moving. The water must have just stranded them a little while ago. But it shouldn't smell this bad."

The stench worsened as they approached. Finally they could see why. None of the fish were alive—the movement they'd seen was larvae squirming. They shifted in their seats in a fruitless effort to escape the stink. Marella couldn't identify the fish, which were silver with bar code-like stripes, each a couple of feet long. Elizabeth didn't volunteer the species.

"This is messed up," said Noah. "Water on one side, cliffs on the other, and one zillion dead fish in front of us."

"We must be slightly higher up than we were when we started off," said Elizabeth. "They've been out of the water for at least half a day if there are maggots."

"Then why aren't they all dried up?" asked Marella.

"I don't know," said Elizabeth. "I do know that the sea must have gotten too warm for them when it became shallow. It doesn't take much change to kill off marine life."

"This is disgusting," said Noah.

"We'll just have to drive through it," said Marella.

"Go fast," said Elizabeth. "We don't want to get stuck."

Noah made gagging noises. "Driving on a road of rotting flesh. Never thought I'd do that."

"Something to tell your grandkids," said Elizabeth.

He pretended to speak like an old man. "Little ones, gather 'round. Let me tell you about squashing fish guts during the Aguageddon." He spoke normally now. "You should probably get a running start."

Marella laughed nervously, backing up the truck. "Okay. Squashing fish guts. Here we go." She punched her foot on the gas. They zoomed forward, the truck hydroplaning when it hit the fish. Glop shot upward, slapping against the windows. "Oh shit, it's deeper than it looked."

The truck slowed halfway through. "Keep going." Noah waved ahead.

"I'm trying." Marella pumped the gas. The other three vehicles rumbled past.

The truck stopped. Noah groaned. "Tell me this isn't happening."

"It isn't happening." Marella's response was automatic, an attempt at a joke, but too full of despair. They had finally been making progress. And now this. She tried reverse. More glop flew up and hit the window, making her jump.

"We're definitely stuck," said Noah.

"We'll just have to get unstuck." Marella could barely speak though her disgust. "Brace yourselves." She opened the door. The smell made her turn her head. *Don't think about it. Don't breathe too deeply.*

She stepped down.

"Wait, don't," Elizabeth reached toward her. "The bacteria."

"Too late," said Marella, clenching her jaw as she sank knee deep. Goop coated her skin and filled her shoes. The movement of the larvae felt like sickly fingertips stroking her ankles.

The stink rose in a moist cloud, coating her nostrils. Her stomach churned so strongly it was all she could do to keep from vomiting. Breathing in shallow gasps, she waded through putrid fish flesh. Flies landed on her as if she were dead too. She swatted them away with a frenzy.

"Holy shit," said Noah, "I can't believe you're really in that stuff."

Marella's voice shook. "Come on in, the water's fine. Bring the laundry basket."

Noah groaned in disgust, but followed her into the muck trailing the basket. "Oh jeez, it's like they're fondling my legs."

"Think about something else," said Marella.

"Like what?" asked Noah.

"I don't know. Baseball."

"It's like walking through diarrhea. With bones."

Marella stepped awkwardly, turning her ankle. Pain shot up her leg; she slipped, falling face down into the rotting fish. It tasted like butcher's slop and felt slippery as mud. The goo filled her mouth and nostrils, choking her. She couldn't breathe. She couldn't get traction on the slick ground with her limbs sliding every which way.

She panicked, flailing, losing the sense of up or down. Something sharp jabbed her cheek. Her body jerked with the effort of trying not to suck rot into her lungs.

Arms gripped her, pulling her up. She stood awkwardly, feet splayed like a newborn calf, eyes shut tightly, spitting, blowing goop out of her nostrils. She sucked in air and slime went down her throat, then came up as vomit. Brutish noises burst from her mouth. Swiping her eyes over and over, she tried to clear them, but to no avail. "Can't see! Can't see!"

She felt cloth smoothing her face, somebody wiping it. Her cheek stung where the fish bones had poked. She blinked her eyes open. Through strings of slime on her eyelashes, she saw Noah planted front of her, a worried look on his face. He had used his ragged shirt to clean her eyes.

"Thank you," said Marella gratefully.

Her shoes had come off. She placed her feet more firmly underneath herself, looking around to get her bearings. The swath of fish stretched out ahead and behind. To Marella it seemed as if the world itself had begun to decompose, starting with this layer of fish. Next the sand and rocks would decay, and the Earth itself would rot away in time-lapse jerks, bit by bit, until there was nothing left.

She didn't want to move for fear of slipping again or cutting her bare feet, but there was no other option. She had to get the truck free.

Somehow she found a reserve of fortitude. She turned to the truck, bent down to the tire with the laundry basket, and began scooping glop into it. Noah waded over to another tire to help. Now Elizabeth joined them. They grunted in discontent as they worked.

Noah's look of worry stuck in her mind. It helped her more than he could know that he cared. And with Elizabeth joining them, it felt like a team. A real team, the way Elizabeth had always talked about at the office. Marella repeated one of Elizabeth's maxims. "Alone we can do so little, together we can do so much."

"Helen Keller," added Elizabeth, blowing upward to get hair out of her face.

"Oh, we're doing sayings?" asked Noah. "Well then, 'He who walks among maggots should be prepared to pluck them from between his toes.'"

"Ugh," said Marella with a strained chuckle.

When they'd cleared enough fish to see sand in front of the truck, Noah said, "I think we're good now. Let's try it."

They got back in the truck, clothes heavy with slime. Palms together, Noah gazed upward. "Lord, if we ever needed a favor, this is it."

Elizabeth egged the truck on as Marella stepped on the gas. They moved forward. The truck resounded with their cheers. When they reached the sand, Marella stopped near the water and they poured out.

Noah made a show of kissing the ground. Marella strode into the cobalt and iron waves, gasping at the cold. The salt stung her scraped skin. She frantically scrubbed off the dried, caked-on slime, cleaning her clothes and the bandage that was wrapped around her ankle. Noah and Elizabeth plunged in and cleaned themselves as well.

The water sloshed around her. A memory popped up: she was a child in some community pool or other and Mom was using the water's buoyancy to lift and toss her, laughing her shutter-stop laugh. She remembered the playful shouts of other children. The joy of the memory took the edge off.

Preston and his group gathered as the three emerged from the water. "Are you all right?" asked Olivia.

"Sure," said Noah. "I love fish guts. It doesn't get any better than this."

"I lost my shoes," said Marella.

"We look about the same size," said Edie. "I've got a pair in my truck that might fit you." She retrieved a pair of hiking boots, which Marella donned gratefully. So what if Edie seemed standoffish? Her action showed compassion.

They wiped the truck's seats and continued on. Though the ground here was flat, single granite slabs towered upward, creating a crooked barnacle-covered Stonehenge. They drove across the shadows of the strange monoliths.

"That would be a great photo to post," said Noah. The thought seemed ridiculous to Marella. She clearly remembered doing such everyday things, but couldn't imagine ever caring about them again.

• • • •

THAT AFTERNOON, OFF the coast near Port Angeles, Marella and Elizabeth gazed at the water spread out below, the scene fantastical, as if they'd gone abruptly from two dimensions to three. In places, widely spaced rock shelves stepped down to the water, as if designed for a giant's stride. On one side of a bay, rock spires rose like a castle with only half a moat.

A quarter mile ahead, a royal blue cargo ship was grounded in the water, its orange and red containers stacked six high. The ship was so still it seemed under a spell. To Marella, it was a statement of failed human ingenuity. All that effort to build something so large, only to abandon it. It made her feel as if her own efforts would also come to nothing.

She shook her head at herself. She couldn't think like that.

They had seen other vehicles during the drive, but had kept their distance from them all. Now those cars were nowhere to be seen and the water was blocking their way once more.

"We should have followed those other people," said Noah. "We wouldn't be stuck here."

"They could be stuck too, wherever they are," said Elizabeth.

Noah went down to join Olivia and Edie at the shoreline. He called to the ship. There was no answer.

Marella watched a black and white duck floating and preening itself. She wished she had wings like that bird. How could she get to the island more quickly? A feeling of restlessness overtook her, making her pace. She had the overwhelming desire to run to the beach and plunge into the waves. Swim all the way to Wisdom Island.

"Maybe you should sit down," said Elizabeth. The same thing she had told her mother so many times. This must have been how her mother felt. This need to move on. It was nearly overpowering. So then...had Mom been seeking something by moving from house to house? She had thought that her father's death had done the damage, making her so restless, but maybe the need had been there all along and Dad's presence only tamped it down.

Marella crossed her arms and squeezed them tightly across her torso. "I feel like the dam's about to burst and I'm going to pour through. I just want to go."

"Patience," said Elizabeth.

"We can't just sit here and do nothing," said Marella. "We need to get to the island." Then somehow, some way, get back to her family. Together they would find a place to build a better life. One where she wasn't thirsty, hungry, tired, and sore.

"The world won't see me in a good light," said Elizabeth, changing the subject abruptly, her voice filled with regret. "They won't understand I was trying to do good."

Marella wrestled with how to respond. She understood that Elizabeth meant no harm, but couldn't help assigning her some of the blame. Yet what was done was done. A morose Elizabeth would be counterproductive. "You didn't design Project Athena."

"No, but I supported it. I was too starry-eyed about it. It's a pattern repeated over the years. People not directly responsible for destructive products and their repercussions, yet indirectly involved. Weapons. Leaded gasoline. The dumping of byproducts in rivers."

"You didn't know."

"I didn't ask."

"I don't believe that," said Marella. "You're the queen of asking questions."

"You're right. I asked questions, just not the right ones. And I accepted certain answers when I should have delved deeper. I'm ashamed to admit that I couldn't always follow the discussions. I'm not even sure which theory of multiverse they based Athena's design on. They were so brilliant I often got lost. I just assumed I would never understand completely, not being a physicist. That's the problem with people. We base our decisions on so little information. I shouldn't have supported it without trying harder to understand."

"I supported it too, in a way," said Marella in an attempt to make Elizabeth feel better, expecting Elizabeth to brush off her culpability.

"Yes. You might get blamed too."

Marella looked at Elizabeth sharply. Perhaps she was right. Marella had been an unwitting assistant, but in the aftermath scapegoats would be needed. She began to slide toward despair. She couldn't afford to lose hope. That could lead to failure.

"We can't worry about that now," said Marella. "We have a goal. Get the flash drive to Wisdom Island. Run the shutdown program."

"It's just good to be prepared. So later you can act instead of react."

"There's being prepared, and there's dwelling on things we can't do anything about right this minute."

Elizabeth sighed, then smiled wanly. "That's wise. Very wise." She pulled something out of her pocket. The flash drive. She examined it carefully.

"Is it okay?" asked Marella.

"Seems fine. Although we should have made a backup." She looked back at the truck. "What was that?"

"What?"

"I thought somebody was over there."

Marella saw some mallards waddling toward the water. "Just some ducks. There's nobody but us here. Everybody else is on the shore or in their cars."

Elizabeth slipped the flash drive back in her pocket.

They hiked down to the rock spires. Red mosaic-patterned shellfish were clustered on them. Marella wrestled one off, turning it like a jewel. "What's this?"

"A gooseneck barnacle."

"That's a barnacle?" said Marella. "It's the size of a mussel."

"Don't sound so disappointed. They're edible. You can eat white barnacles too, it's just that there's not much to them. These are called gooseneck because in mediaeval Europe people believed geese grew out of them."

"People thought some ridiculous things back then," said Marella.

"People think ridiculous things now," said Elizabeth. "We just don't know it yet. Gather as many as you can. We're lucky. They often grow where the surf beats so hard against the rocks that they're too dangerous to harvest."

The sudden output of knowledge was reassuring. Elizabeth had bounced right back to her old self. That was the Elizabeth she needed. The one who loved knowledge for the sake of it, and had plenty to spare, always saying she wanted to leave the world smarter than she found it.

Marella retrieved Gabriela's bucket and filled it with gooseneck barnacles. By the time she returned, Gabriela had built a fire, lively orange against the grey sand. Edie and Noah began working the watermakers, pumping ocean water through them to replenish their containers with fresh water. Olivia gave Marella a pot for cooking.

Marella was thankful to be occupied with a task. But while she cooked the gooseneck barnacles, grilling them over the fire, she began to worry about her family once again. What if they were dead and they never found the bodies? She imagined a life of searching. Never knowing when or how they died. It made her feel raw, as if she'd been turned inside out.

Everybody gathered at the fire. Marella distributed the barnacles, then sat on a drift log next to Preston and took a bite of one. It was one of the best things she'd ever tasted. She supposed she shouldn't be surprised that a barnacle tasted good when she was half starving.

Preston plucked a shard of red plastic from the sole of his shoe. "I wonder what this used to be?"

"I don't know," said Marella. "There's so much garbage down here."

"It gets worse," said Elizabeth. "The Great Pacific garbage patch is out there in the Pacific Ocean. Three times the size of France. Twice the size of Texas. And that's only one of the ocean garbage patches. They'll be there for centuries. It takes 500 years for plastic to degrade."

"I heard it's a thousand years," said Noah.

"I heard it's never," said Olivia.

"You could be right," said Elizabeth. "They break into microparticles that are suspended in the water. Fish eat them instead of real food. Or they become nano-size and we ingest them not even knowing it."

"We've been destroying our world from top to bottom," said Preston. "And now we can see the result." He gestured at the dry sand.

Destroying our world. If he only knew who was making the water disappear. She took a deep breath but it was hugely unsatisfying. The air so full of smoke, the cooking fire only making it worse. It made her want to scramble to fresh air, but there was none to be had. In spite of her worry, she was tired. "I'm going to take a nap," said Marella.

"Good idea, me too," said Noah.

Everybody picked a spot in the shade of the vehicles to rest.

Sometime later Marella woke to the grinding roar of the world ripping apart.

Chapter Fifteen

The world's demise shook the ground. Marella curled into a ball, crushing her head between her hands to block the sound. The noise lasted for minutes while her brain whirled through the possibilities. Asteroid. Plane crash. Volcano.

The ship out in the water. Of course. Something had happened to it. When the crashing stopped she uncurled, trying to still her heart and her breathing.

Staggering to her feet, she saw the others heading for the slope. She ran to join them. Reaching the slope's crest, in sight of the bay, she saw the ship on its side, some containers still lashed to it, some spilled.

She also saw why it had toppled. The water had receded, withdrawing all support. The shoreline was now a half mile away. Marella put a hand to her heart. "How long were we asleep?"

"Only two hours." Noah's eyebrows knit together; he gestured, palms upward. "Why is the water disappearing? And why so fast?"

They had needed the water to recede further so they could continue on, but now that it had, it was horrifying. The way had opened up, but the meaning was dire. At this rate no water would be left by the time they reached Wisdom Island. There would be no world to save. Just a desert planet.

It seemed like proof that Marella wasn't up to this challenge. She wasn't the type of person to save the world. How could she when even somebody with Elizabeth's knowledge was falling short?

"Don't lose all hope," said Elizabeth as if reading Marella's thoughts. "Just remember Puget Sound is like a trough. Deeper in the middle, shallower where it meets the ocean. The water in the Pacific won't be disappearing quite as fast as here in the strait. But we still have to hurry."

Hope. She had to find hope to outrun this disaster. She thought of Brielle, who always seemed to have hope, even the time she broke her leg and couldn't participate in her beloved sports. Marella pictured her saying, "I just have to get through this and someday everything will be better."

Having so little hope of her own, Marella borrowed Brielle's. She looked at the situation through Brielle's eyes. They just had to get through this and everything would be better. Marella took a few breaths, pumping herself with resolve. "Let's go," she shouted. "Come on everybody!"

They drove down the slope and alongside the toppled container ship. Its rust-red bottom, black sides, and white tower loomed high above them. Its grand scale astounded Marella. "I haven't seen a ship this big since we left Seattle," she said.

"It's as long as a skyscraper is tall," said Elizabeth. "Sometimes it truly amazes me that people build things so large."

"Some of the containers have broken open," said Noah. "There might be food."

"We don't have a lot of time for foraging," warned Elizabeth.

In spite of herself, Marella imagined cartons full of grape juice. The sweet purple liquid pooled in her mouth. The chances were slim they would find exactly that, but still she was hopeful they would find something. Preston and the others were still reticent to open any more of their canned food when they didn't know how long the disaster would last. Maybe there would be something to eat in the spilled containers. Her stomach gurgled in anticipation.

Preston's camper stopped. He got out.

Some of the containers still hung precariously from the ship. Marella pulled up as close as she dared. They descended to examine spilled packages of light pink. Marella picked up a stubby plastic unicorn. "They're toys."

"Useless," said Elizabeth, kicking a package, disgust on her face.

Several person-size pods also lay on the ground. "Space capsules," said Noah. "So aliens took our water."

"Emergency rafts," said Elizabeth.

"I know. I was trying to lighten things up."

Emergency rafts. The ultimate workaround. "Help me load one of these onto my truck," said Marella.

"That's a ten-person raft," said Elizabeth. "I'd guesstimate over a hundred pounds. We'll use more gas. It'll weigh us down."

"You're always talking about contingency plans," said Marella. "This is ours. For if we get to Sekiu and the boat's gone."

"It better not come to that," said Elizabeth. "A raft would be slow going." Still, she and Noah helped load it.

Marella said to Preston, "There's another raft over there. Can you use it?"

"I've got one already."

Marella raised an eyebrow. How prepared could one person possibly be? It was as if he'd known the Aguageddon was coming. But of course that was the definition of disaster prepper. Certain that catastrophe was on the way.

• • • •

THEY CONTINUED DRIVING on the seabed through the Strait of Juan de Fuca. Fire still raged on land. As they drove, Puget Sound shrank alongside them, becoming a string of narrow lakes. It gave them more room, which helped because the terrain was uneven and tricky to navigate, like the inside of a shark's mouth, with jagged rows of teeth, the ground an undulating tongue.

The terrain morphed to low dunes. "They're like burial mounds," said Noah.

"Don't say that," said Marella. Suddenly demons lurked at the edges of her thoughts.

Noah tilted his head. "You don't seem like the type to believe in ghosts."

"Can we talk about something else?"

"Sorry."

"Never apologize," said Elizabeth.

Noah seemed perplexed. "Are you serious?"

"Quite serious. It diminishes you. Instead you should thank someone for their patience or understanding."

"Let me try this out. I'm late getting home. I say, 'Mom, Dad, thank you for your patience.' You know, they've never beat me but I think that would make them start."

Elizabeth seemed annoyed at his mocking attitude. "Here's some more advice. It's about advice. When somebody with experience in this world gives you some, at least consider its value before you throw it back in her face."

Noah bristled. "You think I don't have experience? I've been through shit you'll never, ever have to deal with."

Noah was about to continue, but Elizabeth spoke first. "Thank you for understanding how straightforward I can be."

Noah's mouth hung open for a moment, then he laughed accusingly, jabbing his finger at her. "You just apologized!"

Elizabeth rolled her shoulders, unable to hold back a smile. "Not necessarily."

Noah laughed again, real laughter this time, and shook his head as if to say Elizabeth was incorrigible.

Marella was relieved. She needed them to get along. Strife now could have devastating consequences.

She navigated among strange white objects that were scattered on the ground. "Whale vertebrae," suggested Noah.

"Cloud sponges," corrected Elizabeth. "They can be hundreds of years old."

"Sure, but they look like vertebrae. Right Marella?"

Hell no. She wasn't going to take sides, even on something so minor. "They look like vertebrae *and* cloud sponges."

To their left was the Olympic Peninsula, the part of Washington that looked like the lower jaw of a mouth on a map. The tops of the Olympic Mountains came into view; she was encouraged that a bit of snow still showed on their peaks. That meant there would still be snow on Mount Rainier for Mom and Brielle.

She thought of joking with Elizabeth that they should have built Project Athena on this peninsula, on Mount Olympus, so that Athena wouldn't have to commute, but Noah was there. What also held her back was the admittedly ridiculous notion that Athena might overhear and punish her for it. The thought of penance and the sight of more fire turned her thoughts back to the idea that even now she could be dead in Hell and just not know it.

Goddesses. Hell. Why was she thinking about them? Could they just get this over with? It was taking so much longer to get from point A to point B than it should. She had never appreciated roads enough.

"Where is everybody?" asked Marella. "There aren't as many cars out here as I would think."

"It's not easy to drive around," said Elizabeth. "We're lucky you have a truck and that the tires have held up."

"I'd hoped the rain forest would escape the drought," said Noah. "I just don't understand. Why now? How did this all happen? What started the drought? If you're going to drop knowledge on me, that's the kind I could use."

Marella wondered if she should pretend to guess. Change the subject. Elizabeth ignored Noah's questions, wiping dirt from her blouse. Why didn't she say something?

Finally Noah answered his own questions. "Maybe climate change finally caught up with us. They kept warning us. But did we listen? I mean, even now we're all driving around burning fossil fuels. But I wonder about the anarchists. They love destroying things. Maybe they had something to do with it. But what?" Noah sighed. "Where are you trying to go with the boat? Who are you trying to save?"

"A lot of people," said Marella. "That's all I can say."

"Why? Is it something to do with your job? Where do you work?"

"You'll have to be content with the information we've given you," said Elizabeth.

Noah rubbed his temples as if unsure what to think. "Okay," he said in a have-it-your-way tone.

As they got closer to Sekiu, Marella began to brace herself for more disappointment. With everything on fire, it was unlikely the boat would still be there. Still, when they arrived at the cove where Sekiu used to be, finding only a smoldering marina and a hillside furrowed with flames, it felt like she had been body-slammed by an invisible force. The boat had burned. It was gone.

She watched the flames, her mind going every which way. No boat. Just her truck and a tiny raft, which realistically would never get them to where they were going.

The sounds of the wind and cracking fire seemed different now, as if the Aguageddon had nudged noises into a different key.

She wished her phone was working. She wanted so badly to call her Mom, to at least tell her and Brielle goodbye. Tell them she tried to help but was a miserable failure. This was her fault. If she hadn't suggested driving on the shoreline, they wouldn't have ended up here. Another person might have come up with a real solution that would have gotten them to the island in mere hours.

Still, she felt the need to move, to travel. Going forward was doing something. If she remained here, waiting for inspiration that might never come, she would go mad. She spoke dully. "We'll just have to keep driving."

Elizabeth was pressing her hands on her thighs as if she, too, had been body-slammed. She seemed to collect herself. Then she keyed some numbers into Marella's GPS. "Yes. Keep driving. We need to get from Puget Sound to the ocean, launch the raft, and get past the continental shelf before the water lowers that far. The underwater drop-off at its base could be thirteen hundred meters. That's fourteen thousand and something feet."

Marella's mouth hung open. "Oh my god. I didn't think of that. We can't drive all the way because the continental shelf is giant cliff."

"You're trying to cross the ocean?" asked Noah. "That's not possible."

"We're trying to get to an island," said Marella. Elizabeth gave her a look. She gave her one back. That wasn't giving anything away.

"How are you going to help people on an island?" asked Noah. "We're the ones who need saving."

"It'll all make sense later on," said Elizabeth. "But you don't have to come with us. Preston would take you in."

Marella felt a ping of dismay. She didn't want to leave Noah behind.

"How many people are you trying to save?" asked Noah. "Ten? A hundred?"

Marella raised her eyebrows at Elizabeth, indicating she should say something. Elizabeth pinched the top of her nose, shaking her head.

"A thousand?" asked Noah. "A hundred thousand?"

"That's closer," said Elizabeth. Marella tilted her head, satisfied. That would do.

"You're trying to save a hundred thousand people?" said Noah, awed.

"At least," said Marella.

"How? What are you going to do?"

"That's all we can tell you right now," said Marella.

Noah thought for a while, rubbing his face and shifting his position. Finally he said, "Okay, I'm in. I think you could use my help, so I'm coming with you. Besides, you saved my life. I still owe you."

"You don't owe us anything," said Elizabeth. "You saved me from the dog."

"I haven't saved Marella's life yet." He looked at Marella with such loving concern that she blushed and looked away. This wasn't a time for romance, but it pleased her that he might have such thoughts.

"You rescued me from the fish guts," she offered.

"That doesn't count," said Noah. "Unless you can stink yourself to death. But anyway, since we're going to be driving some more, you should ask Preston for more gas. You're getting low. He'll give it to you. He likes you."

"He likes all of us," said Marella, uncomfortable with Noah's suggestive tone.

"I see the way he looks at you, and the way you look at him. I get it. There's something special about him. You could do worse."

Marella shifted uncomfortably. She must have misread Noah entirely. He had no romantic feelings for her, and what was more, it felt like he was pushing her away by connecting her with Preston. Or was he probing to see how she felt about him? But none of that mattered now. "I'm just grateful that he saved my life. Besides, Elizabeth identified the yellowstripe goatfish and the gooseneck barnacles. He knows she's more important than I am."

"Not trying to dis Elizabeth, but he's definitely got a thing for you."

"He's right," said Elizabeth, putting a calming hand on her arm, probably seeing Marella's consternation. "You ask him for gas."

Annoyance crept into Marella's tone. "Okay. Next time he stops." She put the car back into drive, accidentally revving the engine in her hurry to catch up with Preston and the others.

When Preston sat next to her in the camper she had been so uncomfortable, but since then she had somehow talked herself into thinking his attention had been fatherly after all. Now she had to admit it wasn't. She would have to be careful not to put herself in a position to be propositioned again.

They passed a two-story stone arch that looked like it belonged in a fish tank. Sharp purple anemones congregated at its base.

* * * *

THE SKY DARKENED. THEY were trying to eke out the last bit of light before night made driving too dangerous. Edie's car was ahead. Smoke began surging from its hood.

"No, no, no, no, NO!" Marella pounded the steering wheel.

"That's the last thing we need," said Noah.

"Fire extinguisher," said Elizabeth.

Edie stopped the car and began unstrapping Baby Faith. Marella stopped her truck, retrieved her fire extinguisher, and rushed to help. Noah thrust open the hood of Edie's car. Flames shot up. Marella sprayed. The smoke spread, engulfing Marella as if angry at her attack. She staggered back, but then forced herself forward again, holding her breath, spraying back and forth.

The fire out, Edie and the others joined Marella, anxiously examining the blackened, fire retardant-covered engine.

"It's toast," said Edie, her voice quavering.

Marella felt a chill. What if that happened to her truck? They would be stuck and unable to reach their goal. She'd been lucky so far. Would that last? A blanket of exhaustion unrolled over her.

The others looked stricken as well.

"You can ride with Olivia," said Preston. His calm soothed Marella.

Edie reached into her car for a bag.

"It's late," said Preston. "We'll load your things into Olivia's car in the morning."

"We should do it now so we can leave at first light." Marella reached for Edie's bag.

"No," said Edie. "We'll do it in the morning."

Marella was tired. She didn't feel like moving Edie's possessions. Still, it grated that she wouldn't listen to her.

Several seagulls stood near each other in the twilight, like cocktail party attendees unable to think up any small talk.

Olivia brought out a metal slingshot with black rubber cords and an arm brace. She placed a rock in its sling.

"That looks powerful," said Elizabeth. "Be careful with it. You could hurt somebody."

"Really?" Olivia looked at it with a concerned expression, and then at Elizabeth gratefully. "Thanks for the tip."

Elizabeth gestured melodramatically at Olivia. "Did you hear that, Noah? That's how to gracefully accept advice from a peer."

"Oh, we're peers now?" said Noah wryly. "I've been promoted."

They both smiled as they'd each won an argument.

Holding the slingshot out, Olivia snuck toward the seagulls. She shot. A seagull fell to the ground, a pile of white and light gray. Olivia reloaded quickly but the others had already flown off.

Olivia whirled. "I got one! I got one!" It was exactly how Brielle would have acted.

"You're a pro," said Marella. They trotted up to the kill. The seagull's little head was gone, with bits of blood scattered about as if it had exploded. Marella's stomach squirmed.

Noah raised his eyebrows. "Wow. Take no prisoners."

Olivia lifted the animal's body gingerly. "Ew." She scurried off with it. "Edie, look!"

Marella regretted not having at least a few more survival items stashed in her truck. "They were so prepared. I would never have thought of getting a slingshot."

Elizabeth screwed up her face. "Seagulls eat garbage. It will taste nasty."

• • • •

THEY SAT ON THE SAND around a fire, faces smudged in the light like half-polished silver. The night was black behind them, shrinking the world to this small circle. The wind nudged her as if to move her along; she wished she could heed its request. Edie scratched the bug bites on her lower legs, fingers splayed like gardening fork tines. Noah rubbed the stubble on his chin. Marella sipped water, but it didn't completely quench her thirst.

The Aguageddon magnified everything. Losing a car would be bad enough under normal circumstances, but out here it could be deadly. Having truck problems would mean the difference between making it back to her family or not. Even a minor inconvenience could ruin everything. Like running out of gas. She really needed to get some more, but she worried that Preston might ask her to visit to his camper again. She had no indication he would expect something from her in return for the gas, but she might as well be cautious and wait until morning to ask.

The Aguageddon was disaster enough, but it didn't preclude other catastrophes. Anything could happen. She looked up, as if something might drop from the sky. An asteroid, a space station. Or maybe the sky itself would fall. She saw only darkness.

Gabriela, who seemed more and more sluggish by the moment, stood awkwardly. "I'm going to go to sleep," she said.

"Eat something first," said Edie, who was cooking the seagull on the fire.

"I'm not hungry. You all can have mine." She headed to her truck, then stumbled, catching herself. Marella, who was closest, rushed to help her. Gabriela waved her away. "I'm okay." She climbed into the back of her truck, closing the canopy door behind her.

"Is she all right?" asked Elizabeth when Marella returned to her spot.

"So much driving," said Marella. "It's tiring. At least we three can switch off sometimes."

"I wish she would let one of us drive for her," said Elizabeth. "I've been worried about her ever since the eel bite. It isn't healing well. She needs more rest than she's getting."

Marella felt a jolt of shame. Elizabeth didn't know that Gabriela had been chasing a crab at her urging when she was bitten.

Elizabeth turned out to be right about the seagull. It tasted rank and fishy, and for its size seemed to have little meat, so there was only a bite for each of them. Preston opened a can of kidney beans and gave them each a couple of spoonfuls. It only made Marella want more.

"I wish I knew what was causing the Aguageddon," said Noah. "It makes no sense."

"It's part of God's plan," said Preston.

Marella furrowed her brow. When people said such things it was like they were blaming God somehow. "How can this be part of a plan? Why would God be so callous? It doesn't make sense. And if you're going to kill people, why make everyone suffer so much? Why not just flick a finger and give people aneurisms?"

"Sing something, Edie," blurted Olivia.

Olivia was smart to keep them from getting into a debate. Brielle would have done the same thing if she were here.

Edie shifted in her seat and began to sing, the notes pure and haunting. Marella was drawn in by the words, about the water receding, looking away for a second and it being gone. The song left Marella with a sense of longing. "Did you make that up?"

Edie shook her head. "It's 'Je Suis Pret,' a Brooke Fraser song."

"It's like she predicted the Aguageddon," said Marella.

"Nobody could have predicted this," said Noah.

There was silence. Marella imagined her own family in front of a refugee camp tent, looking out over a mountainside packed with other refugees, wondering about Marella's fate. At least they would be above the tree line, away from forest fires. If they had made it there. And who knew what craziness a place like that would hold. A refugee camp was its own world to navigate and suffer through. They wouldn't be having an easy time of it.

The sense of longing for them built until it seemed to fill the whole basin, all around them, like the smoke.

• • • •

IN THE MORNING MARELLA woke when the sky was barely light. Noah and Elizabeth were still asleep.

When she got out of her truck nobody was stirring except Preston, who was kneeling in the sand, head bowed. She trod over to him. "Are you all right?"

Preston turned toward her. His eyes had the blank stare of a wax figure. "Gabriela is dead."

Chapter Sixteen

Marella let the words hover, not wanting to let them in. They squeezed through anyway. Gabriela was dead. The living, breathing vibrant woman who had comforted her and been a bright spot in the midst of uncertainty was gone, never to return.

She looked in the open canopy hatch of Gabriela's truck. Gabriela lay on her side, her eyes open, her hand limp in front of blue lips. Marella couldn't seem to catch her breath as memories and the present merged in her mind. Her dead father, staying dead no matter how much she pleaded to him not to be. Gabriela, who was now dead. Alive and loving one moment, and gone the next.

If this could happen so quickly to Gabriela, it could happen to anybody. Marella could be next. Elizabeth. Noah. Preston. And her family of course. The ever-present dread about their fate hovered like a false angel.

The wind sounded too much like demons whispering. Marella squashed the urge to run. Demons weren't real, she told herself. Just a childhood fear. Just pictures in a book. Still, she stepped back.

"What did she die of?" asked Marella, hoping that he would declare something other than infection from the wolf eel bite. That this wouldn't somehow be her fault.

Preston rose and leaned back against the car. "I was responsible for keeping her safe. For keeping all of you safe. I failed. I'm to blame."

Marella knitted her eyebrows. She understood that he felt a patriarchal responsibility for all of them but he was taking it too far. "Of course you're not to blame."

Preston shook his head, "Would you please wake the others? We need to have a ceremony."

She nodded even though it meant that she would be the one to inform them Gabriela had passed. She swallowed nervously as she headed back to her truck. What should she say? Whatever words she chose, she would need to do it quickly. Also, a ceremony would take more time. Yet how could she protest such a thing? In any case, the sooner they got to it the sooner they could leave.

She opened the truck door. Elizabeth lifted her head drowsily and said, "We should get going." Noah stirred also.

"I have something to tell you," said Marella.

They looked at Marella with concern. "What's wrong?" asked Elizabeth.

"Gabriela..." Marella's throat tightened, making it hard to speak.

"What? What about her?" asked Noah.

"She's dead."

Elizabeth sprang up, jumping past Marella and across the sand, with Noah close behind. At the sight of Gabriela's body in the truck, she stood still for a time, then deflated as she turned away. She spoke quietly to Preston, who shook his head. She then leaned into the back of the truck—apparently to examine Gabriela—but Preston touched her arm, shaking his head again, and she backed up. Marella was both relieved and anxious that she might not learn whether the wolf eel bite had killed her.

But then, did it really matter? Wasn't this like her father's death, where she couldn't see the future and so she couldn't have saved Gabriela?

Noah gazed at Gabriela's body and then bowed his head, eyes squeezed shut. He was praying.

Edie. She had to tell her now. Marella trudged to Edie's car and tapped on the window. Edie woke. Marella gestured insistently for her to come out. Looking alarmed, Edie glanced at her sleeping baby, then opened her door gingerly.

Marella's throat was still tight. She forced the words out anyway, speaking quietly so that Baby Faith wouldn't wake. "I'm so sorry to have to tell you this. It's Gabriela. She died."

Edie gasped, putting a hand to her mouth. She looked over at Gabriela's car, where Preston, Elizabeth, and Noah stood, heads hanging. "No," said Edie. "No, no, no, no, no." She ran to Gabriela's truck. She pounded on the tailgate, calling, "No, Gabriela, no, wake up! You're supposed to bring in the new world."

Marella wasn't sure what she meant. Perhaps she was just confused. It was as if Marella watched a reflection of herself at her father's death, screaming words, any words to get her father to react. Elizabeth tried to console Edie, to no avail. She continued crying and screaming.

Edie's frenzied entreaties turned Marella's dread to panic. She'd managed to control herself to keep from doing exactly what Edie was doing, but now her emotions threatened to overcome her. She pressed her hands to her temples, trying to calm herself.

Baby Faith began wailing, giving her a reason for restraint. She scooped the infant up, feeling her warmth. The baby snuffled, then quieted, but the sound of her mother still pleading with Gabriela made her start crying again.

Drawn by the noise, Olivia emerged from her truck. Marella was relieved she didn't need to tell her, though it was painful to watch her discover it for herself then turn away, gripping her forearms and turning from one side to another, like somebody trying to walk off a stubbed toe.

Marella walked away from the cars, rocking and comforting Baby Faith, telling her, "It's all right, it's okay." Though Marella didn't believe her own words, the infant seemed to. She quieted.

She looked out over the landscape, as dry as the surface of the moon. What if Preston was right, that everything was going according to God's plan, and nothing she did would change that? And if the plan was for all of them to die, who was next? Who after that? Which of them would be left alone in the middle of all this nothingness? She felt hollow.

She gathered herself, stuffing her fears into a compartment. They had to move on quickly or those fears would come true. Then none of them would survive, not even the baby in her arms.

She strode up to the group, determined to press forward. Her voice warbled with sadness in spite of her intention to be firm. "I'm sorry everybody, we have to leave." She handed Baby Faith to Edie. "You should drive Gabriela's truck. We'll help you move your things."

"What about Gabriela?" asked Edie.

"We should bury her," said Noah.

"No," said Preston. "We have to cremate her."

Cremation. The ramifications seeped in. Gabriela burning right in front of them. Marella's imagination had demons reveling in the flames, dancing with jerky, spiteful movements, chanting throaty songs.

Even without her imagination working overtime, the prospect was appalling in this context. They had escaped the flames in the city, only to subject Gabriela to them. Of course Gabriela could no longer feel pain, but Marella couldn't suppress her revulsion, unable to avoid thinking of it as grilling Gabriela the way they had grilled the gooseneck barnacles.

Of course not exactly the same way. There would be a ceremony. Words would be spoken. But burning people out in the open wasn't how they did things in this part of the world. She understood that in some countries it was normal, but she'd had no preparation for such an event. It was too raw. Too primal. And most of all, it pointed out how much things had changed in such a short time. In normal times it would not be allowed.

To Marella's relief, Elizabeth spoke up, "We don't have time. We need to get to the Pacific."

"It's her religion," said Preston. "She has to be cremated."

"She would understand that we have to leave," said Elizabeth.

"I can't do that to her," said Preston. "She won't go to Heaven."

How could she counter such a statement? Marella looked at Elizabeth. but she too seemed nonplussed.

It was bad timing to ask for a favor, but it had to be done. Marella cleared her throat. "Well then, could you please give us some gas so we could keep going?"

"The infection might have caused her death," said Preston, matter-of-factly. "If you hadn't taken her with you foraging, she might be alive today."

Marella's insides went cold. She stared back at Preston and his wooden expression. Her emotions swirled. She wasn't truly to blame. Her voice cracked a little as she spoke. "I didn't know Gabriela would get bit."

"Of course you didn't," said Preston. "But you are a part of her journey. It's only right that you be a part of this ceremony. After the cremation I'll give you gas."

"We'd better start gathering driftwood to burn," said Edie.

"That'll take a long time," said Elizabeth. "There's not much here and it's all spread out."

"It must be done," said Preston.

Marella was desperate to get them all moving. They had five days before the machine passed the point of no return. Besides that, the longer they took, the more people would die of thirst. How bad it was, she didn't know. A thousand a day? A thousand an hour? Or maybe the deaths could be counted by minutes.

She wished she possessed Preston's trait that made people listen. She needed the power of persuasion. If only she could tell them that they were extending the Aguageddon by tarrying. That every moment they spent here meant less water in the world.

Could she tell them? She felt little allegiance to HemisNorth, not after all she'd been through. She didn't need to keep their secrets. The truth would come out sooner or later.

Marella pulled Elizabeth aside. "They don't understand the urgency. We need to tell them why we're in a hurry. We need to tell them we're trying to stop the Aguageddon."

"You'd be telling them HemisNorth is responsible for all this. They would ostracize us. They wouldn't give us more gas and we wouldn't get the flash drive and the shutdown program to the island."

"We only have to tell them we're trying to fix the Aguageddon," said Marella. "We don't have to give them those details. Or we could tell them we're trying to save people, like we told Noah."

"It's been hard enough keeping the details from Noah. A whole group of people wouldn't be satisfied until they knew the details. Trust me. We're not telling them."

Trust me. Marella trusted her boss before, along with everybody at HemisNorth. And look what happened. She clamped her jaw shut, trying to tamp down her anger. But then maybe her reaction proved Elizabeth right. It was too easy to be angry. Too easy to blame. If it was that easy for her, it would be that easy for them. Still, if Preston knew their mission, they might already be on their way.

"Besides," added Elizabeth. "They know how important it is to keep up with the receding water, and they're still taking the time for this. It's that important to them. Nothing we can do will move them along any faster."

Marella rushed to gather driftwood with the others, her anxiety mounting. She helped arrange the pieces into a bench-like pyre and arrange kindling underneath. Preston retrieved a flat can from his camper and squirted its liquid onto the wood, rhythmically, ceremonially. The sharp smell of lighter fluid reached Marella. It was all wrong. That smell belonged to barbeques and to sunny days at Lake Washington. Not to this.

The reality sank in further. *Gabriela will lie on this wood. They'll burn her.* How could she watch such a thing? It would be like seeing her die. Her hands began shaking. She grasped them together to still them. *Get a grip on yourself. It'll be over soon.*

Preston put his hand on Noah's shoulder. "The women are going to wash Gabriela," he said.

"With water?" said Noah. "We can't waste it like that."

"It's what God would want," said Preston.

Noah nodded. Marella looked to the sky in frustration. She wanted to shake sense into them. And surely they didn't expect her to participate.

Edie spoke up, "Olivia and I will do it."

Marella was thankful to avoid such a tragic task, though a twinge of bitterness over the rejection surprised her. But above all, she was exasperated about more delay.

She went to her truck, opening the hood to check the oil and make sure nothing was loose. She didn't want anything else to slow them once they got going again. She examined the tires. They looked fine. Finally she sat in the truck with Elizabeth, watching Noah and Preston standing quietly near the camper, heads bowed in prayer, lips moving silently.

"Why are they insisting on cremating her?" Marella made a wild gesture of resentment.

"Some religions are like that. They believe that cremation releases the soul from the body."

"But she's Christian. I saw her wearing a cross."

Elizabeth just shook her head, fidgeting, legs shifting. "I want to get going too."

"Then talk to him again. You're good at that."

"No. He thinks you had a hand in Gabriela's death."

Marella raised her face up in frustration. "He also said he was to blame for not keeping her safe."

"He seemed to be at a tipping point. If I badger him, he might not give us gas at all."

Elizabeth had always been able to motivate people into action. Why couldn't she now, when it was most important? It reminded her that much of people's power came from others giving it to them. Nobody was giving power to Elizabeth or Marella, and they were giving their own power to Preston by heeding his wishes.

Edie and Olivia eased Gabriela out to the tailgate. Marella caught glimpses of bare skin and a sheet. She thought of Gabriela wrapping her bad ankle, which now hurt worse than ever, as if Gabriela's passing had erased all the good she had done in life.

Suddenly Marella didn't want things to get over with. She wanted to stop time, never go forward, never get to the burning. She began rocking, trying to shift away the bad feeling, then stopped. It made her feel too crazy.

"She was younger than me," said Elizabeth. "It makes me think."

Marella looked sideways at Elizabeth. "That doesn't mean you're next."

"I prefer burial," said Elizabeth. "But it doesn't matter that much. Once I'm gone, I'm gone. What I'm most afraid of is dying alone."

Marella crossed her arms over herself. The statement surprised her but she didn't know why.

Elizabeth took a deep breath, as if preparing to confess. "It's the one thing I'm afraid of more than anything else. I was often by myself when I was young. My parents would go out and party. When I was six years old they were off who knows where and I was pretending to play hide and seek with my stuffed animals. I locked myself in a cupboard somehow. My parents didn't come home that night." Elizabeth's voice broke. She put her hand to her eyes. "Or the next."

Marella breathed shallowly. She wished she could go back in time and comfort Elizabeth as a scared little girl.

"I was sure I was going to die." Elizabeth dropped her hand to her lap, where it lay open, just like Gabriela's hand in the truck. As if the two older women were linked, death leaching from one to the other. Marella felt a wave of dread. She reached over to grasp Elizabeth's hand partly to staunch her superstitious thoughts, and partly to comfort.

Elizabeth squeezed back gratefully. "I thought I would dry up and be a little spot of powder that would blow away as soon as somebody opened the cupboard. When they finally came home they spanked me for peeing there."

Marella imagined Elizabeth as a small child locked in the dark, pushing on the door, yelling, kicking, begging to be let out. Nobody coming. Alone. The same way Marella had felt in the woods when her father died, except Marella had the option of running. It made her feel like running now.

"I hate being alone too." Marella described her father's death. Elizabeth listened, her expression soft and wistful, then brushed a lock of hair from Marella's face. "Well, when you feel abandoned like we have—and you've divested yourself of family, as I have, the corporate world is a good place to be. There's always some networking event, conference, client dinner, charity fundraiser. You make friends. I've managed to fill up my life with people. Some of them would visit me on my deathbed. My ex and his family too. But out here..." she gestured at the expanse of sand. "Promise me if something happens you won't let me die alone."

Marella shivered. She'd been trying not to visualize their death. "Nothing's going to happen. We're going to get to the island and fix this."

Elizabeth straightened, her voice matter-of-fact. She seemed to be returning to her self-assured state. "Well then if you're sure nothing's going to happen, you can promise without fear."

"Promising would jinx it. Make it happen."

"Don't be ridiculous. You have too much common sense to be superstitious."

She hadn't mentioned the demons. Marella's eyes watered. She wiped them quickly, but they were already dry. Best to agree so they could move on to another topic. "Okay then, I promise."

Elizabeth looked satisfied. She slapped her hands on her thighs. "Good. I have every faith in you. You'll keep your word if you need to."

"I won't need to. You can't die. Two employees have to turn off the machine because of the biometrics."

"I have a workaround for that. If something should happen to either of us, there's an employee on the island right now."

"You can't mean..." Marella felt her gorge rise. She couldn't say it.

"Yes, Victor."

"But he's dead. How would it work if he's dead? He can't look into the camera."

Elizabeth spoke firmly, as if to instill Marella with composure. "We'd have to help him. Arnie and Delphine are options except they will have been dead for longer."

Marella felt a sob building. She had to lighten things up or she would break down. "Well if Gabriela gets cremation and you take burial in the ground, I guess I'm stuck with burial at sea."

Elizabeth tilted her head.

"I was joking," said Marella.

"Oh, of course. Nothing like a morbid joke to get through something terrible. I suppose if I were creative I would come up with a good one about a tailgate party."

Marella glanced at Gabriela's body on the tailgate, surprising herself by smiling.

"Which reminds me," said Elizabeth, "if anything happens to me, just remember that the computer username is Project Athena, with initial caps, and the password is Hemi$phere180, the 'S' is a dollar sign. Repeat that back to me."

"Project Athena, with initial caps, and Hemi$phere180, the 'S' is a dollar sign."

"On Wisdom Island there's a road that leads to a green camouflage building. Inside there's an office, where Victor is."

Marella imagined arriving at the office without Elizabeth. Alone. She felt a wave of anguish. But then, Noah would be with her. He could help with Victor. And besides, she wasn't going to let anything happen to Elizabeth. All three of them would be there.

Elizabeth continued. "There's a door that leads to the operations room. Project Athena's workings are in there, protected by shatterproof glass. They don't look like you'd think. They're like a steampunk chandelier. There's a control panel with a keyboard and a camera. We put the flash drive in the slot on the control panel, then follow the directions on the screen."

"What if there's no power?"

"There will be. It has a geothermal system." Elizabeth gazed at her, almost lovingly, the iguana stare long gone. "I'm glad you're here. I was right when I saw the potential in you."

Marella looked away, suddenly embarrassed. She glanced back; now Elizabeth looked at the smoky sky, reminiscing. "When I was your age I was a lot like you. I didn't have a degree, didn't know what I wanted to do. A woman at work took me under her wing. She made me feel like I could make something of myself. I always thought I would pay it forward. In a way, I did. I've mentored plenty of young people along the way. Most of them were already on a path. But you're different."

"Because I needed a lot more work."

"In some ways, but that's not what I meant. You were the first one that came along who I thought could make a real difference in this world. Don't ask me how or what. It was just a feeling. Maybe even wishful thinking, at first. It turned out you didn't need me. I needed you. You and your workarounds. It's humbling."

Marella was about to tell her she was wrong. Workarounds were one thing, making a difference was another. But a crack opened up. The way she thought about herself. Could Elizabeth be right? A little?

She pushed the idea off for later. The validation made her feel special, but she already had enough responsibility without Elizabeth loading more on her shoulders. And if she was so capable then why didn't people listen to her? "I did need you. We need each other."

"Sappy but true." Elizabeth pressed her lips together in a wan smile.

"Where's the woman who mentored you?"

"We lost touch. That was thoughtless on my part. But there was no social media then. Not that there had to be. I could still have made the effort. A postcard or something now and then. She's the one who taught me the importance of a handwritten note." Elizabeth squeezed her eyes shut. It looked like she might cry. Instead she burst out, "Why the fuck am I talking about handwritten notes?"

Marella leaned back, surprised by the sudden outburst.

Elizabeth craned her neck. "They need to finish this nonsense. We have to go."

Olivia motioned for them to come. Elizabeth marched to the tailgate, Marella following nervously. Gabriella was wrapped in a blanket like a rolled-up rug. She smelled of lemon and sage. A faint rumble sounded in the distance. Not demons, she told herself.

Olivia and Edie slipped their hands underneath Gabriela, then looked at Elizabeth and Marella. It seemed to be understood that the four of them would carry her body to the pyre.

She could do this. To move things along. To honor Gabriela. Taking short, shallow breaths, she reached under.

Now Gabriela's legs lay in her arms. It seemed wrong. Gabriela wasn't an object to be carried. She was a person. Marella tried to picture Gabriela in a better place, but that seemed wrong too. It wasn't right to accept death like that. Such an acceptance was giving up.

Marella shook all the way to the pyre. They set Gabriela reverently onto it. Again the smell of lighter fluid. All wrong. Preston said some words that she barely heard at first, too occupied with the thought of what was to come. But then he spoke loudly, "From fire comes death. From death comes life." She shivered. His voice sounded like a preacher's.

He ended forcefully with, "This is what comes from tampering with God's will. God will strike down sinners and lay them low. Only the faithful will remain."

Marella and Elizabeth glanced at each other. He didn't really believe that, did he? That Gabriela deserved this? Noah's eyebrows knitted. He too seemed surprised by the words.

Preston took a moment to compose himself. He took a deep breath, then ceremoniously handed them each a candle, lighting them one by one, then nodding at the pyre. With dismay she realized that they were all supposed to light the fire. She was supposed to make Gabriela burn. Well then, she would do it. So that Preston would give her gas. So she could save her family. Whatever it took.

They approached the pyre. Holding out the candles seemed too much like campers about to roast marshmallows. At their touch, the lighter fluid sprang into flame. All at once Gabriela's body was wreathed in fire. Marella eased back from its heat, heart pounding.

Within the conflagration, the blanket edges peeled open, revealing glimpses of the white sheet, which turned black, then burned away. Abruptly Gabriela's body was as visible as if it had never been shrouded. Torso, limbs, face, all perfectly clear, the skin fading to gray then blackening.

Gabriela's head moved. Marella gasped. It turned slowly, smoothly. "She's alive," said Marella, hand to chest.

"No," said Elizabeth. "She's not. Her muscles and tendons are contracting."

Gabriela's head now faced Marella directly, as if to tell her something. Warn Marella of her own fate, or perhaps blame her for the wolf eel bite. Was that really what killed her? But it was no longer Gabriela's head, it was something the shape of a skull, steam rising from sizzling eye sockets. So much steam—not just from the eyes, but also the brain, Marella realized. She dropped to her knees, hugging herself. She had thought this would be difficult but had never expected it to be so grisly. She tried not to think of demons scuffling underground, or of Hell as a giant cavern inches under her feet.

She tore her eyes away, looking at the others, who also appeared stricken. This was hard for everybody. Still, nobody made a move to leave. To honor Gabriela, she supposed. Which was difficult when she smelled like burning lunch meat.

Marella rose to her feet, eyes drawn back to the pyre. She couldn't stop herself from looking. She tried to think noble thoughts, but it was difficult with burning chunks falling away, revealing oozing red flesh below, which in turn burned black and fell off. Now she could see Gabriela's ribs and the vertebrae of her neck.

Gabriela's legs rose—just the thigh bones, the knee attachments having burnt through. Her back arched. Her jaw opened wider and wider. Just the muscles and tendons contracting, Marella told herself, but it looked like the embodiment of pain.

She closed her eyes, but then imagined her mother burning in place of Gabriela. She blinked, opening her eyes once more.

The images of the burning body—its various stages and arches—fixed themselves in her mind. They would be there for as long as she lived. However long that might be.

Chapter Seventeen

Marella had been at the pyre for hours, watching Gabriela burn and shrink, the gruesome odor of charred internal organs infusing Marella's skin. Now all that remained was a skull and a mound of bones. The wind picked up, blowing sand in their faces. She hunched from fatigue. Her lungs felt coated with death. Twice she had suggested leaving but Preston had ignored her, standing as still as the nearby rock outcropping

Now he wiped his hands over his hair and shook out his legs. *Finally*, she thought, but instead of preparing to go, he climbed into the back of his camper, shutting the door behind himself.

"Give him a little more time," said Noah.

"We're fresh out," said Marella testily. She trod over and knocked on the camper door, then gingerly opened it. Preston was sitting on the bench, head in hands. She climbed in, closing the door against sand blowing in with the wind. It was hard to ask when he was still so distraught, but she had to do it. "Can I please get some gas from you?"

He seemed not to hear. "All the suffering. All the death. It's just overwhelming. I didn't know what it would be like, surviving when others are dying."

He was right. It was hard. Overwhelming. And if calm, capable Preston couldn't bear it, how would she? She fought her own distress, trying to sound encouraging. "We can't let it get to us. The water is still receding and we have to keep up with it or we'll all die of thirst."

"I don't know if I want this burden. I may not have the strength to bear it. The Aguageddon is going to continue until most of the people of this Earth are gone."

She squeezed her fingers, fidgeting. How was she going to turn this around? She didn't have the words to bring him out of such dark despair. But she had to try. Lift him out, somehow, some way. She glanced helplessly around the camper, hoping for inspiration. She saw unlabeled cartons. The box with the raft Preston had mentioned, with a picture of people whitewater rafting. The water looked refreshing.

She sat next to him. "No, it's not going to be like that."

"It will though. The water is going to keep disappearing until God stops it. I don't have the courage for this. Maybe I don't deserve to live."

"What do you mean? You're not thinking of hurting yourself, are you?"

"Maybe that would be better. Then somebody else could take this on. Somebody who could keep you all safe."

"That doesn't make any sense at all." Marella patted him awkwardly on the shoulder. "Don't talk like that. You saved my life when you gave me water. We need you."

"You'll be better off without me."

"That's not true at all."

He looked upward, as if he could see through to heaven. "I don't know what God wants."

"Well then maybe you should stick around until you figure it out."

Preston bent once more, as if the weight of his trials was physically pushing him down.

He had told her a few things about his life. What did he have to live for? His parents didn't understand him. But he had been a teacher. He had lit up when talking about kids opening up to new ideas. "Think about the children. They need you."

Preston groaned. "I can't save them."

She felt a sense of desperation. She'd never talked somebody out of suicide before. She didn't know how it was done. And his misery was pulling her down. Things were bleak. Unfathomably difficult.

"Look, I understand how you feel. It's hard. When people die it seems senseless, and it makes you think about your own death. But you have to keep going."

As she spoke, she felt the truth of her words. She herself had to keep going. She had a mission. She couldn't let Preston's hopelessness get in the way. She had to do everything she could to move it along.

She knew exactly what to say to make that happen. She leaned close to him to emphasize her words. "I promise you everything will be better soon, because Elizabeth and I are going to stop the Aguageddon."

Preston looked up, eyes watery. "What do you mean?"

Marella watched him hopefully, anticipating a smile when he finally understood. She spoke with excitement. "We know what's causing the Aguageddon, and how to stop it."

"That can't be true." Preston's voice had a spark of astonishment.

She livened her tone to fan that spark. "Yes! It's true. I can't tell you the details, but you have to believe me. That's why we're going west."

Preston looked at her searchingly, as if the answer to his question was written on her face and he had only to find it. "How is it possible that you could stop the Aguageddon?"

"I can't explain it to you now. But when we get to the place we're trying to get to, we'll stop it. So please give me some gas so we can go."

Preston shifted in his seat, seeming to have a realization. "Your flash drive with the shutdown program. You plan to stop the Aguageddon using your flash drive."

She leaned back. How did he know about that? She hadn't said anything to him about it. When she had been talking to Elizabeth about getting the flash drive to the island she thought she'd seen somebody. Had Preston been eavesdropping then?

It didn't matter. He was emerging from his despair. She needed to pull him up the rest of the way. She continued. "You just have to trust that it won't be much longer before the Aguageddon ends and we can all begin to pick up the pieces. We can make things better."

He seized her wrist, holding it too tightly, his voice rumbling like an engine. "Where are you taking the flash drive?"

The abrupt change in his attitude startled Marella. "That hurts, let go." She yanked her wrist from his grasp.

His face transformed, his forehead wrinkling, his eyes narrowing. This was rage. "Tell me where you're taking the flash drive."

She breathed hard. Who was this person who seemed to have taken Preston's place? She spoke quickly. "You must have heard me wrong. We're trying to fix things. Stop the water from going away. Why are you mad at me?"

"It's not your call to stop the Aguageddon. The Aguageddon is God's will." He spoke viciously but quietly, which made him all the more terrifying, like a dragon holding back fire.

It dawned on her that she hadn't known him very long, that her version of his character was a concoction assembled from filled-in blanks. She didn't know most of his history, or if what little he told her was true. And yes, he'd saved her life, but after first denying her. He had only given her water after she'd crawled on her hands and knees begging like a dog.

He stood, his head close to the camper's ceiling. He towered over her, seeming barely able to contain his fury. She shrank back. She had to get away, now, but feared any abrupt move would trigger an explosion. She edged toward the door, but there was little room in the small camper, and Preston blocked her easily.

She was trapped. The camper felt too small. "I didn't mean to upset you. I should go."

"You think you can counter God's will," said Preston. "But the divine wrath is here."

Divine wrath. The words terrified her. She tried to launch herself past him, but he grabbed her arm. As she opened her mouth to call for help he seized her throat, cutting her scream short. She struggled, kicking and hitting in panic, but he didn't seem to feel it. The pain of his grip was excruciating, as if he were squeezing her soul from her body.

She was faint. Fading. There was one last bit of fight left in her. She put all her effort into a solid stomp on his foot.

He grunted, letting go. She fell back, gasping for breath, chest heaving. He was coming at her once more. She tried to yell but only a garbled sound emerged from her damaged throat. She reached out, grabbing things from the shelves, hurling them desperately as she backed up. Cans, a pillow, books, shirts, shoes. He ducked them like a prizefighter evading punches.

Suddenly she was throwing gold fabric at him. A cascade of it fluttered onto him, covering him. She could see a sleeve. A collar.

It was a robe. A gold robe. The memory of people falling from the Space Needle returned in full force. The gold robes fluttering in the sky.

Time froze while she put two and two together. Zokara's Chosen wore gold robes. Was Preston a member of that cult? Had he escaped, perhaps, refusing to jump from the Space Needle, refusing to burn Seattle?

But even as this idea jelled, she had another that was much more appalling. Preston's charismatic personality. The way the others deferred to him. This sudden anger. Could he be the cult's leader? The one who had sent some of his following to their deaths from the Space Needle and probably others to set fires all over Seattle?

She needed a weapon, or she wouldn't escape from him. Elizabeth and Noah wouldn't learn of the danger. Her Mother and Brielle would die. And billions of others.

While he wrestled the robe from his head, she lunged for a toolbox, trying to get it open, but she was shaking and nauseous from the near-strangulation, and her position was awkward, kneeling on the bed. So much seemed to hinge on this one moment. She felt her gorge rise. She was close to vomiting.

Just as she got the toolbox open, he pulled the robe off. She fished out a screwdriver, which he snatched from her hand. She pulled back, quivering with weakness and fear. Now he would use it on her.

Instead, he looked remorseful and spoke in an anguished tone. "I'm sorry. I'm so sorry. When the divine wrath comes over me, I can't stop it. I didn't want to hurt you."

She was too shocked to respond. What had just happened? He was not evil, then evil, then not evil. And what next? Evil once more?

She was still trying not to vomit as a babble of words poured out of his mouth, his voice cracking with grief. "God spoke to me. He warned me that disaster was coming. He commanded me to gather the righteous together. To sacrifice some of them, and save the rest to found a new world, a better world. Then he sent the Aguageddon. And when the water drains away, Zokara will be revealed."

The truth of it sank in, hot and heavy. Preston was a dangerous cult leader.

He continued. "And then he sent you to me. I knew you from a dream I had. And because your first name and last name both mean water. And you arrived with a man named Noah. These were all signs. You are going to be mother of the new humanity."

This was all so dizzying. She no longer knew up from down. She was having a hard time reorienting herself to this new view of Preston. A madman. A murderer. Sending people he purported to love to their deaths. It was like biting into a lovely red apple with a razor blade hidden inside.

He gazed at her with a horrifying combination of admiration and lunacy. "You and I are going to live in Zokara together. In one place, like you wanted, a permanent home."

She felt a stab of anger. Her fists balled up. He was using her own words against her. But she had to humor him until she could get out of the camper. She coughed. Her throat hurt so badly. She croaked the words though the pain. "Yes, Zokara. We'll go there."

Surprisingly, he seemed to accept her abrupt conversion as if it were only natural. He beamed like a lover. "First comes fire, then the cleansing. Say it with me."

Fire. She'd almost succumbed to his fire. The explosion at the Duwamish River. He had caused that. Marella struggled to contain the fury that ricocheted through her. Her own divine wrath. "First comes fire, then comes cleansing."

"You understand now? You can't stop the Aguageddon." He took her hands in his.

She shivered with disgust, trying to keep her voice level. "I understand." She fought to keep revulsion from her tone. As if she liked him. As if he hadn't just tried to kill her. As if he hadn't just revealed his true being.

He spoke like a preacher to his flock. "Life on Earth began in Zokara because the ground there is so fertile and the sun so nourishing that the plants grow lush and green. Its bounty tastes unlike anything you've ever eaten here in more barren lands."

The singsong quality grated, while the eerie tone made her shudder.

"When you stroll through luxuriant groves where fruit hangs abundant," he continued, "you have only to reach up and pick a globe." He reached a cupped hand upward. "And its juice bursts into your mouth with every bite. At the center of Zokara is a freshwater lake, from which four rivers flow, each toward the four directions of the world. The rivers are warm and wash away all illness." He paused, as if a response was required.

"It sounds wonderful." She could hardly get the words out. All this time she had seen him as their savior. Why was she always so naïve, giving others the benefit of the doubt? Why couldn't she intuit the evil around her? Instead, she sat in his grip, shocked by the profound change that revealed him as a psychopath.

His chin lifted. "The sun has a golden cast that can't burn you. The birds sing so sweetly their song fills you with light. Reeds grow that you can pluck to make beautiful music, to play duets with the birds. But outside of Zokara, the world is full of evil. People spread their nonbelief like a virus, so that there's no longer meaning in this world. We'll start over. We'll bring meaning to the world."

She looked at the door. She had to find a way to get out. Talk him into letting her leave. But how could she negotiate with a madman?

He spoke urgently. "The world is full of sinners who have to perish so their nonbelief will die with them. Then you and I will found a new world together. We have to let God have his way, as much as it hurts us. Don't let all these deaths be in vain."

He cupped her shoulder with one hand. She couldn't stifle a raspy wheeze of fear. He was looking at her with love and hope slathered with crazed intensity. He smelled sweaty and peppery. His hand brushed her chin lightly, making her want to jerk away. She held steady, fearing that any more indications of resistance might set him off once more.

"You and I are the beginning," said Preston. "But you mustn't tell anybody about you and me. Only God knows."

Another rush of emotion, sorrow this time. This was how he worked. Making people feel they were special. And then convincing them to jump off the Space Needle or to set buildings on fire. Marella had the feeling that if she wasn't vigilant he would hypnotize her into her own death. She feared his eyes, refusing to look into them.

"I want you to do something for me," said Preston.

She swallowed painfully. Would he ask her to die? Put on the gold robe and leap to her death? "What?"

"Destroy the flash drive. Let the Aguageddon take its course, and then you and I can go to Zokara."

She nodded. "I will."

He leaned aside to let her by. He was actually going to allow her to leave. Her heart pounded harder. In just a moment she could be free. She moved toward the door. Put her hand on the doorlatch.

"Marella?" asked Preston.

She froze. "Yes?"

The madman leaned close to her. The sour smell of his sweat was overpowering. His breath tickled her ear. "God is waiting."

Chapter Eighteen

M arella opened the camper door. She was about to step through.

Behind her, Preston bowed his head. He whispered, "From fire comes death. From death comes life."

She shuddered so hard she nearly stumbled. Stepping carefully out, she shut the door behind herself. She breathed in the smoky air as if it were freedom itself and gave a quiet sob of thankfulness to be out of the close confines of the camper. Her nausea eased, but tension made her run stiffly.

Elizabeth and Noah were standing near her truck. They looked anxious when they saw her rushing toward them, breathing in gulps of air as if having nearly drowned.

"What's wrong?" Elizabeth reached a hand out.

"Get in. Now. We have to go." Talking was like rubbing sandpaper on her throat, but the words came more easily now.

"What's going on?" asked Noah. "What happened?"

"Hurry," said Marella. "Preston is evil. A cult leader. Zokara's Chosen."

Noah stood his ground, shaking his head. "That's not possible."

"I saw the gold robes," Marella forced her voice out. "He said we were going to Zokara. He said God brought the Aguageddon. He thinks he channels divine wrath. I only got away from him because he thinks I'm going to destroy the flash drive. We have to leave while we can."

"How does he know about the flash drive?" Elizabeth's eyebrows knit in consternation.

"What flash drive?" asked Noah, perplexed.

Preston opened his camper door. He was coming this way, seeing her urging them into the car. Knowing she wasn't destroying the flash drive as she promised.

He carried something in his hand. Metal. Curved.

A machete.

Marella's blood turned cold. She imagined the slashing blade. Red blood spurting. She had no shield. She couldn't even hold up a grocery basket as she'd done to ward off the businessman in the store.

"Both of you shut up and get in the truck if you want to live." Marella spoke forcefully, herding them into the truck. They let her, mouths open in surprise at this sudden danger.

Now Preston was running. Only twenty feet away. Marella flew into the driver's seat and started the engine. Preston's face wrung itself into anger. The divine wrath. It was back. His features twisted. His shoulders raised in ire. Marella's nausea returned.

She pulled away just as Elizabeth and Noah shut their doors.

"Holy shit, he looks mad." Noah twisted to watch Preston as he fell behind.

"You told him." Elizabeth slapped the dashboard and raised her hands with an exasperated gesture. "Why? I warned you not to."

"Told him what?" asked Noah. "What the hell is going on?"

Marella spoke through the pain in her throat. "He was so sad he was going to kill himself. It was the only way. I didn't know he'd get angry. I told him we could stop the Aguageddon, but I didn't tell him about the flash drive. He must have heard us talking."

"This is insane." Noah's voice cracked. "You're not making any sense. We need him. Why did you have to piss him off?"

"He's following with in his camper," said Marella. She pressed the gas pedal harder. The truck careened over the hard sand, bouncing on its uneven surface.

Elizabeth's eyes widened. "I'm starting to understand. If he's that cult leader, that explains so much. Edie and Olivia jumping to do his bidding. Looking at his feet rather than his eyes. Agreeing with everything he says. The constant nodding. I thought they just looked up to him."

Marella nodded. "He's the man who told people jump to their deaths from the Space Needle. He's a cold-blooded killer. And now he's coming after us."

"I should have seen it." Elizabeth pounded her fist. "The bastard. He asked me to tell him something I wouldn't tell anybody else. That's what cult leaders do to keep their grip on you. I knew that and I still didn't see him for what he was."

Noah thrust his arms in the air for emphasis. "Preston's not a cult leader. He's not like that at all."

"Olivia's car is behind us too," said Marella. "We have to make sure she doesn't get the flash drive either."

"What flash drive?" Noah was yelling now. "What are you hiding?"

"Tell him," said Marella. "He deserves to know."

Elizabeth raised her hands in a calming gesture. "All right, all right. The flash drive has a program to stop the Aguageddon. When we get to the island we can run the program."

"What? That's it?" Noah threw a hand in the air and spoke mockingly. "Of course. You'll just run a computer program and the disaster will go away."

"It's because a machine is accidentally causing the Aguageddon," said Elizabeth. "The program can shut the machine down."

"A machine?" Noah sounded incredulous. He pointed at the desert surrounding them. "Is causing all this? A machine that powerful would be huge. It would be all over the internet. You'd see it in satellite photos, or from airplanes or drones."

"It's not obvious from the air or sea," said Elizabeth. "First of all, the island is only about two miles long. The modules have a kind of stealth camouflage that was developed along with the other technology. And the modules are each about forty feet long. Smaller than you'd think because Project Athena is based on quantum physics."

"That's crazy." Noah threw himself back against the seat, then winced at the pain in his back. "You're both crazy."

"What she says is true," said Marella. "We work at HemisNorth. They invented a climate machine. An employee confessed to us that he recalibrated sampling instruments so they didn't know the machine was screwing up. It was supposed to take carbon dioxide away, but it takes water instead."

Noah crossed his arms. "How is that even possible?"

"The concept is that the components that make up a given molecule could be in our universe or in other universes," said Elizabeth. "The machine makes the locations of specific particles undefined. A molecule is not in our universe but also not in a parallel universe. It has the potential to be in either one, but is not."

Marella kept glancing back. Preston still behind. Oliva passing him. No sign of Edie.

Noah thought for a time, then asked, "Why wouldn't it take the water from our bodies? We should all be nothing but dried up husks."

"I don't understand the intricacies of the science," said Elizabeth, "but it doesn't take water that is contained, such as in our bodies or bottles."

"There's more," said Marella. "We have to get to the machine in five days or a runaway reaction will take place. The water will keep disappearing no matter what. Everybody on Earth will die."

In the rearview mirror Marella saw his expression. Like she'd just told him that pigs fly using chicken wings. Marella understood. Saying it out loud made it seem so farfetched.

Noah's tone was belittling. "Things don't work that way. Quantum mechanics affects miniscule stuff. Smaller than molecules. Smaller than atoms. But let's say it's true. A machine is causing the Aguageddon. You don't need a program to stop it. Just destroy the machine."

"We can't." Marella's tone was hard. He shouldn't speak to them that way when they were trying to save his life yet again. "Damaging the machine would also cause a runaway reaction."

"Regardless, it's not possible for us to destroy it," added Elizabeth quickly, "The modules and their controls are built to endure a tsunami or a terror attack."

"You're wrong," said Noah. "A single machine didn't do all this by itself."

Marella glanced in the side mirror. Olivia was getting closer. She could feel the stress in her body. As if all its little quantum-size bits had expanded and were fighting amongst themselves for space.

Marella explained how she had come to believe Project Athena had caused the Aguageddon. Elizabeth described their discovery that several employees had sabotaged the data. Noah was silent as he took it in, looking from Marella to Elizabeth, his eyes growing wide with comprehension. Finally he said, "You're telling me the Aguageddon is your fault."

Marella winced at his accusatory tone. She had somehow joined the *them* of *us vs. them*. But her feelings didn't matter. "The important thing is to shut off Project Athena."

Noah slapped the seat in frustration. "Why would you build such a dangerous machine? If you leave it alone it'll drain the Earth. If you destroy it, it *might* drain the Earth. My money is on destroying it. Bomb it, nuke it from outer space, I don't care. You should have called somebody to make that happen the second you figured out it was the cause."

"We tried to get hold of people," said Marella. "We couldn't."

"Okay, then just take away the power source," said Noah. "Pull the damn plug."

"Its geothermal energy source is also protected," said Elizabeth. "It's an enhanced closed loop system, all underground, even its energy system."

They drove past rock towers that rose awkwardly from the ground like stalagmites that had lost their cave. Gargoyle-like growths sprouted from their sides. The two vehicles were still behind. Marella felt like a goldfish in an aquarium being chased by piranhas.

Noah's voice went higher. "I had dreams, you know. I was going to do big things. Lucas and Marius and I were going to start a business together. How am I going to finish college now? You burned it down."

"Preston did that," said Marella,

His voice sound almost as if he were pleading. "Seattle was dry enough to burn because of the Aguageddon. My back is burned because of you. How are you going to make it right for us? We worked hard to get where we are. We didn't get a free ride. We picked apples, mowed lawns, babysat. Ever since we were kids we were out there making money when everybody else was having fun. The three of us were going to be something. And now I don't even know if they're alive." His face worked as if he might break down in sobs. "Fuck HemisNorth and its stupid climate machine. What were you guys thinking to make something so deadly? You should have asked me." He slapped his chest, furious. "I would have told you not to."

"Ask Elizabeth," said Marella, furious in turn. "I only just found out myself."

"It's quite simple," yelled Elizabeth. "People had been blindly moving forward on a path of doom, and my co-workers were trying to save the world's people from themselves. Trying to keep entire cities from being inundated. The oceans from turning acidic. Hurricanes from rampaging."

Noah threw his hands in the air. "You're killing a mosquito with a nuclear bomb."

"Climate change is not a mosquito." Elizabeth emphasized the consonants.

"Climate change is irrelevant now," said Noah. "Soon there won't be any climate."

The tension in the car only added to Marella's distress. She gripped the steering wheel as if that could keep her from exploding. She tried speak calmly. "What's done is done. We have to fix it now."

"Just tell me how you can build a machine that's supposed to take CO_2 from the air and instead it takes H_2O?" asked Noah. "Those are two completely different things."

"We'll never know because the people who made it are dead and everything's burning down," burst out Marella. "Oh shit. The gas warning light just came on," She pounded the steering wheel. "What do we do?"

Elizabeth leaned over to look at the gas gage, then twisted back, looking at their pursuers. "Keep driving, we'll think of something."

Marella pictured Preston and his machete. "We can't let him reach us. He'll kill us."

"You're right," said Elizabeth. "He sent dozens to their death. He could have any number of weapons in that camper."

"But how can he be the leader of Zokara's Chosen?" asked Noah. "The chances that we would just happen to run into him are so remote they're laughable. There must be some other explanation."

"It's him. He went on and on about Zokara." Marella tried to see through the dust raised by Olivia's truck. "Wait—I don't see him anymore. Is he back there?"

"No, just Olivia," said Elizabeth.

Marella watched, but Preston's camper didn't show up in her rearview mirror. She began to breathe easier. "Olivia's still coming. She's dangerous. She'll do his bidding. That slingshot she has would work just as well on people as it does on seagulls." Even as she said it, she didn't know whether she meant it. Olivia was sweet, caring. She couldn't picture her doing anything wrong.

"She's not a threat," said Noah. "If Preston is as evil as you seem to think he is, then she's a victim. And so is Edie. And now she and Baby Faith are alone back there. I hope they'll be alright."

"We can't trust Edie either," said Marella.

"We don't have a choice," said Noah. Again that belittling tone. "We're going to run out of gas. Olivia's right behind us."

The sand became ragged, as if the cavalry had just crossed by. Marella gathered her thoughts. Finally she said, "All right, here's the plan. We stop, get out of the truck as if we just want to talk to her. Elizabeth will have the pepper spray ready. You and Noah keep her away while I get one of the gas cans from her truck."

"Let's think about this," said Elizabeth.

"No time," said Marella. The truck began rolling to a stop. They were out of gas. Marella got out of the car. Her legs felt weak. She shuffled in place a little. She had to be ready to run. Unstrap the gas.

Olivia's truck stopped right behind them. To Marella's surprise, she spilled out of the car, shouting, "Save me!" She ran straight to Marella and dropped to her knees, begging, "Please let me come with you. I'm so scared of him." Her words poured out between sobs. "I've been so afraid."

It was true, Olivia was a victim. Marella's heart melted. Remorse filled her. She wanted to console Olivia, but saw dust rising in the distance. Preston would catch up soon. Thankfully Noah was already retrieving the gas, lugging the can with fast, heavy steps. Elizabeth sprinted to the side of the truck to open the gas cap. The fuel glugged as Noah poured.

Marella pulled Olivia to standing. "Get back in your car and drive along with us."

Olivia nodded gratefully and rushed to comply.

As she climbed in the driver's seat, Marella allowed hope to seep in. She'd nearly lost. She'd almost been strangled. But she'd made it this far, and she was going to succeed. Nothing was going to stop them now. They would get to Wisdom Island no matter what waited ahead or followed behind.

Chapter Nineteen

It was early evening. Marella, Noah, Elizabeth, and Olivia poured out of the vehicles at the Pacific Ocean. This was so different from Puget Sound. Marella hadn't expected the waves to pound the shore as if they meant it harm. Stupidly, she'd imagined it would be calm as a Hawaiian vacation spot.

The wind slashed her hair into her eyes. It also seemed to mean harm, trying to topple her. Further down the beach lay a dead seal, a flipper raised as if to get Marella's attention. The colors of everything were oddly saturated. The reds too red, the greens too green. Even the smoke haze hanging above them seemed overly brown.

Several fish with fins like sails flopped helplessly on the sand. They were the gold of the robes of Zokara's Chosen. She eyed them apprehensively. An omen? Good or bad?

Noah looked at one up close. "Red Irish lord sculpins," said Elizabeth.

He bristled. "You don't have to instruct me. I'm not your employee."

Olivia snuck Marella a look. *Uh, oh.*

Elizabeth talked over her shoulder as she headed to the back of the truck. "Knowledge is never a bad thing."

She didn't sound irritated, which seemed to spur Noah's annoyance. He joined them as they began to unload the truck. "You're just assuming I don't know anything."

Marella had enough stress already. Drinking no longer relieved her thirst and she worried that Athena's effects would be too powerful to overcome. The sight of all this undrinkable salt water only worsened her craving. The arguing threatened to send her over the edge. "You're both hella smart. So drop it."

"I just wish this was a dream," said Noah. "We'd wake up and it would be over."

"That would make me the woman of your dreams," said Elizabeth.

Olivia giggled. Noah guffawed. They were back to getting along. Good.

"Let's get the raft," said Marella. "Come on, we don't know how close Preston is."

"I don't understand. Why abandon the cars?" Olivia motioned past the dead seal. "Why not just keep driving along the shore?"

"We're almost at the continental shelf," answered Elizabeth, pulling bottles of water from the truck.

Olivia's eyes went wide. "Wow. I didn't think of that."

"How are we going to launch a raft with the surf so strong?" Noah gestured toward the crashing waves.

"Paddle like hell," said Elizabeth dryly.

Together they heaved the hundred-pound lozenge from the truck, lowering it to the ground. They piled their backpacks and bags on the shore with the watermaker, bottles and jugs, a carton of soup, a few tools, a knife and utensils, a sheet, and three blankets.

"What if we spring a leak or flip over?" asked Noah.

"Oh, so you'd like some knowledge?" Elizabeth sounded pleased.

Noah sighed, then pressed his hands together, speaking deadpan. "Yes. I'd like knowledge. Please instruct me oh wise one."

Elizabeth resumed a practical tone. "They regularly inspect these rafts. You saw the seal on the outside. Plus there will be a patch kit. Also there will be ballast bags to keep it upright."

"Hm." Noah seemed unconvinced.

Marella understood his reticence. When she came up with the idea to bring the raft, it was with the practical, problem-solving part of her mind but she hadn't thought it all the way through. Now she imagined the raft as a tiny speck floating on the vast, churning water. The sheer power of the waves was daunting even from shore.

How much worse would it be further out, completely at the ocean's mercy?

Marella took a last look at her truck. When she made the down payment on it, she had so much hope. She had a job and a stable future. One where she wasn't floating from place to place. But now, ironically, here she would be floating again, literally this time.

She looked east. No sign of Preston on the flat sand. At least there was that. Once they got on the water it would be impossible for him to find them.

Elizabeth lifted a strap that was connected to the raft pod. "We need to put the pod into the water, then pull on the strap for it to deploy."

They carried it into the surf. Waves surged around their legs, the foam like curdled milk. Elizabeth yanked the strap and the raft unfolded magically, becoming an orange hexagon ten feet across. A canopy covered the entire raft, leaving a square opening a few feet wide.

Noah's tone was doubtful. "I've been on that ride at Disneyland."

"We need to do a quick check of the raft's contents, then start loading," said Elizabeth brusquely.

"I've got this." Marella waded into the freezing water, sucking in air at the shock of the cold, then vaulted awkwardly through the opening into the strange orange interior. The smell reminded her of a wading pool she and Brielle played in as children. She stepped forward, holding out her arms to keep her balance. An inflated bench wrapped around the whole inside, with straps to hold onto. Bags of supplies were labeled with a large black font.

"Do you see paddles? Life vests?" asked Elizabeth.

"Yes," said Marella, pawing through the bags. "Four paddles. Ten life vests. Also a bailer and sponges, an air pump and repair kit, a solar light, seasickness tablets and bags, one-hundred foot rope."

"Get the life vests," said Elizabeth. "Wear them at all times. Ten minutes after you fall in the cold water you start to lose the ability to swim. You have to keep afloat until you can be saved."

"It's an adventure," said Noah robotically, as if trying to convince himself.

"An adventure," repeated Olivia, also seeming uncertain.

"An adventure," said Marella, over-the-top like an old-time announcer.

"An adventure." Elizabeth's tone rose and fell. The wrap-up.

The exchange seemed to bolster Noah, who scooped up some water bottles and waded into the surf singing an adventure tune, which morphed into noises of discomfort. "You aren't kidding about this water. It's even colder than Puget Sound." He handed the bottles to Marella, who stashed them and reached for more. The three of them continued handing supplies to Marella, bucket-brigade fashion. The raft lifted and lowered with the waves, making the chore awkward.

As they worked, Marella tried unsuccessfully to quell her dread. This was actually dangerous. She wasn't sure how much of her shakiness was from unsteadiness on the raft and how much from nerves.

"Have we got everything?" asked Elizabeth. "The GPS too? Then all aboard."

Because of the attached canopy, the only way to paddle was to lean out the front opening. Olivia handed out the paddles. All four of them leaned out and set to work. The waves curled in front of them like a series of shelves. Getting past the first ones would be the most difficult.

"Ready?" said Elizabeth. "Go, go, go!" They dug the paddles in. The raft moved surprisingly fast, but the water before them swelled upward, rising higher and higher. As a wave unfurled overhead, it seemed to be reconsidering whether it wanted to break or not.

"Oh Shit," said Noah.

Olivia whimpered. Elizabeth clutched onto her. "I've got you."

"Stay back, stay back," whispered Marella. But the wave ignored her plea, breaking onto them. It was more of a collision than a splash, pounding Marella like a crash test dummy, ramming her back into the raft. Water thudded down all around. She sputtered and grunted, wiping her eyes. Her body shuddered in the frigid water, now a foot deep.

The others had kept their positions by clutching the strap that ran along the side.

"That was so freezing!" cried Olivia.

"Keep going!" urged Elizabeth, her voice warbling from a shiver.

Marella scrambled to rejoin them. They dipped their paddles into the white Rorschach-patterns, pulling hard. Marella tried to match her strokes to Elizabeth, who worked with a speed Marella wouldn't expect from a fifty-something year old, her small but powerful biceps bulging under her wet sleeves.

Marella was fortified by the presence of the others, straining and grunting with their paddles. But then she saw the water curling above them again. The wave forming. There was nothing she could do to stop it. She cringed.

"Get ready, it's a big one," said Noah.

Marella held on to the strap. The raft tilted. This time the wave didn't pause before smashing them. It was a brutal punch to the face, leaving her gasping for breath. They all coughed and spit.

The water was now knee-high. "Get the bailer," said Elizabeth. "Looks like a bicycle tire pump."

Marella searched out the tube-like object. She plunged it into the pool of water, directed one end through the raft opening, and pumped. A rooster tail of water shot out.

"Pump as if your life depended on it," said Elizabeth.

"It does," said Noah. Marella worked furiously while the others paddled, watching warily for the next wave.

Another curl of water rose ahead of them.

"Visualize success," shouted Marella.

Elizabeth sounded affronted. "Don't you dare throw my platitudes back in my face."

"I meant it," said Marella, exasperated.

"Just paddle with all you've got," said Olivia.

"Less talk, more work," shouted Noah, his voice husky, shoving the paddle down as if digging a fence post.

Marella gritted her teeth. She wrapped her elbow into the strap, still pumping. The wave rose high. It was claustrophobic. She cowered.

The wave burst onto them, icy and startling. Marella screamed.

"You bastard," sputtered Elizabeth.

The raft was perilously full of water. The next wave could fill it. Marella wished she hadn't come, but it was too late. Like jumping off a cliff and changing her mind halfway to the ground, she was here and there was no going back.

As hopeless as it seemed, she resumed pumping, panting like an escaping wild creature. Her face stung, but she endured it rather than reach up to rub it. She watched for the next wave. Where would it rise? Along that dark line in the water? Or closer in?

The moments passed. She kept watching. Kept pumping. No wave rose high.

"Are we okay?" asked Olivia. "I think we're okay."

"We're past the waves!" said Noah. "We did it!"

They all whooped with joy, high-fiving each other, still breathing hard from their efforts. Their eyes glinted. They were a team, the underdogs coming through for the win.

"No laurel resting," said Elizabeth. "Let's at least get out of sight of the beach. And then we have to make darn sure we get past the continental shelf."

Noah grunted. "You think those waves were bad. If there's a storm, this raft will be tossed around like a salad crouton."

Marella tried to keep the fear from creeping back in. How would they survive worse? "Maybe there won't be any storms. No clouds, so no rain."

"But there's more wind than ever," said Noah.

The water rolled like battered aluminum in front of the raft, as far as the horizon. They took turns, three of them paddling at a time, the other bailing.

The sea raised one side of the raft, then the other, as if sweeping dirt under a rug. The odor of their own sweat mingled with the polyurethane. Gusts of wind blew the smoky air through the canopy opening. The waves hitting the raft sounded like a dog sniffing on the other side of a door.

During her turn at bailing, Olivia began to sing. The words, in a language Marella didn't know, evoked another time and place. The tune was dreamlike, hopeful, and otherworldly all at the same time. Marella was glad they had saved her from Preston.

After an hour a barking noise sounded outside. "Steller sea lions, I believe," said Elizabeth, standing up to look back east over the canopy's curve. "Oh good god." She sounded shocked.

Marella joined her, clutching the canopy to keep steady. She saw the sleek brown heads of two sea lions, but that wasn't what held Elizabeth's attention. She was looking at a line in the water.

"What's that?" asked Marella.

"Looks like a ridge," said Noah, joining them.

"But it goes on forever," said Marella.

Olivia clutched onto Marella to get a look. Marella wrapped an arm around her for support. She felt like Brielle, which was a small comfort.

"I'm pretty sure we're looking at the top edge of the continental shelf," said Elizabeth.

Marella's stomach felt like lead. How could that be? "No way. The water has receded that low, that fast?"

"One hundred and fifty meters," said Elizabeth as if she couldn't believe it herself. "Nearly five hundred feet down."

Noah looked stricken, as if told he had only a week to live, which Marella realized could be true. He lowered himself to sitting, the knowledge seemingly too heavy to bear. "How will people survive this?"

Elizabeth shook her head. Her face turned blotchy like somebody crying. She covered her eyes.

"This is really awful," Olivia squeezed Marella more tightly. Her voice sounded poignant. Lonely.

Marella clenched her jaw, their sorrow sparking her anger. Project Athena's designers had gotten off much too lightly. Len and Shauna should be here suffering too. She guzzled some water, then went back to stabbing the ocean with a paddle. The water splashed all over.

Over the next two hours, a cliff face appeared behind them, its growths shockingly colorful. As the water level lowered, more and more sea life showed: red, orange, and pink blotches like the aftermath of a brutal paint ball fight.

"Look how high it is even though we've paddled so far away," said Marella. Her anger hadn't abated. It only grew to encompass the obstacles themselves. The water, Project Athena, and her own human frailty. She was exhausted. Her lungs wheezed like a broken accordion.

"The water's dropping fast," said Noah. "The continental shelf must be, what, a hundred feet high? If the ocean is receding this fast, then how long before the Earth is dry?"

She imagined an endless Sahara all around. Blustery wind. Nothing but her dusty bones to show she'd ever been alive. Bones that still felt fidgety and restless, as tired as she was. They had to go on.

Debris floated past them: a drift net. A buoy. Hundreds of dead fish, one of which Elizabeth identified as a painted greenling. No green in spite of the name; rather, decorated in red and white barber pole stripes. "Normally I'd be surprised to see that right here," said Elizabeth, "but everything's different now."

"It smells foul," said Noah. "I could really use a cologne-soaked bandana. Or a speedboat. Yeah, a speedboat would be better. I'll take that instead."

Night settled around them abruptly. For a short time they used a solar light, which seemed as harsh as an interrogation lamp. They all laid down as best they could along the inflated benches that lined the raft's interior, huddling under blankets they'd brought from Olivia's car. As tired as she was, Marella couldn't fall asleep. She listened to the water slapping against the raft, thinking of all the sharp-tooth creatures that might be swimming below. Only the raft bottom separated her from them.

She tried to picture telling her story to Brielle and Mom when the Aguageddon was over. An adventure tale. "I was terrified," she would say. "But I thought about you guys and that made everything better."

But it didn't. She could only imagine them as burnt corpses on a charred road.

Where were they? What were they doing? Were they alive? Were they suffering? How would she find them when this was all over?

She remembered her mom cutting pink dahlias from the yard, watching a ladybug. Naming it Spot, then changing it to Sylvia, then Rodger, because there were male ladybugs you know. That only made Marella want to sob, to the point where she had to get up and do something, anything. Carefully, so as not to wake the others, Marella made her way to the raft's opening and looked out from under the canopy flap into the darkness. The smoky sky meant no stars, no Milky Way. Just a black night that could contain anything. The awful smoke stench only added to her misery.

She returned to her blanket. Finally sleep settled over her, like falling ash.

Chapter Twenty

Marella dreamed the raft was heading for a whirlpool, but she was too mesmerized to react. Looking into its vortex felt like looking into infinity, and she could only stare into its void with mounting terror. Just when she reached the edge, the raft tipping downward, she woke with a start.

The light in the raft was dull orange. It was morning. Olivia was bent over Elizabeth, holding something silver.

"Hey," said Marella, confused.

Olivia straightened. Her hand closed around the object just as Marella realized what it was: the flash drive with the shutdown program. The world's only hope. The reason they were all out here on a raft in the middle of nowhere. The thing on which their survival depended, contained in a single, compact unit. And Olivia clutched it in her hand.

It took Marella a fraction of a second to understand Olivia was stealing the flash drive. She had bamboozled them all. Put on a show of being a victim. In reality she was dedicated to Preston. Doing his bidding. As evil and devious as he was, if not more so.

Marella jackknifed up.

Startled, Olivia yelped, shoved the flash drive in her pocket, bounded to the raft opening, and tossed the flap upward. Light streamed in, showing that Olivia was wearing her backpack. She glanced back like a suicide jumper on a ledge, a frightened expression on her face.

Elizabeth had warned them that the cold water could steal their ability to swim in ten minutes. Was Olivia trying to kill herself, weighed down by her backpack? Take the flash drive with her to her death? "Olivia, wait. Let's talk."

"Hey!" said Noah.

"What's going on?" asked Elizabeth.

Abruptly Olivia turned and jumped. The raft bounded up and down in reaction.

"Olivia!" In a panic, Marella stumbled to the opening, frustratingly clumsy in the raft. Olivia was already swimming away.

There was no time to think about it. Marella plunged in after her. The ocean encased her body all at once like a suit of frozen armor. She powered forward anyway.

Yet Olivia already had a big lead, streaming forward as if part dolphin. The backpack didn't seem to weigh her down at all. So much salt in the water, probably—Marella too felt lighter in the water.

It was a race now, for Marella to catch her before they both succumbed to hypothermia. The cold was already stiffening Marella's joints.

Suddenly Marella caught a glimpse of a river raft maybe two hundred feet away. Cold gripped her heart, colder than the water. Preston! There was his noble-looking face. He had not only made it to the ocean, but had somehow found them in this great expanse of water. Impossible. Yet there he was.

So this wasn't suicide. This was Olivia bringing Preston the flash drive. A trophy for her master. If this were merely a game, Marella would concede and hope she would be better at a different one. Her opponent was too good.

But there was no giving up, and now fury drove her. Olivia had betrayed them all. She was trying to kill them. Kill everybody. Marella cut through the water, the chill weighing her arms like invisible chains.

She heard Elizabeth and Noah calling for her to come back, the splashing of their paddles in the water. They didn't know Olivia had the flash drive.

Churning through the water, she got close enough for Olivia's kicks to splash water into her face. She stretched with each stroke, finally latching onto Olivia's ankle. She had her. All she had to do was get the flash drive from her pocket.

Olivia turned, clamping onto Marella's arm with unexpected strength. Even though she was younger and smaller, somehow she pushed Marella down. Marella managed to gulp in a big breath just before they went under together.

Get the flash drive, she told herself, fighting to control her panic. The cold made it hard to open her eyes. She did so for a moment, enough to orient herself. With her free hand she reached for Olivia's pants pocket. She shoved her fingers inside and felt something—the flash drive. Yes! She hooked it with her fingers and pulled. It was coming out. She almost had it.

Olivia corkscrewed her hips away. Marella lost hold of the flash drive. No! She peered through the green water and saw it suspended in the ocean. Right there. She could get it. She reached for it.

Olivia wrapped her legs around Marella's torso, forcing air from her lungs. Marella heard her own grunt muted underwater. Bubbles streamed upward. Her lungs filled with fire instead of oxygen. She hammered on Olivia's legs angrily, frustrated when water slowed the motion.

The girl was evil. She refused to die because of her. Reaching out, she grasped Olivia's arm, pulled it to her mouth, and bit down on the firm flesh.

Olivia loosened her legs, pushed away, and kicked toward the surface.

Marella, too, fought her way upward, her lungs about to burst. She broke the surface gasping.

Olivia was there, also gasping. Marella's instinct was to attack and punish her for her deceit. But the flash drive was still somewhere below. She took several catch breaths, then a big one, and dived back down.

Where was it? The cold stabbed her eyes. She turned her head this way and that. Silver fish bulleted back and forth, cluttering the underwater world. They were the same size and color as the flash drive, making the task nearly impossible. Still, Marella scanned the depths, spotting a small object. Was that it? Veering left and kicking downward, she reached out to grasp it. Only a piece of plastic. She had been deceived.

She twisted in place, becoming more frantic. It was here. She had to get it. All was lost if she didn't, but her lungs burned.

She was the wrong person for this. She wasn't capable. And because of that, her mother would die. Her sister would die.

She saw an object the right size. Just another piece of debris, she feared as she kicked towards it. But there it was. The flash drive. Silver, and the blue and purple HemisNorth logo.

And there was Olivia, reaching for it. Marella's lungs were beyond taxed, her limbs leaden from the cold, but she fought through and headed for the flash drive.

Suddenly Olivia pulled back without getting the flash drive. She ran out of air, thought Marella jubilantly, kicking forward. She would win this game after all.

Oddly, the flash drive seemed to be behind a bead curtain, crystalline like the one her mother had lost years ago in a move. But of course it wasn't a curtain. No, she realized, those were tentacles, undulating; above them pulsed a translucent body with orange and yellow innards. A living creature, a massive jellyfish, bigger than she was. It looked deadly. Like it could pull her into its gelatinous body and digest her whole.

The cold had saturated her bones. She could feel herself slowing even more. There was no time to waste—this would be her only chance. But to get the flash drive from its terrible fortification, she risked death.

The choice was anguishing. No choice at all, really. If she didn't get the flash drive, she would die for sure. She had to try.

She kicked forward and thrust her arm among the strings. She closed her fingers around the flash drive. She had it. She possessed the thumb drive! But the triumph was obliterated by the pain searing her arm. The jellyfish had stung her. She was poisoned. She clenched her mouth to keep from screaming.

She kicked away, terrified that the tentacles would bind themselves onto her and pull her in. They must have found her ankles because suddenly they were on fire too. She flogged the water in her desperation to get away.

Breaking the surface, she choked air in, coughing and thrashing, flash drive in hand. She was free from the jellyfish and had saved the flash drive, but what would come next? Paralysis? Death? She floundered forward, somehow making it to the raft and getting hold of the boarding ladder.

Noah yanked her upward. His grip on her forearms felt like slashing swords. She choked and sputtered, moaning with pain. Red welts branched across her arms.

She looked back. Olivia was climbing onto Preston's raft, which was now only fifty feet away.

"Marella." Preston's deep tone was like a sorcerer. Commanding. Frightening. Marella recoiled.

"Creepy bastard," muttered Elizabeth.

Noah sneered. "Let's get out of here."

The two of them snapped up the paddles and got to work. Marella wanted to help but pain kept her huddling in the raft.

A minute later Marella heard a splash like a fish jumping in the water.

"What was that?" asked Elizabeth.

Noah stood, looking back at Preston's raft over the canopy, then dropped back down, speaking quickly. "Slingshot. She's shooting at us."

Marella remembered the slingshot. How easily she had killed the seagull.

"The little bitch," cried Elizabeth. She and Noah paddled furiously.

Marella listened for the sound of a strike. She heard water sloshing. Elizabeth and Noah's alternating exhales.

There was a thunk, then another.

"She hit us!" said Noah.

She heard a sputtering noise. Air escaping. "We're going to sink!" said Marella.

"Calm yourselves," said Elizabeth in a not-so-calm tone. "We have to get out of range before we can patch it, but we've got a little time."

"How much?" asked Noah.

"I don't know, but there's a lot of oomph in this raft. It's not going to be immediate."

A few minutes passed. Then a few more. Were they getting away? She couldn't see.

"What happened to you?" asked Noah.

"Jellyfish," said Marella. "Bigger than me. Orange. Yellow."

Elizabeth sounded troubled. "That would be a lion's mane jellyfish. That's not good. Not good at all."

Noah glanced back at Marella, dismayed. "Will she die?"

Not *will she die*, but *how long will she suffer beforehand*, thought Marella.

"No, but she might wish she had." Elizabeth spoke with rebuke. "Marella, you shouldn't have gone after her. We could have lost you."

"She had the flash drive," said Marella. "I got it back."

Their expressions turned to horror as it sank in. They had almost failed. Elizabeth paused, then quickly resumed paddling. "Oh my god. Thank you."

"It's all wet," said Noah. "It won't work now."

"No, it's waterproof," said Elizabeth.

The leaking raft sputtered like a distant engine. Marella lay shaking so hard the raft trembled. She didn't deserve this. The pain, the fear. None of it.

"Marella!" Though faint, Preston's voice sent a chill down her spine. "I'll find you wherever you are."

Chapter Twenty-One

N oah's voice was strained with dread. "I can't believe I'm going to die over a flash drive."

"She's not trying to kill us," said Elizabeth. "She could have done that while we slept. They want to sink the raft so we'll swim to his."

"We should be able to stay ahead of them," said Noah. "He's got to be tired after all that paddling by himself."

"But how did he catch up to us?" Elizabeth sounded exhausted.

"He gets strength from his belief," said Noah.

"You're a believer too," said Elizabeth. "As am I."

"Yeah, well," said Noah defensively. "It takes a certain kind of crazy to tap into it like he does. The raft is getting soft."

"We might be okay," said Elizabeth. "Each of the rings is manufactured to hold the raft up by itself in case the other one gets damaged."

"Yeah, well, both of the rings are soft."

"We've got a patch kit. Marella can you get your hands on it?"

How could she possibly move? Even breathing was too much motion when the skin on her arms and ankles felt like they'd been flayed. Yet Marella dragged herself to the supplies that had come with the raft. She took a moment to recover from the searing pain, then pawed through the bags until she found the right one. "Got it." She clutched it like a life preserver.

Elizabeth tore through it. "Aha!" She pulled out some tiny orange cones.

"What are those?" asked Noah.

"Leak stoppers." Before Marella knew it Elizabeth had scrambled down the boarding ladder and into the water. Marella's heart skipped a beat as she imagined a giant lion's mane jellyfish lying in wait.

"Be careful," said Noah, also sounding surprised that Elizabeth had gone in so unceremoniously.

Elizabeth's voice came from the other side of the raft. "Bubbles spotted." After a couple of minutes she returned to the raft opening and Noah helped her in.

"I think we're good," said Elizabeth. Then, "My clothes are already starting to dry."

"Mine are dry too," said Noah. "That's ridiculously fast. I don't like it."

Marella's clothes were dry too, but the chill remained. She realized she had been tensing her muscles. She told herself to relax. They wouldn't sink to the bottom of the ocean, not in the next few minutes anyway. Elizabeth and Noah returned to paddling.

Marella's arms and ankles hurt so badly she thought she could hear them sizzle. "I hate that man. I want to tear him apart."

"Later," said Elizabeth. "We'll do it together."

"How did he find us?" asked Noah.

"I don't know," said Elizabeth. "I didn't think he could in this vast ocean, and yet he did. He knew we were headed west. We used the solar lamp last night. He could have seen us then."

Marella's shivering made her voice quake. "I feel stupid for trusting him."

"How could you have done otherwise?" said Noah. "I remember him giving you that water after we first drove up. How kind he was."

"I feel worse for not keeping a closer eye on Olivia," said Elizabeth. "But how was I to know she'd steal from me while I slept?"

After a half hour Elizabeth stood, looking back over the canopy. "I don't see them anymore. Noah, I need your help." She rushed to retrieve an empty jug, filled it with seawater, and handed Noah a credit card. "Marella, sit at the opening of the raft. Noah, scrape her welts with this while I pour water on her."

"You can't be serious," Marella recoiled.

Noah winced. "Can't we just call Telehealth?"

"We have to get the stingers out. Hurry up. She'll only get worse until we do."

Marella straddled the edge of the raft and squeezed her eyes shut. It felt like waiting for a firing squad to shoot. Noah scraped her welts with the credit card as Elizabeth poured water. Marella shouted and writhed.

"It's a platinum card so that's good enough," joked Noah after they'd done each arm and leg, though clearly the process pained him. He retrieved a blanket and wrapped Marella in it as gently as he could.

"You'd better drink," said Elizabeth, holding water up to Marella's mouth. She sipped gratefully.

Noah and Elizabeth resumed paddling the raft westward. Marella lay wheezing, wishing she could fast forward time. By focusing on her breath she somehow got from moment to moment. She gazed up at the orange canopy, saying to herself, *Mind over matter, mind over matter.* She watched Elizabeth and Noah through slitted eyes as they toiled, trying to distract herself with the details that she might someday recount to her family. Elizabeth's shirt, filthy, clinging to her thin body. The Antarctic burn shape on Noah's back, his shirt tatters flapping in the wind. A memory popped in, uninvited. Arguing with Brielle over a shirt she wanted to borrow. It seemed so petty now. Why couldn't she think of something pleasant?

"There's a bunch of debris up ahead," said Noah. "And some blocks that look like white coffins."

The mention of coffins disturbed Marella, and apparently Elizabeth too, because she responded coldly. "They're not. They're polystyrene blocks. They use them for road foundations. Must have spilled off a ship."

They paddled through the debris, with Noah narrating for Marella's benefit. "Boat floats. Plastic hose. Kitchen sink." He looked back to see if she got his joke. She could only smile wanly.

The wind blew harder. A succession of waves gushed in. The salt water felt like knife tips on her skin. Slicing. Gouging.

The water in the raft was ankle-deep in no time. While Noah closed the canopy opening, Elizabeth retrieved the bailer and set to work pumping water.

The raft lifted and dropped forcefully, as if trying to launch itself into the air. The supplies shifted from place to place. Noah wrapped rope around the water jugs to keep them in place, and fished out a seasickness tablet for each of them.

They wedged themselves into the seat straps, careful to lean away from the sides so that the ocean debris couldn't hit them. The jellyfish welts burned like branding irons.

The swells grew steeper. She felt as if she were on a roller coaster cart that had sprung its track and gone rogue. When she was four, she had ridden the Sky Caster, a loop de loop she was too small for. There were sickening moments of weightlessness and the terrifying pull of gravity. She had been sure she would be tossed from the ride. Now she felt the same way, expecting to be ejected into the cold sea any moment. The water that pooled in the bottom of the raft kept rising up as a single wedge to splash her, dousing her face, making her gag, firing up her wounds. Her hair stuck to her face.

"Good time to plan our next theme park visit," said Noah, his voice strained with fear, jerking with the motion of the raft.

Elizabeth seemed too terrified to answer, then finally said, "I'm in."

Marella took a deep breath. *Try to sound brave.* "Is there one called Wet World?"

The raft tilted nearly perpendicular. A water jug escaped from the rope, striking her shin. She howled from both pain and fear. This was it. They were going to overturn. The raft would fill with water. They would be trapped. The irony of it all. She was trying to save the water, and it was water that would kill her. *Please please please.* She sent a prayer into the ether, hoping for once it would be answered. *Don't do this to us.* She strained to keep herself in place, holding her breath as if that could stop the sea's motion.

"Oh my god," said Elizabeth, over and over.

The raft opening's flap suddenly broke open. Cold water slapped Marella in the face.

"That's known as a wake up call," said Noah, reaching over to tie the flap back down.

"I'm awake," said Marella. "It worked."

Chapter Twenty-Two

The storm calmed in the middle of the night. They bailed the water. There was no need for the sponges that came with the raft because the last inch of water dried the rest of the way by itself. Still, it was freezing cold with only the raft bottom between them and the icy ocean. Marella lay shivering.

"Hypothermia is a real threat for all of us, but especially you after your injury," said Elizabeth. "We're going to have to make a Marella sandwich." They both snuggled their bodies against her. She felt their warmth begin to soak in.

"You're shaking like an old-time exercise machine," said Noah.

"The kind with the strap that vibrates the pounds away," added Elizabeth.

Marella was about to say, "Sorry," then remembered not to apologize. "Thank you for warming me up." Her shivering slowed to the occasional shudder. The pain from her stings kept her awake for a time, but eventually she slept.

• • • •

IT WAS MORNING, FIRST light. Elizabeth and Noah rose. Marella sat up, sucking air through her teeth when the skin on her arms and ankles stretched, renewing the pain. Her skin was sunburned now, which added to the irritation.

She pulled herself to the raft opening and looked out at the smoke-fuzzed horizon. No sign of Preston. "It's so calm." Dead fish and a myriad of random trash dotted its surface. Dozens of the polystyrene blocks were scattered everywhere, like an exploded Ziggurat. It smelled like the liquid at the bottom of a garbage can.

Aside from the debris, the surface was so flat it was hard to believe they floated on water. It seemed solid, as if they were embedded in a mirror. Marella felt small and insignificant. A bug carried away by floodwaters.

"Come on, we have to get going." Marella drank deeply. Her mouth felt like a crusty cave no matter how much she drank. She plucked a tin from a box that Olivia had left behind. Sardines. Her stomach rebelled at the thought of eating dead fish. She tossed it back, wolfing down a granola bar instead.

She thrust a paddle in the water, her muscles hardwood-stiff. She hadn't gotten enough sleep. Still, she paddled as if just starting a race. Noah and Elizabeth joining her made it somehow more tolerable.

"I don't understand it," said Elizabeth. "The lack of water in the atmosphere is why it's been so windy. There should be even more wind. And now there's no wind at all."

"It feels bizarre," said Noah. "Like a whirlpool is going to appear any minute and suck us down."

"It's like the doldrums where old-time sailing ships would get stuck," said Marella.

"Yes," said Elizabeth. "The inter-tropical convergence zone, near the equator. I hope it keeps up like this."

"Yeah but didn't it make the sailors go crazy?" asked Marella.

"We're already crazy," said Noah. "You can't go through all this and not be. The only question is, how much crazier are we going to be when all is said and done?"

"It's the smoke in the air that's making me crazy," said Marella. "I'll never complain about rain again."

Marella gazed at a spot where water had splashed onto her arm a couple of minutes earlier, the salt stinging her. The welted skin was no longer wet. She kept having to blink to wet her eyes. "Is it just me or is everything drying even faster now?"

"Definitely faster," said Noah.

"Because we're getting closer to the machine?" asked Marella.

"I don't know." Elizabeth puffed with effort.

"How long would we have before we end up like Victor?" She remembered his head on the desk. The raspy breathing, then silence.

"You're not going to end up like him." Elizabeth sounded testy. "He was there since the start."

"Who's Victor?" asked Noah.

"An employee," said Marella. "He died."

"What, because of Project Athena?" Noah sounded aghast.

"Possibly," said Elizabeth. "But he'd been on the island for quite some time."

"Have you got anything else to tell me about?" asked Noah, aggravated. "Get it all out now. I was never a fan of trickle-down theory."

"That's all there is," said Elizabeth.

"Except..." said Marella.

Noah sounded apprehensive. "Except what?"

"There was a Project Athena prototype in Building C when it exploded, right?"

"Right," said Elizabeth hesitantly.

"You said damaging the big Project Athena would cause a runaway reaction. What about damaging the little one? Would that have also caused a runaway reaction?"

"You don't have to worry about that," answered Elizabeth. "Len and Eshana shut it down."

"When?"

Elizabeth paused before answering. "Just before the explosion."

Cause and effect. A shutdown. An explosion. Marella froze as the ramifications set in. "If using the shutdown program on the prototype triggered the explosion, then we could cause a huge explosion by shutting down the one on the island."

Noah stopped paddling. He stared at Elizabeth intently.

Elizabeth also stopped paddling. She screwed her eyes shut. What did that mean? Was she angry with Marella? Worried she'd hit the mark? "I don't know," she said finally.

"So there's a chance Project Athena could explode after we run the shutdown program?" asked Marella.

"Holy shit." Noah threw his paddle down. "Is this a suicide mission?"

"No," said Elizabeth, seeming to fight to remain calm. "I hope not. But we should be prepared for anything. Even an explosion."

Noah held his hands palm up, yelling, "How big an explosion? Are we talking terrorist attack size? Nuclear bomb size? Or is the whole world going to explode? Now you're adding pyrotechnics and I still don't really understand where the water went."

"I told you," said Elizabeth. "The water molecules are not in our universe. They're not in any universe. Not here, not there."

"I'm not asking for an explanation. I'm asking you stop hiding things."

"You know everything now," said Elizabeth.

Which was that Marella could die saving her family. And then there would be no reunion. No future where the Aguageddon was nothing but a terrible memory. Mom and Brielle would be alone. Marella's thoughts threatened to spiral. She struggled to control them. If she succeeded, they would live. That hadn't changed.

She spoke with resolve. "This is what we know. Elizabeth and I both have to be on the island because the biometrics require two employees. Noah doesn't have be there. If we live, we return with him. If we don't..." her voice caught. "Let's go." She picked up a paddle and shoved it into the water.

She tried to calm her anxiety by thinking of other things. The ocean reflected the red sun. It reminded her of the gray house with the red door that her mother loved because it meant good luck.

There had been lilacs in the yard—white, pink, and dark purple—so many that the scent wafted over the whole yard.

But here it smelled of dead fish, the stink concentrated. Ahead, transparent muck covered the water surface. "Stop!" said Marella, backing away from the raft edge. "Jellyfish." The welts from the lion's mane jelly burned. Noah and Elizabeth also lurched back.

But the raft was already gliding into the muck, which now surrounded them. Elizabeth scooped some of it up with a paddle. The transparent mass quivered like gelatin. "It's not jellies, it's dead fish. Since the ocean is saltier, perhaps. And the ocean pressure is lessening. Some fish explode with no pressure and some don't. They say there are over a million undiscovered species in this zone."

"Yeah, and they're all floating right here." Marella moved to the front of the raft and resumed paddling. Each plunge brought a burst of stink. She felt the paddle click against fish bones.

She noticed her arm was mucky. She brushed at it frantically, suddenly sure that she, too was starting to explode like the fish. It was a momentary confusion, but enough to leave her panting.

"Are you okay?" asked Noah. Before she could answer, a rumbling noise sounded. They froze to listen.

"Sea monsters." Noah was joking, holding up a paddle as if ready to fend them off, but his voice warbled.

"Earthquake?" asked Marella. She scanned for the source, but saw nothing.

Elizabeth's voice was flat, as if she was trying to hold it steady. "The ground is used to having tons more water on it."

The rumbling continued into a crescendo. "I can feel it in my teeth." Marella felt panic bubbling up. "How is that possible through the water?"

"Will there be a tsunami?" asked Noah.

Elizabeth scrutinized the ocean's gray expanse. She spoke quickly, as if to get the words out before being interrupted by a catastrophe. "If a seismic event occurs in the right place, and then it depends on the shape of the ocean floor."

Marella examined the horizon in one direction then another, watching for a killer wave. It could come from anywhere. Danger ahead, danger behind. She started breathing too fast. Dropping down, she pummeled her thighs with her fists, trying to beat her anguish away. Anguish over the constant stink, the constant dread, the constant pain. She wanted so badly to stop fretting over too much water, or not enough. Over injury. Over death. She continued to pound her thighs, over and over. She just wanted it to stop. Let the tsunami come. Let it wash her terror away.

Elizabeth tried calming her with shushing noises. She stroked Marella's hair.

Noah took Marella's fists in his hands. "It's going to be okay. We'll get through this. It's hard, I know. But it's going to be okay." He kept murmuring comforting phrases, his low tones grounding her. Maybe he was right. Maybe it would be okay. Marella's breathing slowed; her fists relaxed into Noah's palms. She glanced up. There were tears of compassion in his eyes.

Marella was grateful Noah was there, and that his attitude towards them had changed. She squeezed his hands back. But then she had a sudden thought.

"What's wrong?" asked Noah. "Are you going to throw up?"

"If the water isn't in our universe, then what's taking its place?" asked Marella. "Wouldn't the atmosphere drop down to where the missing water used to be?"

Noah stared at Marella, mouth open. "Oh my God. That's right. All the water that used to be here where we are now is gone. If the atmosphere drops, there's no oxygen up high, and everybody on Mount Rainier will suffocate. Marella's family is there. And maybe my family and friends. They'll die."

"And if the water level keeps on dropping there will be no more oxygen at sea level—what used to be sea level—either." The panic that had overtaken Marella threatened to return. She took deep breaths. She couldn't lose it like that again. *Breathe. Breathe.*

"I don't know," said Elizabeth. She pinched the bridge of her nose, apparently trying to think it through. "The calculations showed only a negligible drop in the atmospheric level with the data we had. But again, we were working with the wrong data because of Victor. A bigger volume is disappearing than we would have lost if it were just CO_2. The atmosphere lowering to take the water's place—that makes sense. It also explains why the atmospheric pressure isn't crushing us."

Elizabeth looked up, eyes wide in alarm. "It's a real danger. They could all suffocate."

Noah fell onto his knees, clutching his head. "No, no, no. Make it stop. Make it all stop."

Marella was paralyzed, imagining Mom and Brielle suffocating on a mountainside, their chests heaving. Dropping to the ground. Their eyes going blank. Were they already dead?

No. They were alive until she knew otherwise. And as long as there was the tiniest bit of hope she had to keep going. She scooped up a paddle, rushing to the raft opening.

• • • •

HOURS LATER, THEY WERE calmer. Marella and Elizabeth were paddling.

"I can't believe the University of Washington is just gone," Noah's voice warbled with the exertion of pumping the watermaker. "I keep thinking of it as still standing."

"What did you say were you majoring in?" asked Marella.

"Real estate. I want to develop property."

"I didn't know that was a major," said Marella.

"What drew you to that?" asked Elizabeth.

Obviously the money, thought Marella, but Noah's answer wasn't that simple. "I like having something to show for my effort. Developing new buildings, so I can say, 'I did that.' And I want to lift myself up so I can lift up others." Marella thought he meant people of color, but then he added, "Especially people with disabilities."

Elizabeth glanced back at Noah, eyebrows raised. "Because?"

"I have Meniere's disease," said Noah.

Marella had never heard of it. It sounded like "miner." She imagined Noah's lungs black with coal.

"I'm not familiar with that," said Elizabeth.

Noah seemed oddly pleased. "Oh, so there's something you don't know?"

"Just tell me," said Elizabeth sarcastically.

He spoke with a more serious tone. "It's an inner ear disorder that gives you vertigo and hearing loss."

"But you seem okay," said Marella.

"It comes and goes. When I was little, every time I had a hearing screening I was fine. I didn't know what was wrong until I was a teenager. It messed up my childhood. I couldn't always hear teachers. People spoke to me and thought I was ignoring them. They thought I was faking the dizziness, or that I was on drugs. Lucas and Marius were always there for me."

The friends they hadn't gone back to rescue when they were in Elliott Bay. Marella felt a prickling of shame. She'd thought she had Noah figured out. Young black man ready to defend any possibility of injustice to himself, which was understandable because of discrimination he'd endured. Somewhat self-aggrandizing, at times. But there were layers to everybody. Endless layers.

"Are you experiencing any symptoms now?" asked Elizabeth.

"No. I can hear fine. I was dizzy during the storm."

"You didn't say anything," said Marella.

"You couldn't have helped me."

Suddenly the water churned like a pot of water just before boiling, its foam a dirty meringue. Marella stiffened. "Whoa, what's that?" Her first thought was that the tsunami she'd feared was coming. She grabbed the raft strap.

Noah joined them. "I see a fin," said Elizabeth. "And another."

The sea pulsated with animal life, just as it had in the basins of Puget Sound. Not a tsunami, but a different crisis. Marella cried, "We can't be at the bottom of the ocean."

"We better not be," said Elizabeth. "That would mean sea level has dropped another thirteen hundred meters."

"Oh no, there's land!" said Noah, jabbing a finger west towards a trampoline-sized patch of rock rising from the ocean.

"Could be an underwater ridge," said Elizabeth

"Paddle hard," said Noah. "We'll be grounded if we can't get past it. Then we'd have to carry our hundred-pound raft over it."

Marella grunted with each stroke. "How far are we from the island?"

Elizabeth retrieved the GPS. "Twenty miles. We must have gotten lucky with a current, we're closer than we would have gotten just by paddling. Maybe a day by raft or by foot, assuming no obstructions. Four days before the runaway reaction. We'll make it." It sounded like she was trying to convince herself.

"There will be obstructions," said Noah. "It's the Aguageddon."

A hump of land began to rise. Marella stood to get a better view. There were similar humps in every direction. "Left!" she called.

They paddled madly, with no rhythm to their strokes. The splashing water made them squint. To the right more ground appeared, growing, expanding, seeming to come for them, trying to overtake the raft. Marella gasped. "Go, go!"

Noah shouted a battle cry. They passed several mounds, but then more rose, growing into hills.

Like time lapse photography, patches of ocean lowered, then shrank away.

"It's not a ridge," said Marella. "It's the bottom of the Pacific. The water is going away too fast. It'll be gone in no time. This will be the end of everything."

"Maybe it's a plateau," said Elizabeth.

Marella felt the paddle clunk on something hard. "I hit bottom."

"Me too," said Elizabeth.

Her family might already be dead. They were far from the island. They would never make it. She was worn out. Her bones ached as if she was being stretched on a rack. What was the point of even trying to overcome this newest obstacle?

"This can't be happening," said Elizabeth, her voice full of rage.

"Why, why, why?" Noah asked the sky, his tone anguished.

The raft creaked as it settled onto sand. The sudden stillness stirred a feeling in Marella. As if the world itself had stopped turning, and the only way she could get it moving was to get herself moving. Though deathly tired, she couldn't be still. She had to get up, had to run, fight, punch, *something*.

She clawed herself out of the raft and shoved her arms under its edge, struggling to lift it. Noah and Elizabeth followed her lead. Together they raised it, wobbling forward, trying to sync their steps. The awkward position made Marella's back ache. She tried to shift, and dropped her end. She lifted it again, returning to her original posture. Her back would just have to ache. It was the only way.

The shore was now dozens of feet from the raft. Rivulets of water were draining away. Fish flopped all around, some silver, some transparent as glass. A two-hundred-pound halibut lay wrapped in kelp as if to cover its nakedness, mouth opening and shutting uselessly.

With the raft bouncing in their grasp, they tramped over the scum left by the ocean, which looked and smelled like sour turkey gravy.

The minutes passed. The need to move dissipated like a fog. Marella felt her very being start to drain as well, as if it were following the water. Soon it was no longer her carrying the raft. It was a hunk of flesh that used to have hope. The only thing grounding her to that flesh was the pain radiating through her body with each step, each stumble, each breath. She focused on the pain. It was real. She was real.

Keep going. Keep going.

Chapter Twenty-Three

After they'd been so long afloat, Marella was unsteady on her feet, like a sea creature trying to support itself on its own fins.

"Be careful not to snag the ballast bags," said Elizabeth as they crablegged toward the receding water. Debris and flopping fish made them stumble.

"This is a nightmare," said Noah.

We'll never make it, thought Marella. But as long as there was a possibility her family still lived, she had to try.

Noah kicked a crab trap out of the way, his voice tight with exertion. "You'd think there would be less garbage in the middle of nowhere."

Marella tripped over a driftnet, yelping at the pain in her ankle.

"It appears that we have reached the twilight zone," said Elizabeth, grunting with effort.

"Which episode?" asked Noah. "Not the Death Ship, I hope."

"I mean we're thirteen hundred meters deep," said Elizabeth.

"I know what you mean," said Noah. "I'm trying to lighten the mood."

"The Death Ship," said Elizabeth. "That's pretty light."

They scurried between large sand dunes, past construction debris. Rebar embedded in concrete. Metal pipes, PVC pipes, drywall.

"Welcome to the ocean, the world's personal dumping ground," said Noah.

Elizabeth dropped her side of the raft, which forced the others to follow suit. "I can't do this much longer." Elizabeth's voice was breathy with exhaustion.

The ocean continued its escape, receding even further, revealing clusters of rock towers and more piles of flopping fish.

"It's useless," said Noah. "We're going to have to walk the rest of the way to the island."

"We should leave the raft," said Elizabeth. "It's slowing us down."

"How are we going to carry our water?" asked Marella. She answered her own question. "I guess we could cut a piece of the raft. Drag the bottles along on it."

"That would be difficult," said Elizabeth. "It would still be a chore. Getting it past the garbage."

"What if we made a sled?" Marella nudged a piece of PVC pipe.

"Not with that," said Noah. "The open end will catch on the sand. I think I see something we can use." Noah trotted over and picked up a double metal railing that curved at the end. "Look at this. It's perfect. Like God put it here for us to find." His voice had a tinge of awe. Marella could see why. It was a big coincidence that this type of debris was here with exactly the piece they needed. Marella envied him his belief. That he knew somebody high up was watching over him. She couldn't be sure that a divine being had dropped the railing in their path; still, she was relieved to have such a handy solution.

"Let's hop to it then," said Elizabeth firmly, using the same voice she used at the end of meetings when she ordered everybody to work on their action items.

They loaded their water jugs, a carton of canned food, the watermaker, blankets, and other supplies onto the makeshift sled. Noah tied on the rope that had come with the raft and insisted on taking the first turn pulling.

The terrain became rugged. They circled around ridges that curled upwards like petrified waves. After an hour Marella said, "That's a ravine ahead. You both rest for a minute. I'm going to climb those rocks and see how to get past it." It would be hard with an injured ankle, and she wasn't sure how to dredge up the energy for such a task. She could have asked one of them to do it, but Noah had been pulling the sled and Elizabeth was drooping with fatigue. Besides, not being able to see ahead, she felt trapped like a mouse in a maze. She needed to rise above.

Marella stepped carefully onto the pink-splotched rocks, avoiding coral and other blobby growths. She climbed, ankle throbbing, the wind biting her skin, until she was two stories high. A maze of stone and ravine stood between them and the ocean, but she could see a good route with a smooth alleyway of sand. "Veer left. It opens up that way."

They got past the ravine. Another hour went by as they hauled the sled through uneven terrain. Marella took a turn pulling. It was unwieldy, but better than carrying everything.

"Mush, mush!" joked Noah.

"My lungs feel like sandpaper," said Marella.

"Those rocks look like Easter Island statues," said Elizabeth.

"They're guarding their territory," said Noah.

Marella looked at them anew. The hollows like eyes. It felt like being watched. Marella wished Elizabeth hadn't said anything. Things were too fantastical out here. As if they traveled within a myth, where such things could come to life. She leaned into the rope, staring at the sand, thankful for the appearance of a dented cola can. Something normal. Just litter at the side of a road.

They lumbered through sandy desert punctuated by stone slabs and layered with dead fish that were all either white or rotting their color away; the stink coated the inside of her nose.

"Someday I'm going to own a helicopter," Noah gazed at the smoky sky as if one were on its way.

So he still had hope. That was good, thought Marella. She examined herself for hope as well. It was there. Barely.

The sled crossed streamers of green-brown kelp, reminding her of finger paintings Brielle made when she was three years old, never happy until she had zigzagged her fingers through the entire, gloppy mess. The kelp crackled with each step.

She created a fantasy of Brielle waiting for her on Wisdom Island, arms crossed, foot tapping, pretending to be annoyed because Marella was taking so long. It gave her fuel she didn't know she had. *Get to Brielle*, she told herself with each step. It became a marching mantra. *Get to Brielle. Get to Brielle.*

The ground rumbled as if their passage disturbed it. Marella started, looking every which way.

"Another earthquake?" asked Noah, his question answered by shaking before he finished the words. They dropped to the sand. The pulses seemed to sync with her heartbeat, which terrified her. It was as if the earthquake had entered her body to wreak its havoc from the inside. She would have thought they were safe out in the open where nothing could crash onto their heads, but it felt as if the ground would split at any moment to swallow her whole.

When the motion stopped, the earth groaned twice in a kind of curtain call, and then all was silent. She remained kneeling though something hard dug into one knee. Was the earthquake really done or was that the precursor to worse?

They lurched to their feet and continued, up a colossal dune. It smelled like vinegar, which she used to clean the bathroom mirror. At home Mom refused to use store-bought cleaning products, the kind that HemisNorth manufactured.

Bleached coral sprang randomly from the sand like misshapen bones. The beauty of it surprised her, lifting her spirits. "Those are like the Chihuly glass sculptures at Benaroya Hall."

"You go to the symphony?" asked Elizabeth, surprised.

"Field trips," said Marella, annoyed at Elizabeth's implication she had no culture, and annoyed at herself that it mattered. Who cared, when the world could end? "Anyway you can see them through the windows from Third Avenue. I mean, before the fire."

"Downtown Seattle," said Noah. "People walking on sidewalks, cars driving by. It all seems like a former life."

It was. And they would never have it back again even if they stopped the Aguageddon.

She could no longer see the water ahead of them. A sense of loss lay over her like a shroud. Nothing would be the same. So many people dead. The rest would be fighting over whatever reserves of water remained. What did that mean for Mom and Brielle? How could they possibly be alive?

And yet, people survived disasters.

But there was still a big unknown: when they shut down the machine would the water come back, or would Earth be left with a fraction of what it had before?

Marella stepped over what might have been a bike handle. Her ankle twinged and complained. The jellyfish welts were getting better, but the injury she'd gotten while falling in the grocery store was worsening. It didn't flex well, forcing her into a stiff, Frankenstein gait.

"I keep thinking about my uncle," said Noah. "He used to watch me and my brothers race. It's like I can hear his voice now. "Fire up the burners! Fire up the burners!"

"It helps to have something to keep you moving," said Elizabeth. "I've been playing the 1812 Overture in my head. The part with the cannons."

"Is that what they played at your high school prom?" asked Noah.

"Very funny," said Elizabeth. "The interesting thing about ageism is that those who commit it will someday experience it."

"Only if they're lucky," said Noah.

"You know, Noah, you remind me of my ex-husband," said Elizabeth.

He grimaced. "Sorry to hear that."

"I didn't mean it like that," said Elizabeth. "He's...quick-witted, let's say. I'm worried sick about him. Him and his whole damn family."

"Oh," said Noah, nodding off kilter, like a bobble-head doll.

Before the Aguageddon Marella hadn't known much about her boss. She had felt too much like a peon to get to know her on a personal level. Now Marella kept seeing her human, vulnerable side, as opposed to her composed corporate image. It was a shame it had taken a disaster for that to happen.

They took a quick break to eat chicken noodle soup from the can and drink water. The ocean was invisible, somewhere beyond a plain strewn with thousands of colorful objects. At first Marella mistook them for tropical fish gone astray. Then she saw they were flip-flops.

"A gyre must have put them in our way," said Elizabeth, exasperated.

"Or God," said Noah.

"Or God," agreed Elizabeth.

Marella imagined God—the traditional western bearded man in a robe—directing a dump truck to this spot and directing it to spill its load. Then picking out a pair of flip-flops for himself.

They trod on top of them, pulling the sled as best they could.

"When I was a kid we called those thongs," said Elizabeth.

"So when I'm your age, they'll call thongs flip-flops," said Marella.

"And what will flip-flops be called?" asked Noah.

"Cheap footwear that's in my way," said Elizabeth, yanking the sled to get it unstuck.

Finally they reached bare sand, which had dried so quickly that the foot-long worms that burrowed beneath also dried up. The wind blew away their sand shrouds, revealing fossil-like bodies. Fish bones also jutted from the sand, as did the occasional shell.

"Sharp shell shard, sharp shell shard, sharp shell shard." Noah said, tripping over his tongue. They passed a cracked bucket, and thousands of drinking straws that were scattered like pickup sticks.

Everything that touched the air felt drier. Skin, eyes, sinuses, mouth. How would it be when they got to the island? Would the machine damage her the way it had Victor? How much time would she have on Wisdom Island before she could no longer recover from its effects? She licked a crack in her lips and pressed them together. *Don't think about it. Move forward.*

Wind gusts blew the flour-fine sand and rubbish into their faces without warning, irritating the sunburn on Marella's face. "The sand is getting weird. It has colored bits and smells like plastic."

"Because of the microparticles that used to be suspended in the ocean," said Elizabeth. "They've settled here."

Marella covered her mouth and nose with a t-shirt. Squinting, she blinked dust from her eyes. "I feel like there should be an oasis, with palm trees and water springs and camels."

"Well," said Elizabeth, "there's the way things are supposed to be. And there's the way things are."

"Smell that?" asked Noah. "There's a big mess ahead. I know, because I'm becoming a connoisseur of rotten."

"A sommelier of stink," said Elizabeth.

"Yeah, that," agreed Noah.

The ground in front of them was mottled white, like a cake frosted while still warm. "See, I was right," said Noah.

"More exploded sea life," said Marella.

"Lovely," said Elizabeth wearily.

Oddly shaped mounds rose above the muck like giant heads. "Brain coral," announced Elizabeth. "It's not supposed to exist this deep."

Marella didn't like the look of them. They felt like a warning. As if any hapless humans wandering by would be trapped and buried up to their ears, their skulls opened up to reveal the inner workings of their minds.

They walked ankle deep in the muck, stepping over fish ribs, fish spines, and fish jaws stuffed with needle-sharp teeth. Marella feared it would deepen and she would flounder like she had in the fish guts, but as they trekked, the muck dried. "It's like walking on rice crackers."

Wind gusts ballooned their clothing, including the t-shirt covering her mouth and nose. She tucked it into her collar and leaned into the wind, determined not to let it slow her down.

Beyond the valley, frayed rope strands waved like fingers in the wind. A buoy tilted like a roly-poly toy with the bigger wind gusts.

She spotted a kitchen sink lodged half in, half out of the sand, the faucet curved in an upside-down "J." For a fraction of a moment she felt giddy. A source of water!

But even as she trudged up to it she knew that her brain betrayed her by allowing her such an irrational thought. She reached down to turn the cold water handle anyway. Nothing happened. A sense of betrayal filled her. She deserved a miracle. She deserved water from an unconnected faucet.

A dried white shrimp body fell from the faucet to the sand. Marella jumped, startled.

"Don't leave the water on," Noah called back, already twenty feet ahead.

"My bad," said Marella. She bent and tightened the faucet, out of a superstitious feeling that if she didn't she would be furthering the Aguageddon.

Elizabeth looked back at her with a sad expression. Feeling like she'd disappointed her in some way, Marella ran to catch up. When she did, the wind died down.

"You turned off the wind," said Noah. She'd gotten her miracle, but the wrong one.

After a while, Marella glanced back at the faucet, already small against the landscape.

"Let's move it!" said Noah. "We have to get there before we all dry up and blow away."

She imagined the blood drying in her veins, the red blood cells flattening to the consistency of dried jellyfish. Her muscles shrinking to cords. Her brain contracting to the size of a walnut and rolling around in her skull. It made her think of a song, but she couldn't remember the lyric. How much of that memory loss was fatigue and how much was from getting closer to the machine?

"Damn," said Marella.

"What?" asked Noah.

"I can't look anything up without my phone working. I'm stuck with what I know."

"And with what I know. Go ahead. Ask me."

"What comes after, "I've hit bottom, I'm at the end of the road?"

"Hmm," said Noah, "I don't know that one. How about this?" He began singing *It's a Wonderful World*. None of it was true. There were no skies of blue, no red roses, no trees of green. But Noah's voice, though scratchy from desiccation and smoke damage, was comforting. While he sang, she floated above her pain. For just a little while their desperate situation was fuzzy around the edges.

They passed an outcropping covered with cream-colored growths the size of serving bowls.

"Goblet sponges," said Elizabeth.

"It looks like a table set for dinner," said Noah.

They crested another dune. Ahead was a forest of rock towers and arches, as tall as skyscrapers and packed too tightly together, as if somebody had plucked all the landscape formations from the States of Arizona and Utah and deposited them in one place.

"Incredible." Noah spoke with awe.

"I've never seen such a thing," said Marella.

Elizabeth sounded perplexed. "I've gone rafting in the Grand Canyon. It's narrow like this...but this is so much stranger."

As they got closer, Marella became edgy. Large rocks were wedged in gaps high above them. Arches were shot through with cracks. "It looks dangerous."

"So precarious," said Noah. "I don't see how they're still standing."

"If the currents ate away softer stone, that would leave the hard stone to create these configurations. They must be sturdier than they look." Elizabeth didn't sound convinced by her own words.

When they reached the towers, Marella had to strain her neck to see their tops. "Can we really get through? It's only as wide as an alleyway between some of these. It might get narrower further on."

"Those bulges look like they could break off and drop on us," said Noah.

"I don't see any way around." Elizabeth got her phone from her bag. "But the GPS won't work in there. We won't have line of sight to a satellite. I've got a smidgen of battery left on my phone. My compass app should get us through."

Still, none of them made a move to enter the strange place. Marella gazed right and left. The towers seemed to go on forever in either direction. She rubbed her temples. *Think. There must be a better way. A workaround.*

"Abandon all hope, ye who enter here," said Elizabeth.

"Isn't that on the entrance to Hell?" asked Noah.

"Oh, you've been there?" asked Elizabeth.

Noah guffawed mirthlessly. "I'm there now."

Marella thought Hell could take on many forms. There was the fiery hot version of Seattle ablaze, and the fortress-like version in front of her. In either one, demons lurked. "You two aren't making this any easier."

Should they have gone a different way, taken a different turn? She looked back to the east. Saw movement in the distance. Was that a person? And another? Her back prickled. How could it be? She grabbed onto Elizabeth's arm. "I think I see Preston and Olivia."

Noah whirled. "That's not possible. How would they find us?"

Elizabeth tensed. "I don't believe it. The chances are one in a million. Yet who else could it be?"

"It's them. It's definitely them," said Noah.

"Let's go." Marella picked up the sled strap, took a breath as if to go underwater, and plunged into the forest of rock.

Chapter Twenty-Four

Noah and Elizabeth followed Marella between the towers. Abruptly, all was cool and dark. The feeling she had earlier of being a mouse in a maze returned. She glanced upward and around as she rushed forward.

"This is freakish," said Noah. "And it smells so bad I can taste it."

"I feel like I'm on another planet," said Marella.

"Yet even here there's random trash to remind us we're on Earth," said Elizabeth, bypassing a plastic thermos and a dock cleat.

"At least it's not as hot," said Noah.

"I don't like those." Marella pointed at white blobs that hung on the tower formations. They glowed as if acid-filled and sagged as if they would drop at any moment.

"I can't identify them." Elizabeth huffed as she ran. "Steer clear."

White worms also hung from the tower walls, wriggling like medusa hair. "Not going near those either," said Noah.

Marella imagined the formations toppling on her, entombing her. Fear corseted her chest, stealing what little breath she had. She didn't know how to force herself onward, but she knew she must.

"This better not be a dead end," said Noah.

The formations creaked like the settling of an old house. The space between them narrowed to ten feet, turning it so dark that Elizabeth and Noah were merely shapes. The worms glowed eerily, curling and uncurling like ghostly fingers gesturing for her to come. She cowered, running in a crouch.

This was hopeless. They would reach a dead end. Then what? She fought a feeling of claustrophobia. It was hard enough to breathe already without buying into the fear. Instead she focused on the fact that Elizabeth and Noah were there too. They had each other. One plus one plus one equaled more than just three. She listened to their labored breathing and followed Elizabeth's directions to turn this way and that.

"It's getting harder to see," said Noah.

"Let's hold off on lights as long as we can," said Elizabeth. "We don't want Preston and Olivia to find us. Just watch your step."

A rumbling started up. They froze.

"Earthquake coming," said Noah, his words clipped.

"Please, not here, not now." Marella felt Noah's hand on her arm. She was grateful for the gesture.

"Drop and cover." said Elizabeth. Marella and Noah did as told, throwing their arms over their heads.

The shaking started abruptly. It felt as if the ground was being lifted and dropped, over and over. Bits of grit fell on her, stinging her skin like bees. Something dropped sharply onto her leg. She yelped, curling into a tight ball.

The rumbling's source seemed to come from far below. From the underworld. She imagined demon hordes pounding drums, the details much too vivid in her mind. Their skin garnet red and slug-slimy. It seemed as if the weight of the water had previously held the underworld door closed, but now it was flung open, the inhabitants marching upward.

Marella clutched at handfuls of sand, desperate to flee. She knew from experience that would be the wrong choice. As a child, when she'd run away from her dead father, she'd been lost for three days. But it was hard not to scramble forward, even while the earth shook. The details of her imaginary demons had only become more real in her imagination over the years. The teeth more sharp, the growls more vicious. And now it was as if she could smell their stink. Marella dug her fingers deeper into the sand. *There are no demons.*

There was a dull noise, and then grinding sounds. Something hit Marella sharply on the back, making her jerk. Something else fell beside her. It sounded like a shovel striking dirt. Like the start of a grave being dug. Soon she would be buried. Buried alive. More debris fell. She shook it off frantically, praying. *Keep us safe. Help us get through this.*

Finally it quieted. Marella took a deep breath, then held it when Elizabeth let out a moan. "I'm stuck." Her voice was ragged.

Noah shined his phone's light and they scrambled to her. Marella gasped at the sight. Chunks of tray-sized rock had fallen onto her, so many they would have to dig her out.

They rushed to toss away the pieces. As they did, she flashed back to a house her mother rented that had a pile of broken concrete chunks in the yard. Her family had used them to build a raised garden bed, in which they planted sunflower seeds. They hadn't even sprouted before Mom moved them to a new home. She hoped that Elizabeth wasn't hurt badly. That this task wasn't just as futile as the garden bed.

They pulled the last chunks off of Elizabeth. Noah shined the phone light along Elizabeth's skin. There wasn't as much blood as Marella expected, just a splotch on her arm.

"Can you get up?" asked Noah.

Elizabeth moved her legs. Her face scrunched with pain. "My stomach. Can't move."

A sea snake of anger wove its way through Marella's body. She'd prayed to keep them all safe, and it hadn't worked, as if God, like the GPS, needed line of sight to perform. So they were left to their own devices in this hell of a place. Abandon all hope my ass. She wasn't going to let God's inability or unwillingness—whichever it was—stop her. She would get through Hell and out to the other side, one way or another.

"Lift her onto the sled." She rushed to position their supplies so Elizabeth could lie on them as comfortably as possible, turning the bottles and jugs sideways and padding them with the blanket.

Elizabeth moaned as they moved her. She seemed so light, as if her injuries had taken a part of her away. The term will-o'-the-wisp came to mind. Perhaps she was always that lightweight, Marella thought. She had only given the impression of being larger than life.

As Noah pulled the sled, Marella skittered ahead shining a light, clearing debris out of the way, heartened by her own determination. They would get Elizabeth to the island whatever it took. She whispered, "It's going to be okay." When they jostled the sled, Elizabeth groaned. "Sorry," said Marella.

"Never apologize," said Elizabeth. A good sign. She was still educating them. Still, it was slow going.

"Are we headed the right way?" asked Noah.

Marella checked Elizabeth's compass app. "Yes."

After an hour, it was lighter ahead. Marella's spirits rose. They would soon be out of this oppressive place. When they trudged abruptly out into the open it was liberating to be free of the imposing formations, yet at the same time she felt horribly exposed.

In the brighter light Elizabeth looked much worse than Marella hoped, draped like a rag doll over the sled. Now there was blood in the corner of her mouth. Her arm hung wrong. Her breathing was shallow.

Elizabeth could die, realized Marella, unless they got her to a hospital. It felt like a stab in the gut. Like fate had made her get close to somebody she ordinarily wouldn't have, only to snatch her away.

A memory came to mind. Elizabeth in a conference room with Marella, combing through a biology report, her face scrunched in concentration as she explained how to tighten the text and make it understandable. "Don't use the word 'utilize.' It's technospeak for 'use.' It means exactly the same thing."

Belinda had tornadoed in. "Elizabeth, can I get your help with something?"

"I'll be done in about ten minutes," Elizabeth responded.

At the time, Marella interpreted it as a bit of a power play—putting the CEO off for something that wasn't critical. Only now did Marella realize the truth. To Elizabeth, teaching Marella had been that important. Because she cared about Marella's future.

Aside from her feelings, there were other reasons she couldn't lose Elizabeth now. They needed two employees to pass the biometric screen, and Marella had her doubts about using Victor as the second employee. Also, a hitch could arise on the island that only Elizabeth could solve. The computer systems at HemisNorth were quirky. There was always something you had to know to get them to work. Some setup that had to be bypassed. A folder filed in a less than obvious location. Elizabeth had praised Marella for her workarounds, but Elizabeth had plenty too. All her sayings about teamwork were true. It took more than one mind to solve some problems.

As they plodded too slowly west, the towers shrank in the distance. The smoky sky swirled like spoiled broth. There was no sign of Preston and Olivia. Yet.

She thought about how prepared they had been. How unprepared she was for these events. "I should have learned more," said Marella.

"About what?" asked Noah.

"About everything. First aid, so I could help Elizabeth. Flying a helicopter. We could have avoided all this. Computers and physics. Who knows what I'll need to know when we get to Project Athena?"

Noah tilted his head in a maybe-so, maybe-not gesture. "You can't learn everything."

"But I could have learned a lot more."

Noah sighed. "Me too, I guess. But I was trying. I was really trying."

• • • •

IT WAS NEARLY SUNSET. They'd traveled for hours, pulling the sled mostly uphill, which slowed them even more. They looked back constantly, worried that Preston and Olivia had made it through. Occasionally Noah murmured encouragement to Marella or Elizabeth, which no longer buoyed her after Elizabeth coughed up more blood. Maybe Marella didn't know much about medicine, but she at least knew that something inside Elizabeth was bleeding. Something they couldn't access to fix.

At first Elizabeth had enough strength to bolster them by telling them that steeper terrain meant they were closer to the island. Later, she didn't have the stamina to speak. She couldn't lift her own hand. Her eyes had a glassy look. They lifted her from the sled to the ground and draped the blanket over her.

"Not going to make it," said Elizabeth weakly.

The words filled Marella with despair. If Elizabeth didn't try to fight through it, then she would surely die, and things would be bleak beyond measure. What words would uplift her? What would convince her to rally? She floundered, then remembered Elizabeth's own words to her. "You can make it. I have every faith in you."

"Can we do anything to make you more comfortable?" asked Noah, sounding stricken.

Elizabeth ignored the question, whispering, "You have the flash drive still?"

Marella nodded.

"Remember the username and password?" asked Elizabeth.

"Project Athena, Hemi$phere180, the 's' is a dollar sign. But it might not work without you. We need two employees for the biometrics. You have to push through. You have to live."

When Marella first met Elizabeth, she knew her new boss would become an important figure in her life, but never dreamed how much. Together they had survived against terrible odds. Escaping the women with the guns who were robbing a line of cars on

FifteenthAvenue. Enduring the storm in the raft. Sharing stories of their difficult childhoods. Even before that, she had been a constant teacher and mentor. While she'd only known her boss six months, that was twice as long as she'd known most people in her life.

Marella felt as if a piece of herself was shearing off, falling to the ground.

Elizabeth moved her fingers. Marella took her hand. Elizabeth screwed her eyes shut. Marella had the odd feeling that Elizabeth was trying to transfer all her knowledge into Marella through her touch.

Marella tried to be stoic. To appreciate the time she'd had with her. Instead she felt as if her stomach had turned to stone.

Elizabeth opened her eyes. "You and Noah will have to save humanity."

"That's above my pay grade," said Marella.

Elizabeth smiled. It looked angelic. She soaked the image in. That was the picture Marella wanted to keep always. Tears fell, drying halfway down her cheeks.

"Take my watch," said Elizabeth. "Make sure you get there in time."

Marella started to protest, then decided against it. She took the watch, slipping it on her own wrist.

"How much time is there?" asked Elizabeth.

"Four days and..." Marella glanced at the dial, "four hours."

Elizabeth had a long coughing spell. Blood colored the corner of her mouth. "Remember your promise. Don't let me die alone."

The request was jolting. She'd only made the promise to get Elizabeth off the subject of death. At the time, it hadn't seemed necessary. In retrospect, it seemed prophetic.

"Tell me," said Elizabeth. "You won't let me die alone."

As a child Elizabeth had been alone, afraid she would turn to dust. Of course she wouldn't put her through that again. "I won't," said Marella.

The distress must have shown on Marella's face, because Elizabeth said, "I'm sorry."

At that, Marella clenched her arms to her sides to keep from breaking down. Elizabeth, who always said, "Never apologize," was doing just that. It was close to the end.

Elizabeth became too weak to talk. Marella tried to give her water, but she wouldn't respond.

"I don't think it will be long now," said Noah.

"Maybe she just needs rest," said Marella, knowing she was grasping at straws.

Noah brushed a strand of hair from Elizabeth's face, then put his head in his hands. "No, She's done in this world. This is such a hard part. Waiting for it to happen."

"You've been through this before?" asked Marella.

Noah spoke sadly. "A grandmother and an uncle."

Marella hung her head. There was no hope for Elizabeth. Her friend—yes, friend—would die. She wasn't going to reach the island alive.

After a time Noah spoke. "This is really hard for me to say," he took a deep breath, then blew it out slowly. He looked at the sky, then the ground. "We're going about half the speed we would be. We can't afford that."

"What are you telling me?"

"I'm saying that in the morning we might have to leave her behind. Even if she hasn't died yet."

The thought pained Marella's heart. "We can't do that. We need her for the biometrics."

"She's not going to make it to the island alive. And you said there was another employee there. Victor. The biometrics will work for him."

"You heard her. She asked me not to let her die alone. It was the thing she feared the most."

"I get that. Nobody would want that. Still." He raised a hand, gesturing west. The direction of their goal. Wisdom Island. "We're going way too slowly."

"That was to keep from hurting her," said Marella, hearing the desperation in her own voice. "Now she's in a coma we can speed up."

"We won't be able to. It's getting harder and harder. That machine is doing something to me. I can feel it. Every extra pound makes a difference."

She shivered. He was right. Fatigue dragged her down, but there was more. It was as if she struggled against an invisible force. Even at first, pulling Elizabeth's hundred-and-something extra pounds felt like playing tug-a-war with an elephant. It had been hard enough this far. It would get even harder.

They couldn't risk billions of lives for a single promise. But it tore at her. Elizabeth's words replayed themselves in Marella's mind with an insistent tone. *Don't let me die alone. Don't let me die alone.*

"It's probably moot," said Marella despondently. "I don't think she'll live much longer."

She removed her boots carefully. Edie had given her these when she'd lost her shoes in the fish muck. What would happen to her Baby Faith now that they were left behind? She rewrapped the ace bandage on her ankle.

Noah removed his shoes gingerly as well. They could add blisters to their long list of physical pains. It was a small thing compared to Elizabeth's impending death, but each added trauma was exponential, making it that much harder to endure.

The heat of the day lasted into the night, and there was no need for them to huddle against Elizabeth to keep her warm. Marella should have been relived. She wouldn't wake up with a corpse in her arms. She felt nothing but sorrow.

The sunset was like an iron door shutting in the distance.

• • • •

IN THE MORNING, MARELLA woke before Noah. When she sat up, he didn't stir. She didn't want to be the one to find Elizabeth dead, but she was the first to wake. She would have to muster the courage to check.

A few feet away, Elizabeth lay still, dried blood on her nostrils. Marella leaned closer; she was breathing. Still alive, but barely.

It was a relief of sorts, but not a good thing, in the end. They would have to leave her here. The chance that she would wake up and find herself abandoned was miniscule. Yet even a tiny chance was too much.

She remembered the terror of being alone in the woods, of thinking she would never see another human being again. That would be Elizabeth's fate. It would be evil to knowingly subject her to that.

There was no question of taking her with them. They couldn't. She knew she would barely be able to get herself to the island, her muscles felt so weak.

But another option stole its way into her thoughts. A horrifying option. One she wished she hadn't conceived of. One she would never have considered had Elizabeth not been fearful of dying alone.

Marella had once worked in a warehouse. A pest control company had deployed glue traps: hand-size plastic trays, each with a strong adhesive layer. A rat had stepped on one and was stuck fast. Her co-workers found it, still alive, struggling so hard that it had torn off whole chunks of fur and skin yet couldn't get free. It was going to die from its wounds, but it would be a long and painful death. Her co-workers seemed incapable of action. They could only gawk, horrified by its suffering.

"Put the poor creature out of its misery," somebody said, but nobody moved to do so until Marella filled a bucket with water and dropped the rat into it, still stuck to the glue trap. She left, not wanting to watch its death struggles, but came back later to throw the dead rat into the garbage.

Her actions had been logical. At the time, she couldn't help being a little proud of her fortitude. She hadn't wanted to, but she had stepped up and done the difficult deed. Still, she was left with uneasiness. Why was she able to kill the rat when others couldn't? Was it some sort of failure of conscience?

She looked west for a sign of the island, but there was only sand, with a few rock slabs rising from the landscape. There was so far to go.

She glanced at Noah. He was still fast asleep a few feet away. She rose, kneeling beside Elizabeth. Her breathing was light, almost nonexistent.

How could she even consider doing what she was about to do? Could she really follow through with something so unthinkable, so final?

One life versus seven billion lives.

With assisted suicide, a doctor had to be involved and the dying person had to not only agree to it, but also do the deed herself. There were no doctors here, and Elizabeth was beyond all that. Her directive, however, had been more than clear. "Don't let me die alone."

"Elizabeth," said Marella in her ear, so as not to wake Noah. "Elizabeth? Elizabeth?" She nudged her. There was no response.

Slowly, deliberately, Marella reached out. Her heart was racing. Was she really going to do this with Noah lying asleep right over there? With one hand she pinched Elizabeth's nostrils together and with the other she covered her mouth. Elizabeth's lips felt dry and cracked.

You can't do this. You can't take a life. Stop now. But if she let go to reconsider, she knew she wouldn't be capable of trying again.

That would be impossible. Continuing was also impossible. It was too final. It would bring demons.

She rocked with anguish but kept her hands clamped onto Elizabeth's face. After what might have been half a minute Elizabeth went into a weak seizure, her body fighting for air. She almost hoped Elizabeth would be strong, that she would come out of the coma and force Marella's hands away. Ridiculously, Marella imagined saying, "I'm sorry," and Elizabeth telling her not to apologize.

But Elizabeth didn't wake. Her body's reaction was mild, so there was no hope of failure. Marella was about to succeed at a goal she would never have set for herself. Killing another person. But it wasn't murder. It wasn't. It couldn't be. Marella was a virtuous person. This was trying to do good.

Marella glanced over at Noah. Still asleep.

The seizure continued. A weak struggle for life. *Lie still. Please lie still.* Marella herself began to shake with anguish. She was actually killing another human being. Because she cared for her—yes, that was true. Again she imagined herself abandoned in this wasteland, dying alone; the sadness of it overwhelmed her. She could feel the terror Elizabeth would experience upon waking and finding that they'd abandoned her. She couldn't let her go through that. This was more merciful.

The longer the seizure lasted, the harder it was for Marella to continue. She would remember this always. Remember snuffing out a person's life. Remember Elizabeth convulsing under her hands. Again Marella looked over at Noah, almost hoping that he would wake up so she would have to stop. But he was motionless, in contrast to Elizabeth's shuddering.

Elizabeth's eyes opened. Marella gasped. But her boss's eyes didn't focus. She wasn't awake. She didn't see Marella. *Put the creature out of her misery. Put her out of her misery. Out of her misery. Misery. Misery. Misery.*

Finally Elizabeth lay still. Was she dead? Marella kept her hands in place to be sure, but began envisioning spike-tooth demons howling with pleasure at this phenomenal crime. She tore her hands from Elizabeth's face and backed away.

Her thoughts went in circles. *What have I done?* Then: *How could I know life would bring me to this?* Then: *You never know what you're capable of.* And then back to: *What have I done?*

Her hands burned from Elizabeth's blood and spittle. She wiped them frenziedly with sand. Bits of grit stuck to her palms. She tried to wipe them away, but only succeeded in gathering new grit. Why wouldn't they dry? Everything else did. It seemed to prove that she would never erase the deed.

Now she stood and walked three steps, then back, then away again, holding her hands out as if they weren't part of her. Her appendages had committed the crime, not her. Burying her mouth in the crook of her arm, she allowed herself to sob silently.

Finally she returned and stared at Elizabeth's lifeless body. She no longer seemed real. It was as if she had been replaced by a life-size doll. Her soul had vanished. Or was it "not here and not there" like the water?

Marella looked east at the horizon from which they'd come. Innocent people had died in the disaster. Yet she lived on.

She knew now what she didn't understand back when she'd killed the rat. She was guilty not just of killing it, but of being capable of killing it. And the same held true now. She'd always had it in her. Whether she'd killed or not, she would always have been guilty. But wouldn't anybody be capable, under the right circumstances? Her thoughts flipped like stranded fish, alternately condemning her crime and justifying it.

Guilt was good, she told herself. It meant she wasn't a psychopath. But now it threatened to overcome her, and she couldn't let it, because then Noah would find out. She couldn't bear his judgment.

Her imagination kept conjuring demons. Why was she terrified of something she didn't believe in? She needed more time to cope with what she'd done, but didn't have it. Instead, she put up a wall in her mind. Against guilt, against sorrow, against all feeling. Against thoughts of demons, and thoughts of Hell. It was the only way to go on.

That done, she trudged over to Noah, woke him, and pointed at Elizabeth's body, unable to speak.

He leaned up on his elbow and saw that Elizabeth was dead. He went closer, reached out to touch her, then didn't. He began crying, deep sobs that threatened to tear down the wall Marella had erected, but she shed no more tears. The wall held for now. She half expected him to notice this and become suspicious. He only said, "At least she went peacefully."

They pushed sand over her, burying her quickly, then started west, dragging the sled.

Marella left the dead woman behind, but her crime accompanied her. She would wear it always, like a second skin.

Chapter Twenty-Five

Noah pulled the sled, which hissed like a sleigh on a sandscape so white with salt it seemed like Antarctica. There were no plastic bags. No coral, no driftwood, no dead fish. Just the flat dried undersea hooded by a smoke-hazed sky.

"It's taking so long," said Marella. "We only have three days left."

"We're ten miles from the island. We'll get there."

Eight jugs of water remained. She drank regularly, making sure to stay hydrated. Although thankful for Noah's presence she felt helpless without Elizabeth. She thought of her trudging alongside, pulling the sled, as strong as Marella even at her age. She missed her more than she ever imagined missing a person who wasn't family. The guilt of the mercy killing pushed at the wall Marella had built, threatening to burst free.

"It seems like this just goes on forever," said Noah. "It's so strange. It feels like we're the only people left alive. And it's so hot."

"Yeah, but it's a dry heat."

Noah guffawed, which heartened Marella.

"You're red as a beet," said Noah. "Does it hurt much?"

"Probably not like the burn on your back. How's that?"

"Still hurts. Everything hurts."

Two orange-beaked black and white birds came from the north, flew overhead, then veered west. "Caspian terns," said Noah sadly. "Elizabeth taught me."

Marella didn't trust herself to answer. She listened to the hiss of the sled and the huff of her own breathing as she labored. She had the feeling of being watched. She looked around, but there was nobody there. Still, Preston's voice echoed in her thoughts. *I'll find you wherever you are.*

Knee-high rock slabs rose from the sand, scattered randomly. There were more as they moved along, and then they started to see garbage. Just plastic bottles at first, but as they traveled various pieces of trash were scattered everywhere, like the aftermath of a weekend music festival.

"Is that an engine block?" asked Marella.

"I don't know, but those are some big bolts," said Noah, kicking a fist-size one out of his way. "And I recognize that plastic tray from my school's cafeteria. There must be thousands of plastic bottles. No, millions." He tried to veer around several.

"Just run over them."

The chalkboard-screech sound of metal running over plastic made her insides squirm. More birds swooped overhead.

"Those geese are acting weird," said Noah. "Kind of frantic."

"Don't they usually fly in formation?"

"That's it, that's what's wrong. They're all out of order."

"Maybe they sense another earthquake coming," said Marella.

But it was quiet, the ground still. "The wind stopped," said Noah.

They detoured around door-size rock slabs. A hundred feet ahead, larger hut-size pieces jutted from the seafloor.

"That's not good," said Marella. "I hope they don't block our way. We'd have to abandon the sled and climb them."

"We can't. We need it to carry the water." Noah shivered. "Does it feel colder to you?"

She would have rubbed her arms but the jellyfish welts were still sensitive. "A lot colder. Twenty or thirty degrees colder. I don't get it."

"The sun looks the same as it has all day. Kind of orange behind the smoke."

Marella shaded her eyes. "But it's freezing out, like somebody replaced it with a photograph of itself."

More birds—sea gulls this time—came from the north, their squawks sounding like warnings. Marella glanced over, then stopped abruptly. In the distance a mile-high mass of clouds filled the horizon, billowing as if giant fists punched from inside.

She couldn't quite connect what she was seeing with real life. This didn't happen in the northwest. "Sandstorm." Her dry mouth could barely say the word.

Noah snapped his head around to look, then exclaimed in surprise. "We have to get to cover." He strained against the rope and dug in with his feet. "It could be here in minutes. And sandstorms can last days."

"It better not. We don't have that long."

The sandstorm rolled closer as they ran, a roiling mass, oddly quiet, stalking them. As if it thought itself invisible and was determined to take them by surprise.

The sled jerked to a stop. "Come on," said Noah, yanking the rope.

"It's stuck on some old netting," said Marella, puffing hard.

They yanked the sled backwards, but it wouldn't come free. Seconds went by as Marella cut it with a knife. They would never make it to the slabs at this rate. The storm was still so quiet that she could hear her heart pounding.

She freed the sled, but the roiling wall was now only a hundred feet away, closing fast. Static electricity made the hairs stand up all over her body. It felt like a message from the storm. *Be terrified. Fear me.* As if it meant to punish her for doing euthanasia. It seemed like overkill. This ridiculously enormous retribution coming for her.

As if switched on, the metal on the sled glowed like neon. They scrambled away. The storm's electricity forced them to leave the sled behind.

"We have to stay together." Noah reached out, but when their hands touched, the static electricity knocked them both onto their backs. They struggled to their feet. Noah whisked a blanket from the sled and sprinted towards the ridge. "Come on."

Marella hesitated. The flash drive. It was in her backpack on the sled. Careful not to touch the glowing sled rails, Marella tugged at the backpack, but it was stuck. She'd tied it on with a piece of rope, and now the knot was too tight. She took precious seconds trying to untie it, but it was impossible, and now there was no time to cut the knot.

The sandstorm was almost there; she knew without looking because the wind started up, blowing every which way, slapping her hair against her face. She pulled her t-shirt up over her nose and mouth and started toward Noah, who had reached a rock slab. He called to her, but the gusts stole his words away.

The world collapsed around her. One moment was bright sunlight; the next black as a cave. She couldn't see her own body. She lost all sense of direction. Even with the t-shirt over her mouth and nose it was like breathing cotton. Grit sandpapered her stomach, forehead, hands, ankles, neck. The noise was a factory gone wild, clacking and screeching, terrifyingly machinelike.

Buffeted by gusts, she fell to the ground. She used one arm to prop herself up, the other to shield her head. She scrambled forward, wanting to call out but stifled by the wind, which dipped into her lungs to steal her breath. The storm steered her in one direction, only to demand she switch to another.

Debris smashed into her side, then her head. She crawled, if only to not stay where she was. The wind clanked, the factory broken, the machines out of order. The world itself seemed shattered, its shards striking her. She felt so alone. So lost. Her heart pounded as if it would never stop.

Now Noah's shouting sounded amid the clamor. She wasn't alone! She veered in that direction, the storm raging and fighting her all the way. She bumped into something hard—a stone slab. Then Noah's voice was right there, though she couldn't see him.

Remembering the static electricity, she didn't try to touch him. Somehow she managed to reply. "Noah!"

"Here," he called. "Grab the blanket." She felt for the loose end. They pulled it over themselves, forming a sort of tent, their backs to the stone wall. The storm, seemingly furious they had taken shelter, clawed at the blanket's edges, trying to snatch it away.

It was a relief the sand was no longer grinding into her skin. She spit and coughed in the darkness.

"Don't rub your eyes," Noah bellowed.

She let them water without touching them, feeling grit caking around them as they dried.

As the storm continued its onslaught Marella imagined the sand burying them, the ocean surging back over them. They would lie under its weight as flattened, mummified strips. Two-dimensional things. No, three-dimensional, if she counted the dimension of time, which seemed to go on forever, like this sandstorm. Somebody once labeled them the four winds, but they were more like the thousand winds. All thousand of them whined, cajoled, complained, and roared.

Marella roared back. She roared at the wind. She roared at the injustice. This wasn't her fight. She hadn't caused this. She shouldn't have to endure this. She roared until the dust layered her nasal cavities and lungs like a velvet lining, forcing her to stop.

The anger drained. Only doubt remained. She wasn't capable. She couldn't do this. How could she, when it couldn't be done?

Chapter Twenty-Six

The storm dwindled. Marella felt grit everywhere: teeth, neck, armpits, back, crotch, feet. The light returned, shining through the blanket, revealing pinprick holes. Noah's face was filthy, streaked by tears, one eye redder than the other from rubbing.

"I feel like I've been through a meat grinder," said Marella.

"I feel like I've been through one twice," said Noah. "And then a dog ate me and shit me out."

They lowered the blanket. In spite of her discomfort, she was relieved the world had opened up. The sandstorm hadn't lasted as long as it could have. They could still make it to Wisdom Island. She stood, gazing at the expanse of sand.

"Our travel agent sucks," said Noah.

Marella smiled grimly, then frowned. She leaped to her feet, looking every which way. "The sled. Where's the sled? The flash drive is in my backpack."

"Are you serious right now?" Noah's voice was hollow with dismay. "We need that. And the water. And the GPS."

She trudged to what she hoped was the right spot and began digging, scooping away armloads of sand.

"It can't be far," said Noah uncertainly. "It was stuck fast."

• • • •

BY AFTERNOON, THEIR digging had pocked the area with craters. They were tired, their hands and arms raw from scooping the gritty sand. Marella was dizzy; her head pounded. Hope was waning. Her back was stiff, her arms shaking from exertion. She pushed herself anyway. Each second counted, as if her own family was buried and she was trying to dig them out.

She understood that their task might be an impossible one. There was too much territory and too little time. And the wind might have pushed the sled away. Still, she was going to dig until her muscles gave out.

"Look!" said Noah.

Marella's hopes skyrocketed, until she saw a rock in his hand. He hadn't found the sled. Still, he seemed so excited that she went to see. His thimble-size find was half black rock and half white agate, fused perfectly together. "That's you and me!" said Noah. "It's a sign. A good luck charm. I'm keeping it." He slipped it into his pocket.

She resumed digging with renewed vigor. His excitement spurred her on. When her hand hit something solid, she almost didn't believe it. She prepared herself for disappointment. It could be a rock, or plastic junk. Then she uncovered the rope. "It's here! It's here!"

Noah staggered across the loose sand. They scooped enthusiastically, uncovering the sled, with the backpack still tied on. Marella shook as she unzipped the side pocket. The flash drive. It was still there. Silver with the HemisNorth logo. Relief welled in her heart.

"Put it somewhere safe," said Noah.

"I thought I had." She turned away from Noah and took off her shirt and bra. Cutting a nick in the upper lining of her bra, she slipped it into the cup, shifting it down to the bottom. She put the bra and shirt back on, feeling more secure.

They drank some water. She was still thirsty.

There were only a few hours of remaining daylight. They had spent the whole day traveling, fighting the storm, and digging.

They started off once more, with Marella pulling the sled, amazed at her renewed energy and sense of hope. The empty sand brought up a memory. "In Tacoma we lived in a house where the backyard was all dug up. My sister and I played desert. I was the camel."

"I thought you were from Seattle."

"I'm not from anywhere," said Marella. "We moved fifty-two times."

"Fifty-two times? That's a lot."

"When I was little, Mom would ask if we should move to the place near the candy store. I would tell her no. I didn't want to lose my friends again. But then she'd get antsy and I knew it wouldn't be long." She would give anything to be with her mother now, even if she were fidgeting and ready to move again.

Noah said, "My mother became agoraphobic—she won't leave the house. We were going to get her some help. Then this happened."

Marella realized she might have more in common with Noah than she'd thought. Both their mothers had serious psychological problems. It then occurred to her that she might have more in common with the whole human race than she'd thought. Her isolation at being the new kid. Her irrational fear of demons. Isolation and fear. She'd been told those were universal.

She tried to imagine her own mother staying in the house, never leaving, but could only picture her carrying moving boxes out the door. The thought of it made her heart ache.

They passed a door lying on the sand. It almost looked as if they could open it and descend to a root cellar, perhaps.

"My father carves traditional Kenyan wooden doors. I wish I could show you."

"When this is all over," said Marella.

"My parents would love you."

Marella's eyes welled with tears, then dried up. "My Mom would love you too."

"No father?"

Marella shook her head, but didn't explain. She didn't want to think about death. "I wish we could talk to our families. Tell them we're alive. I hope it's not true about the atmosphere lowering."

"We can't think about it." He spoke firmly. And he was right. The strain of it was too much along with the pain and fear. And then there was the heat, which was only bearable because of the wind.

"It's just that every time I think life couldn't get worse, it does," said Marella.

"So you're saying it's going to get even worse than it is right now," said Noah.

"I suppose."

"Well then, these are the good times."

It struck her how right he was. She hadn't appreciated her life enough when her basic needs were met. She hadn't appreciated her life at each step of the Aguageddon so far, even though she saw now how good she had it in comparison with the day before. If she couldn't appreciate her life now—rough as it was—when would she appreciate it?

"So what did you do at HemisNorth?" asked Noah.

"I was an office assistant. My last day I spent copying and pasting stuff into a database. All day long. If I'd have known all that work would be for nothing I'd have slacked off."

"Somebody should have seen this coming. Somebody should have had the foresight to know that some technology or other was going to take things too far. If it hadn't been HemisNorth it would have been somebody else."

She pondered that. She counted herself among those without foresight. Other people were supposed to tackle the big problems, not a small player like her. War, disease, disaster. Making sure that new technology didn't cause Aguageddons.

It struck her that all along she had been thinking too small. Yes, she'd realized along the way that she could have done more with her life up until now. Learned more, experienced more, appreciated more. But this new realization was different. She had always thought of herself as a small cog. There were plenty of people who were more clever than she was, so let them figure out the solution to world problems. She wasn't the "type."

This was much more than regret for what could have been. This was an understanding that from here out, she had to look at things differently. Do things differently. She had to not only stop the water from going away, but be instrumental in the world's recovery.

First things first. Get the flash drive to the island. Initiate the shutoff program. Somehow find the courage to position Victor for the biometric scan. And hope she didn't die in an explosion.

Marella had the feeling that somebody was behind her. She looked back. There was no sign of Preston and Olivia. But he'd found them before. He could find them again.

• • • •

IN THE EVENING THEY reached a high dune and trudged upward. At the top they stood catching their breath. Below them the ground stretched out in a cracked gray mosaic that was so dry it seemed the Aguageddon had lasted decades. In the distance on either side, cliffs rose, forming a bowl. Nothing moved. No birds, no breeze, no plastic bags. It was forlorn. Being alone in such a place would drive her mad. "I'm glad you're here."

Noah smiled his lopsided smile. "I wish I wasn't. But since it turns out I have to be, I'm glad you're here too." He cocked his head. "I was thinking. What we need is condensed water. We put it in a bag and seal it up. And when we get to where we're going, we..."

"Just add water," Marella finished.

"Exactly." Marella felt in sync with Noah. This moment was something to treasure when everything else was such a struggle.

Ahead a smattering of boulders broke the landscape's monotony. Beyond them, several buttes rose from the emptiness, barely visible in the smoky sky.

She took out the GPS. "We're five miles from the island."

"That's encouraging."

She glanced back, seeing movement about a mile away. Her heart fluttered. The moving thing split into two. "Preston and Olivia."

"Hurry." Noah yanked the sled down other side of the dune, which would hide them, but only for a short while. "We have to make it to real cover. Past the boulders up ahead to the buttes. I don't believe this. How did he find us? It's like he has a tracking device or something."

"A tracking device." Marella's eyes went wide. "Oh my god. I can't believe I didn't think of it before. The necklace." She plucked her backpack off the sled.

"Why are you stopping? What necklace?"

She dug frantically. "He gave it to me. Said he made it. I should have known. It probably has a tracking device." She yanked the blond wood cross from the bag and held it dangling as if it were poison.

He snatched it from her, examining it, then dropped it on the hard ground. He stomped, splintering it into pieces. He sorted through the jumble of splinters. "There's only wood. No tracking device."

She rubbed her forehead in disappointment, then scooped sand over the pile. "Let's go."

"I'm not running from him anymore. I'm going to fight him. I can beat him any day of the week."

She also wanted to take a stand, but it wasn't logical. "Fists against a machete and slingshot. That wouldn't go so well."

Grunting with displeasure, he grabbed the rope to pull the sled forward.

She hurried along with him. If Preston and Olivia caught up, they would have to fight whether they wanted to or not.

Chapter Twenty-Seven

"Let's go. Hurry," said Noah. Marella joined him in pulling the sled toward the boulders, feeling as if a sandstorm chased them once more. They headed for the boulders, glancing back to see if Preston and Olivia had crested the dune.

She remembered Preston's hands gripping her throat. The look in his eyes as the divine wrath overcame him.

There was a stench like spoiled meat. "What's that?" Noah waved a hand as if to wipe it away.

Marella covered her nose. "Oh shit. Those aren't boulders."

As they neared it became clear. They were carcasses of hundred-foot-long blue whales, bloated like balloons in a Thanksgiving Day parade, the majestic creatures reduced to caricatures of themselves.

Marella's stomach turned, with nausea from the smell, but also from dread. Whales were smart creatures. It felt like a warning that this wasn't a place for living beings.

"They've been dead a while if they're this bloated," said Noah disgustedly.

"Maybe they died before the water disappeared."

"Then they should have been eaten up by undersea creatures. Nothing makes sense here."

They gagged as they rushed behind the first whale, out of Preston's line of sight. In spite of the bloating, characteristic ridges still ran along its length. Barnacles rimmed its rheumy eye. They passed another whale, then another.

Noah peeked back around whales. "They're closer."

"How close?"

"They could be here in twenty minutes."

She raised her eyebrows. "How are they going so fast?"

"I don't know. They're pulling a sled too. Maybe theirs slides better." He swore under his breath. "Olivia has her slingshot out and ready. Preston's got that machete. If they want us to join their cult, why are they so ready to kill us?"

"He's crazy. Whatever he's doing makes sense to him."

"We can't outrun them. We have to fight."

"I have an idea." Marella ran to one of the whales. Three times her height, it trembled at her touch like a water balloon. "We can hide in it."

"Hell no." Noah sliced his hands for emphasis. "They're ready to explode. Haven't you seen the videos?"

"That's the plan. We cut one. The insides flow out and give us cover."

Noah frowned in disgust. "I'd much rather fight."

"With what?" Marella glanced at the sled with its remaining jugs of water. "We have a knife. They have a machete and slingshot. Got any other ideas? We need a workaround."

Noah swiveled his head. "Not enough time to make a whalebone spear. Or dig a trap. I don't know. I've got nothing."

"I can hear them. We have to hide in a whale."

"All right." Noah took hold of the sled's rope. "I can't believe I'm agreeing to this."

While he dragged the sled to the whale's side, she retrieved a knife. It had been disgusting to flounder in dead fish guts. This would be worse. She hoped that some other idea would jump into her head. A better workaround. One that Elizabeth would have approved of. None did.

Marella planted her feet beside the whale. "Here we go."

"Are you sure you want to..."

No. Hell no. "Yes." Grasping the knife in both hands, she stabbed the creature as hard as she could. The carcass hissed, spraying an ammonia-strong gas. She staggered back, shielding her mouth and nose.

The knife was still in the whale. Noah rushed to it. Reaching up with both hands and turning his head to the side, he cut downward, a mad scientist pulling a lever.

All at once the whale exploded with surprising force. A hot mudslide of dead flesh pushed her off her feet and carried her backward, making her flail. Slippery muck surged out, burying her legs, arms, and torso, and flowing to her neck. She pushed herself up to standing, then threw up, the vomit mixing into the sludge.

She looked around desperately. Noah was nowhere to be seen. "Where are you?" she hissed. "Noah!" She saw movement and waded toward it, finding only exploded gut matter shifting and settling.

A hand rose from the mess. Marella plunged forward, scooping aside intestines and blubber. Muck was still surging from the carcass, making the going difficult. Seconds passed. He would suffocate if she didn't get him out. He would die.

And she would be the one who killed him. Her second homicide of the day. She growled with determination, pulling great armfuls of glop aside.

Finally she reached him. She pulled a thick intestine away and his head burst upward, like a calf being born, goop spilling off. He gasped for air, then vomited. He tried to scramble past her.

"Stay here," whispered Marella, grabbing onto him. "Preston's coming."

"I can't," said Noah, his voice garbled.

"We have to do this to save our families."

He stayed. Marella confirmed that the sled was covered, then she and Noah crouched down. The whale's flesh was furnace hot from decomposing bacteria. The sting from her injuries made her skin feel as if the bacteria were decomposing her too.

She heard Preston's voice but couldn't make out the words. Then a response from Olivia, also unintelligible.

"They aren't far," she whispered to Noah. Only their faces were free, hidden behind glistening intestine. The smell was so bad her eyes teared, distorting the grays, whites, and pinks of the decaying flesh that surrounded her.

Suddenly she remembered the flash drive. Was it still in her bra or had it slipped out into this mess? She was about to check when she heard Preston loud and clear. "All plants and animals began in Zokara. Those in the rest of the world are only the few meager varieties that spread into the less fertile areas of Earth, where they have to be cultivated."

His words made her stiffen with anger. Such nonsense. As odious as the waste she was buried in. She was suffering because of his lies. She wanted to spring forward and stuff this awful muck down his throat.

She was still holding Noah's arm. His muscles hardened in her grasp. He made a low, throaty noise, probably of anger. She tightened her hold on him, feeling a soldier-like camaraderie.

"The reduced fertility makes every plant and animal we know of smaller, weaker. But in Zokara there is a fantastic variety of plants, and they all grow without labor. Thousands of different fruits, each more delicious than the last. Plants that heal every ailment known to mankind. Pools of liquid that put any beverage you've ever tasted to shame. And you will enjoy this as the mother of all humanity."

Now Olivia was right in front of her holding a GPS unit. Marella had a flash of understanding. They knew Wisdom Island's coordinates because Olivia had seen them in the raft. It was no miracle Preston had found them. They were both headed the same way.

How could she stop them? She had the ridiculous notion of lassoing them with a whale intestine. Why couldn't she think of a real solution? And what about the flash drive? Was it in her bra lining or somewhere in this mess of guts?

Preston strode into view, machete in hand. She stifled a gasp. She felt trapped. She watched for them to turn their heads just the right way and spot them. Reveal a sign of recognition. Take aim with their weapons. She cupped her hand, ready to fling gunk at their eyes. It was all she had.

"I don't see them ahead of us anymore," said Olivia. Her voice angered Marella. The little traitor. It galled her to think she'd compared her to Brielle. The notion brought her fresh pain, but the wrong move now would mean never seeing her sister again.

"They could still be here," said Preston. "I'll go this way. You look there."

Marella could feel Noah's pulse alternating with hers, making one continuous pounding too fast for a normal heart.

There was silence. For too long. Noah jerked as if to resist vomiting. *Not now.* Marella squeezed him harder.

Something slithered against bare skin where her shirt had slipped upward. Something muscular, like an eel or some other writhing creature of the deep. It nuzzled her stomach, making her shudder.

A fish biology book at HemisNorth featured the lamprey. An eel-like fish that clamped onto its victim's skin and then chomped its way inside. The unlucky victim would be eaten alive. It fed on fish, but Marella was here now. If it was a lamprey—or something just as hungry, she would be its meal instead.

Marella squeezed her eyes open and shut, clasping harder onto Noah, expecting whatever it was to latch on. She hoped it was too picky to want human flesh. *I taste bad,* she tried to tell it telepathically. *Move along now. In fact, everybody just go. I can't take this anymore.*

Now Olivia was visible again, looking down at the sand. "Are those tracks?"

Marella couldn't breathe. Had they left tracks? How could that be? The ground was cracked it was so hard. At any rate, she wasn't going to give up that easily after all she'd been through. Slowly, carefully, she positioned her hands. When they came for her she would hurl gunk then leap out and try to grab the machete. It wouldn't work, but she would go down fighting.

The creature squiggled at her stomach. Marella held still.

They came no closer. They walked off, eyes on the ground. She relaxed. A thread of relief wound through her as she realized they were following a false track. They were leaving.

She pulled away from the wriggling creature, careful to remain hidden. Then she reached her hand up to her bra, checking for the flash drive.

She felt its edges. It was there. She closed her eyes. *Thank you. Thank you!*

Preston and Olivia headed toward a butte. It was taking so long for them to get there. The wait seemed interminable.

"Let's go," said Noah.

"I still see them," she fought her own urge to push free.

It took an hour, but finally their pursuers were gone and they slopped their way out of the goop, pulling the sled out with them. White matter drooped from the rope as it emerged, like cheese stretching from a pizza. Gunk streaked Noah's face and his cheek bled where he had nicked it on something.

With quiet noises of disgust, they sloughed the mess off.

Noah tilted his head, cleaning stuff from his ears. "I could have died in that filth. That's not the way I want to go out."

They stripped down, mindless of their naked bodies, and rubbed themselves with sand, though it stung. They wiped each other's backs. She cleaned goop from his burn, which looked red and angry. Noah gritted his teeth. "Pain is inevitable. Suffering is optional."

"Who said that?" asked Marella.

"I did," said Noah. "But I think Buddha said it too."

Marella wiped the flash drive clean then returned it to her bra. They wiped their clothes, the sled, and water jugs as best they could, then dressed and pressed onward. The stink felt permanent, as if it had soaked inward to her bones.

Preston and Olivia had gone to the left of one of the buttes. When Marella and Noah reached it, they went to the right.

As they advanced, they drank the water they carried. Her thirst remained as if she'd had nothing at all. It was their proximity to Project Athena. How much worse would it get when they were there?

At twilight they crossed some dunes, reaching an area of rocks, ravines, and coral shaped like saguaro cactus. It looked like the old west, missing only cowboys on horseback. As the sun was setting the dunes behind them looked like burning coals. The wind was even stronger this time of evening.

"We should try to keep going." Marella was too fatigued, but hoped to find the strength somehow.

"We'd have to use a light. They might see us."

"They're miles away from us on the other side of the butte."

"We won't be able to see far enough ahead. We'll go the wrong way and it'll take extra time to retrace our steps."

Exhaustion kept Marella from arguing. She was too tired to take off her boots. She started to pull the blanket from the sled, then stopped. "The blanket stinks. Can I huddle up to you instead?"

"Of course."

She started to lie down, but something poked her. She reached in her back pocket and pulled out a key.

"Is that for your apartment?" asked Noah.

Marella nodded.

"Get rid of it. It'll just make you sad."

She smiled, just a little. "No, it reminds me of when things were better." She rubbed the rough edges on her palm. "And maybe...maybe it's a good luck charm."

"We could use some good luck. What about your car key? That's bigger. Even more luck."

"I lost it."

She snuggled up to his back, draping an arm along his. When he shifted to accommodate her, his back muscles tensed against her belly. It was comforting and—in spite of her fatigue—sensual.

She could hear the smile in his voice. "I could get used to this."

"Me too."

Marella lay daydreaming that they were an ordinary couple, in bed after a long day. In the morning, they would wake and make love, then sit drinking coffee while they decided what to do. Go out to breakfast? Visit friends? Go to a movie? Play video games? All of the above! And more. It felt good to shed the disaster in her imagination.

After a few minutes, Noah said sorrowfully, "Don't take this the wrong way, but it's probably just as well Elizabeth died. If she helped cause the Aguageddon, then it wouldn't go well for her. People would crucify her."

Marella had managed to put her mercy killing out of her mind for a short time. Now it came rushing back. She had killed Elizabeth. No, helped her. No, murdered her. Her legs shook. She pulled away so Noah wouldn't feel it.

It was as if she were killing Elizabeth all over again. She remembered the feel of her hands on Elizabeth's face. Her seizing.

"I'm sorry." Noah touched her shoulder. "I shouldn't have said that."

Marella pulled away, turning her face and clutching her arms to her chest, trying to bring back the mental wall that was crumbling away.

"Marella, I know it's hard. But it's okay. She went in her sleep. And we were there. She wasn't alone."

Marella had to confess. She had to get it off her chest or it would bury her. She turned back. "No. She wasn't alone because I helped her to go. I made a promise and I stuck to it."

Noah sucked in a breath. "What do you mean?" His tone was harsh. Not what she hoped for.

But it was too late. She'd already begun. She spoke softly. "I did what she wanted."

"You...you killed her?"

The horror in Noah's voice crumbled all that was left of the wall that Marella had put up. She couldn't hold back sobs. "I couldn't let her die alone."

Noah stood. He took a step away, then a step back, then a step forward, holding his palms out in supplication. "My god, Marella. When somebody tells you they don't want to die alone, they're not asking you to kill them."

She spoke angrily through her sobs. "Don't patronize me. You know the situation just as well as I do."

"But to out and out murder her."

Marella tried to speak evenly. She had to make him understand. "It wasn't murder. It was mercy. I'm tormenting myself enough over this. I don't need you to do it too. Do you think it was easy for me? It'll haunt me for the rest of my life."

Noah furrowed his eyebrows. His voice got louder. "All the things you hid from me. The machine, the island. And now you killed a person while I was sleeping right next to her. I can't believe you about anything. What's really on the island? What are you really going to do there?"

How had this gotten so out of hand? She should have kept her mouth shut. Borne the burden alone. Now things were so much worse. She stood and faced him squarely. "I told you the truth. We're going to stop the Aguageddon. Please trust me."

"Trust," said Noah with disgust. "That's a fine word. I've heard it before. Any time somebody tells me to trust them, that's a red flag. I shouldn't have come with you."

Marella cringed as if he'd stabbed her. He'd taken it too far. He'd gone from saying Elizabeth would be crucified to crucifying Marella. "You should have stayed and burned? We saved your life, don't forget that when you're talking about trust."

"Saving my life doesn't mean you can use me for whatever devious purpose you want." His eyes widened as if he'd just realized something. "All those things you said about Preston. That he's a cult leader, a killer. Were you lying to me because he found out the truth? You were afraid he would tell us why you're really going to Wisdom Island."

Marella's mouth hung open. The accusation was like a punch in the gut. As if she was still some stranger, and they'd shared nothing together. She grasped for a response. "It wasn't just me. You heard Olivia say he was Zokara's Chosen's leader."

"Olivia was pretending to agree with you to get the flash drive away from you. What's on that flash drive? Why were Preston and Olivia trying to stop you? That never made sense to me, you going all that way in person just to shut something down. And the stuff about a runaway reaction. It's contrived."

Noah turned one way, then another, as more thoughts struck him. She could see his revulsion building. "What is this, some HemisNorth world domination thing? For all I know you're trying to keep the Aguageddon going. How do I know you're trying to save your family? You could have made that all up." He looked at her as if she were a pile of shit he had been about to step in. "All that moving around you said you did growing up. Was that some over-the-top lie? Was it supposed to make me feel sorry for you? Are you really some rich kid from Bellevue?"

Rage flowed through Marella like molten steel. After all the pain. All the fear. And after confessing to Noah, baring her soul to him, trusting him, to be accused like this. "I'll tell you what's over-the-top. You taking Preston's side. He's a mass murderer. You conveniently forget that we heard him talking about Zokara."

"I never heard him say a word about it."

"At the whales, when he and Olivia were close."

"I couldn't understand them. My ears were full of whale guts. You could be making that up."

"Right. I'm so goddamn devious. I'm out here making shit up. And, oh yeah, risking my life. For world domination. Maybe I should confess. Is that want you want? For me to tell you my true aim, to dominate a world where—oops—everybody's dead?"

She stared at him, seething, breathing hard. Challenging him with her eyes.

His pulled his head back, seeming surprised by her fierceness.

Marella continued, shouting and gesturing wildly, "Think about it. Really think about it. I nearly died. More than once. No amount of money or power is worth dying for. I'm here to save my family, and believe it or not, to save your family too. I told you about Elizabeth because I thought you'd understand. But you don't. So the hell with you."

His energy seemed to drain. "I don't know. I don't know what to think anymore."

Her tirade fatigued her. She felt heavy. "Let's go to sleep. We still have a ways to go so I can fucking dominate the world."

"Am I going to be alive when I wake up?" Noah lay down, sounding annoyed rather than angry, as if she'd made her point. Maybe they had worked it out. Maybe he believed her.

"Yes, you'll be alive when you wake up. You damn well better be. I need you." She lay down a few steps away from him, but heard whispering underground. *Demons.* She jerked herself upwards into a spider pose, heart pounding. "Something's under there."

Noah spoke tiredly. "It's the dunes shifting. Singing sands, like in the Sahara."

She lay gingerly back down. The sound, like slurred words, disconcerted her.

Marella slept, then woke to a hand on her mouth.

Chapter Twenty-Eight

Marella's first thought was that Elizabeth's ghost had come for revenge. Fear sloshed through her veins like cold water. She had murdered. With her own hands. Now she would pay. Elizabeth was sucking Marella's soul out through her mouth to take it for judgement.

But when her eyes flew open she saw Preston, a look of triumph on his face. Her body reacted before her brain could process what was happening, her hands grabbing his wrists, but somebody—Olivia?—wrenched her arms away, pinning them behind her back. Preston stuffed a gag into her mouth and tied it too tightly. She couldn't yell. She grunted, trying in vain to make enough noise to alert Noah, who lay deep in sleep, out of reach, mouth open, hand relaxed near his face.

She bucked and twisted, trying to understand. How had they found her? They had gone the other way! She kicked hard, but Preston held onto her ankles. Pain shot through the bad one, the pressure of his grip like a bear trap clamped to her bone.

Olivia trussed Marella's feet together. How could the girl be so stupid as to follow a madman?

The gag stank of dried mold and made it hard to get air. She grew dizzy. She had to stop moving to catch her breath.

It was bright out, she realized with anguish. It was their own fault Preston and Olivia had found them. They had slept way past sunrise, leaving ample time to be discovered.

She looked at Olivia, eyes pleading. *Please be like my sister. See the wrong in this.* Olivia merely gazed at her inquisitively as if Marella were an unusual shell on the shore. So unfeeling. It made Marella's stomach churn. She was capable of anything. She could reach over and suffocate Marella merely by pinching her nose. Marella knew how well that worked. Guilt and fear intertwined. Did she deserve what was happening to her now?

Preston strode to where Noah lay, standing over him. What was he going to do? A horrible image came to mind. Preston lifting his foot. Stomping Noah's head. It would be so easy with Noah so fast asleep. So vulnerable.

Marella took a deep breath through her nose and grunted as loud and long as she could. It was too muffled to have any effect. Noah lay just as still, just as defenseless. She twisted, rolling to her knees. Olivia pushed her back down much too easily. She grunted as she landed, hitting her shoulder, wincing with the pain of it.

There was hope though. Noah was bigger, stronger. He would be harder to wrangle. Once he woke, he would fight them. Overcome them, then free Marella.

With a swift move, Preston rolled Noah to his stomach and pretzeled his arm behind him. Just like that, all hope was gone. They didn't bother gagging him because Marella was already incapacitated, and so he could sputter out his confusion. "What the hell! Stop! Ow, shit, don't."

Preston removed the rag from Marella's mouth. She worked her dry tongue around in her mouth, wetting it so she could speak. "Let us go!" It came out as a furious demand. But then she clamped her mouth shut, regretting her tone. What if his wrath emerged once more? She swallowed hard.

"Let us go," echoed Noah, barely containing his rage. "Just untie us. We can talk like human beings. We all want the same thing. We all want to get through the Aguageddon. We can help each other."

"Where is your flash drive?" asked Preston.

Marella froze. What should she say? Would he believe her? "Olivia dropped it in the ocean. I tried to get it but a jellyfish was in the way. You can see it stung my arms and legs."

Preston shook his head. "I see through your lie." He was filthy, his hair a pile of seaweed. His eyes seemed crazy. There was something missing there, as if he'd left a part of himself in the dry ocean bed along the way. She shrank away, struggling for air, unable to hold back choking noises. She'd lost. Preston would take the flash drive from her and destroy it.

He leaned closer. What if he searched her? His grimy hands touching, probing. A wave of nausea washed through her.

Preston reached out, placing a hand on her side. She jerked involuntarily. The heat of it radiated through her skin. He was too close to the flash drive. As if God was leading him to it. He stank of urine.

She began to retch. Preston jerked his hand away and backed up.

"She doesn't have it," shouted Noah, flopping like a fish in his struggle to get free.

Preston turned to Noah. "That also is a lie. Do you know how I know?" A beatific smile spread across his face. "I am the father of the new era. Many years ago God flooded the Earth with water to destroy the wicked. This time, he's taking it away to destroy the wicked. You are all here to help found the new era. Marella, I saw you in a vision and then you arrived. Bringing Noah. His name is a message that you both were to be spared."

Marella closed her eyes against his all-encompassing gaze. It was such a conundrum. If he hadn't believed her special back then, he might not have saved her by giving her water, and she might have died. But now she would die anyway because of him.

Unless she had resolve. She opened her eyes. There had to be a way. Could she somehow convince Olivia to help? But there was madness in her eyes as well, as if she was looking both near and far. Why was it only emerging now? Or had been there all along and she had missed it?

She tried anyway. "Olivia, he'll kill you like he killed the others. He's using you until he doesn't need you anymore. Then he'll toss you away. Like Edie and Baby Faith. He left them behind to die. Just abandoned them." She watched Preston for signs of wrath, but he was calm.

Olivia merely shook her head as if declining seconds at dinner. She attached a burner to a small green propane bottle.

"Edie and Baby Fay are safe," said Preston. "God led them to safety, just as he'll lead us."

Marella burst out. "It's not true! Olivia, how can you believe this nonsense?"

Olivia gazed at Marella as if she were an idiot. "It's right before your eyes and you choose not to see it. God led Elizabeth, the creator of the Aguageddon, Destroyer of Life, directly to Preston, Savior of life."

"Elizabeth didn't create it."

"You and she are from HemisNorth," said Preston, "which made the machine. That's not a coincidence."

The statement confounded Marella. Yes, it was a big coincidence, but how did that prove anything? Marella wasn't sure how to counter a statement of fact being used to bolster up lunacy.

Preston began talking about the new era, while Olivia turned away, cutting something she couldn't see—some kind of food?

Despair began to take over. Tears rose in Marella's eyes. There wasn't time for this. Project Athena was taking the water away. Each moment lost meant more water gone. Soon it would be too late.

Olivia twisted a knob on the tiny stove, then held a lighter to the burner; blue flames rose in a circle. She balanced a small pan on top. The knife she had used was sitting on the ground, between the camp stove and Olivia's backpack. Could she reach it somehow?

The smell of cooking fish reached her. She needed to think her way out of this but she was running on empty. The smell distracted her.

Olivia helped Marella sit up, then held a cup to her mouth. She drank. Olivia gave her spoonfuls of fish. Marella ate it, though it was tough and dry. Maybe it would help her think clearly.

Noah, too, accepted the food, biting quickly, like a koi snapping up an insect.

Preston and Olivia lowered themselves to the sand. The way they watched her was disconcerting. As if they expected her to explode.

She began to feel strange. There was something wrong with her limbs. Marella tried to imbue her voice with reason. "I can't feel my hands and feet," said Marella. "I'm tied up too tight. Just take these off. I won't go anywhere."

"I told you," said Preston. "I can tell when you're lying."

It almost seemed as if he could. It was true he was able to read people well enough to manipulate them. Maybe that was his secret power over his followers.

Was it hopeless then? She couldn't break free yet couldn't talk her way out of bondage. It was like trying to persuade a river not to flow. And the knife that Olivia used on the fish was out of reach.

It was so frustrating it made her belly ache. Or so she thought, but then the pain intensified. She was ill. Dizzy. Had the fish been spoiled?

"Something's wrong with me," said Marella. "My stomach hurts."

Preston nodded. "That's God working through you."

Surprisingly, he untied her legs, then her arms. Marella pushed her hands against the ground, telling her body to rise, to run, to escape, but she couldn't. It felt as if her intestines were being twisted around a stick.

The knife was still on the ground. Through fierce concentration Marella brought her legs under herself and stood, staggering a few feet forward. Olivia easily beat her to the knife. A wave of pain brought her to her knees next to the remains of the fish that Olivia had fed them. Its skin had a single black blotch, like smudged ink. It was a yellowstripe goatfish, which Elizabeth had warned would cause cramps and hallucinations.

"You poisoned us," said Marella, not sure her mouth actually formed the words. She tried to stick her finger down her throat, but Preston stopped her. She was too weak to resist.

Now they untied Noah, who reached out like a blind man. "Everything is warped. Like you're made of waves."

"Marella." Preston's voice tinkled like chimes. It confused her. Why did evil sound so sweet? "I only want what God wants for you. It's so beautiful. I wish you could see it through my eyes, how it will be. The splendid glory. We are the chosen. The new era is in all of us. We need only embrace it." He held his arms out as if to enfold the sky.

It was frightening that belief gave him a license to do anything, from kidnapping to destroying an entire planet.

A prickly sensation traveled along Marella's skin. The sand particles sparkled at her. Something hung in the air, blue and round. A single raindrop had stalled five feet off the ground, where it hung like dew without a leaf.

Marella touched the tip of her tongue to it. Its radiance absorbed into her, and she herself became radiant.

"Do you feel how wonderful it is?" asked Preston.

At his suggestion, the sand emitted a feeling. Something like love, but more subtle, more secretive.

"You are part of the new era," said Preston. He kept talking, a continuous drone, but she had a hard time concentrating on his words because a mirage swirled in front of her, tall as a house. It solidified into a being of some kind. A woman, yet too big to be human. A goddess. Her face hidden behind a jeweled veil. That was best, because to see her face would be overwhelming to a mortal.

"You are part of the new era," said the Goddess. Her shimmering hair became the ocean, her eyes the sky, her skin the sand. She was everywhere, all at once. Marella touched the sand—the Goddess's skin—crying at how smooth it was; her tears flowed, forming one of the world's four rivers that were said to spring from center of the world.

The Goddess led her into the moonlight, showing her the grottos of the gods. Beautiful, foliage-filled caves, with pink and crimson flowers. Marella understood now that this had always been available to her; she had only to come to the bottom of the sea to find it. It was what her mother had been searching for without knowing what it was, without understanding that she needed to submerge herself to find it rather than move from town to town.

"This is Zokara. Preston will lead you here." The Goddess talked for hours, telling her of her role in the new era, and that she had been chosen to live. It was foretold that she would find Preston.

The Goddess twirled a finger, spinning water into tornadoes. She had such power. Such ability to cause disorder. She could do anything. So had the Goddess, rather than HemisNorth, caused the Aguageddon?

"You shouldn't take away our water," said Marella.

The veil lifted, revealing the Goddess's eyes as bottomless pits. The ground lurched and rolled. She was angry at the challenge. Angry that Marella thought it wrong to remove the ocean. Angry at her insolence. The deity roared, "You are part of the new era."

Marella ran. She climbed over rocks, traversed great dunes, and splashed through ebbing puddles that tried to suck her into the underworld. For eons she ran, the Goddess always right behind. Then she felt her feet lifting from the ground. The world fell away. She rose higher, higher, higher, until she could see Earth's curvature.

Black ashes and crusty residue lined the west coast where the North American continent used to end, giving her a startling view of how much the oceans had emptied. The sea floor was scarred like a moon. She could make out the contours of Alaska, British Columbia, Washington, Oregon, California, Baja California.

Something occurred to her: if the Goddess thought her special enough to be a mother of humanity, Marella might have more power than she realized. She could try to bring the water back herself. She swept her arm wide, motioning for the ocean to spread eastward.

The ocean flowed, following her orders; but as it did, it changed color and intention, glowing red, boiling with malevolence, becoming lava.

No. That wasn't her intent! She held up a hand to command the flow to stop, but it was too late. Once given, the order must be executed. She cried out, but that only hastened the lava sea's pace, and it filled trenches and voids, its roaring sizzle discernable even from this great height.

When it reached the damaged continents, the lava's power was too great. Pieces of Mexico's coast yielded, calving into it. The burning sea mauled North America's entire west coast. Speeding forward, it ate the continent away. Marella watched in horror as it swallowed all land.

The Earth rotated, revealing its devastation. Dusty slag floated on glowing lava, the only evidence that Earth's continents ever existed. Marella's skin gleamed red in the light of the dead planet.

The Goddess spoke. "I am Athena."

• • • •

MARELLA WOKE, EYES closed, body weighed down, not yet connected to her limbs, not yet able to move. Flotsams of understanding floated by, just out of reach.

Something was wrong. She was nauseous, dizzy. She opened her eyes, saw Noah sprawled next to her, mouth partly open, asleep.

She was part of the new era. They were the chosen. These were facts, but something about them didn't match. Like they were a story, not reality. They were words she'd been hearing. Words Preston had been saying while she was drugged.

She had eaten that fish. Her stomach muscles ached from cramps caused by the poison. Preston's continuous blur of words was meant to brainwash her. They hadn't taken hold completely, but they were hard to remove from her psyche, like thorns in clothing. She needed to carefully extract herself without letting them dig in further.

A thought emerged from the fog in her brain. Her family was in danger, and Preston and Olivia were keeping her from saving them. Marella gulped for air as if surfacing from a deep dive. What was the mission? She was going to an island. Wisdom Island. Taking the shutdown program there.

She swiveled her head, surveying her surroundings. They were in a different place than where they'd eaten the fish. Dunes behind, rock formations ahead. Olivia and Preston were not in view, but their boots and Olivia's backpack were there, so they were somewhere close.

She rose with difficulty, as if she was being exhumed. She was still wearing her boots from the night before. Her feet felt hot and sore.

The flash drive. Marella sucked in a breath as dread coursed through her. Did she still have it? Or had Preston found it? She reached up.

It was still there in her bra lining. She bowed her head in relief.

How long had she been out? She looked at the watch Elizabeth had given her. They had lost an entire day. They had only twelve hours left to use the shutdown program. "Oh my god," Marella whispered.

They needed to subdue Preston and Olivia, quickly, while they still had the element of surprise. She dropped to Noah's side, shaking him, whispering into his ear. "Wake up. You have to wake up."

Noah grunted, curling into a ball, then uncurling. His head hovered an inch from the ground. "What's going on?" His voice sounded mangled.

"Come on. Get up. Quickly. Be quiet."

Noah clutched his head. "We are the chosen."

"Shhh. Noah, shake yourself out of it. We lost a day. We have to go."

"We will found a new civilization."

It seemed true. She lost herself for moment trying to think why. She felt a strange mixture of adoration and loathing for Preston, wanting both to kiss his feet and bash him with a tire iron. The brainwashing had succeeded just enough to confuse her.

She pulled herself out of it. "No, that's wrong. Olivia drugged us. She fed us yellowstripe goatfish. It made us hallucinate."

"I've always believed in Preston," said Noah. "Always known I would find him. It was foretold."

Every word he spoke echoed in her brain. She'd heard them before. Over and over. "Shake it off. That was brainwashing. Get up."

Noah rolled to his knees, then right back to his side. "I've got vertigo."

Marella raised her chin to the sky in despair. Either the Meniere's disease or the drug. Maybe both. What now?

She peeked around an outcropping. Olivia and Preston were sitting next to each other about ten feet away looking into each other's eyes. Adoringly. Like lovers. He lay his hand on her face, kissing her mouth, then pulled away, smiling. Olivia smiled back. Marella's skin crawled.

The machete lay on the ground next to Preston. Too far away for her to get it.

A weapon. She needed a weapon.

She stumbled to the backpack and ripped the zipper open, pawing through it. It contained the mini propane bottle and its camp stove attachment, a lighter, and water bottles. No knives, no weapons, no slingshot. She looked at their boots. Laces could strangle. But bringing shoelaces to a machete fight was preposterous.

She went back to Noah and shook him hard. "Come on, get up." He barely reacted, sunk back into his drugged state.

He couldn't help her. It was up to Marella, and Marella alone, to fix the Aguageddon. The responsibility felt heavy, as if her clothes had turned to lead.

She turned her head from side to side, looking for inspiration. What now? She had no weapons. The rocks were too big to lift. The small propane tank in the backpack was all she had.

Two of them against one of her. And there was Preston's machete to fear, and Olivia's slingshot. She wouldn't win.

She had to leave. But she would make it harder for them to follow. She bent to scoop up Preston and Olivia's boots, then realized that Preston could just take Noah's shoes to wear. She gathered those up as well.

Now Noah would be stranded barefoot with the enemy in a world of sea urchins, shells, fish bones and other sharp debris. *I'm sorry. I'm so sorry.* Donning the backpack and clutching the shoes, she ran.

Chapter Twenty-Nine

S he rushed west among the rock formations, not knowing how she kept up the pace, except that she was running for her life. For her family's lives. If there was ever a time to find reserves, this was it.

Dumping the footwear in a ravine, she winced inwardly, imagining Noah when he realized what she'd done to him. She hoped he would forgive her. If he survived.

By noon she could only keep up a fast walk. Dunes stretched out like sea star legs. Marella saw hundreds of tiny pools, like molten tin. Mirages. The plastic microparticles mixed in with the sand stuck to her boots, reeking of the oil and other rubbery-smelling chemicals they had absorbed.

She was alone. Horrifyingly alone. Every shadow was a crouched demon. Every gust was Athena hissing at her to be gone.

It was ironic how difficult it was to be alone, given how hard she was working to keep it that way. Alone so she could finish the task. That was, if she could find the island without the GPS. She knew it was not far now, but what if she went right by it?

The earth rumbled, then shook. She dropped to the ground to ride it out. She growled back at the earthquake. She wouldn't let it defeat her.

When the earth stilled, she rose and jogged forward, stopping to catch her breath when she had to, then propelling herself forward once more. She thought about how each stage of the Aguageddon made her long for the previous, unappreciated stage of her life. "These are the good times," Noah had said. She used to think she had it bad with all their moves, but that was heaven compared to now. So much happiness mixed in with the difficulties. Then came the start of the Aguageddon, then life on the Puget Sound seabed with the group, then life with Noah and the bare essentials to survive; and now, life alone, ankle aching, skin burning, thighs cramping, lungs smoldering.

Did that mean that in death she would look longingly back to this moment? Should she appreciate what she had now, though it only encompassed pain and anguish, because the future always held worse? And once she died, would each stage of death be more horrifying than the previous?

Just as she thought she couldn't take any more, the island appeared. She clasped her hands to her face. A swirl of emotion overtook her. Joy that her goal was finally in sight. Triumph that she had made it far enough to see this fantasy world. The sea life on its lower slopes as colorful as a candy mountain, its upper slopes parched, and its top sprouting with brown-needle pines.

Within moments dismay overtook her once more. The top of the island was so high above. With the undersea portion no longer surrounded by ocean, it was as daunting as Mount Rainier.

Doubt flooded her mind like dirty seawater. How could she possibly find the stamina? She was so tired. Everything hurt, including the blisters on her feet, as if her boots were cheese graters. Even if she made it to the top, what if the program's flash drive didn't stop the Aguageddon? And if it did, what would happen to her? She would be stranded with a dead man.

She scooted forward as if to outpace her negative thoughts. In reality, the island wasn't nearly as tall as Mount Rainier. Even though they had descended to the twilight zone, she had been going back uphill for some time. It looked like she could make it in half a day. She glanced at her watch. She had ten hours.

Anyway, it was better not to get too far ahead of herself. She had to get to the base of the island first, then make the climb, then deal with the machine itself. She could almost hear her mother's words: "One foot in front of the other. No tripping allowed."

She powered forward, concentrating on the task at hand. Avoiding sea urchins and other spikey creatures in the sand. Finding the best route past piles of dead fish and mounds of undersea debris.

After another hour, she saw that the sand ahead had a strange, shifting color like velvet rubbed one way and then the other. When she reached it she scooped up a handful and saw why. Here there was no sand at all, only plastic microparticles. They were green, blue, orange, and other random colors, some iridescent. When she poured them from her hand, the lighter bits blew away like a mist.

She stepped forward onto the microparticle beach. Her foot sank several inches. She continued onward. It was like walking in soft snow. After a few minutes, the strange stuff was up to her knees, but she plowed through it anyway, grunting with exertion. She didn't know how she would make it to the island with each step such a struggle. She could only hope that it would get easier further on.

She looked around. No sign of Preston, Olivia, or Noah. Still alone.

Then, with one step, she sank to her thighs, unable to pull her knees upward. It felt like the earth reaching up to swallow her, to take back its own. She jerked and flailed, but the more she struggled, the more she slipped downward. The stuff compressed her legs, securing them in place.

She forced herself to freeze, arms extended like a tightrope walker. She wasn't going to make it to the island, not from here. Her only hope was to make it back to where she had started sinking. Once again, the enormity of being alone engulfed her. She began to hyperventilate. There was nobody to help. Nobody to lift her up. Her family far away. Elizabeth dead. Only the empty vastness of land surrounding her.

She gazed at the island as she tried to calm her breathing. Forced herself to think it through. Be rational. But what could she do? It was like standing on a land mine that would detonate if she moved.

She realized that even though the microparticles were plastic, they had the qualities of quicksand. A video had circulated among her schoolmates. How to get out of quicksand by yourself. The man in the video had used small, careful movements to raise one leg, then the other, and then lean down into a military crawl position. She would do the same.

Even though it seemed wrong, she made herself lean forward to push gently on the surface ahead of her with her hands. Her hand sank in. She pushed with her other hand. Now both were stuck.

This wasn't working. She realized with horror that she'd done exactly the wrong thing. This wasn't quicksand. Quicksand was made of sand and water. There was no water here. This was more like a ball pit, where weight made you sink to the bottom. There was no video answer for this.

She sank further, elbow deep. Her heart was beating so fast. As if to get all the beats in before she died. *Alone. She was so alone. Nobody could save her.* She nearly succumbed to despair. She had been given an impossible task, to save the world without superpowers, but she couldn't even save herself.

Still, there was nothing she could do but try. She was frozen in lizard position. *Think. Find a workaround.* The backpack. Could she use it as a tool? The motion of shrugging it off would only sink her deeper. Or would it?

Marella leaned to the side. Her left arm sank several inches further, but by wiggling her right arm as she pulled upward, it came free from the microparticles. Now she contorted herself to get free from a strap. The backpack shifted, settling onto the microparticles. She twisted, extracting her left arm and shoulder from the other strap.

She had both hands free of the microparticles. It felt liberating in its way, but she'd traded one position for a more precarious one. Her torso lay directly on the particles. Whatever she did next would either save her or be the end of her. Her throat felt tight, her windpipe as narrow as a straw.

The backpack lay on the surface. In one slow, delicate, continuous movement, she reached both arms over and grasped its top. She pulled, hauling herself forward a hand's length, her legs leveling slightly.

It was working! "Thank god." Her voice broke. She pulled herself forward until the pack was level with her belly. Her legs leveled further.

Now she needed to turn back, to where the sand was solid. The trick would be to move the backpack without pushing herself the wrong way. By holding her arm out and pulling at an angle, she managed to do just that. Then she grasped the backpack and hauled herself forward again.

She continued pulling and hauling, curving around until she struggled back to where the ground was solid, pulling herself completely out of the microparticles.

Finally free, she allowed herself to go wild. As if possessed by a wild beast, she ripped off her shirt. Microparticles stuck to her skin; she thrashed at them like biting insects. She tore off the boots Olivia had given her, hurling them onto the ground. She yanked off her slacks, beating them against the ground as if they were the cause of all her woes.

In the middle of a beat, she froze. The flash drive! Did she still have it? Her hand went to her bra. She felt for it. There were the flash drive's edges. It was still there. She dropped to her knees, gulping breaths in. Gathering herself. There wasn't time for this nonsense.

And yet...she felt the need to know that she also had her good luck charm. She felt in her pants pocket. Yes, her apartment key was still there.

She glanced back as she dressed once more. No sign of Preston. She turned back toward the mountain island, seeing now that the microparticle landscape surrounded it like a moat. She had to find a way past this obstacle. She needed a major workaround.

Snowshoes might get her across, but there was nothing to fashion them from. No debris, no coral, no shells, no wood. A snowmobile might have done the trick. A hovercraft. A helicopter. A time machine.

Nothing that came to mind was remotely obtainable. Marella's thoughts kept going in circles until she was forced to admit there was no way to the island.

A sense of failure settled over her like falling ash, covering her bit by bit until it buried her, forcing her to her knees. This was proof that she was the wrong person for this impossible task. She wasn't capable. Never had been.

The germ of anger began to grow. It started as a tiny heat in her solar plexus, then expanded into a spinning ball. The entire world teetered on the brink of death because of Eshana Collins and Len Janderson. Marella wished they were alive to see the damage they'd done. To suffer along with everybody else. Belinda Waverly and Elizabeth were also culpable even though they hadn't invented the machine.

As the minutes passed, the heat eased. They had been trying to do good. Trying to fix humanity's mess. It was humanity she should be angry with. People who insisted on spewing carbon dioxide into the air, regardless of the consequences, forcing others to come up with a solution, which in this case had gone atrociously wrong.

People manufactured plastic things. And people bought them. And people dumped them. This mess blocking her way was everybody's fault. Everybody was to blame.

She had known that people produced a lot of garbage. She'd passed so much of it on the ocean floor. But the sheer scale of the microparticle disaster was unbelievable, even when it lay right in front of her. She thought about the times she'd thrown things away, never expecting to see them again. Now they were represented here, spread out in front of her, a testament to her indifference.

That thought jolted her to her feet. She was the one to blame because she was the only person she truly controlled. She held her hand to her forehead. *Me. I did this.* She dropped back to her knees and scooped the microparticles with both hands. She saw tiny white bits representing the thousands of plastic bags she had used in her lifetime. Blue bits, the plastic toy train set she had bought for Brielle because it was cheaper than the wooden set. Clear bits, the syringes used to vaccinate her and keep her healthy.

She flung the microparticles away. She couldn't blame everybody else, because she had played just as much a part in it. She could only account for her own actions and her own needs. She had done this just as much as anybody else. That was why she had to repair it.

But how? She paced, limping parallel to the microparticle beach. She couldn't have come all this way for nothing. All this effort, just to die alone.

Perhaps she was already dead. In Hell, it seemed, where she had been since Seattle. The Hell where she could try and try and never succeed. Like Sisyphus pushing the boulder up the mountain, only to have it roll back down again. Or Tantalus stretching out an arm to pick fruit, the branches rising just out of reach. She would forever be trying to stop the Aguageddon, without ever reaching the island.

It had been eight days since she'd left Seattle. The city was a faded dream; only the fire that destroyed it was real. She could picture vividly the embers raining into Elliott Bay, the trees and buildings burning all along the shoreline as they drove north, then west, until they'd reached the ocean. Billowing smoke rising from walls of red flames.

Marella sat, hugging herself, trying force her thoughts back to solving the problem. Instead she obsessed about fire. She thought of Gabriela in the pyre, the flames wrapping her. Marella began rocking.

It felt like her own head was on fire, like the flames would melt her brain. She couldn't stop imagining flames everywhere.

Marella stopped rocking. She loosened her arms from around herself. *Flames everywhere.* Could that be the answer?

Such a simple idea. Such a horrible idea. But what if worked? What if got her to the island?

Again Marella scooped up a handful of microplastic. Plastic burned. Especially if it absorbed oil from the ocean. She could eliminate the microparticles by setting them on fire. That would clear the way to the island.

She had the means. Olivia had used a lighter to light the camp stove. It was in the backpack Marella had carried here.

Marella furrowed a finger through the handful of microparticles. Would it work? And even if it did, would she survive the smoke and fumes?

The wind was blowing to the west. But what if it shifted? She'd watched a health and safety video at work that warned that burning plastic put hydrogen cyanide into the air. What would happen if she burned this much plastic? How poisonous would it be? Her lungs were already damaged from smoke. Could she survive more?

Marella took a deep breath into her cottony lungs and blew it slowly out. She had no other options. She was dead if she didn't do something. Billions would die. Including Mom and Brielle. She pulled the lighter out of the backpack.

This was it. This was the moment of truth. Almost a point of no return. Marella's heart beat with kettle-drum force as she held the flame down to the microparticles. Her hand shook. The microparticles melted away from the lighter so she moved the lighter forward. More microparticles melted, but didn't catch fire.

Marella grunted and tapped her leg anxiously. She thought of Elizabeth back at the office, before the Aguageddon, saying, "This is doable." And somehow those doable things got done.

Elizabeth. Marella had put her out of her misery. Guilt welled up. Elizabeth should be here, but she wasn't. She couldn't change that. But if she were, what would she do?

She would ask Marella for a workaround. And Marella would come up with one. Marella would examine her resources, and inspiration would hit.

Her resources. She lifted the small propane bottle and its platter top out of the backpack, thankful she hadn't jettisoned them. She attached the platter top to the propane bottle, then turned the switch. It hummed as the gas flowed.

She held the lighter to the propane. A ring of flames sprang up with a tiny whoosh. She turned the knob all the way up. The fire rose three inches high.

Making a mound in the microparticles, she set the canister against it. The flames made contact. A glowing rim appeared in the mound, as if a baby dragon had breathed fire onto it.

Something huffed. Startled, she jumped back. The glowing rim expanded to the size of a bicycle tire. Flames jetted upward, their odor thick and acrid. It was working. "That's good," she murmured without truly rejoicing. The fire alarmed her. She'd seen enough of it to last a lifetime.

Now flames crept toward her. Feeling heat on her face, she skittered back. To her surprise, the fire kept advancing.

She turned, sprinting away. She'd made a terrible mistake. She hadn't considered the mixed sand and microparticles to be flammable, but it was, so now flames sprang up ankle-high at her feet.

An image came to mind. A plaster cast of a Pompeii volcano victim. Caught in death trying to rise from the ground. The cast had no features, just a shape where a woman had once been when the disaster overtook her. In the same way, the burned plastic remnant would encase Marella's body. Take on a shape that would survive her.

Empty, for people to gawk at. Except that there would be nobody to see it. They would all be dead.

Chapter Thirty

The fire roared. Marella raced along, suddenly sure that Gabriela had felt the flames while she was dead. Sure that Gabriela could feel them now, because everybody was a sinner, so everybody went to Hell. Marella would be there soon.

Abruptly there were no flames at her feet. She glanced back, seeing a wall of fire. Dark gray smoke roiled high into the air. She gulped for breath, safe for another moment. It felt precious. She needed more moments, more life. She kept running.

A horrendous boom sounded behind her. Something whizzed past her ear. Marella threw herself to the ground, covering her head. The propane tank exploding? Ear to the ground, it sounded as if the earth were shifting, about to crack open.

There were more loud bangs. It didn't feel safe to stand, but smoke billowed overhead. She couldn't stay there. Leaping up, she ran once more.

Minutes later she reached a rocky area and dropped to the ground, chest heaving. She watched the smoke anxiously as it swelled in the west. What would her world look like when this was all done? Would the fire clear the way, or make it even more impossible to reach Project Athena? Would it create a sticky mess like the glue trap the rat had died on? She imagined herself stuck to the ground, ripping her skin off to get free.

• • • •

TWO HOURS LATER MARELLA was still on the rocky area, assessing whether to continue to the island or not. It looked as if acid had eaten the ground away, leaving blackened mounds and valleys. Swaths of land still fumed in seeming anger at their defilement. It stank of burned plastic and salt, and other caustic things she couldn't identify.

She was running out of time—she had only six hours left—but feared venturing into the smoldering wasteland too soon. What if she sank into a pocket of scorching material the way she had sunk into the microparticles earlier?

She rubbed her forehead as if that would help her conceive of a faster plan. Her skin felt gritty.

Marella looked eastward. She'd been watching for the others, thankful of her lead. Now she spotted the three of them behind her like toy soldiers coming home from war, bedraggled and unorganized. She crouched low, relieved to see Noah, but aggravated by this compounded threat.

Memories flooded in. Olivia stealing the flash drive. Preston's hands around her throat. Marella made fists so tight her fingernails dug into her palms. Her face grew hot. They had betrayed her. By running the shutdown program, she would be saving their lives too, but they didn't deserve it. They didn't deserve rescuing.

And now they were forcing her onto a burnt wasteland before it was safe.

So be it. She rose, running toward the ravaged landscape. At its edge she took a few tentative steps. The ground held her weight. A few more, then a few more, then she scurried forward over the wounded earth, her boots blackened by carbon. The ground's heat enveloped her, irritating her sunburn and jellyfish stings. A burnt rubber smell prickled her throat.

As much as she feared her pursuers, what was ahead was worse. She could feel the machine affecting her—dry mouth, dry eyes, dry throat, but it was more than just dehydration. It was as if something malevolent awaited her on Wisdom Island: the terrifying Goddess Athena of her drugged visions.

Project Athena. Such a choice for a name. Athena was more than just the goddess of wisdom. She was the goddess of war, amassing her forces to win.

She pushed the thought from her mind. Athena was just a marketing concept. Nothing more. Just a name. If they'd called it Project Lulu, would things be different? An image came to mind: a 1920s flapper dancing the Charleston. She allowed herself a quiet, hysterical laugh. It didn't change her situation, but helped her to press on.

She reached the mountain's candy colored slope with its corals and sponges. Dollops of exploded deep ocean creatures smelled like rotten eggs. Shelves jutted randomly, leaving no direct path. It was steep, the footing treacherous. While she was glad to be out of the gray ashes, the dead and dying sea creatures looked toxic. She had only traded one danger for another.

Marella launched herself ever upward, thankful for a smoke haze that kept her out of view of her pursuers. In places the footing was solid; in others it was like stepping on dinner plates filled with granola.

Three hours passed as she climbed ever higher. She slipped, falling onto a red sea urchin, a spine stabbing into her palm. The pain was electric, radiating all the way up her arm. Her shout came out as a hoarse bark. Was it poisonous?

She clenched her teeth, counted to three, and yanked the spine out. The pain was sharp, then dull and heavy. Now she could barely move her thumb. A single drop of blood fell from the wound, crimson against gray lichen. She didn't have time to be more careful. She had only three hours left.

She passed the husk of an air conditioner, an aluminum can, and two oil drums. A dozen dead eels were strewn across them like streamers after a raucous party. Orange, twelve-legged sea stars clung to the undersides of rocks, along with green and red Christmas anemones, withdrawn into dried cushions.

Every muscle in her body ached. Her hand and ankle throbbed. Her head felt like a just-rung iron bell. Nausea prickled at her. It seemed as if Athena was causing it all. Warning her away.

No, that wasn't true. She needed to remember it was Project Athena, not Goddess Athena. Still, she kept slipping back into a fear of the Goddess, like slipping back into a dream in the wee hours of night.

A jagged fish with razor teeth swam in front of her eyes. She jerked away. How was that possible without water? Then another zipped by, until a school of the malicious creatures surrounded her.

Marella waved her arms to fend them off, even though she knew she was hallucinating. Now a hammerhead shark loomed. Sea snakes undulated forward. Marella slowed, fearful that her motion would make them strike. They circled her, seeming to be timing their attack.

A machine was causing her symptoms. She had to keep that straight. With a burst of courage, she rushed forward. The images scattered in shreds, then faded away.

It was a relief; still, the fact remained: she was traveling towards the epicenter of Project Athena's influence. Three dead people waited for her there. Victor had looked so emaciated. The water was being sucked from her, just as it had been from him. Her skin felt thin, merely draped over the scaffolding of her bones. Her own death awaited if she couldn't get the shutdown program to work.

She looked back once more. At first she saw nobody, then the haze parted and she spotted three figures a quarter mile away. Preston way in front, Olivia lagging behind him, and Noah, much further behind, using both hands to steady himself on the slope. They had tied clothing to their bare feet, and walked awkwardly.

The smoke fell back in place like a shutting curtain. It was as if she had been given the glimpse as a warning to hurry.

And so she did. Hallucinations be damned, sea urchins be damned, pain and fatigue be damned, she would make it to the top before them and run the shutdown program. As Elizabeth had complained to the coffeemaker when it failed, "You had one job." This was Marella's one job, her one task. Perhaps the reason she had been born.

She jetted up the slope for another hour but had to stop twice for leg cramps. She passed a rusty washing machine covered with barnacles, sitting perfectly upright as if positioned for mermaids to use. Then the ground leveled somewhat; finally she reached the island's former beach, in what would have been a cove if the water were there. She allowed herself to rejoice. She had made it to the island itself! There was hope. As long as the others didn't stop her, and as long as the program worked, and as long as the biometric workaround succeeded.

Her feet crunched over oyster shells and walnut-size rocks, which made her run in slow motion. The noise of her steps unnerved her. Could they hear her?

She was so close to her goal! She ran alongside a massive dock, which thrust outward over the dry beach. Newer looking, heavy duty. They'd have used it to haul building materials onto the island. Further off was a smaller float-supported dock, lying uselessly on the sand. A cabin cruiser—named the *Drawing Board*—lay askew next to it as if in a drunken stupor. Marella clambered over a line of driftwood and logs, the former high tide line. She was nearly there.

A chain link fence stopped Marella short. It triggered good memories: batting practice with Mom and Brielle; being up to bat with schoolmates cheering her on. But this fence was topped with razor wire, and held warning signs. *Private Property. No entry.* She hooked her fingers into the holes at its base and pulled upward with all her might, but the wire was extra thick. It didn't budge. Idiots! They made a fence that works. Why couldn't they have made a machine that works? She wanted so badly to punch somebody for making her struggle even more impossible.

The fence stretched a hundred feet away to a cliff edge. How could she get through it? What would be her workaround?

Marella raced back to the high tide pile of driftwood. She clambered through it, finding a piece about five feet long. Dragging it to the fence, she wedged it underneath and pushed down. The fencing gave a couple of inches. Encouraged, Marella repositioned the driftwood, then pushed as hard as she could. The fence gave some more. She slid underneath, swearing when the wire scraped her leg.

She climbed to a paved road lined with solar lights that resembled London gas lamps but were only knee high. Now she could see a plume rising—steam, not smoke. Elizabeth had said the geothermal heating system vented steam. As she ran the pines rained brown needles with each gust of wind. She heard a thin whining sound. Faint but aggravating. Her skin crawled as if maggots squirmed underneath. Such a horribly odd feeling. What was causing that?

After hurrying to the top of a hill, she abruptly broke through to a clearing. She stopped, hands on thighs, catching her breath, stunned by the scale of the development in front of her.

The machine's modules stretched across the two-mile island like a fleet of grounded ships. The forty-foot-long blocks were the black of a stealth bomber. Each module had its own twenty-story loop the size of Seattle's Great Wheel.

The nearest loop loomed above her. Within its circle a whirlpool swirled, just like the one in her recent nightmare. She gasped at the similarity, as if the dream had been a premonition. The view into its vortex felt like looking into infinity. Terrifyingly disorienting. She felt that it could suck her in.

How had the designers missed the machine's danger? Why hadn't they seen its horrible potency the moment they turned on the prototype? Marella's very soul felt in jeopardy. Straightening slowly to keep her balance, she held up a hand to shield herself from the sight.

The road led down to a utilitarian building painted in green camouflage. Elizabeth had said the computer she needed would be inside such a building. She ran toward it, wobbling like a stilt walker, not knowing how she found the fortitude to approach the building where Victor died, except that it was a relief to escape the sight of the strange loops. She kept an eye out for two bodies—Victor had spoken of Arnie and Delphine, killed by Athena. Where would they be?

At the door she gathered her courage. It wasn't locked; she burst through. Stink billowed out, like rancid butter, yet dry and stale. It was dark, the room stuffed with shadows.

As her eyes adjusted to the low light, she saw Victor on a chair, his head on the desk in front of a computer monitor. His skin had dried to a dusty gray; his eyes mere sockets. The rancid butter smell intensified.

Her stomach did a backflip. She swallowed back bile, then gritted her teeth. She had to keep control. Nobody else could do this.

There were two employees here: Marella and Victor, but would the biometric scan work with his eyes gone? She remembered back to when her own face had been scanned for HemisNorth's records. A grid of polygons had overlapped her facial features. It was the shape of her face that was important, not the presence of retinas. She hoped.

Marella locked the door behind her. Shutting herself in with Victor smacked of locking herself into Hell, but she couldn't chance being interrupted so close to her goal. She leaned her head against the door, gathering courage. She could do this. She breathed shallowly so as not to inhale death too deeply into her lungs.

Where was the operations room? She looked around. The desk was lit by a small window gridded with protective reinforcement. There was a bobble-head Mariners baseball player, jiggling mildly. Above that, a calendar with a picture of a Swiss village nestled in green hills. How could such mundane things exist in such terrible times? To her left were the gray utility cabinets and whiteboard she'd seen in the video conference.

Keeping her distance from Victor, she moved into the room. She spotted the door Elizabeth had told her about. It looked heavy, made of steel, but it was open.

"System maintenance is past due." The recorded woman's voice made Marella jump. "Shutdown required in one hour." Essentially it was telling her that the point of no return was coming, and therefore the end of the world, but in the soothing tone of a bedtime story.

Marella scuttled past Victor and through the door. She was in the operations room.

Elizabeth had said Project Athena's workings were here behind shatterproof glass—and they were—but she said it looked like a steampunk chandelier, which was much too tame as a description. Hanging from the ceiling was a ten-foot-wide copper cylinder. Dozens of thin pipes descended from it, connected to one another by coils. Hundreds of transparent wires also hung from the cylinder.

The machine was unnervingly similar to the lion's mane jellyfish that had caused her so much pain—perhaps a steampunk version—giving it an air of evil. Marella's bones threatened to turn to rubber, but there was no time for irrational fear. It was a machine. Nothing more.

In the room with Marella there was a control panel with a keyboard, monitor, and camera lens. She touched the keyboard and the monitor screen blipped on. That was good. The computer requested a username and password. Marella tried to remember through the haziness of her thoughts. She knew them. It was just so hard to concentrate. Finally she typed in Project Athena, Hemi$phere180.

She slipped the flash drive out of her bra lining. Uncapping it, she inserted it into the USB slot. She held her breath. Had the flash drive held up through all her travels?

An icon appeared on the screen labeled *EndAthena.exe*. The shutdown program. It was right there. She exclaimed in jubilation and clicked on it. Words on the screen asked her if she wanted to run EndAthena.exe.

She did. But in doing so, she might also end herself. If the machine exploded she might not have time to escape. Her hand shook as she clicked "enter." She told herself that billions of lives in return for hers would be the best deal she had ever made.

She waited, finally remembering to breathe. What would happen next?

An image popped up. A live feed of her own face looking into the monitor. A caption read: *Biometric authentication required.*

A box appeared around the image of her face. A glowing grid of polygons overlapped her facial features and the image froze in place. She looked so robot-like, for a moment she felt unreal. But the pain she felt was real. Her thirst real. Her anxiety real. What was she supposed to do now?

The screen read *hit enter for authentication.*

Marella jabbed at the enter button. The grid disappeared. The screen read: *Authentication successful. Second biometric required.*

She whooped. "It worked. Now it's your turn Victor. Come on. Don't be shy."

She rushed to the dead man in the other room. She had to get his face in front of the monitor's camera. That meant moving him. Touching a dead body. Like summoning demons. Her stomach turned again. She began shaking. "It's okay, Victor. Don't be scared. It'll just scan your face. That's all. It's not painful."

Victor was in a rolling office chair. She grasped the chair back with one arm; the other she wrapped around his upper chest, clamping him against the chair as she began to move it. He felt like badly made papier mâché, crinkly and dry. A fine powder poofed up as if she had stepped on a puffball mushroom. She coughed, waving the dust away and screwing her face against the rancid butter stink. "Damn, Victor. Next time use deodorant."

Marella crouched awkwardly as she rolled the chair into the operations room and into position in front of the computer camera. Now she would have to touch him with her hands to align him. *Don't think. Just do it.* Quickly she grasped his head and pulled, shuddering at the feel of his powdery skin, but it didn't move. Instead the sides of his face crumbled away like dried feta cheese. She jumped back, frantically wiping the chalky residue from her hands.

What had she done? His face was damaged. He was a broken sculpture. How could the biometric software work now? She grasped the chair instead, tilting it precariously until the camera caught Victor's facial features and locked on. A glowing grid emphasized his chin, forehead, and what remained of his cheeks. Marella quickly reached over to hit *enter*.

The screen flickered. It read: *Authentication unsuccessful. Try again?*

Marella tried again and again, holding the chair closer, then further back. It didn't work.

There were other dead employees here—Arnie and Delphine—but they could be anywhere. There wasn't time for a search, and their biometrics were even less likely to work.

There was no way to shut the computer down, and so now Project Athena would reach the point of no return. After that, the water would keep disappearing. Never to return.

She had failed. After all her efforts and workarounds, after all her pain. It had all come to nothing. Her family was going to die. She stood rooted to the floor, unable to tear her eyes away from Victor's damaged face. She and her family would look like that soon. Eye sockets empty. Cheekbones protruding from missing flesh. Forehead rutted. Lips fixed in a grimace. It gave Victor an expression of blame.

And rightly so. She had caused the Aguageddon. By assuming that those around her had the intelligence to avoid disaster. By accepting that all progress was good progress. By allowing herself to stay ignorant. By thinking she wasn't the type of person to improve the world. She'd left that for others, and now it was too late to fix.

She thought she heard whispering. Maybe the wind outside. Maybe demons coming for her. *These are the good times. It will only get worse in death.*

"System maintenance is past due," said the computer voice. "Shutdown required in forty-five minutes."

Marella jumped, startled. *Don't give in to despair.* Her family deserved better. They deserved somebody who would try to the bitter end. She shoved Victor's chair aside, then tapped at the computer, looking for a workaround. Her stomach churned like a washing machine. *Victor, dead. Right next to me.* It felt like he might reach over at any moment and clutch her arm. Drag her down with him to Hell.

She opened a list of folders. Their names had technical terms that she didn't understand. She continued to scan them anyway, finally seeing one labeled *Human Resources.*

It gave her an idea. She returned to the main screen and checked the icons. There was the program she was looking for. She had a possible workaround.

She would need Noah's help. But first, she needed something to protect herself while she went to find him.

Rushing out of the operations room and into the office, she yanked open a metal cabinet. She didn't know what she was looking for but whatever it was didn't seem to be here. HemisNorth cleaning supplies. Paper towels. Various small tools. Plastic tubing.

A key hung on a rack. It had a small float attached labeled *Drawing Board*. That would be for the cabin cruiser. She put it in her other pocket, thinking how smart it was of her to plan ahead, yet how futile. She probably wouldn't survive long enough to use the boat. And the water might never come back.

She yanked out a cardboard box labeled *boat supplies*, dumping its contents on the floor. In the pile was a brand new bright orange flare gun, packaged along with four orange tubes—flares.

A flare gun could be a weapon. She freed it from its packaging, took some precious moments to glance at the directions, then pivoted the barrel upward to load it. She stuffed the extra flares in a pocket. Just holding it made her feel powerful in a way she'd never felt. Like she had some control over her situation.

She unlocked the door. She needed Noah, and she needed him now.

Chapter Thirty-One

Marella peeked out of the operations building, watching for movement. Dead pine needles stirred in the wind. Dead salal bushes slapped the tree trunks. Dead blackberry vines—like patches of brown barbed wire—shifted in a strong gust.

She was about to step outside when dozens of long-legged albino crabs appeared out of nowhere, floating in the air. She jerked back, shoulders tight. Delusions, she told herself. They're not real. She closed her eyes, then looked out again. No crabs. No people.

She slipped out to the road and hunched as she ran—as if that would keep her from being seen! Zooming up the hill, she scanned the haze for looming forms, ready to take cover behind wide cedar trees.

At first having the flare gun fortified her. She was bringing a gun to a slingshot fight. But her confidence waned as she considered her inexperience. She had never shot a gun before, and besides, she'd heard flare guns were not particularly accurate, made for shooting in the sky, not taking out enemies. Plus she had only four flares, and would have to reload after each shot.

She didn't want to kill again, just incapacitate. But what would happen if she actually hit Preston? Would it turn him into a living Fourth of July spectacular? Pass through him, leaving a hole like in a classic cartoon? Bounce off his chest like Superman?

She reached the top of the hill, still scanning. Nobody. She needed Noah. Where was he? The shifting smoke haze made it difficult to see.

Over her shoulder a Project Athena loop loomed. That she could see all too clearly. In its center the vortex swirled. Its sense of endlessness made her feel faint.

"Your flash drive didn't work, did it?" She jumped at the sound of Preston's voice, which growled with anger and triumph. He and

Olivia appeared on the road, a half block away, emerging from the haze as if transported there instantaneously. The fabric tied to their feet was tattered. They'd suffered getting here.

Preston carried the machete. The sight of it made Marella's heart lurch.

Olivia raised her slingshot and launched a stone before Marella could move. It hit a nearby tree with a loud thunk. Marella dashed behind a cedar, the dry ferns crackling under her feet. She pointed the flare gun but didn't fire. She was too wobbly and they were too far.

Seeing the flare gun, Olivia and Preston also took cover behind a tree, leaning out to watch Marella.

She didn't have time for a standoff. She had to get them to go away so she could get Noah inside when he arrived. "No, the flash drive didn't work, so go on. Zokara is waiting for you."

"You're coming with us."

"No thanks."

"Come. Now," rumbled Preston.

Her frustration with this useless back-and-forth spewed out, her words heated. "You go on. I'll catch up."

Preston's tone changed. He sounded anguished. "Don't make me do this. Don't make me keep you from running away anymore." He held up the machete. "God will make you the mother of the new humanity one way or another. If I have to cut your feet off to stop you then I will. Don't make me enforce God's will."

A shiver traveled down Marella's back. It was both ludicrous and horrific. He would mutilate her in the name of God. His demeanor—righteous determination—was somehow more frightening than anger. As if he truly had patronage that she didn't.

"No," wailed Olivia, "I'm the mother of humanity."

Preston froze, except for his eyes, which turned left, then right. He had blundered. He had told them both they were special and now his duplicity was revealed.

Could Marella use this error to turn Olivia against him? She spoke flippantly. "Sorry Olivia. Preston made me the mother of humanity."

"Marella, be quiet," said Preston.

Flustered, Olivia looked back and forth between Preston and Marella. "No, I am. God said it. I am the mother of the new humanity."

"Preston doesn't agree with you. He must not think you're good enough. He told me I'm the mother of all humanity. Not you."

"Marella," warned Preston.

Olivia's shoulders raised. She spoke through clenched jaws. "You're wrong."

"You're nothing to him," said Marella. "He doesn't care about you. Everything he told you was false. He lied to you. Because you're just a thing to him. Something to manipulate. He used you and then moved on to the next female."

Olivia's teeth bared. Her lips stretched. Like Preston in his camper when Marella had told him they were going to stop the Aguageddon.

She's getting the wrath, Marella realized. *How? Preston is the delusional one.* But there was no time to ponder. Olivia charged forward, slingshot raised and ready. Not turning on Preston, but coming for Marella. She was now twenty feet away and coming fast.

Marella stepped from behind the tree and fired. Smoke poofed. The flare burst from the gun, hitting Olivia in the sternum, bouncing onto the road and into the blackberry stickers, where it sputtered yellow, then fizzled down. Orange flames rose in its place, reaching up through the blackberry vines.

Olivia clutched her chest, grunting in pain, but remained standing, her eyes blazing like the flare. So it didn't kill her. And she still had the slingshot. How long would she need to recover?

Now Preston was charging forward, machete in hand. Marella pulled a flare from her pocket but the gun barrel stuck, refusing to pivot upward for loading. There wasn't time to fumble with it. She spun around and ran, imagining him slicing her to pieces. Her limp slowed her. She couldn't outrun him.

She ran behind a long, thigh-high storage bin. He was running straight for her, as if to hurdle the bin. Quickly she flipped it open.

A rancid butter stink spilled out. She glimpsed two dead bodies, curled around each other like awkward lovers. Arne and Delphine, the other employees who had been on the island. Dead, just as Victor had said. Their eyes hollow, faces distorted as if chunks had been bitten off.

She reeled backward. The bodies themselves were bad enough, but now she imagined demons pushing them aside and rising from the bin. Ridiculously, she also imagined directing them to Preston, telling them to grab him instead.

Now Preston was rounding the bin, only a few feet away. Something clattered like hailstones all around them. God raining down his wrath now, guessed Marella despairingly, but Preston swung around, clutching the back of his neck.

And there was Noah! Holding a square piece of metal like a shield, wobbling toward them, throwing what was apparently his second handful of pebbles. She saw now that the shield had barnacles. It was a washing machine lid, from the machine she'd passed on the way up. Good thinking!

With Preston distracted, Marella tugged at the gun; this time it opened. She loaded it, but then a ghostly hammerhead shark swam up, making her jump back. Another delusion. It wasn't real. She couldn't afford such a distraction. She gathered all her courage, telling herself to ignore the beast, but it was too fearsome. So big. Circling her.

Olivia charged her, knocking her onto the pavement. The gun and flare went flying. Olivia straddled Marella. Her breath stank of rotten tuna and decaying seaweed. She made angry noises like a wounded beast.

Marella pounded Olivia's ear. Howling with pain, the girl scrambled off. Marella rushed her, but Olivia used Marella's impetus to slam her against a pine, then forced her face against the rough bark. Marella's own teeth gouged the inside of her mouth. Dry brown needles showered them. It was wrong to smell Christmas and taste blood at the same time.

A clanging noise startled Olivia, allowing Marella to break away from the girl's hold. Noah had managed to fend off Preston's machete strike with the washing machine lid, but Preston circled him. One well-aimed slice and Noah could be dead. All would be lost. She had to help him, but Olivia was right in front of her now, throwing a punch. Marella jerked backward to avoid it, throwing herself off balance. She stumbled and fell, nearly hitting one of the knee-high solar lights on the way down. As she rose she wrenched the light and its foundation stake out of the dry ground. She swiveled, turning its sharp, dusty point outward, then charged.

There was a sickening thunk as the stake plunged into Olivia's gut. Blood fountained, warm and wet on Marella's hands. Olivia's gasp seemed to come from Marella's own throat. She thought she tasted iron.

Incapacitating Olivia had been the goal. But the girl wouldn't survive this. Her demise became chillingly real. Marella flashed back to killing Elizabeth. Pinching Elizabeth's nostrils together and covering her mouth to speed her death. How dry and cracked Elizabeth's lips had been. How Elizabeth's body had seized under Marella's hands.

Marella had sworn she would never kill another human being, but this would be her second slaying. In spite of all her anger at Olivia, at one time she had thought of her like a sister. It felt almost as if she was killing Brielle.

It seemed that Marella couldn't save her family's lives without trading her own humanity away. It was a horrifying exchange, but she had made it. Thoughts flew about in her mind, threatening to land like vultures, to pick at whatever sanity she had left. She was an assassin. Evil. Vile.

Not wanting to watch the last light leave Olivia's eyes, she backed away. This was not the time to let her deed envelope her. Not the time to imagine demons bursting through the earth's crust.

There was another loud clang, the machete hitting metal again. She whirled. Along with the washing machine lid, Noah held a short piece of rusty rebar, giving him the air of an underequipped Roman centurion. He teetered, looking dizzy, mouth open as he gasped for breath.

Where was the flare gun? Nowhere to be seen, but there was the slingshot, right in front of her. Scooping it up, she fit a rock into its sling and raised it, trying to aim at Preston, but he kept moving around.

Preston swung the machete. Its tip struck the washing machine lid hard, knocking it out of Noah's hand. It clattered to the ground. Preston's lip raised into a sneer of effort as he drew the machete back, level with Noah's torso.

She aligned the slingshot sights to Preston's head. This was it. Her only chance before Noah was sliced to death in front of her very eyes. She shot. The rock flew out.

Preston clutched his ear, roaring with pain. As Marella scooped up another rock, he turned, spotting Olivia on the ground, drenched with blood. He had already been angry, but now the wrath entered him like a bolt of lightning. His face glowed with such an evil light that Marella could almost believe he himself was a god of retribution. He charged toward her with a weapon made sharper by his righteousness. There was no stopping him, no escaping him. As powerful as the slingshot was, it seemed a child's toy in the face of the power now bearing down on her.

She aimed and shot, hitting him in the cheek, but he didn't seem to feel it. He kept coming.

Suddenly a yellow flame burst from Preston's side, as if his skin could no longer contain his inferno of anger. Marella could only surmise that the fury of his wrath, in physical form, had finally been too much. It had burst free from its human container.

But then she saw Noah lowering his arm. He had shot the flare gun, hitting Preston in his side, where the flare now stuck fast. It caught Preston's clothing on fire. Flames draped him with astonishing speed. He became a burning pillar, writhing, teetering. He staggered back until he fell into the dry underbrush, which in turn caught on fire.

Burning things. Burning cities, burning land, burning dreams, and now a burning soul.

Noah looked nauseous. Marella guessed that he was overwhelmed by his deed. She glanced at the watch Elizabeth had given her, then grabbed his arm, pulling. "I need your help. Only ten minutes left."

Running drunkenly, the two rushed into the building.

In the operations room, seeing Victor slumped in the chair, Noah gave a strangled yelp.

"Ignore him," said Marella quickly. She clicked the icon on the screen.

"What are you doing?"

"I'm going to set you up as an employee. We can scan your face and you can be the second biometric."

She clicked on *Add new employee*. A fillable form appeared on the screen. A banner at the top read *Biometric scans must be taken in a HemisNorth office location.*

Her throat tightened. It was another failsafe. To keep somebody from shutting down the system. To keep *her* from shutting it down. A feeling of helplessness threatened to paralyze her. "It won't work."

Along the way she'd thought she'd failed but then came with workarounds. But there were no more to be had. She'd done all she could. She was too tired, too confused. This was the end. She looked down at Noah's feet. The material he'd wrapped them with had fallen off and they were bare and bloody. That was her fault, because she had taken his shoes. She'd made him suffer.

"System maintenance is past due," said the recorded voice. "Shutdown required in five minutes."

"Let's think through this," said Noah, shaking his head as if to clear it. "Victor's driver's license would have a photo."

She spoke despondently. "No, the scan works three-dimensionally."

"Right. I remember Elizabeth saying that. It's just so hard to think. What we need is another registered employee, another one of you. Clone yourself or something, quick."

It wasn't a real suggestion. They needed two different employees, not two of her. Yet it seemed like a clue somehow. Something that would save their lives if she only understood why it would help to copy and paste herself.

Copy and paste.

Her mouth opened. She stared at the keyboard. Could it work? "I've got an idea." She scanned the folder names, clicking through into a subfolder.

"What are you doing?"

"Cloning myself. Every employee is assigned an employee number. If I can copy my information to somebody else's number... I need to find the right folder."

She clicked on a folder marked *Biometric data*. There were subfolders with employee names and employee numbers. She found her name, and clicked on it. *Right click. Copy.* It was a strange feeling to do such a familiar action when the world was about to end.

She exited her folder and opened a different employee's. *Paste.* Now she had replaced the other employee's information with hers. Minimizing the folder, she returned to the biometric scanning screen and clicked on the words *Try Again?*

The camera captured her face, presenting it on the monitor. A glowing grid of geometric shapes overlapped her facial features; the image froze in place.

The screen flickered. A line of dots traveled like ants across the screen. Then more dots. Then more.

What was happening?

The screen read: *Shutdown initiated.*

Marella stared at the words. Two words that meant everything. Two words that said she hadn't failed. Yet.

"It's working!" said Noah, sounding incredulous.

A timer appeared on the screen, small but potent. It was counting down. Sixty seconds. *Fifty-nine. Fifty-eight.*

She thought of the explosion at Building C. This machine could explode too, but she couldn't leave. She had to make sure the shutdown happened.

Turning to Noah, she pulled the cabin cruiser's key from her pocket and thrust it at him. "This is for the boat if the water returns. Hurry, go. Now before everything explodes."

Noah pushed away the key, sounding offended. "I'm not leaving you here alone."

"You have to tell my family what happened to me."

"We wouldn't have gotten this far without each other. Something could still go wrong. This is the last chance. I'm staying."

He sounded adamant. And he was right. There was no room for gallantry on her part. There was too much at stake. The two of them together were more likely to succeed than just one alone, but it was anguishing to think he might sacrifice himself too. It felt like her fault.

Forty-five. Forty-three.

Marella tapped on her leg anxiously. *Make it work. Make it work.*

"I killed a man," said Noah, sounding wretched.

Marella put her hand on his shoulder. "You had to. Preston would have stopped us. You saved me. And your friends and family." She hoped.

He nodded, but she understood that words were little comfort. She herself had killed twice. Once would have been an anomaly. Twice was a pattern. Would they both find themselves in Hell a minute or so from now? How long did it actually take to get there? And how much worse would it be than her recent life?

"Now I know what you were going through when you confessed to me. I should have listened instead of judging you. I'm sorry I treated you that way."

"It's okay."

"I care about you more than that. I just want you to know."

"I care about you too. I wish it didn't have to be like this."

Thirty-one. Thirty.

They reached for each other's hands at the same time. All four clasped together. Their raspy breathing alternated, completely out of sync.

What would it feel like to explode?

Fifteen. Fourteen.

"It's been nice knowing ya," said Marella, her voice shaking.

"See you on the flip side." He squeezed tighter.

The screen went blank. What now?

Shutdown complete.

What that it? No fanfare, no hokey "you win" computer sound? Had they actually succeeded?

A thin whistling noise touched her eardrum. It felt like the end of a needle, a small pain that quickly strengthened.

"It worked, let's go." Noah pulled her. They rushed for the door. The noise pierced its way through to her brain. She clutched her head, rushing through the office and to the outside.

The trees were burning on the side of the road where Preston had fallen, an inferno, smoke billowing. As if they had instantaneously arrived in Hell after all. They coughed, forced to run through the underbrush.

Fear spurred her on, in spite of her injured ankle. Noah, too, raced as if he wasn't barefoot and bleeding. They reached the top of the hill, within view of a module loop. So enormous. So dominating. Its whirlpool turned faster now, frenzied, as if being stirred by a great force, as if something powerful was about to happen.

She stopped, transfixed. A bolt of lightning burst from the loop. Rather than strike all it once, it coursed through the air going one direction then another, as if searching for her. Frozen, she watched in horror. It came closer.

It hit her head. Her skull felt cracked open. She screamed.

"Come on!" Noah pulled her arm, making her stumble along. She clutched her head.

The pain faded, leaving bewilderment. How could her skull possibly be intact? She only knew that she would still be standing there if Noah hadn't broken whatever spell was holding her.

They ran further. She was still taking stock. She'd been hit by a bolt of energy coming out of the machine. It seemed real, not a hallucination, yet she wasn't hurt by it, except that her brain felt thick, as if wrapped in a towel. Dust billowed up from the dead underbrush. Scraggy pine branches dropped around them. The ground beneath her feet felt hollow, as if she stood on a thin crust that might crack and collapse at any moment.

There was a tremendous boom. More than just sound of an explosion, it seemed like universes colliding. They dropped to the ground, covering their heads. A car-size chunk of twisted metal crashed down only twenty feet away, propelling them back to their feet.

The dock was ahead, solid, massive. A haven. If they could reach it. They clambered through the opening under the fence, then leaped over a torn yellow plastic laundry basket and around a table-size Styrofoam float. Something fiery hit the ground beside her. She screamed and corkscrewed her body.

They reached the dock, diving under it. There they huddled, entangled as a single being against the machine's rage, heads bent. Like a fireworks display, explosion followed explosion as each blast vied to surpass the previous one.

More metal slabs slammed against the ground, as if trying to shove the Earth out of orbit. A sheet of viscous liquid struck the sand; fire curtained upward. Marella could feel its heat on her side. She folded herself in, pressing even harder against Noah.

Death seemed only moments away. Images flashed before her eyes. Her father picking her up and swinging her around. Brielle challenging her to a race. Mom welcoming her into a new house.

The explosions slowed. Like popcorn in a microwave oven, each time Marella thought they were done, another blast startled them, making them tighten their grip on each other.

When it was finally quiet, Marella and Noah rose warily. Blackened tree trunks fanned over the beach like fallen fences. The few trees still standing were tipped with yellow auras of quiet fire. Pieces of machine lay everywhere, broken and twisted. Black smoke rose to the sky to mingle with the brown smoke already there. It smelled of ozone and burned plastic.

Marella no longer felt nauseous. Her head felt strange, like her brain was too big for her skull, but not painfully so. Her thoughts began to clear. Most noticeably the pervasive dread was gone, as was the feeling of being watched.

Now that the immediate danger was over, it finally sank in. They'd done it. They'd accomplished what they came to Wisdom Island to do: run the shutdown program. In spite of thieves and murderers. In spite of a monstrous jellyfish, a mile-high sandstorm, a crazed cult leader, and so many other obstacles. By truck, by raft, and finally by foot. She'd beaten the odds and cheated the gods, or at least one goddess. Athena was no more.

The phrase tripped through her mind. *Beaten the odds, cheated the gods.* She felt one big weight gone from her shoulders, while another one settled in. They weren't safe yet. They were marooned on an island miles from water, miles from civilization. But whatever happened next, the mission was complete. She felt clear. Open. Expanded. She wished Elizabeth could be there to experience it. She wished her family could know what she had done.

"Are you okay?" Noah had the rejuvenated look of somebody emerging from a deep sleep.

"I think so."

They made their way to the cabin cruiser. "It's called the *Drawing Board*," said Noah. "I get it. You're always going back to it."

Walking around the boat, they saw it was intact. The falling debris had spared it.

"It's a miracle," said Noah, with a tone of awe.

Maybe, thought Marella. She might never know if miracles were real. In any case, things had gone wrong for so long that of course it seemed like a miracle when something went right. "When the water comes back we've got transportation. We can get—" she almost said home. Instead she said "somewhere."

Noah gazed off in the distance, though it was too hazy to see very far. "*If* it comes back."

Marella nodded. She gazed at her hands, their creases still stained with Olivia's blood. She had killed again. Maybe she deserved to die. But her family didn't deserve for her to die. And the Aguageddon wouldn't have ended if they hadn't stopped Olivia and Preston.

As if he could hear her thoughts, Noah said, "Hey, it's not every day you save billions of peoples' lives."

In the boat's cabin they found a first aid kit and some nut bars, but were too thirsty to eat. They sat on a cushioned seat bank and Marella cleaned Noah's feet and the burn on his back.

They climbed back up the beach to the road, walking slowly with their injuries. The blasts had ripped the modules and pitched the pieces everywhere. The destruction was astounding, as if the earth had vomited sharp, coal-black bile.

Marella took a shuddering breath, then released it. What now? It felt like a strange limbo. No wind. Quiet.

Noah put an arm around her. She leaned into him. They stayed together for minutes, staring at the wrecked landscape.

Marella's skin tingled. A sheen moistened her arm. "I'm wet."

Noah looked down at his arm, which also glistened.

"Is the water coming back?" Marella tried to tamp down any hope as best she could. She didn't want to let herself believe it, only to be disappointed. What if some unusual aftereffect of the machine's destruction caused the sheen?

"Look!" shouted Noah. Waves of fog came into being, looking like a mesh curtain of dew. The fog swirled, dissolving then reforming, then washing over them. The tiny drops felt like light pinpricks. She licked her lips—they were wet. Hope filled her, too strong to contain. Water! Actual water!

It was warm on her skin. More fog swirled over her, drenching her.

"It's coming back!" Noah stretched himself out as if to touch every drop, a look of ecstasy on his face. "Thank you God! Thank you!"

Marella laughed, the peals bursting out. Streams trickled past their feet, then flowed. Puddles were everywhere.

The water's unusual beauty was mesmerizing, illuminated by prisms of light, as if to reveal colors that weren't normally visible. "The rain is so beautiful," said Marella.

"It's not rain," said Noah. "There aren't any clouds. It's like you said. All these particles were undefined. Not in our universe or in other universes. And now they're suddenly being defined. So they aren't 'not here and not there,' anymore. They're here. They're here!"

The smell of burned debris gave way to the smell of wet soil, which was enchanting, like the smell of Spring, holding such promise.

The feeling of awe was overwhelming. At having summoned water. At having succeeded at the impossible. It felt like a flower opening, like walking after being bedridden, like life renewed. It was magical.

A waterfall began spilling over a bank. At first it was a ribbon of sooty liquid, but then it cleared. Marella reached into it, feeling its silky smoothness and rubbing her hands together. The blood and dirt dissolved and flowed away. They drank from it, big gulps. It tasted fresher than seemed possible, as if it had been purified—the woes of the world removed—by being suspended between the universes.

They let it pour over their heads. Soon they were washing the grime out of one another's hair, then cleaning one another's bodies, and then they were kissing.

For so long the evil of the Aguageddon had been perched on her shoulders, its talons demanding attention. But now, Marella could be there with Noah. Nothing demanded to be solved. There was only him.

* * * *

AS WONDERFUL AS IT was to have water, the world had become a humid sauna, and after a time they went back to the *Drawing Board*, happily finding that the boat's cabin wasn't as wet. Sitting side by side, they ate nut bars.

"There's a reason this all happened," said Noah. "Maybe someday I'll know why. But one thing I do know, is that you're amazing. You figured out why the water was disappearing, and you brought it back. If my family and friends are alive, it's because of you."

"We did that together. You were ready to die for me and my family. You wouldn't leave me even when you knew the machine could explode."

"Still." He pulled the black rock and agate from his pocket. His good luck charm. It gleamed even more while wet. "I want you to have this."

Marella closed her fingers around it and held it to her heart. It felt warm, as if its luck was throwing off heat. "If you're giving me your good luck, then you'll need some too." She pulled her apartment key out of her pocket and handed it to him.

Noah gazed at the key sadly. "Your apartment is gone. You don't have anywhere to go." He brightened. "Come to Spokane with me and stay with my parents. Your family too."

Marella hadn't been thinking beyond the disaster's end, except to picture herself safe with her family. "Would they be okay with that?"

"No question. They're always taking in strays. Not that you're a stray."

Marella smiled. "I'm as stray you get right now. It sounds great." More than great. It sounded wonderful. To put all this behind them and start anew.

• • • •

THE NEXT MORNING THE air was still thick and humid with returning water, but the ocean hadn't reached them.

"What if the water coming back is a runaway reaction, and it just keeps coming and never stops?" asked Marella.

"Too many worries are taking up space in my head," said Noah. "There's not enough room for more of them."

He was right, but as hope for themselves waxed and waned in her mind, Marella agonized over who might have survived. She couldn't help but think in terms of tradeoffs, like Brielle liked to do, asking, "Would you rather lose an arm or a leg? Would you rather be a genius or drop dead gorgeous?" Now, as if success required a cost, it might be, "Would you rather that you survive, or your family?"

She tried to be content that Noah was with her. They'd been victims together, and now they were victors together, no matter what happened next. Still, she couldn't stop wondering what the world was like now. "I wonder how many people died."

"We might find out soon enough."

"A lot of animals died too. It'll be hard to find food."

Noah nodded. "All those dead fish. And the salt concentration got so high in the water. Only the toughest, ugliest fish survived." He screwed up his face to show what that looked like.

Marella laughed. "Like the ratfish."

Two more days of relentless water-filled air passed. They were sleeping in the boat's cabin when Marella woke. Something was different. She peeked out. Overhead, for the first time since the fires began, she could see stars. With the air clear of smoke and moisture, there was nothing to hide the Milky Way, so it shimmered its way across the sky.

Noah stirred and peeked out as well, his voice tinged with wonder. "It's clear out."

"Look! The moon."

The moon's reflection on the water was breathtakingly beautiful, but it meant so much more. The ocean had almost reached them.

"The water came back so fast." asked Marella. "It took twice as long for it to disappear."

"Maybe it's like a dam. It takes time to fill a reservoir, but when the dam breaks it all comes at once."

"We can't tell anybody about the climate machine," blurted Marella. "Not yet."

"Why not?"

"Preston might have some followers left, and we really don't want them to find out about it. Or terrorists. It's better if nobody knows such a thing is possible, at least until we know that any of the plans have been destroyed."

"You have a point. I'm good with that, for now. But people need to know HemisNorth is to blame. Hell, they might already know."

"Maybe so."

By morning the *Drawing Board* was floating. The sun rose on water that sloshed steadily against the dock pilings. It brought debris, revealing yet more garbage that the ocean had hidden. It seemed as if the trash was no longer content to remain at the bottom of the ocean. In a burst of poetry, Noah called it, "The detritus of all our lives laid bare."

"Edie and Baby Faith are still out there somewhere," said Marella.

Noah nodded. "Rest in peace."

They were able to start the boat's engine. There were no hitches. No cult members to stop them. No Roman goddesses to hold them back. They headed east, toward the mainland. Once they reached the coast, where all was burned, they headed south to Grays Harbor. There, in southern Washington State, the raging fire had stopped, and the towns and forests had survived.

Chapter Thirty-Two

D ozens of people were packed into a multipurpose room in a community center in Aberdeen, Washington. Marella flashed back to the crowd that had nearly crushed her in Occidental Square. Her instinct told her turn around. Get away from all these people.

But now Marella looked—really looked—at the faces. Some hopeful, some tired, some happy, some sad, but none angry. How unique each person appeared. A woman with a round face and straw hair. A man with large ears and a tiny forehead. A knock-kneed child. And so many more.

These were the people she and Noah had saved. The struggle, pain, and final triumph had all been for them.

Marella didn't believe in fate, but she believed in the feeling of it. All the times she'd moved, all the people she'd met and lost, and each moment of each day of her life, good or bad, had led to this moment. Even the death of her father had contributed to her choices. She would have been a different person without it. Her fear of the dead and her fear of being alone were both a part of the path to the island. She could let go of those fears, now that they had served their purpose in forming her and carrying her all the way to the present.

Marella and Noah slumped in blue plastic chairs. The room smelled of HemisNorth Springtime floral scent cleaning spray. They waited two hours for a volunteer to check for news of their families. Were they alive or dead? Lost or found? Would it be good news or bad?

A doctor had examined them in the hospital. Marella's ankle was strained but not broken. She'd described the slow lightning bolt that had hit her in the head, suggesting it had caused the strange, stuffed feeling in her head. Finding no burns on her skin, the doctor rejected that idea, and said her head would clear once she was better rested.

The burn on Noah's back and the cuts on his feet had been cleaned and bandaged. They'd been given clean secondhand clothes to wear.

Now finally, in the community center, most of the others who had arrived before them were taken care of. There was only one other climate refugee in the room, a sunburned man with an arm in a sling. "I was on Mount Rainier," he offered, after hearing they'd spent their time on the seabed.

Marella sat up, leaning towards the man. "My family was headed there."

The man nodded. "A lot of people were there. Thousands, at least. Maybe more, I don't know. Even so, we had enough water. But then it got hard to breathe, because the atmosphere was lowering, taking the place of the ocean. We had to leave quickly."

"So then some people didn't make it," said Marella. "How many?"

The man shrugged, then looked at the floor. "Well...it was a little crazy, it's hard to know. Your family is probably fine. They might even be here—most of us were brought here because the hospital and aid agencies are here."

There was silence for a while. The man fidgeted. It seemed he didn't want to leave things where they were. "We have a lot to be thankful for. The Aguageddon is over, and there'll never be another one."

Marella and Noah looked at each other. "How do you know that?" asked Noah.

"You didn't hear? It was a Concurrent Alignment. The perfect storm, so to speak. Solar flares, global warming, alignment of planets, alignment of galaxies. Everything happened at once and it made some kind of alignment vortex. I don't understand the science, but it can't happen again, at least not for a million years, and so now we can all move on with our lives."

"It's not going to be that easy," said Noah. "Most of the world dried up. Most of the fish are dead. And a lot of other animals. Crops must have dried up."

"Yeah, it was horrifying for seven days. But the worst of it was on the West Coast, because that was where the vortex was centered. So yeah, that all happened, and everybody was out for themselves. But suddenly everybody's coming together. You see how people got taken care of here." He waved an arm at the nearly empty room.

Paulette, the volunteer, appeared in the doorway. She wore a tie-dye caftan and a big smile. "Marella and Noah, your families are on the safe list. They're alive and well."

Marella leaped to her feet, turning to Noah, then back to Paulette. She was speechless.

Noah's voice shook. "Oh my god. They're really all right?"

"Yes!" said Paulette. "Noah, your family is still in Spokane, and your two friends have gone back there also. Unfortunately there's no way to talk to them right now, but we'll get word to them that you're alive."

To Marella she said, "Your family is here in Aberdeen." She handed Marella a slip of paper with an address. Marella could barely read it with her eyes filling with tears. Mom and Brielle were alive. She finally spoke. "They're okay." A tear ran down her cheek, followed by another, then another. Noah wiped her cheek, and she wiped his.

"I'm almost done here," said Paulette. "I'll drive you in a bit."

"See?" said the man. "People coming together. It'll be a bumpy road, but we'll get through it."

• • • •

PAULETTE PULLED UP to a treehouse. Not a child's treehouse, but an architectural marvel with round windows, a shingled roof, and an attached deck, built around a giant tree.

"I don't think this is the right place," said Marella. "It looks too expensive."

But then Mom and Brielle appeared on the deck, faces bright with amazement. "Marella! You're here!" Both rushed down the stairs that wrapped around the tree. They nearly knocked her over with their embrace.

Their arms felt strong and right. Her mother pulled back as if to make sure it was really Marella. Her smooth hands felt Marella's cheeks.

"I knew you'd make it through," said Mom.

"Me too," said Marella. Funny how saying it made it true.

Breaking free of the embrace, she ran back to Noah and pulled him forward. "This is Noah. He saved my life."

"And she saved mine," said Noah.

Mom and Brielle looked at Noah searchingly as the importance of Marella's words sunk in. Then they rushed to him and hugged him too.

"Come on." Mom waved them all forward. "I'll show you the place."

"It's only temporary," said Brielle.

Isn't everything? "Of course," Marella replied, waving goodbye to Paulette, who drove away.

She felt the warmth of Noah's hand in hers as they approached the stairs. Brielle's elbow linked solidly with hers. There was no wind. The air smelled fresh.

High above, clouds hung like full hammocks, their bellies full of life-giving water. A drop of rain fell on Marella's face and rolled down her cheek: a tear without sadness. She didn't wipe it away. Instead, laughing with contentment, she raised her face for more.

About the Author

Susan Whiting Kemp is a co-author of We Grew Tales. She earned her Bachelor of Arts degree in drama from the University of Washington. Working as a writer and marketer at environmental companies opened her eyes to the astounding extent that human beings have affected the Earth. Her blog at SusanWKemp.com features writing-related articles and short fiction. She lives in wet and rainy Seattle, Washington, USA.

Read more at https://www.susanwkemp.com.

Made in the USA
Coppell, TX
22 September 2023

21902349R00196